Portia Da Costa is one of the most i
authors of erotica.

She is the author of over fifteen *Black Lace* novels, as well
as being a contributing author to a number of short story
collections.

Also by Portia Da Costa

The Accidental Mistress

PORTIA DA COSTA

BLACK
LACE

1 3 5 7 9 10 8 6 4 2

First published in 2013 by Black Lace, an imprint of Ebury Publishing
A Random House Group Company

The Random House Group Limited Reg. No. 954009

Addresses for companies within the Random House Group can be found at:
www.randomhouse.co.uk

A CIP catalogue record for this book is
available from the British Library

The Random House Group Limited supports the Forest Stewardship
Council® (FSC®), the leading international forest-certification organisation.
Our books carrying the FSC label are printed on FSC®-certified paper. FSC is
the only forest-certification scheme supported by the leading environmental
organisations, including Greenpeace. Our paper procurement policy
can be found at: www.randomhouse.co.uk/environment

Printed and bound by CPI Group (UK) Ltd, Croydon, CR0 4YY

ISBN 9780352347619

To buy books by your favourite authors and register for offers visit:
www.randomhouse.co.uk
www.blacklace.co.uk

Dedicated to the real Alice, gone now,
but never to be forgotten.

Call Girl for a Night

When Lizzie Aitchison first met John Smith in the Lawns Bar of the Waverley Grange Hotel, she didn't realise that he thought she was an escort in search of a client. The chemistry between them was dynamite from the outset, and Lizzie couldn't resist the allure of John's fallen angel face and the way his lean body looked in a sharp business suit. In a daring leap, she decided to play along with his misapprehension and become 'Bettie', the high-class call girl . . . if only for one night.

John, too, was captivated. Shaken out of a state of ennui, he was gripped by an unstoppable urge to possess this beautiful young woman, whose combination of a distinctive vintage style and a bold yet strangely vulnerable personality was the ultimate call to his senses.

The two embarked on an intense, kinky affair for the duration of John's stay in the area on business, sharing pleasures far more intense than either one of them had ever expected. Especially when Lizzie was forced to admit that she wasn't really a call girl after all.

But what was supposed to be a simple, temporary, sex

friendship, just for fun, quickly turned out to be something deeper and more meaningful. And when John returned to Lizzie after a month spent apart, suggesting they try a more permanent relationship, as lovers, the next stage of their passionate journey had begun.

1

An Undiscovered Country

He's come back! He's come back! It wasn't just temporary...He's come back! He's come back!

Lizzie walked beside John, her hand tucked under his arm, and the sun shone overhead, benign and warm. She matched his long stride easily, as if he was giving her some kind of turbo energy boost. In fact, if he hadn't been her anchor, she'd probably have been bouncing around him Tigger-style, or floating upwards like a balloon full of excitement. She couldn't stop looking at him, either. She simply couldn't stop looking at him.

The most handsome man she'd ever seen, the most daring, fascinating, exciting, demanding man she could ever have imagined...he'd come back because he wanted to be with *her*.

Don't go mad, woman. And don't get all gooey. He'll think you're mental!

'Are you OK?' John gave her a sideways smile as they walked, his sandy eyebrows lifting. He could feel her insane excitement, she knew he could. He'd been able to read her like a book from day one. Now, more than ever, she was convinced he'd suspected she wasn't a call girl on that night they'd first met at the Waverley. But being John, he'd played along with her silly masquerade. Because it'd suited him, and he'd wanted *her* to have fun.

But this…this was a new game, with new rules. Infinitely more challenging. The thought of it made her heart thunder, thud, thud, thud.

'I'm fine . . .' Who was she kidding? Fine? What a small, stupid word. 'Actually, I feel a bit giddy…as if I'm in a dream.' No use trying to hide it from him. He knew anyway.

John's grip tightened on her hand. 'You know what? I feel a bit the same…Exciting, isn't it?' He leaned in close, his breath like a zephyr in her ear. 'And I'm dying to fuck you. It's been a long hard month, gorgeous girl. *Very* hard. I thought I might die of frustration.'

'Me too.' No point in denying that either.

'Well, won't be long now. Here we are.'

They'd reached a car. John's car. Half expecting the limousine, Lizzie was taken aback. The vehicle they were standing in front of was still substantial and luxurious, a sleek black Bentley Continental, if she wasn't mistaken, recognising the badge from a car owned by a friend of her mother.

Goodness, he drives. He drives himself. *I thought . . .*

John gave her a searching look as he opened the passenger door and she slid inside, settling into a deep, leather-upholstered seat, as comfortable as a Scandinavian armchair, and as cradling as if it'd been tailored to fit her.

The driver's door closed with a soft, perfectly engineered clomp as John settled himself at her side. But he didn't start the motor. Instead, he turned in his seat, a quizzical yet serious expression on his face.

'It was over twenty years ago, love.' His eyes were steady, and he looked calm, but there was a hint of something stark and melancholy, far back in his expression. 'You don't think I'd ever have got back behind a wheel if I wasn't completely sure I'd learnt my lesson, do you? There isn't a day that goes by without my thinking about what I did. You're perfectly safe. I'm not the man I was back then.'

They'd never discussed this, not properly, but no doubt he knew that she'd Googled him. So he must know she'd discovered his troubled history on the road. The car crash in his twenties, his conviction for dangerous driving. And the fact that he'd lost his licence for several years too.

'I trust you. I know you'd never do anything bad deliberately…you're not that kind of person.'

John laughed; a short, brusque sound. 'Well, now you're giving me far too much benefit of the doubt, woman. I'm no angel. But buckle up anyway, and I'll drive you to the Waverley like a punctilious maiden aunt. Never over twenty miles an hour, promise.'

'Actually, that sounds more like my mother.' Lizzie grinned, thinking of her *über*-cautious parent. 'She's the slowest driver in the entire world.'

'Well, I'll drive like her, then.' John gave her a quick, salacious smirk, and then fired the engine. 'I bet your mother would probably have a fit, though, if she knew what I've got planned for her daughter when I get her to the Waverley.'

The smirk became a wicked wink, and then was gone in an instant. As if a switch had tripped, John's face straightened and he was all attention to the road: sharp of eye, serious, completely focused. The junction out of the car park was an awkward one, but within moments they'd smoothly negotiated it and were scudding on their way, heading out of town, towards the Waverley Grange Country House Hotel.

I do feel safe.

It was true. The momentary blip she'd experienced was gone. Behind the wheel, John was as assured, confident and as unassailably competent as he was in all things. Not that she'd experienced John in many 'things'. She knew him almost exclusively from the bedroom, and sex…and from the way he'd taken charge and got her back home within an hour when her friend and house-mate Brent had tried to commit suicide. The circumstances couldn't have been more different, and yet in both, John had excelled, and been supreme.

He didn't speak while he drove, and she wondered whether that was for her benefit, so she'd feel confident in his total concentration. Only while waiting at a junction did he glance sideways at her, with a smile.

The silence gave Lizzie the chance to ogle him.

Slyly, and out of his sight-line, she pinched her own thigh. He was a dream. A beautiful, golden, alpha-male dream with the profile of an archangel and the gilded curls to match. During the month they'd been apart, time after time, she'd almost managed to convince herself that he'd been a figment of her fantasies, and that the emails and thoughtful gifts were imaginary too.

But now, the fantasy was reality. John Smith, billionaire, aristocrat and world-class sexual genius was beside her, and whisking her away to his hotel room to make passionate love to her.

And after that, who knew? An undiscovered country…

It didn't take long to reach their destination, even though, true to his word, John didn't drive particularly fast. But here they were again at the Waverley Grange Country House Hotel, the place she supposed they could call their old stomping ground. The place where a different life had begun.

In the lobby, astonishingly, John almost seemed hesitant. Good grief, surely he wasn't as big a bag of nerves as she was, was he?

His hand tightened around hers. 'Lunch…or room service?'

I shouldn't. You shouldn't. We should talk, really, not just throw ourselves at one another like a pair of randy animals.

And yet, out came the words, 'Oh, room service, please.'

John's blue eyes flared, and he led her towards the lift. Usually the coolly contained gentleman in public, he was in a rush now, fingers gripping hers almost to the point of pain again, just as in the car park. It was as if he feared she might break free and bolt.

'Oh, love,' he sighed as the lift doors closed. Taking her in his arms, he brought his mouth down on hers again, the taste of his lips, oh God, so delicious, so right. Lizzie opened her own mouth to welcome his thrusting tongue.

And that wasn't the only part of him that was thrusting. Had he been erect all the way here, since the car park? She'd hardly dared look. Now, though, even such a short ride up was plenty long enough for him to pin her against the lift wall and mould his body to hers. She almost laughed against his lips. *This* was the elevator scene she'd joked about on that very first night when they'd met in a hotel bar and he'd easily persuaded her to go up to his room. A thousand times more meaningful than it could ever have been back then.

John no longer had to hustle her along. She was with him all the way as they hurried to his room, and the door was no sooner shut than they were pulling at each other's clothes, kicking away shoes, wrenching at buttons and zips. Then, kissing her again, and still in his underwear, John fumbled like a youth with the hooks of her bra as he walked her backwards to the chintz-covered bed and tipped her on to it.

'Oh, hell, yes,' he growled, hitching sideways across the bed then climbing on, spreading himself on top of her like a living quilt. He kissed again, deep, deep, deep, exploring her mouth while he rocked against her, his cock like an iron bar in his trunks, rubbing against her hip.

Oh, hell, yes!

Beside herself with excitement, Lizzie spread her thighs so he could press against her pussy instead, hot and hard through the thin fabric of their underwear.

Oh John, I want you…I love you…even if it's crazy.

Her brain whirled, critical faculties fighting to survive, and failing.

He smelt divine. His body was perfect. He kissed like a god.

Her own body was shaking, shaking really hard now. She was out of control. She couldn't think. What the hell was happening to her?

It's too much. I think I'm going to faint.

Immediately, as if he'd heard the thought, John sat up beside her. His eyes were dark, yet lambent, his cock enormous in his jersey trunks, but there was concern on his face, an expression that looked ascetic, almost pure.

'Lizzie? What is it? Are you all right?'

She sat up too, still shaking. Shaking very hard. Was she in shock? John's blue eyes narrowed and he dragged a soft blanket from the bottom of the bed and draped it carefully around her shoulders.

'I…I'm sorry…I just feel a bit odd.' It came out in a thin,

wavery voice, but he took her hand, and instantly she felt stronger. 'I…oh, this is stupid. I'm stupid.'

'You're not. You're the least stupid person I know.' John's arm was around her shoulder, holding the comforting blanket in place. 'Now, tell me what's wrong?'

'Nothing…I don't know…I'm really not sure myself.' She wasn't. Not right now. He was still temptation incarnate, and yet the intersection of a month's worth of dreams and longing with the warm reality of John and his beautiful body had sent her into some kind of emotional tailspin.

'I think we need a little drink. Even if it is early.' John squeezed her shoulders again, and then slid off the bed, heading for the sideboard. For a special guest like him, there was a silver tray with various bottles upon it, plus a selection of crystal and a rather splendid cut-glass ice bucket. He picked up a familiar green bottle and gave her a questioning look.

Gin. Why not? 'Please . . .' she responded.

He sloshed a measure into two glasses, then looked back at her again. 'I bet you really prefer it with ice and tonic, don't you?'

'Um . . .yes, I do, actually.'

He smiled and then added tonic and ice to hers, along with a slice of fresh lime from a small dish.

'Cheers!' They clinked glasses. Lizzie took a long sip, feeling the spirit settle her and put the brakes on the strange whirling sensation. She hadn't had gin since she'd last been with John, and now she realised how she missed it. But it *was* much better with ice and tonic.

'Better now?'

'Yes, I think so.' She tweaked the blanket round her shoulders and took another little sip of her drink. 'I'm sorry. I had a bit of a turn there.'

John reached out, and did some blanket tweaking of his own. 'You gave me a bit of a scare. You went quite white.' He brushed his fingertips gently down her cheek, making her shiver in an entirely different kind of turn. 'You have the most gorgeous creamy skin, love, but that icy white was way too much.' He cradled her chin, looking into her eyes, searching. Concerned.

Oh, this is ridiculous. I want him to jump my bones, not turn into a nursemaid!

'I'm OK now, John. In fact…I feel great! It's just that it's not every day that someone like me gets a handsome squillionaire for a boyfriend. I'm entitled to go a bit funny!' She turned her face so she could kiss the palm of his hand, parting her lips against his skin. 'But I'm all better now. Completely recovered.'

'Oh Lizzie, Lizzie, I'm all right too. So all right that I'm bloody desperate to f—' He shook his head, making his golden curls dance. 'Sorry…I'm bloody desperate to *make love* to you. I just want to touch you and hold you and be in you. No funny stuff…just plain old missionary…Well, that'll do for the moment.' His blue eyes twinkled in the wicked boyish way that she loved.

'Don't worry, a fuck works for me.'

She wanted to say more but the words wouldn't form. She opened her mouth, but a silly grin got in the way. She couldn't stop smiling long enough to communicate verbally any more, so the only thing to do was to use actions instead. Putting aside her glass, she reached for his hand, then shuffled backwards on to the bed, dragging him along with her as she went and swivelling around so she was lying against the pillows.

'Oh Lizzie, Lizzie,' he murmured again, and like a horny

schoolboy, he almost threw himself on top of her. Claiming her mouth in a messy, frantic kiss, he rocked his pelvis against hers. Lovely heat bloomed, born of the friction, her pussy loving the pressure and his hardness, her body quickening in familiar, rampaging lust. Cupping his muscular buttocks, she pressed herself even tighter against him, using him to shamelessly work her clit, knowing she was but a breath away from coming after only moments. Such a rocket-ride to orgasm was as absurd as the entire situation, yet it was happening, boy, how it was happening.

But how could it not happen when she loved this man so much?

Kissing her hard, John ran his hand up and down her body, supporting himself on his other arm. It was a frantic exploration, as wild and inaccurate as the kisses, but as rousing as his most complex and sophisticated sex games.

When he thumbed her nipple, and jerked his hips, knocking her clitoris with the knot of his cock, she growled against his lips, coming quick and hard.

Holding her tight, he let her soar, pulsing with pleasure. The peak lasted just a few moments, but when she descended she was smiling, renewed and energised. Her funny turn was a thing of the past, and she was ready to go again, and take him with her this time.

'Well, that was very nice, John, but I thought you wanted to fuck me?' She tugged at the waistband of his underwear.

He laughed. 'Of course I fucking well do, you minx!' Rolling on to his side, he wiggled out of his trunks, still managing to look elegant while his erection bounced free and slapped against his belly. As Lizzie reached for it, he tapped her fingers gently aside and went for her knickers too, helping her out of them. Moving against her, pressing his body to hers, he kissed her hungrily, then drew back, even while she was winding her arms around him again and squirming against him.

John grinned then kissed her again. 'And you're a demanding madam, Ms Aitchison. Perhaps I should spank your luscious bottom first for being so forward.' Sliding his other hand beneath her, he squeezed her bum.

'Later, maybe…But let's do the wild thing first, eh? I've been gagging for it for a month.'

'So refined,' he said with a laugh, adjusting their positions so he could slide his hand between her thighs. 'Now, let's concentrate on the job in hand.' Twisting his wrist in a clever, clever way, he slid a finger inside her, and rubbed her clit with his thumb.

'Please do. Although could we possibly engage some of your other anatomy…you know…further south?' She rocked, pressing herself against his cock.

'Hell, yes!'

He clasped her sex in a brief hard squeeze, making her gasp, then shifted around with a swift mammalian grace. Sliding his hand beneath the pillow, he pulled a condom packet out from under it.

'You were sure of yourself.' She watched him handle himself, sliding on the contraceptive. 'Condom always at the ready, eh?'

'Hopeful, rather than sure, love. One always lives in hope,' he said, adjusting the fit, then, happy with it, rolling between her thighs.

Leaning his weight on his arm, he kissed her, his mouth soft, beguiling, and loving. Between her thighs, he guided his cock to her entrance, notched himself there, and pushed in, working his hips in a long, smooth shove.

Lizzie clove to him, bringing her knees right up, tilting her pelvis, coaxing him, *commanding* him to go deeper.

'Yes. Oh God, yes,' he chanted, starting to thrust. It wasn't eloquent, but to Lizzie it was music. She added mutterings and encouragements of her own, swinging herself against him as he plunged into her. On instinct, she locked her ankles at the base of his spine, straining against him and drawing him in deeper.

Grunting, gasping, and happily cursing, they rocked and slammed against each other, every one of John's thrusts knocking against her clitoris, again and again.

It didn't take long, and within moments, she was coming again, shouting out loud, barely coherent, praising his name as her body rippled and clenched and embraced him. Her fingers gouged at his back and buttocks as she climaxed, and she knew, in a clear high-floating part of her mind, that she was hurting him, but she could no sooner stop doing it than stop breathing.

'Oh my lovely, lovely girl . . .' John's voice cracked as his hips hammered, the unmistakable strokes pounding into her as he seemed to come and come and come, taking her up, flying high with him again.

'Oh my lovely, lovely man,' she echoed, laughing with pleasure and going limp as they floated down together, spent.

2

What Now?

'So, what now?'

It had to be said, but still Lizzie froze, waiting on tenterhooks. Back in the car park, at the station, he'd been all about her 'taking him on', but what did that really mean? They led completely different lives, located in completely different places. How on earth was a proper 'relationship' going to work?

John gave her a crooked grin, and a shrug, and her tension ebbed. The gesture was so boyish, so not the all-powerful businessman, that it always got to her. She loved him as the dominant one, and her sometime master. But seeing glimpses of this other John, the cute, slightly unsure, slightly younger incarnation, was just adorable . . . and another huge turn-on.

Focus, woman.

'Well, to be honest, love, I haven't really thought it all through yet. I just decided to drop everything and come north, when Brent said...well, when he said you were missing me.' He poured tea into two turquoise china cups, then added milk. He'd rung down for room service after they'd made love, and it had arrived while Lizzie had been showering. Now they were sitting together on the bed, bundled in towelling robes, nibbling the Waverley's delicious home-made biscuits, the tea tray their impromptu 'what next' picnic.

'And I thought I was the impulsive one. You're usually the man with the plan right out of the gate, being Mr Business and all.' Lizzie grinned at him. It was always fun to tease him. She knew what it often led to, and that was something simple and thrilling and relatively uncomplicated, compared to the tangle of 'relationships'.

'Indeed I am. Just shows what you do to me, you perplexing madam.' John grinned back, his face alight. She'd never seen anyone with a smile quite like his. Always new, it had that magic quality of lighting up a room. Her hand shook as she reached out for the cup and saucer he held out to her.

The tea was perfect. Milk, no sugar, just as strong as she liked it. He'd clearly noted her preferences a month ago.

'It's quite a kick to be able to send a grown man, and such a mega alpha male, doolally. I've never quite managed to do that before.' She took another sip of her lovely tea. Why did a simple cuppa taste like nectar after sex? Or even *before* sex? The glint in John's eyes had subtly changed. 'I could really get a taste for driving you to distraction.'

'Careful, little escort girl, don't get above yourself.' His tone was teasing and husky, and there was desire in his gaze again. A fond kind of desire, but still fiery enough to make her heart rev up and her own lust gather low in her belly.

'Ah, but I'm not your escort girl any more, and I can do what I want now.' Shooting him a fierce look of her own, she reached for a biscuit and nibbled a bit. It was heavenly, but gorgeous as it was, she wanted something *more* heavenly. And just as delicious.

'Is that a fact?' replied John, his voice arch as he set aside his cup and saucer on the tray, and gave her cup and saucer a look as if to say they were superfluous, and that she was blatantly defying him by hanging on to them.

Favouring him with a slow, provocative smile, Lizzie sipped her tea in a leisurely, savouring fashion, and ate more of her biscuit.

John shook his head in mock despair.

'I think you owe me something, Lizzie.'

'Since when?' She knew what it was. She couldn't help but smirk.

'Since when we were at the party at the mansion, Ms Wicked, and don't grin like that at me.' He sat so still, and his face had a slightly stern look now, even though there was laughter in his eyes. 'I granted you a rare privilege, and now it's your turn to pay me back.'

Excitement surged, a sharp, high wave inside her. For a while, memories of that party had been a blur, and it'd felt wrong to revisit them in the face of what had happened afterwards. But now that Brent was well and happy, it was OK to look back, and the erotic thrill of dominating John – albeit temporarily – was a treasure she recalled with profound relish.

He was in charge now, though. And probably would mostly always be. It was a sweet thrill all of its own and one that she'd missed during the weeks since he'd left. Not knowing if she'd ever see him again, she'd banished all thought of being spanked or played with in the way John had spanked and played with her...because she knew there'd never be a man she'd allow to do it to her again.

'I don't know what you mean.'

'Oh, I think you do, Miss Aitchison, and it's payback time.

Now take that tray and put it on the sideboard, then come back here.' His eyes still fixed upon her, he slowly rubbed the palms of his hands together, as if assessing the rigour that they might inflict on her. Watching him made Lizzie's desire roll, like a pot of thick honey on a flame. Her sex fluttered, as if already anticipating the reward she'd receive for her…endurance.

'Come on, be quick about it,' he added.

Sliding to her feet as gracefully as she could, she snatched up the tray, making the cups and spoons rattle. Her gaze shot to his, and he gave her a mock frown. At the sideboard she set the thing down as gently as she could, but there was still another clatter. Her whole body was trembling in anticipation.

Walking back towards him, to where he now lounged on the bed, she lifted her head, staring back at him boldly. She couldn't help it; she knew she was the most useless submissive really, but perversely, her master seemed to like it that way.

John shook his head slowly, making his blond curls dance, and a smile haunted the corners of his beautiful, plush mouth. 'Remove your robe, slave.'

That word always made her want to giggle at first, but his eyes blazed so fiercely at her that she lowered her gaze, and obeyed.

Oh God, it was always the same. The deep, randy surge of desire. Baring herself to John was new every time, always like the first time, when she'd undressed for him while masquerading as an escort, freshly picked up in the bar downstairs. She'd never been vain about her shape, and always ruefully admitted that even though she looked a bit like the 1950s glamour model Bettie Page, she didn't have that goddess's incredible figure. But seeing the reflection of herself in John's brilliant eyes, her self-esteem soared and she *loved* being in her own body.

Slowly, and with a bit of a burlesque flourish, she let the thick, fluffy robe slide down her arms, then straightened her spine and set back her shoulders, to present herself to the eyes of her master.

'Beautiful,' said John softly, drawing in a deep breath, as if she were Venus rising from the waves, or even the great Bettie herself, reborn to her glory days. 'Now touch your breasts. Put on a little show for me. Let me see how you pleasure yourself when I'm not around.'

'Well, I don't stand up to do it, and that's a fact.'

Oops, a slip-up. Insubordination. She could already imagine the impact of his hand, hot on her bottom. Retribution.

John sighed, a gusty theatrical sound. 'Did I say you can speak? No. And if I desire you to play with yourself while standing up, you play with yourself while standing up. Do you understand me?'

Lizzie nodded, snagging her lower lip between her teeth as she braced herself up and went about her task.

First, she cupped herself, cradling the slight weight of her breast and flicking at the nipple with her thumb. Just that small action made her gasp, sending a sharp silvery jolt of pleasure right from the tip of her breast to her aching clit. She couldn't help but rock her hips, and she daren't look at John, knowing he'd have seen the movement, as he saw everything.

'Be careful. Be very careful. Now, pinch your nipple. Do it hard.'

Swallowing, she obeyed, shocked by the pain, yet in the eternal paradox, also loving it. In all the brief time they'd spent together, she hadn't completely figured out why she could both dread and enjoy punishment. In normal logic, it didn't make any sense, but in a beautiful chintz-clad bedroom at the Waverley Grange Hotel, it was exactly as it should be.

She pinched harder, suppressing her gasp as her clit throbbed, almost as if that were being squeezed too. Maybe that was next?

'Touch your pussy with your other hand. Rub and squeeze at the same time, caress your clit.'

Again she obeyed, shocked at the wealth of slippery, silky fluid between her sex lips. As she stroked her clitoris lightly, she held her breath. She was incredibly close. As a woman with a fairly average relationship with her orgasms – sometimes easy, sometimes not so much – it always astounded her that with John, they were always within reach. Sometimes, he only had to look at her and she was on the brink. If anybody had suggested that was possible before she'd met him, she'd have told them not to be so daft. But with him, strange miracles could happen.

'No climax. Not yet. Not until I've spanked you.' His wonder-smile was devilish, a wicked icon to her eyes. 'But try and get as close as you can without orgasming. Go right to the edge.'

You swine! You perverse swine!

She railed at him inside, but she obeyed him, loving the perversity, loving the way he pushed her. Her clit trembled beneath her fingertip, and she tried to back off a bit, rub a bit to one side. Could he see what she was doing? She was often convinced he had X-ray vision, and that he could see every secret of her body, and sometimes even her heart.

'You're cheating, Lizzie,' he said, swinging his legs off the edge of the bed. The bathrobe he wore was thick and luxurious, but she could still see the prominence of his erection. Its tantalising promise took her mind off her own problems. Soon…soon…she would have him again.

'The game's rigged.'

'Tut tut…I never said you could speak. When I was in the army, we'd have called that insubordination, young lady.'

Despite his instruction, her fingertip stilled, and her other hand dropped away from her breast. 'You were in the army?' Curiosity skyrocketed, and the desire to know more of his life outside the bedroom momentarily made her forget about sex.

Slowly shaking his head, John favoured her with another despairing grin. 'You really are the most incorrigible submissive, Lizzie. And yes, I was in the army once. But only for about a fortnight, so I didn't rise all that far in the ranks.'

'What happened?' She imagined him, however briefly, in uniform, his curls brutally shorn. He'd still have looked fabulous, and despite his pampered lifestyle, she knew his mind and body were rigorous. Why hadn't he stayed in?

John reached out for her hand, drawing it away from her body. 'I'll tell you one of these days. But now can we get back to the matter in hand? I think you need your bottom smacked, to get you back on track.'

'Yes, sir. Just as you wish, sir.' She feigned a subordinate, military tone.

'I do wish,' he said, tugging gently on her arm, guiding her towards the classic position, across his lap. It seemed so natural and easy, and in the blink of an eye, she was lying belly down, stretched over his knees, her head dangling, her hair a black curtain around her face. John caught her hands together at the small of her back, holding them in one of his while with his free hand he started stroking her naked bottom.

Softening her up . . .

Inside, Lizzie trembled, even though she tried to keep still, and not be that oh so incorrigible submissive. Being motionless, pliable and obedient was a great goal to shoot for, but not easy. It was John's fault, though. He was too gorgeous when he was stern, or acting that way. His faux severity induced a volatile reaction, mostly the near uncontrollable desire to wriggle about and rub her body against his. The compulsion gripped her now, the need to work herself against his cock, through the thick cloth of his robe, and excite his flesh as much as he excited hers.

'Hush. Be still.' His voice was soft, authoritative but not harsh. His hand stilled on her bottom, fingers shaped to clasp the outer curve of it.

Lizzie quieted down, but it wouldn't last for long, that she knew.

'Oh, you beautiful woman, how I've missed this.' He squeezed a little, as if savouring the resilience of her musculature. 'All the time we've been apart, I've fantasised about touching you like this. Touching and stroking this gorgeous arse of yours. It's just perfect.'

'I hope you've thought about the rest of me too.'

'Of course I have. The rest of you is perfect too, but you know what a horny old dog I am, love. My mind tends to run to sex, and to doing kinky things with you.'

'Me too.' It was the truth. She had fantasised too. And she'd played with herself, dreaming of a moment like this, even if she'd not truly expected it to arrive. The truth of it overwhelmed her again, and a few tears formed in her eyes.

I am so lucky!

'Did you dream of me touching you?'

'Yes, all the time.' Not strictly true, but near enough.

There'd been times when all she wanted was just a glimpse of him again, a sight of his smile.

'And did you touch yourself, thinking of me touching you and spanking you?'

'Hell, yes!'

'Me too.' She could hear that longed-for smile in his voice, and feel the desire in his exploring hand as his finger slid into her cleft from behind, gliding and tickling. 'Do you want an orgasm now, before we start?'

She did, but she didn't. She didn't know what she wanted. Just anything really, if it came from him.

'No...it's OK. It'll be better after.'

Not sure if she'd made the right choice, she shuffled on his lap, ruffling up his robe and dislodging it. Bingo! Where the panels slid apart a bit, there was bare thigh beneath, with a bit of body hair...and his cock pressing hard, pressing hot.

'Naughty, naughty.'

Without warning, the first slap landed like a thunderclap. She'd barely had time to register his fingers quitting her pussy before they'd struck her.

'Oh!'

It stung. How it stung. The heat from one simple blow was enormous. No matter how much she'd thought about this in the last month, she'd forgotten its intensity. Before she knew it, she was squirrelling about on John's knee, fighting his hold on her hands, and bumping and jostling his erection.

But he was unswerving and resolute. He spanked her steadily, his rhythm and aim breathtaking, spreading an even veil of simmering heat across both her buttocks within the space of a minute or two.

Even though she was the one being disciplined, Lizzie was in awe of *his* discipline. His control. His quiet composure in the face of extreme provocation, mainly in the form of her rubbing herself against his cock so shamelessly.

When her bottom felt as if it were about to combust, he stilled his hand, fingers resting on the fury. 'Oh my God, you're amazing. You look so gorgeous, Lizzie. Your skin marks like a dream.' Nearly bending himself double, he pressed his lips against the crown of each hot round in two little kisses. 'Perfection...pure perfection,' he breathed against the heat. 'I've got to have you again, love. I've got to have you *now*.'

'Thank God for that,' gasped Lizzie as he released her hands. Desperate for him, she shuffled on to her knees on the soft rug beside the bed. Looking over her shoulder at him, the sight of his stiff cock made her want to purr. From between the folds of his dressing gown, it jutted, so eager, so hard, and a perfect fit for her. *The* perfect fit.

'Come on, I'm waiting,' she commanded him, full of sudden power. The switch was automatic. Submitting to John filled her with strength and confidence, and the power to order him about in return. With a happy laugh, he tumbled on to the rug behind her, and draped himself across her body. The press of his skin against hers, and the texture of the towelling robe . . . both stirred the heat in her spanked buttocks. She hissed through her teeth, but the sensations only excited her more than ever. Made her want him more and more. She dished her spine, pressing her bottom and her sex against him, loving the rock-hard feel of his erection pushing against her.

Leaning on one arm, he explored her with his free hand, caressing, squeezing, arousing. He fondled her breasts, her belly and her thighs, then slid his fingers into her sex, finding her silky wetness and stroking her clit.

'Oh...Oh God,' she crooned as he pleasured her with his

fingertips, stroking and circling the tiny organ, touching and teasing with exactly the right pressure and action. Within seconds, the pent-up yearning fractured and her sex flexed and rippled in a hard, deep orgasm. She pitched forward on to her forearms, overcome, tossing her head from side to side, making incoherent sounds, some of which just might have been, 'John! John! John!'

With his body pressed against hers, the pleasure was contained and magnified, but after a few moments, some semblance of thought returned. 'Please . . . oh please, fuck me,' she gasped. 'I want you in me.' It sounded so wanton, yet her heart soared, loving her ability to command him, the dominance *he* provoked in *her*.

'Nothing would make me happier,' he whispered in her ear, then fell back a little, lifting away from her to rummage in the pocket of his robe, and then shuck it off.

'Another handily placed condom?' She lifted up a bit, turning to look back at him, grinning. He was always prepared, and was already rolling on the latex.

'Do you blame me?' he said, flashing her a quick, hot look, then concentrating on his task, snagging his lower lip between his teeth as he smoothed the fine rubber over himself. Like that, he looked boyish again, like a horny but responsible lad, suiting up ready to shag his first love. For a moment, Lizzie remembered his story of Benjamin, John's heavy crush back at public school, the one he'd said he'd loved for about two weeks. Had Benjamin been his first sex partner ever? Or simply his first man? Maybe one day, when they knew each other better, she'd ask him.

But not now. Now, all she wanted was him. He was *her* first love. Her first real love. She'd thought she'd loved before, a boy or two, a man . . . yes, even Brent. But fond as she'd been, and no matter how much she still cared for her house-mate, it wasn't this. This wonderful, all-consuming, all-encompassing emotion she experienced with John Smith, the miracle man she'd found completely by accident that first night here at the Waverley.

Not wanting him to see the raw love on her face, she collapsed on to her forearms again, offering herself to him. She did love John, but she couldn't expect him to love her back in quite the same way, if at all. He'd said he didn't do the hearts and flowers thing, but he *did* care in his own fashion, she was absolutely certain of that.

Especially when she felt the hard push of his cock against her entrance. Hard, but measured, thoughtful of her, not greedy. He eased in, making her his, entering not simply her body, but her very heart and soul.

With a gusty sigh of happiness, she let him in, relaxing to ease his progress, and then, when he was right in, lodged deep, she clenched actively around him, embracing his hardness.

'Oh Lizzie, yes, yes…you beautiful woman, yes!' He gripped her by the hips, his strong thumbs pressing against the soreness in her bottom, making her growl with the pain and the perverse delicious thrill of it. She clasped him harder, tensing her inner muscles, and he let out a fierce oath, then thrust, deep and hard.

He was wild, a force of nature, and she responded with a savagery of her own, giving as good as she got, pressing back against him as he pressed into her. Still she squeezed him as best she could, but it was getting more and more difficult to concentrate, like being in the centre of a whirlwind.

'Touch yourself, love,' gasped John, still pounding. 'Touch yourself . . . I want you to come. This's not just for me…it's for you too.'

He always thought of her. Always. Even when he was half-blind with lust, on the point of orgasm, he thought of her. Half sobbing, she buried her face in her forearm, and with her free hand reached back to touch him, to grab at the flexing muscles of his thigh, telling him with the simple contact what she couldn't speak to him in words.

That done, she obeyed him, sliding the hand to her own body, finding her clit, giving it a little rub. It was all she needed.

Sweet sensation bloomed again, and she rippled around him, seeing stars and his beautiful face in her mind's eye. Gasps and little cries fell from her lips, and she collapsed forward, only to be held tight around the belly as John came too, hammering into her, painting the air with divine profanities as his semen pulsed and spurted.

Time seemed to muddle, but somehow, they ended up in tangled heap together on the rug, spooned and breathing heavily. The steady lift of John's chest against her back was reassuring, like a wave slowly beating against the shore. His raw cries of pleasure seemed to echo still in Lizzie's ears, unfettered. She loved that about him. He was a sophisticated man...and a primal male. Like no other lover she'd ever had, and none she'd even imagined.

Oh, God, how I love you . . .

Why not just tell him? Just whisper it now, put it right out there, while they were both mellow?

But her gut told her it was too soon, and maybe, perhaps, always would be.

3

Diamonds are a Girl's Best Friend

He missed her. She was only in the bathroom, yet he missed her. The sensation was so intense, it almost made him dizzy.

Oh Lizzie, what have you done to me? I haven't felt like this for years, and I'm not sure I wanted to feel like this when I did...Yet still, I can't turn away. I can't not want you as much as I do.

The tea in the pot was long cold, but he would have loved a cup. Anything to settle him, any normal act, to get him out of this hyped-up state so he could think straight. He took a bottle of water from the mini fridge and sipped slowly. It was fresh and pure and cool...and goddamnit, that only reminded him of her.

Fresh and young, cool and composed, and still pure even when at her most carnal.

When he'd received that email from Brent Westhead, the one that seemed to clarify the younger man's relationship with Lizzie, John's heart had begun to sing. And even while such an out-of-control state alarmed him, he'd still exulted, knowing she was missing him as much as he was missing her. With barely a moment's hesitation, he'd rearranged his schedule as best he could. Then, he'd flung some clothes in a bag, fired up the Bentley, and just set off north. He hated to think how many anxious voicemails, texts and emails would be waiting for him when he turned on his phone again, and he'd specifically asked the staff at the Waverley not to forward any but the most urgent messages to him, while he was in residence.

He had a huge, unavoidable meeting in New York in a couple of days' time, and no desire whatsoever to be there. All he wanted was to be here: looking at Lizzie, talking to Lizzie, touching and kissing and fucking her.

And spanking her too. Oh hell, yes…how he'd missed that. Not once in his years of exploring BDSM had it ever been the way it was with her. With Lizzie, even the simplest and most playful games had moment, and significance.

Was it wrong to feel like this? This driving urge to possess her utterly, and make her his, even knowing his own shortcomings? The need was so strong, he feared he might crush her with it, and that must not happen. He needed to keep control of himself, and take things slowly with her, for *her* sake.

It's not all about you, man. You mustn't overwhelm her and you mustn't just fuck the living daylights out of her because she makes you so horny. Behave like the gentleman you're supposed to be, even if you've never believed you are one.

And yet, the lust was there. He wanted her now. His cock was hard beneath his robe. Again. Still . . .

Striding to the window, he opened it, breathed in the fresh air from the garden. There were techniques he'd learned, to regain control of himself, and to calm fears and urges, and he tried them now.

Their effect was minimal.

But he would not, should not, exhaust Lizzie with his

demands. It wasn't all about sex, sex, sex, and he must never make her feel that was all she was to him. He'd told her he didn't do hearts and flowers, and he knew she was too smart to expect that, but still, he ought to try, at least a bit.

And he was capable of some of the trappings of romance. He turned towards the bags and boxes he'd retrieved from the wardrobe. The booty that was the only other thing he'd paused to stow in the Bentley on his departure.

These were the gifts he'd so carefully selected for her while they'd been apart. Not the little fun items he'd sent to her at home, but the other ones. The treasures he'd been choosing for her in a sort of irrational dream. Lovely things he'd lavish on her if she were ever to become his girlfriend, his mistress…or whatever it was she was to him. A status that was far more than girlfriend or mistress, but much, much less than she deserved.

Eyeing the packages, he smiled. She'd resist, of course. He still remembered the almost pitched battles he'd had with her over money, when they'd still been doing their call girl and client dance, only a month ago. Lizzie wasn't materialistic. Not like certain other women he'd known.

But she deserved good things. All good things. Everything he could give her.

John smoothed the shiny paper of one of the carrier bags, straightening the tiniest of creases that marred its perfection.

He was a persuasive man, and he'd use all the charms he had at his disposal to coax her into accepting these…even if he knew that it was something else, something far less tangible, yet far more significant that he wished to God he might have been capable of offering.

*

What the hell would the Waverley think of them? All these showers, all these wet towels, all this hot water. Lizzie ran her broad-toothed comb through her hair, and smoothed it into some semblance of a style. Her fringe was a bit floppy, not Bettie-fied at all, but it was the best she could manage at the moment.

At least the twinkle in her eyes and the subtle glow on her skin were flattering. The by-products of being freshly and very thoroughly fucked made-up for many deficiencies in the hair and make-up department!

As had become a habit with her, after her kinkier dealings with John, she flipped up the back of her robe, and checked her bottom. A bit pink, but weirdly, almost pretty looking. It was just a gentle glow now; there was no longer any real pain.

She pressed her finger against the rosy coloration, but still nothing of significance. John was clever that way. He knew how to hurt but not hurt, a very rare skill, she guessed. Letting the robe drop again, she reached for the pot of fragrance-free moisturiser from the hotel's complimentary basket of bath and beauty products.

Hmm...they must have assumed that one of their most favoured customers was likely to have his 'companion' with him again, regardless of whether or not she was supposed to be an escort this time. There was a broad selection of high-end female goodies in and amongst the products that John might be expected to use.

Out in the room, their cosy haven of chintz and sex, Lizzie found John partially dressed. She'd urged him to shower first, so she could loll around a while and get her breath back. Now, he looked positively edible in a pair of fantastically fitting jeans and one of his favourite soft blue shirts. He hadn't fastened it yet, and so there was still a nice wedge of firm, muscular chest on view.

'I thought we might go down to the restaurant for dinner. For a change of scene, and to give me a chance to show off my beautiful girlfriend.' He beamed at her, looking so masculine and so possessive. She'd never really liked the latter quality in previous boyfriends, but somehow with John, it was a positive not a negative.

Girlfriend, eh? Was that what she was?

But Lizzie didn't feel quite polished enough to be shown off. She'd never expected to see John when she'd set out, only this morning, to see Brent off at the station, so her jeans and simple top were a bit on the casual side for dining out. John was wearing jeans, of course, but *he* could get away with anything, anywhere. He had the unshakable self-confidence born of wealth and power and looks.

'I'd love to, but I didn't exactly dress for a posh dinner at the Waverley this morning. I…I never expected to see you.' *Ever again*, she almost added.

John crossed the room, and stood in front her. 'You look like a goddess whatever you wear, sweetheart. And even if this place had a dress code, I think they'd pretty much be prepared to waive it for me, and anyone with me.'

'What do you mean? You haven't bullied them into letting you buy the hotel, have you?' Lizzie wasn't sure how she'd feel about that; she'd felt a contrary satisfaction in the fact that the management of the Waverley Grange had resisted her lover's millions, preferring their independence.

'No, alas not. The Guidettis have stood firm.' He shrugged, and gave her a quirky smile, as if he'd read her thoughts. Lizzie remembered the handsome man with long black hair, the one she'd originally assumed was the manager of the Waverley. She'd since discovered that he owned the hotel too, with his wife, and even if she didn't really know either of them, she still wanted them to retain control of their distinctive hotel. 'They won't sell the Waverley itself, but they've been thinking of expanding, and they've got a business plan for a club in town, something a bit metro and fetish, for punters who don't want to drive all the way out here for events. It's very savvily costed, and I think it could work out well with the Waverley's recherché reputation behind it, so I've agreed to float them some capital.' He cradled her cheek with his hand, thumb moving gently. 'So you needn't worry about the filthy plutocrat gobbling up the little guy. It's just an investment by a sleeping partner.'

'Well, I'm glad to hear that.' She turned her face, and kissed his palm, loving the way his long, strangely dark lashes fluttered down as if the touch of her lips induced ecstasy. 'But it still doesn't solve the problem of me looking like a scruff-bag in their lovely dining room.'

John took hold of both her hands in his, and then kissed their backs, one after the other. 'Well, I thought of that. Keep your jeans…mainly because I want to imagine them snug and tight, pressed against your gorgeous rosy bottom, but you might find something amongst that lot to go with them.' He nodded to one side.

Standing by the wardrobe was a pile of large, shiny, very suspiciously gift-like carrier bags and boxes, in white and various colours, all fastened with ribbons. Hanging on the front of the wardrobe was a plain, but intriguing, white garment bag.

'What are they?' She knew what they were. Presents for her. Oh, he shouldn't have. How many times did she have to tell him, *he* was enough!

'Just a few little things I thought you'd like.' He smiled, looking like that young boy again, who, this time, had saved up his pocket money to buy his sweetheart a treat.

Lizzie smiled. How could she be ungracious? John was thoughtful. He didn't expect anything for anything and, if he did, she'd have given him what he wanted anyway.

'Ooh, lovely…it's like Christmas in midsummer. You're very kind. May I look?'

'That's what they're for, doofus,' he said with a laugh, kissing her hands again before releasing her.

Lizzie carried everything to the bed, and spread it out. There was lingerie, *lots* of lingerie. Silk, satin, exquisite froths of delicate lace, but also some fresh, sweet items in white cotton, innocently styled and trimmed with cute embroidered motifs. It was typical of him not to go for all the most obvious looks. Some of it *was* very racy, and almost disturbingly abbreviated, but the fun knickers and bras and camisoles somehow pleased her the most. She picked out a set trimmed with tiny blue flowers.

The garment bag revealed a loose, casually fitted over-shirt in heavy, almost liquid silk-satin. The base colour was midnight blue, but it had a shadow design that made her smile: 1950s motifs, jukeboxes, diner signs, rockabilly cars. Just the job for a casual dinner, worn over her jeans.

John had chosen exactly the sort of shirt she'd have chosen for herself, if she'd had the money. Silk of that calibre wasn't cheap, and though it wasn't an obvious designer label, the workmanship was divine.

The damned man could read her mind…even when she wasn't actively thinking about things.

'It's gorgeous, John. I love it! But how did you choose it?'

He sighed, as if revisiting some sorrow, some ennui. 'I was in Dubai, for a deal. And I felt as if I had to get out of hotels and boardrooms for an hour. I didn't know what to do with myself and somehow I ended up rambling around a shopping complex in a daze. I took one look at that in a boutique window, and I knew it was "you".' He stroked a finger over the silk. 'I was thinking of you . . . missing you . . . and knew you just had to have it.'

Had he really thought about her that much when they'd been apart? He'd said so, earlier, but it was still hard to imagine someone like John wandering aimlessly around a mall, thinking only of her.

'Thank you, John,' she said, leaning over to kiss him, moved beyond the ability to express it properly. 'It's perfect. Wonderful...I'll get changed now. I'm really hungry, all of a sudden. What time is it?'

'I don't know. Around seven, I think.' He consulted his watch on the bedside cabinet. 'Seven-thirty, love . . . Doesn't time fly by when you're enjoying yourself?' He grinned, clearly pleased with the idea that they'd been so lost in passion they'd lost track of time.

'Oh God...Shelley! She'll be wondering where on earth I am. I'll have to ring her.'

Guilt pelted down on her like rain. She'd completely forgotten her friend, her other house-mate, Shelley. Brent might have gone to stay with his parents for a while, but Shelley was still in residence, and if she'd arrived home from a day out at work temping to find Lizzie not there, she'd be wondering what was going on.

This is what happens when you spend the day shagging your billionaire boyfriend, Lizzie Aitchison! She'd completely forgotten she had things to do. Commitments. Heck, she'd even forgotten *meals*. No wonder she was ravenously hungry.

Buckling on his watch, John returned to her and squeezed her shoulder, reassuringly. 'Look, I'll just nip downstairs and have a word with Signor Guidetti. I need to speak to him anyway. You have a chat with your friend. Touch base, reassure her you're OK.' He glanced at his watch, which looked solid, complex, workmanlike and suspiciously as if it might be made of platinum. 'I'll be back up here around eight, and we'll go and eat then, OK?'

So decisive. So organised. Just the qualities that had made him so successful. She watched as he buttoned his shirt, tucked it in, and then put on a light jacket. When he'd stowed his phone and his wallet in his pocket, and slipped his feet into loafers, he gave her a quick kiss, then headed for the door.

'See you soon, sweetheart.'

Then he was gone, and the pretty room seemed ten times as empty as it should have done.

When Lizzie switched on her phone, she found it awash with voicemails and messages from Shelley.

'Nice of you to call at last,' barked her friend, answering Lizzie's call. 'I've been worried sick. No word. Phone off. Nothing. It was only when I called Brent in a panic that I found out. Nice of you two not to mention this secret reunion to me. I'm only one of your best friends, Lizzie. It's really not fair.'

'I'm sorry, I'm sorry, I'm sorry … Really.' She was, knowing how she'd have worried in Shelley's place. 'But to have John appear again, out of the blue … well, I just got swept away, you know. I really am sorry, though.'

Shelley laughed, her voice clear in the earpiece. The other woman never held grudges or got cross for long. 'OK, love, just as long as you're all right. You are all right, aren't you?'

'Yes. Yes, I am, very much … Yes.' And she was, mostly.

Almost completely…Except for the little questioning voice that kept telling her that dreams like this were too beautiful to last for long.

Lizzie, you idiot. Why be such a pessimist? Live for the moment!

'I'm not surprised, you lucky beggar. He's freaking gorgeous. And loaded too! If he'd come back to sweep me off my feet, I'd forget that *you* even existed!'

Lizzie smiled. She could still remember the time Shelley had met John, fleetingly, in the wake of Brent's suicide attempt. The blonde girl had just stared, almost gobsmacked at the sight of him, as if she'd just been introduced to a movie star or to a woman's fantasy of male perfection made real.

'Well, glad you approve. I *am* lucky, I know that.'

'And he's lucky to have *you*,' said Shelley, with emphasis. 'Now, will you be home tonight? If not, don't worry. As long as I know where you are…Which is the Waverley, I presume?'

Now there was a question. John had sleep issues. He'd slept beside her once, but that didn't mean he was miraculously cured, did it? He still might not want a woman in his bed all night, and if he couldn't sleep, *she'd* have to leave. Nobody could function properly without rest. Especially a high-octane lover like John, who invested one hundred and ten per cent energy into sex.

'Yes, we're at the Waverley, but I'm not sure about whether I'll be coming home or not. It's very possible I will. I'll try and phone you again later. Don't worry about supper or anything. We're just about to go and eat.'

'OK, sweetie. Enjoy yourself. Not that there's much doubt on that score. Think about me when you're scoffing posh nosh with a billionaire at the Waverley, and me and Mulder are eating beans and dry bread here.'

'And I'm playing my violin here.' Lizzie smiled to herself, knowing her friend's tendency towards drama. 'Look, you can have my deluxe paella out of the freezer if it'll cheer you up…and there're some roast chicken slices for Mulder.'

The two friends chatted for a few minutes more, and then, with an instruction to pet Mulder the cat on her behalf, Lizzie rang off, and got back to her final preparations.

The shirt fitted like a dream, and despite its superficial simplicity, Lizzie admired the clever darting that made it hang so elegantly on her body. She made a mental note of the positioning and technique, for future reference. With her dressmaking skills, it should be easy enough to adapt a pattern and run up a shirt or two like it, only using a slightly cheaper fabric of a similar weight.

Beneath the shirt, the pretty, floral-trimmed bra and knickers fitted perfectly too. Had John scrutinised the labels of her clothes during their previous time together? He must have done. Either that, or he was so used to women that he could size them up, purely by eye.

Don't think about his other women. Of course he's had them. He's older and too gorgeous and too eligible for him not to have scores of exes…but he's here with you now, and that's what matters.

'Ready to eat?' said John as she finally emerged from the bathroom, with the best attempt at make-up and hair that she could manage with the contents of her bag. Her 'Bettie Page' fringe wasn't quite as accurate as she'd have liked it to be, and her nude lip tint was a bit pale, but lifted by the glorious shirt, she still felt pretty confident that she looked good. She hadn't heard John come back into the bedroom while she was primping, but she hoped he liked what he saw, too.

'Yes, I'm starving. Let's go down!'

'Splendid,' said John, but then he paused and fished inside

the pocket of his jacket. 'You look utterly gorgeous, but perhaps there's just one final touch we can try.'

On the palm of his hand, he held out a small, dark-blue jewellery box.

Oh no, it can't be . . . he said he wasn't interested in all that . . .

Settling her heart, and sternly admonishing her subconscious, Lizzie stepped forward and took the box. There were plenty of other things that came in jewellery boxes; it wasn't just rings.

And this was a pair of earrings.

A pair of diamond earrings.

Diamond earrings…with very *big* diamonds.

Lizzie's heart did a flip-flop. It was too much. *They* were too much. Girls like her didn't wear rocks like these.

John looked a bit worried, presumably by her gobsmacked silence. 'I hope you like them. I noticed that you just wear very plain studs, so I thought something simple like these would be your kind of thing.'

'They're gorgeous . . . They're beautiful . . .'

Simple though the diamond studs were, even with only a slight knowledge of gemstones, Lizzie would have bet good money on the fact that they were worth more than the house she lived in.

'But?' John gave her a steady look, as if he'd read her every qualm.

How to tell him, without seeming like an ungrateful bitch? There probably wasn't a way. 'They're glorious, John. Absolutely exquisite…but you can't give them to me. I mean, they're real, obviously…so they must be worth a small fortune!'

For a moment he looked puzzled, genuinely at a loss. Then he smiled. 'Of course they're real and of course I can give them to you. I like them. I can afford them. They'll look fabulous on you. Where's the problem?'

Put like that, it was simple. And she longed to see the satisfaction in his eyes when she accepted his gift . . . but still.

'OK…OK,' he said. 'Let's try this. You wear them this evening to please me. And we discuss the issue of you keeping them at a later date. Does that sound reasonable?'

So reasonable. You're such a grown-up.

Thinking that, Lizzie almost laughed. He *was* a grown-up. A mature, urbane, sophisticated man, over twenty years her senior. A man prepared to pay for what he wanted without a qualm. As he'd paid for her, that very first night.

'Um…yes, OK.' She gave him a smile, wondering if he understood. 'And thank you, even if for just this evening. They are the most beautiful things I've ever seen.'

Except you.

'Finally! Now pop them in and we'll go down. Do you need me to help?' His smile at having won the point, at least for the time being, was dazzling. His blue eyes flashed, far more brilliant and precious than the gems.

When she entered the restaurant beside John, Lizzie wasn't sure what the women at other tables were looking at most. Her, her earrings, or John.

Mostly John, I should think, with umpteen thousand pounds worth of diamond bling a close second.

They were shown to a table by the window, the one they'd shared once before and which commanded the best view out over the formal gardens of the Waverley, and the long park beyond. Instinctively, Lizzie scrutinised the treeline, looking for the tell-tale gap, and the path that she and John had trod. It was not much more than a month, but it seemed like a lifetime since their wild games in the little dell. First, her spanking with a willow switch; then afterwards, their tumultuous fuck amongst the grass and leaves, her riding John, her bottom still aflame from his fierce attentions.

Happy days.

A different heat flamed in her face now, and when she looked at John he was grinning.

'Good times, eh?' He reached out and placed his hand over hers. 'I can still see you, glaring down at me like a gorgeous Amazon goddess subduing her unworthy subject. That was some afternoon.'

'It was indeed…that switch thing you cut was murder!'

John's slow smirk made her tremble. It was his *I know what you're feeling right now* smile. His X-ray smile. He knew she wanted him again, switch and all.

'And how are you feeling now?' He leaned in close, his voice barely more than a breath, just for her ears. 'Is your delicious arse still tingling?'

'John! For heaven's sake.' She glanced around, wondering if anyone had heard, despite his low tones. Her bottom actually wasn't sore any more, but she certainly didn't want anyone in their vicinity hearing it discussed.

'OK . . . OK . . . I'll behave,' he said, still smirking, mercurial and boyish again. 'Shall we have some wine?' He nodded, over her shoulder, presumably to some waiter hovering across the room and hanging solely on the every whim of the most favoured guest.

'I'd love some. And to answer your question, no it isn't. No ill effects.'

'Good,' he said roundly, as the waiter scuttled over.

The meal they ate was delicious, as everything at the

Waverley was. The hotel might have a naughty reputation, but it excelled in all the good things a normal high-class hotel would, and the dish of poached sea bass in a fennel and butter sauce was breathtakingly yummy. Food, wine, accommodation, a beautiful setting, the Waverley had it all. No wonder John had wanted to buy it.

Mellowed by a little alcohol, Lizzie was able to relax, even in John's eternally provocative company. He too seemed chilled, asking her about her life since they'd last been together, about how Shelley and Brent were doing now, and especially about her sewing and how she liked working at the dress agency.

'How's that working out for you?' he said, laying down his knife and fork, and taking a sip from his water glass. The enquiry seemed casual, but she sensed it was really far from that. 'You sounded quite excited about it in your emails.'

She was excited. Working at New Again was like a gift. 'Fantastic! It's a perfect, steady supply of sewing jobs...and I love working in the shop too. The clothes are wonderful, and Marie is a doll.'

After she'd abandoned temping, Lizzie had popped into the local dress agency on a whim, thinking there was no harm in asking if they needed anyone to do alterations for them, and happily she and Marie, the owner, had instantly clicked. There was plenty of sewing work to do for New Again, and Lizzie had been thrilled when Marie had offered her a chance to work in the shop part time too.

'I hope she's not working you too hard.'

'No, not at all,' said Lizzie firmly, 'and anyway, I'm not afraid of a bit of hard work.'

'Well, then, here's to New Again.' Smiling, John lifted his glass and clinked it to Lizzie's in a toast. 'And to Marie, and plenty of work that's not too hard.'

After a while, they started people-watching, indulging in simple 'couple' fun and eyeing up other diners nearby, just as some were eyeing them up.

'I'm sure that's him off the telly,' said Lizzie in a whisper, glancing to one side, without turning her head. A couple two tables away were chatting animatedly: he, with dark, curly hair and glasses, and looking strangely familiar; she, glowing and vivacious, beautifully voluptuous and clearly besotted with her man. 'You know, the guy who does those history shows…The really cute one. He's usually on BBC2 or BBC4…I've always fancied him.'

'Really? Is that a fact?' countered John, with a mock saturnine quirk of his brow. 'I'm not so sure I like you letching after other men when I'm right here in front of you.' The words were possessive, but his puckish grin told her he was just having fun.

'There's no harm in looking,' replied Lizzie, grinning back at him. 'And what about his lady friend, don't *you* fancy her? She has a gorgeous figure.'

'She has indeed. But so do you. The most gorgeous ever.'

She wanted to tell him not to be idiotic, but it seemed ungracious and combative to keep on rebutting his statements. When he said these wild things he seemed completely sincere…and it *was* nice to be complimented. In her heart of hearts, what woman didn't enjoy being called beautiful?

More importantly, though, John didn't talk down to her, or treat her as if she were some brainless bimbo, easily manipulated by a few pretty words. A man of experience and great achievement, he always addressed her as his equal, except when they were power-playing, for fun.

As the couple they'd been observing rose from their table,

meal finished, Lizzie tried to follow their progress across the restaurant without being too obvious. The historian, Daniel Something, must be accustomed to being recognised, but it was still rude to stare. She supposed John got a lot of that too; even though she'd never seen him on the television or in the papers, his movie star looks and that special, almost regal air of his always drew the eye.

But Daniel the historian and his lady friend had eyes for no one else but each other. Unable to help herself, Lizzie zeroed in on their hands. Yes, matching wedding rings. They were married. As she watched them disappear into the foyer, that fugitive niggle of wistfulness touched her heart again.

Forget it, Lizzie. He doesn't want marriage and commitment, so you'd better disabuse yourself right now of all notions along those lines. And heck, woman, would you even want to get married if he wanted to?

If ever there was a man who came with complications, John Smith was that man.

4

Strangers in the Night

'I think I should go home tonight.'

It was what he'd been going to suggest himself, so why did Lizzie's announcement cut him so hard?

'Do you really want to? Can't you stay here?'

Oh, why oh why had he said that?

Way to sound whiny and possessive, man.

He'd made her feel awkward now, he could tell. She was frowning, her smooth white brow puckered beneath the thick black fringe that he adored so much.

'I'd like to...I really would, John. But I think it's for the best.' She reached out across the table they were sitting at, in the Lawns Bar now, and laid her fingers on his hand. Her touch was soft, almost like living light, but it had the old instantaneous effect on him. His cock lurched to erection, sudden and hard, as if she'd reached into his trousers and touched him there instead. 'This is all so new. I've had a wonderful time today . . . a beautiful time . . . but I don't think we should rush too fast. After all, if you add up all the time we've spent together, we barely really know each other at all.'

But I want you! I want you right now. And I'll want you in the night, even if I don't manage to sleep a wink!

It was the inner voice of the horny, ridiculous young man he'd once been, governed solely by his passions and his cock. The wiser tones of John, the forty-six-year-old who'd made far too many mistakes, told him not to be a petulant idiot. He-man possessiveness had screwed things up for him in the past, and he wasn't going to let that happen with Lizzie.

'You're right…I know…It has been sudden, hasn't it?' He scanned her face. Was she disappointed? Did she really *want* the caveman approach, and for him to metaphorically sling her over his shoulder and carry her back to bed for another round of ruthless, banging sex?

It was difficult to tell. She looked a little young and confused, and very sweet. Bless her, she had even less idea of what to do about this thing of theirs than he had. Which was another reason to give her all the space she needed.

Don't stifle her, you dolt. You know what happened with…with Clara. You were greedy and possessive then, and look what happened.

'Yes, it has. And then there's your sleeping thing too. There's only one room and one bed. We'll both be shattered if we stay awake all night. Especially . . .'

A sugar pink blush stained her cheeks. It both enchanted him and made him harder than ever. She was saying that she'd stay awake for him, and with him, if he wanted her to.

His sleeping thing, she'd called it. Now more than ever he wished he could conquer the problem. For over twenty years, since his incarceration, he'd found it impossible to sleep with someone else in the room. No amount of therapy could overcome the way he'd conditioned himself during those long, terrified nights, and he wouldn't succumb to medication, either. Bewitching as the thought of sleeping in

Lizzie's arms was, in reality, he'd only ever managed to drift off – for a scant few moments – on a couple of occasions. And then his psyche, memory, call it what you will, had roused him, clanging a red alert. If he consciously attempted to fall asleep with her, it just wouldn't happen, and if he lay awake beside her warm, tempting, luscious body . . . well . . . the inevitable reaction would occur.

They'd probably end up fucking the entire night away.

Which was all very well and thrilling in books, but in practical terms, impossible. Although the thought of it still made caveman-John want to leap over the table and shag her right there on that accommodating wide red leather banquette.

Now it was *his* turn to colour up, and Lizzie grinned as if she'd read his intentions.

He twisted his hand and enfolded hers. The shape of her palm and fingers was so slender and graceful. She had the nimblest touch, as befitted a seamstress, but those fingertips could wreak magic on his flesh with their tricky, delicate ways. His cock throbbed, as if subject to that fantasy caress.

'I know…and you know what I'm like. I wouldn't be able to resist you, and then we'd both end up knackered in the morning, when *you* didn't have to be.' God, he wasn't putting this very well, was he? Where was the killer negotiator when he needed him?

Her face was pinker than ever. 'It's not that I don't want you, John, because I do…but, well, you're a very rich and lavish diet for a girl who's not…um…not used to overindulging. I've been living on plainer fare until now.'

A knife of jealousy sliced through him. He didn't like to think about her prior sexual diet at all. Was she still thinking about Brent? Damn it, he'd told himself he must draw a line under any thoughts of the men Lizzie had been with before him. Especially her house-mate. But still that atavistic savage inside him growled.

'You're a delicious dish for me too, Lizzie. But I know what you mean and you're right. We need to do this a tad slower…at a pace where we can enjoy the process like grown-ups.' Her hand still rested in his. Had she trembled? Maybe it was him? Wanting her so badly yet trying to contain himself. 'And *I* need stop acting like a selfish, greedy sex addict. You've got so much more sense than me, love. I need you to keep me in line.' Her eyes twinkled, and he knew she was thinking of that time back at the mansion sex party, where she had indeed kept him in line. Her instinctive dominatrix skills had taken his breath away. 'Well, some of the time…occasionally…You know what I mean.'

She smiled. 'Indeed I do, indeed I do. Sometimes it's nice to mix things up.'

'Seriously though. You *are* right. We both need to sleep tonight. Especially . . .' He took a deep breath, hating what he had to tell her. This lightning visit up north had been shoehorned into a murderous schedule; he hadn't thought of anything but seeing her. 'Well, I have to be in New York the day after tomorrow, love. Something fairly important. I'd put it off, but the negotiations are on a knife edge, and success could lead to a lot of new jobs being created.'

Still the smile, but somehow not as bright. He could see her fighting to be sensible. 'Jobs where?'

'Oh, UK jobs…quite a lot of them. Some of them could be in this area, and I know there's a lot of unemployment,' he said, impressed by her sharp judgement.

'Well, that's excellent. I hope it goes well. It's a good thing.' She twisted her hand again, gripping his and bringing

it to her lips, briefly but fiercely. 'And you should be rested
and at your sharpest.' She released him. 'Perhaps I'd better
be on my way now. Shelley will be expecting me home. I still
feel bad about disappearing without telling her.'

'Let's finish our drinks, eh?' He glanced at his gin, and her
G&T, finding both unappealing.

Why did he suddenly feel he'd let Lizzie down? Why
did he keep on wanting stupid things he knew he simply
shouldn't have?

Why did he suddenly want to take everything about her
life, and make it *his*?

'Do you have nosy neighbours?'

John was walking beside her down St Patrick's Road,
carrying all the bags containing her new goodies, just as if
he was a perfectly normal boyfriend walking his perfectly
normal girlfriend home after a day at the shops. He'd told
the driver of the chauffeured hire car to drop them at the end
of the road, and circle round, so they could cover the last bit
of the way together on foot. Though he hadn't mentioned it,
or made anything of it, Lizzie wondered about the sudden
appearance of a hired driver. She suspected that John never
drove himself anywhere now if he'd had a drink.

'Some of them are a bit like that, though not too bad.
They'd probably have noticed a big car rather than a couple
on foot, so I doubt if anybody will actually be hanging out of
their windows to look at us.'

*Unless, of course, they catch a glimpse of you, in which case,
their eyes will be out on stalks. It's not often a man who looks like a
movie star comes strolling down St Patrick's Road!*

She couldn't keep her eyes off him, either. She still kept
stealing glances to convince herself he was real.

But he wouldn't be here for long. Soon he'd be in New York, and she'd be back leading her normal life.

Better that way, wasn't it? Taking things slow? Being sensible? John would be home again in a week, and then they'd have more time.

But it was still going to be tricky. She *did* have a normal life. And now she had John too. How was she going to integrate them both? Her commitments…and her demanding, possessive man? She couldn't let people down, especially now, when things were going so well at her new job at New Again and with her other sewing work.

John's return was a beautiful miracle, but it wouldn't be without complications, that was for sure. But as she snatched yet another quick glance at him, striding along beside her, swinging the carrier bags slightly, and with the light from the newly lit street lamps making his golden hair shine like a halo, Lizzie felt positive.

Dear God, woman, he's the fantasy of every female who ever had half a hormone! Forget the fucking complications!

By now they were outside her house, number ten, which she shared with Shelley and Brent, about to bid a chaste and polite farewell again.

'Well, I can't see any curtains twitching.' John scanned the houses on either side, then the windows above. 'Looks like someone's home upstairs.'

There was a low light glowing in Shelley's bedroom.

'That'll be Shelley. She's probably reading, or watching YouTube vids on her laptop and cursing at the buffering. Our internet connection is crap.'

Feeling like a nervous teen after her first date, Lizzie felt an urge to scuff her feet, as if an irate parent was going to storm out any minute and catch her with the school bad boy.

'Well, this's it, then. I…um…I'd better get in before she looks out of the window. She's got a sixth sense about these things.' She held out her hand for the bags.

'I'll walk you to the door.' John's tone was no nonsense, and he was already halfway up the path before she could stop him.

'We usually use the back door.' Lizzie nodded to the dark passageway, half-hidden behind a large shrub, which ran between the garage and the house. John took one look at it, then turned to her, transferring all her bags to one hand and grabbing her hand with his other.

Without a word, and before she could draw her breath, he drew her into the deep gloom of the passageway, masked from the road by the shrub, and beyond the reach of all prying eyes, in a cloak of shadow.

They only got halfway along it.

Without warning, John dropped the bags, and swept Lizzie into his arms, pressing her against the garage wall with his entire body. His lips came down hard on hers, not giving her the chance to protest, even if she'd wanted to. Which she didn't.

It was a comprehensive kiss, fierce, rough and complete. His tongue pushed for entrance, filling her mouth, brooking no resistance, owning her. Lizzie stabbed back at him, giving as good as she got, her heart singing, her body alight as if he'd turned a switch. Their awkward farewell had become a bonfire of passion.

Oh yes! Oh yes! No matter how we blunder about doing the 'get to know you' dance, this always works. Right out of the gate.

She grabbed at him, hands surging up and down his back, settling on his muscular buttocks, so firm and tight beneath soft denim. When she squeezed, he made a husky sound in his throat and rocked his pelvis against her. It was impossible *not* to notice that he was rigidly erect, but he seemed intent on making sure she was aware of the fact, just in case.

God, how she loved his cock! She loved the man. That was a given; she couldn't hide it, and she didn't want to. But in a different, primal way, she loved his superb body and the fierce thrust of his penis, always so ready. He roused in the blink of an eye and had the staying power of a man half his age.

Rocking and squirming, she rubbed herself against him, trying to work her sex on the knot of his. They were in a dream, a bubble of space and time that had nothing to do with their location and everything to do with their lust. When he pulled up her blue shirt, thrust his hand beneath it and then pushed up her bra to cup her breast, she growled into his mouth, her hips jerking as he thumbed her nipple.

'You devil,' she hissed when he freed her mouth, and applied kisses to her face and her throat as he caressed her. She didn't care; she had the power to berate him, to goad him into all the outrageousness she craved.

He answered by pinching her nipple and, retaliating, she squeezed his bottom hard, digging her fingertips into the cleft.

'Witch,' he snarled, sucking hard on her neck as if the darkness had turned him into a vampire.

The clatter of a dustbin lid, in a garden somewhere down the road, froze them. But they didn't spring apart, and John maintained his grip on her breast.

'What if Shelley comes out?' she gasped, saying it, but still not caring, her brain on hold.

'She won't.' John kissed her again, quick and fierce.

'How do you know that?'

'I've got powers.'

'I know that.' She pressed her crotch at him, saluting one of them, and snatching a kiss back from him at the same time. 'But seriously . . . we . . . we . . . Maybe we could go inside, sneak upstairs?'

'No, love. That way we'd probably *really* embarrass your friend, because I wouldn't be able to keep from roaring like the King of the Jungle when I come in your beautiful cunt.'

The blatant words made her body ripple, right in the place he deemed so beautiful. She ached for him. She needed to come. Boy, was she going to have to masturbate tonight, her face buried in the pillow to suppress her moans. She wished they'd stayed at the Waverley. She could have slept on the bathroom rug at a pinch.

As if he'd heard the thought, John attacked the zip of her jeans, working it down, then pushing his hand inside, beneath the cotton of the pretty knickers he'd bought her.

'John! What are you doing? We can't!'

Hypocrite, she lashed herself, wiggling about to make his hand's ingress all the easier, ravenous for the perfect touch of his fingertips.

'Yes, we can…and I will…I'm going to give you an orgasm to remember me by, a parting gift for you to dwell on while I'm away. I'm not leaving this stupid alley until you've come. At least once.'

'Oh John…no…you mustn't,' she gasped, every nerve screaming, *Yes, yes, go on, do it! It won't take a moment!*

His finger found her and she moaned, working herself on it. She was silky and slippery, but John still stayed on target, rubbing her roughly, fiercely…just the way she wanted.

'I must. Because you want it. Don't lie.' His finger circled, fast and sure, and he slid his other hand down to grasp her bottom, rubbing the crease through her jeans, tantalising her anus. The pressure stirred the faint echo of where he'd spanked her, and the heat whirled though her pelvis, twining with the jerking pressure on her clit.

A great cry of pleasure surged up, but before Lizzie could utter it, John kissed her, suppressing all sound with his wicked, marauding tongue. Jerking her hips furiously, she clung on to him, one hand digging deep into his soft golden curls, gripping and tugging; hurting him, probably, but unable to stop herself doing it.

The climax seemed to go on and on, but in reality lasted barely a moment or two. It was big . . . huge . . . all-encompassing and, as she descended to earth, Lizzie slumped in John's hold, knees like tissue paper. His hand shaped into a cradling cup, no longer working her sex, but just gentling and holding it. With his free arm, he held her tight around the waist, supporting her and pressing her carefully back against the wall, so she wouldn't tumble.

Her chest heaved as if she'd run a marathon. She held on to him for dear life. Who cared if Shelley came out? Lizzie couldn't move, and didn't want to. John would be gone in a few moments and away across the Atlantic tomorrow. Time was precious.

Against her, John was still erect, and it was that fact which awakened her. She stirred in his embrace, and tried to reach for his crotch, but he said, 'No, don't worry about me. I'll walk it off. It doesn't matter.' Then, rubbing his face against her hair, he muttered, 'Come to New York with me! We can be together. Fuck every night. Don't worry about clothes and packing, just grab your passport and we can buy everything you need when you get there. You've still got the black card, haven't you?'

The request was sharp, urgent, the words staccato as if they'd somehow escaped his higher consciousness and shot out from the depths of his psyche.

What a trip it would be. Together in an iconic foreign city, living the high life that was normal to John, but an unbelievable dream for her. It would be like stepping into a fantasy from a book or movie. She opened her mouth to say yes, even though it was impossible.

'I can't, John. I wish I could. It's wonderful of you to ask me…but I've got things I have to do, and people I can't let down.' It was all true, but even as the words left her lips, she felt – knew – that she was letting down the most important person of all, by refusing.

I'm too small for his life. I can't take off into the blue, just like that. Pretending to be a call girl at the Waverley is the wildest thing I've ever done.

There was a long, charged silence. She expected John to pull away from her, cooling. But still he gently held her pussy, his cradling arm still around her back.

'I know, love…I'm just being crazy, trying to race ahead when I said I'd take things slow. I'm a fool sometimes, but it's just *so* hard to leave you.' His lips moved softly against the side of her face, the contact infinitely tender. Her heart lifted. He wasn't disappointed in her.

Yet still she said, 'I'm sorry.'

'No, Lizzie, no. There's nothing to be sorry about. It's me. It's been a long time since I've been "with" someone like this, and I've forgotten how to do it. You're so delicious, and I just grab like a greedy kid, when I should be acting like a grown-up.'

They held each other for a few moments more. Thoughts, regrets, wishes, crazy longings all turned over in Lizzie's head, and she sensed much the same happening to John. It was all too mad, too sudden. A few days to let it sink in would do them both good. Wouldn't it?

Eventually, John slipped his hand out of her knickers, and fastened the zip and the button of her jeans, neatly 'putting her away' before straightening her bra and shirt too. Then he put both arms around her again, and hugged her against him.

'I'll be back as soon as I can, sweetheart, and then we'll talk properly, eh?' He kissed her, the contact sweet and chaste, despite the fact that he still had a massive hard-on. 'Today's been about our bodies getting back together again. When I get home from New York, we need to let our brains catch up too. We'll have more time then, and you'll have had a chance to catch up with stuff you need to do.'

She didn't like to tell him that there was pretty much a constant demand for her sewing and alteration services nowadays, especially at New Again. And she'd have a double workload tomorrow, after playing hooky with John all day today. She'd have to work something out.

'Yes, that sounds like a plan,' she said, straining to absorb and record the feeling of him in her arms. The solid reality of a man who was straight out of her dreams. 'I think I can just about struggle through a day or two without being serviced by you.'

'Minx,' he replied fondly. 'I hope you've got a good vibrator, so you can use it and think about me. Maybe we can build in some time for phone sex while I'm away. As I recall, you're very, very good at that, Miss Aitchison. I had a very pleasant time of it, on my own, listening to your voice and your exotic dungeon fantasies.'

Eek, yes, that.

'Um…yes, I think I've got a vibe somewhere. I haven't

used it lately. Until I saw you in the Waverley that night, I'd been leading a pretty nun-like life for a while.' A flash of memory popped into her mind. A rather nondescript boyfriend accusing her of being a frigid nun…She felt grateful to him now, *really* grateful. That offhand, nasty remark had been in her thoughts when she'd first met John in the Lawns Bar, and faced the greatest adventure of her life. It'd made her go for it…and go for him. How strange life was.

'Well, your nun-like days are over now, sweetheart. Even if we do spend time talking and getting to know each other properly and all that, there'll still be constant sex as well, you know.' His brilliant blue eyes twinkled in the shadows, and pressed against her body, his still-hard cock stirred. 'If you can manage that?'

'Oh, I'll struggle through somehow.' She let her hand slide around him, until it settled on his erection. 'Look, are you sure you don't want me to do something about this?'

'No, it's all right, sweetheart. Like I said…I'll walk it off. And it'll do me good to exercise a bit of self-control. I'm going to have to contain myself for the next few days. It doesn't do to go waltzing into critical meetings sporting an erection.'

'Oh, I don't know. It might distract the opposition so much that they lose their concentration. And then you can haggle them down and get a better deal.'

John laughed, his chuckle as dark as the shadows surrounding them. 'You may have a point there, love. I might try it if negotiations get tough.'

He kissed her again then, and for a few moments, they continued to kiss. It was going to be a long two or three days.

Eventually, they broke apart, though, and promising to

text, and call her whenever he could, John escorted her to the back door and saw her inside.

'Bye, love,' he whispered, as she stood on doorstep. 'Think of me. I'll soon be back.'

And with one last kiss, blown from the tips of his fingers, he was gone.

5

Girl Talk

The sound of feet thudding through the house woke Shelley from a doze. She'd been reading, futzing about on the internet, and watching some rubbish or other on the telly, all of it done to distract herself from thinking about Lizzie. And what her friend might be doing with that unbelievably gorgeous, unbelievably rich man of hers.

I must not be jealous. I must not be jealous. I love Lizzie and she deserves him. I must not turn into a green-eyed devil because she's getting a ton of sex again...and I'm not.

It was hard, though. Shelley set aside her laptop and her Kindle, and shoved her feet into her slippers. The noise downstairs should have made her scared – there'd been break-ins in the area recently – but she was pretty sure that it *was* Lizzie, returned from her tryst.

Which was weird in itself.

If it was me, I'd have stayed. What on earth have you come home for, you silly mare!

'What on earth was all that racket? I thought we'd got burglars. Shouldn't you be at the Waverley having your brains fucked out by that glorious billionaire of yours?'

Lizzie was in the hall, and she looked up sheepishly as Shelley came downstairs. She was surrounded by suspiciously high-end-looking carrier bags, presents, no doubt. But she was blinking a bit too, as if she'd been crying. Shelley decided there and then that if it was tears, John Smith was going to get a piece of her mind, expensive gifts notwithstanding.

'Sorry, I didn't mean to wake you,' the dark-haired girl said, swooping up her bags as they made their way to the kitchen, the heart of the house and the chapel of tea. 'I was . . . um . . . just rushing to the front window, to get a last glimpse of John. But he'd gone by the time I got there.'

Shelley narrowed her eyes, worried.

'Don't worry, we haven't had a row or anything. It's just that he's off to New York in the morning and I won't see him for a day or two.'

'Right . . .' Shelley reached for the kettle. Better get brewing the cup that cheers. 'Men, eh? Here today, gone tomorrow. But at least it looks as if he's left you some pressies to soften the blow.' She nodded to the bags. 'And that's new too . . .' Lizzie was wearing a beautiful shirt that Shelley had never seen before, insanely expensive by the look of it, although suspiciously rumpled at the moment.

'It's lingerie, mostly . . . and there was this . . . and these . . .' Lizzie swept aside her thick dark hair and Shelley nearly dropped the teapot.

Good God. Diamonds. But then, the man *was* a billionaire.

'Lemme see, lemme see.' Shelley hurried over, and it was her turn to blink, and be dazzled. The diamond studs were *huge*, and breathtakingly beautiful. Pure drama next to Lizzie's inky black hair. 'You jammy devil! They're gorgeous . . . No wonder you let him do all kinds of kinky things to you.'

'It's not like that!' Lizzie's hazel eyes flared. She looked like a lioness, righteously defending her mate.

'I'm sorry, love. I'm just jealous as hell. I only met him for a few minutes, but he seems like a nice guy, even if he is into spanking.' Hypnotised by the gems, Shelley stared into their iridescence, but then noticed something else. 'Good grief, maybe he is Mr Nice…but how old is he, *fifteen*? He's given you a love bite, Lizzie, didn't you realise?' The mark on Lizzie's neck was as red as a brand of ownership. Men, honestly!

'Oh, sod! I didn't realise.' Lizzie flew across the room to the little kitchen mirror, almost tripping over Mulder the cat, who'd just mooched in to see what all the fuss was about, and to check for food. 'Damn, I said I'd work in the shop tomorrow. Now I'll have to wear a tastefully arranged scarf, and you can bet some of the golf club matrons will think I'm taking the piss out of them.'

'But how could you not realise he was biting your neck? He doesn't look like Dracula.'

Shelley knew the answer, though, without Lizzie articulating it. A man like that could just sweep you away, just make you *feel*, without giving consequences the slightest passing thought.

'He just…I don't know…you'd have to have been there,' said Lizzie, touching her throat briefly before she opened the cupboard to get out one of Mulder's Whiskas pouches.

I'd love to be there. Maybe not with John Smith, but some other man, a bit more my type.

That thought stayed with Shelley as the two women chatted over tea. It was a debriefing of sorts, a sketch of Lizzie's day with John, although Shelley had no doubt it was judiciously edited. Envy griddled her, but she tried to suppress it. Lizzie hadn't really had the greatest luck with men – even she and Brent hadn't truly worked out on that score – so she deserved to find a good one.

But don't I deserve someone too?

Shelley lay in the darkness, long after they'd both turned in, unable to stop the swirl of wistful yearnings in her mind. Lately, her dating luck had been worse than Lizzie's had been: either nothing at all, or arrogant gits who seemed only to care about themselves. It was time she got with a man who saw to *her* needs, and *her* pleasure, in the way John Smith obviously saw to Lizzie's. He didn't even have to be rich.

If that were the case, there was a perfect answer, though. A simple, elegant, if rather expensive answer.

I should really do it. Especially now. It's better than going on a chocolate and chips binge and ending up looking like a whale.

It made perfect sense, although if Brent found out, he'd probably go nuts.

Lizzie had trouble sleeping. There was an empty space beside her, even though John had only ever lain there once, and not for very long. He *had* slept here, though, if only for a few minutes.

You're a strange man, John Smith. Probably stranger than I'll ever know . . .

Though she'd sworn off those kinds of thoughts, they resurfaced. It was stupid to question what she had now, but she wasn't a woman for nothing, and women couldn't help speculating. The earliest cavewomen had probably worried about what would happen if their strong, providing mates got stomped on by a woolly mammoth. Or decided to go off with another cavewoman who had wider hips and bigger boobs.

Oh, for heaven's sake.

Sitting up in the dark, she shook her head. As if that might dislodge the stupid thoughts. Peering down towards the bottom of the bed, she looked to see if Mulder jumped on, but there was no sign of the little feline. Probably with Shelley, whose cat she really was.

Just about to lie down again, even if hopes of sleep were very thin, Lizzie jerked in surprise at a familiar sound, ringing at an unfamiliar time. Her mobile. She snatched for it, stabbed the icon and a text opened.

No need to reply. Just wanted you to know I'm thinking of you. J.

Just that? She smiled. It was enough. Gloomy speculations dispersed like mist, and settling down again, and hugging the quilt around her ears, she let the tiredness that had been chasing her since she'd got home catch up with her.

I'm thinking of you too.

She didn't text it, but she drifted off, knowing that he probably knew that anyway.

The next day was hectic, and she was glad of it. New Again was bustling, with lots of ladies shopping for 'gently worn' designer items, and a lot of them falling in love with frocks that just didn't fit them. All of which required a lot of tact and finesse on owner Marie's part, or the plying of Lizzie's dressmaking skills in order to bring dress and woman together in a flattering marriage.

The agency mostly stocked fairly recent items, but the odd vintage 'special' sometimes came along. Today's had been a beautifully constructed Jean Muir dress and coat that Lizzie had fallen in love with, even though it was far from her own usual style. Sadly, a rather overweight solicitor's wife from Kissley Magna, the 'posh' suburb of the Borough, had fallen in love with it too. Unlike some of their other, more status-conscious clients, this lady was a sweetheart, and Lizzie had felt desperately disappointed for her.

'Couldn't you perhaps just make me one a bit like it? I'd be happy to pay.'

This had led to a discussion, and a promise that Lizzie'd try to find a pattern.

'We should do that. Properly,' Marie had said, her clever eyes bright. 'Recreate classics, but with a twist. You could do it, Lizzie, I know you could. Let me do some costings . . . we'd need to do some new advertising. Invest a bit . . . I wonder if I could get a loan from the bank?'

A thought had popped into Lizzie's head, but she'd pushed it away again, not sure. There was no doubt in her mind that she only had to ask...but could she? She'd mull it over, while he was away.

While she was on the bus, going home from New Again, with a dress bag containing a couple of items to work on in the evening, Lizzie thought about John travelling too. Was he in New York yet? She didn't even know the time of his flight. It would have been first class all the way, no doubt, unless he had a jet of his own. He certainly didn't have a helicopter, because he'd once had to borrow one for that anxious night flight, racing home to be with Brent at the hospital.

No, if John had an executive jet of his own, he would surely have mentioned it then.

When she'd reached her bus stop, and was walking the last bit of the way home along St Patrick's Road, Lizzie's phone chimed, almost as if her thoughts had summoned her lover's message. It was a text again, and she stopped dead in the middle of the pavement to read it.

Busy day, my sweet? I wish you were here. I've got boring meetings ahead, but they wouldn't be half so dismal if I knew you were waiting back at the hotel for me, all warm and ready. P.S. Which of your new knickers are you wearing? Thinking of you, your very own dirty old man, J.

Lizzie smiled. He was incorrigible. Why hadn't she gone with him? Just thrown caution to the wind to be with the man she loved? But that wasn't in her nature. Even though she'd let them down badly in some ways, her parents had instilled a sense of duty in her, and Marie had been expecting her in the shop.

Who is this? she texted back. *Who are you, you disgusting old perv, texting innocent young ladies with improper enquiries about their underwear? I'll report you to the police. P.S. I miss you too…and I'm wearing the pink ones. L.*

She tapped in, *I love you,* then deleted it, and pressed send.

Mmmm…I love pink things. ;) Have to go now, gorgeous. Talk later. J.

Feeling hot, Lizzie stuffed her phone in her pocket, swooped up the dress bag, and hurried along the road, her mind running riot. It didn't take much to get her going, where John was concerned. She loved pink things too…Well, a certain thing that was ruddy, more than pink, and that got very big and stiff with alarming frequency.

'Your bloke's been sending you things,' announced Shelley when Lizzie walked into the kitchen.

'What do you mean, sending things? What things?'

Oh, he was so extravagant! She liked it, but it still made her a bit uncomfortable, being used to paying her own way. On and off, all day, she'd been thinking about the diamond earrings too, torn between thinking they were just too much, yet at the same time wallowing in the excitement that she,

Lizzie Aitchison, wearer of plastic beads and the occasional bit of Swarovski, could own something so divinely beautiful and costly. Currently, they were in safe keeping, stowed away in the little home safe Brent had installed beneath a floorboard in the coat cupboard, a holdover from his escorting days when he'd mostly dealt in cash.

Oh, how easy it would be to slip into pampered mistress mode…and keep the diamonds.

'Well, I finished early today and I was home just after lunch,' Shelley went on, 'and it's a good job too. A chap came from Virgin and installed a cable box with about a zillion channels and hyper super-duper fast broadband. I said we hadn't ordered it, and we couldn't afford it, but he said it was *paid for* already.' The blonde girl beamed, like a kid at Christmas. 'Then a courier came with more stuff. Looks like a laptop for you, and more tech stuff, and some other boxes.'

'Oh John! You swine!' Lizzie threw down her bag on the kitchen table. 'Where's this cable box?'

They marched through to the sitting room, and surveyed the technical miracle.

'It's fabulous…it's got everything. I've already watched two movies on the premium channel.' Shelley flung herself down in a chair, snatched up the remote and started flicking through the choices. '*Please* don't say we have to send it back. I know he's your billionaire, but think of your friends, woman! These are some pretty nice crumbs from your table.'

Lizzie smiled. At least she wasn't the only one benefiting here, so that was less of a guilt trip.

'And if you send the broadband back, Brent will kill you!' Shelley continued, not taking her eyes off the screen. 'You know how he's always bitching and moaning about the connection when he's gaming . . . He'll be in hog heaven now, at these speeds.'

But what was in the other boxes?

'I'll make our tea, then,' Lizzie said. Shelley was obviously settled, blissful in her own hog heaven. 'I'll bring it in here on a tray.'

'Ooh, yes, please do that.' Shelley's grin widened. 'And next time you see the golden god, ask him whether he needs a second girlfriend, will you? Or, alternatively, ask him what he's sending us next. A home cinema would be nice, and a new bathroom suite with a hot tub...oh, and one of those big American fridges, if he can manage it.'

'I'll see what I can do,' Lizzie said, though with no intention of doing so. She knew if she said as much as a word, there'd be workmen and more deliveries the next day.

6

Oceans of Time

Lizzie sat cross-legged on the bed, in pyjama bottoms and a vest. Her little clock radio said it was eleven-thirty. So what time was that in New York?

Shelley had been right about some of the gifts being tech. The screen of a glorious new laptop was glowing in front of Lizzie. It was huge, with a blindingly high spec, and all set up ready for her.

She'd just received her very first email, and it had simply said:

Hi, beautiful. See you on Skype later? John.

Was now *later*?

Back on the desktop, she eyed the Skype icon. It looked very small and innocent, but it made her nervous. Talking to John in person made her happy and excited; the prospect of a video call freaked her out, even if it was *him*.

She clicked the link and saw just one contact. Oh well, in for a penny, in for a pound. She waited while the system dialled or whatever it did, feeling impatient, and at the same time half hoping that he was still out at one of his meetings, and not available.

An anonymous-looking icon popped into the window, and John's slightly processed-sounding but unmistakable voice said, 'Hello, gorgeous.' An instant later, there he was; a little bit pixelated, but still handsome as the devil, and smiling just as wickedly.

'Gorgeous indeed,' he said, eyes a little lowered. Lizzie didn't know much about video conferencing, but she knew enough to know that he was looking at her image, rather than the camera at the top of the screen.

'Eek! Oh God, I should have put something nicer on!' Her own image, down in the corner, showed her less than new vest . . . and her nipples clearly visible through the white cotton.

'What you've got on looks plenty nice to me.' John's gaze flicked down again, and she guessed he was enlarging the window. She did the same.

John had got 'something nice' on too, one of his subtle blue shirts, and a very dark grey waistcoat. His hair was wild and tousled as if he'd been running his fingers through it, and she could see what looked like a natural wood headboard behind him. It looked as if he was sitting on his bed in his hotel suite.

'It's not. This vest is ancient, and you can see my tits right through it.'

'That's exactly what I mean.' His smile, across an ocean, and the ether, was dazzling, 'So, how was your day, honey?' he enquired, teasing.

'Oh, all right. Rather busy. Probably boring by your standards, apart from this degenerate old pervert who keeps sending me things, in the hopes that he'll get into my knickers the next time he sees me.'

'Such deplorable behaviour. I don't condone it.' John winked.

'He's very crafty too. Some of the things he sends are things to share with my house-mates, and if I were to try and return them, they'd be very upset.' She fixed him with a mock glare. 'That shows extreme deviousness, don't you think?'

'To a certain extent, but what if he just wants you and your friends to have nice things? With no ulterior motive?'

Gah, that made her feel even more guilty now. Because it *was* the real reason for the gifts. John was just a generous man, as plain and simple as that.

'You're probably right. I'm just being prissy.' She gave him a quirk of a smile, and immediately felt better when she saw his own crooked smile, like the sun rising in a distant New York bedroom.

'You're not prissy, sweetheart. Just a very decent girl. What would make you feel better about receiving such gifts? I'm sure this deplorable pervert would be glad to know. A charitable donation perhaps?'

Exactly!

'Well, our local Cats Protection branch is always in need of dosh,' she said, wondering how worthy he might think that was when there was world poverty and cancer to be cured.

'Consider it done. Well, I'll try to persuade the pervert, on your behalf.' The screen rocked as John shuffled and got comfy, leaning against the headboard. 'Now, can we set these ethical discussions aside for a while, and get to the part where you and I have some sexy talk? I've had a helluva day, and I've spent most of it longing to see you again, if only on a screen.'

Lizzie felt a pang of concern. Even though he was a god to her eyes, John looked more weary and careworn than she'd ever seen him. There were dark smudges beneath his eyes; he looked shattered. It was more than physical, more than just a bit of jet lag, a sixth sense told her.

'I'm sorry . . . and I really am grateful for all the nice things, even if you are a very naughty and very extravagant man.' She ran her finger along the edge of the unfamiliar laptop, wishing she was touching his skin. 'It's just that I've never done Skype before. It's a bit nerve-wracking. Sort of real but not real . . . do you know what I mean? I don't know how to *be*.'

John smiled. 'Don't worry. You're doing fine. Just be yourself, Lizzie, that's all you have to do. You're a breath of fresh air. You don't know how glad I am to see you. In more ways than one.' His grin broadened, and for the time being, at least, the weariness seemed to drop away from him. His blue eyes had that special twinkle again, the one she knew so well.

Have you got a hard-on, Mr Smith?

She'd bet good money that he did, but just from a fuzzed-up web image of her, and a few dark pixels indicating the location of her nipples? Obviously Skyping didn't inhibit him the way it did her. Even so, a little coil of lust suddenly stirred.

'You're blushing, Lizzie.'

'I'm not. It must be something wrong with the colour on your screen.'

'My screen is fine, woman. Don't try to deny that you aren't the tiniest bit excited. I certainly am.' He shifted position again. Was he touching himself, the dirty dog?

'I am, sort of, but how do we know that there isn't some tech support guy somewhere, monitoring this call, just waiting for us to do something rude?' Why had she said that? It was perverse. She almost *wanted* there to be a tech guy to get an eyeful.

'All the more reason not to be shy, gorgeous girl. Try and see it as philanthropy. A service to lonely nerds who might never get a chance to see a goddess like you at play.'

'Unlike the call girl you once thought I was, John Smith, I don't dispense my favours to all and sundry,' she announced pertly, expecting a laugh. But instead, that shadow passed across him again. 'Look . . . seriously, are you all right? You look a bit tired and stressed out . . . maybe you should get some rest?'

With a slow, worldly smile, he replied, 'Worried about the stamina of the old man, are we? I assure you when I get back, I'll leave you in no doubt that I'm not past it yet.'

'I never said that.'

'I should think not, but even so, I'll probably have to spank you when I get home, just to make sure you don't cast any more aspersions.'

'You'd do that anyway. Spank me . . .'

'True. Because I know how much you like it. Now, was there a certain little gadget amongst the things that were delivered? Something purple and white? I've a fancy to see how that item might work.'

Uh oh! Could she? Dare she? Over a video link? Somehow it seemed even ruder than the idea of using it while he was actually in the room with her.

'Oh, come on . . .' His tone was sultry, coaxing. 'You don't have to show me it *doing* anything. You can stay out of camera range if you're bashful. I just want to know if it works. Think of it as a way to relieve *my* tiredness and stress, as well as yours.'

Lizzie shuffled across the bed, and opened the box in question. She'd investigated it earlier and found the contents to be fully charged, and ready for action. 'Is this what you mean?' She held up the thoughtfully shaped little ovoid, the luxury high-end vibrator.

'That's the one. Turn it on.'

She pressed the ON button, on the basic setting, and it hummed in her hand, a soft, provocative buzz. Her palm tingled...and so did somewhere else. 'It...um...feels quite powerful.'

'Excellent. Nothing but the best for my Lizzie. Why don't you give it a whirl?'

My Lizzie. How good that sounded. Even under the circumstances.

'I don't think I can do it with you watching.'

'Then slide out of view. Your voice will be enough to get *me* going.'

Lizzie complied, turning the laptop to face out into the room.

'I see your bedroom is well up to its usual pristine standards,' came John's voice from the speakers, and Lizzie felt as embarrassed about the mess of clothes and books and sewing stuff as she was about the prospect of masturbating for him.

'Well, you know me...and I have been busy.'

'Don't worry about it. Just proceed.' He was a parody of stern now, his voice that of her strict but caring master.

Still nervous, she slid off her pyjama bottoms, and worked her thighs apart. Heart thudding, she pressed the Lelo against herself, parting her sex lips so the business end of it lay against her clit.

'I'm not hearing any buzzing.'

'Give a girl a chance!'

She turned it up. It purred. Her clitoris leapt in an instant surge of pleasure, the delicious rhythm making her gasp. Wiggling against the pillows, she opened her thighs wider, settling the little device close in.

'Good?'

'Yes…very.'

It *was* good. Divinely so. Not organic like the touch of John's fingers, but differently exciting. Clever as he was, he couldn't move his fingers as fast as the vibrations. She squirmed, holding it tight, not able to keep her hips still.

'Good as me?'

Ah, so like a man …

'Different.'

'Ah…tact…even at a time like this.' His voice sounded a little breathy, and over the hum of the Lelo, she could hear shuffling sounds emanating from the laptop's speakers. Was he masturbating? Even as she jerked her hips about, driven by the thrumming vibrator, she hoped so. Pleasure really might help to relax him, and let him sleep and catch up after his flight.

'Are you wanking, Mr Smith?' she asked, gasping.

'Could be …' He was gasping too.

I should hold back, make this last. Prolong the experience.

But, fuck it, she couldn't. She turned up the vibrations a notch, and cried out at the sudden jolt.

'Oh…oh God …' Her body got the better of her, and orgasm bloomed, intense and violent. Unable to contain her moans and cries, she crested the wave, keeping the vibrator pressed close, battling it, subduing it, conquering it. Her hips thrust of their own accord, one, two, three, lifting up off the bed. She shouted 'fuck, fuck, fuck' in time to her undulations, only dimly hearing John's voice in the background, crying out, 'Oh Lizzie, Lizzie…my beautiful girl.'

On two sides of the Atlantic, they lay in silence for a few moments. Well, not quite silence. Their breathing, their heavy breathing, was in sync. Then, as she settled back into herself, Lizzie tossed the vibrator aside, and wiggled back into her pyjama bottoms. She knew it was irrational, but she needed to be covered again before she turned the laptop back around.

'Are you all right?' she asked softly, and was rewarded by John's low, provocative laugh.

'I am now, thanks to you, gorgeous.'

When Lizzie turned the screen to face her again, she saw John had a light flush of pink across his fabulous cheekbones, and he was unconcernedly wiping his fingers with a tissue.

'You dirty devil,' she said fondly, wishing she could reach across the miles and give him a hug.

'Very true . . . but I feel much better for that. Thanks to you, my sweet.' He flung aside the tissue, and Lizzie wondered if his trousers were still open. The angle of the screen made it impossible to see, and it seemed that, despite his claims, he too was rendered as bashful as she by their mode of communication. If he'd been beside her, he'd have been flaunting his cock, even if it was temporarily soft. 'God, I needed that.' As she watched, he subsided against the pillows, his head tipped back. The way his bare throat tautened, framed by his open collar, looked strangely vulnerable. She longed to press her lips soothingly against his skin there. He was more relaxed now, but she could still see that troubled quality in him. To a degree that she wasn't sure she'd ever seen in him before.

'What is it, John? What's bothering you?' She hesitated. Was she crossing an unspoken boundary? He'd said there were things he might never tell her, but she wished he would, so she could help him resolve whatever bothered him. 'I'm sorry, I shouldn't have asked. It's not my business…but I just thought I might be able to help…you know?'

His eyes remained closed, those lashes of his so shockingly and irrationally dark against his cheekbones. Was he practising his bio-feedback? Trying to get control of himself? Perhaps reining in his vexation at her nosiness?

I shouldn't have spoken. But I only want to help.

'I know that, sweetheart. And I know you mean well…but not now, eh?' His eyes snapped open and, to her relief, she saw no rancour, just a hint of sadness. He wanted to tell her – something – but just wasn't ready. Yet.

And he'd also read her mind, apparently.

'You did it again, John. Answered me as if I'd spoken when I haven't.' She laughed, though it spooked her slightly.

'Did I? Sorry…I just feel as if I know you so well. Crazy, isn't it? You don't think you should ask me questions, do you?' He leaned forward, closer to the screen, and she could see the faint lines around his eyes, the laughter lines and the beautiful weathering of his forty-six years. 'I can understand how you feel…I'd be the same. I'm an awkward cuss, I know.' He reached forward, pressing his fingers to the inert surface of that laptop in a New York bedroom. Instinctively, Lizzie did the same to hers, willing herself to feel his beloved touch. 'I…I'll try to tell you more when I get home, I promise, but now I think we both need some sleep.' His lips quirked. 'It's not bedtime here yet, but I'm useless for anything else. Especially now I've had my wicked way with you…after a fashion. And you need to rest too.'

'I am a bit tired,' she admitted. Orgasm did that: the release of tension. Oh, if only she could lie in his arms to nod off. *He* probably wouldn't be able to sleep, but she would. Even knowing his phobia was far from banished yet.

'Of course you are, love,' he said, his voice soft, kind, almost hypnotic. 'And now we're going to say *au revoir*, and you're going to turn your laptop off and go to sleep. And I'll try and do the same. I'll email you, or text or phone you tomorrow, as soon as I get the chance and I know you're up and about.'

How lovely was the way he spoke. So smooth, so musical, so soothing. She felt her eyelids drooping, even though it denied her the sight of his heavenly face.

'Goodnight, beautiful Lizzie, sleep well. I'll be back home with you soon.'

'Goodnight, John . . . goodnight.'

Abruptly, the connection cut. It was like a knife . . . and yet a relief too.

If they'd stayed online longer, he might have seen tears trickling down her face, and that would never do.

It had helped. Talking to Lizzie, flirting, playing a little sex game. Coming with Lizzie, yes, it had all helped. Leaning back against the pillows, John searched for his inner calm and happy place, where she dwelt.

How delectable she'd looked, all cosy and cute, and yet the ultimate temptation. A goddess in her skimpy vest and old pyjama bottoms, her black hair a bit tangled and mussed up, fringe all awry instead of styled with its usual trademark precision. No make-up, no lipstain . . . a perfect, unaffected beauty.

He imagined what he'd heard. Lizzie wriggling about, teased and tormented by the toy he'd chosen for her. Legs akimbo…pyjama bottoms off? Yes, he thought so. There'd been rustling and tussling in the speakers. Her body would arch; her face would be a divine mask of orgasm, taut yet lovely, eyes tightly closed.

It had been easy, and it'd felt so right to stroke himself

as she'd taken her pleasure, an ocean and time zones away. She'd been close, just when he needed her. Absolute solace.

But now he was alone, confined with a source of disquiet and regret he'd not expected to encounter here in the Big Apple. He frowned with distaste at his mobile phone, and as he did so, the fucking thing rang again.

He didn't have to read the name and number to know who it was. This was the fourth time. Why the fuck was *she* ringing? It wasn't as if their first encounter after all these years had been a joyous reunion. He'd managed to be cordial to her, but it had taxed him. He, the tactician, who could always sweet talk the most pugnacious of business opponents, and rigorously contain his anger or distaste in the most combative situations.

But *she* was Clara, the woman he'd once loved. The woman he'd twice loved.

Oh God, the tricks pure chance could play! If only he'd decided to go straight back to the hotel after his last meeting. But no, on a whim, he'd decided to snatch the opportunity to visit his ex-wife, knowing Caroline was at her Manhattan townhouse. And it had been so good to see her. They were still fond of each other, and he valued her opinion and her wisdom. He'd been just on the point of telling her about Lizzie and himself, something he knew would have pleased her no end, when the thing he'd never expected – but which, if he'd had half a brain cell, he should have been prepared for – had happened.

Clara had arrived, and he'd been so angry with himself, for not being on his guard, that he'd felt like breaking something.

You're a half-witted idiot, man. Why wouldn't Clara be there? Caroline's her mother, for God's sake! Of course there's always a chance, albeit slim, that the woman who makes a habit of fucking you over might be visiting her own parent.

And now he was still angry, still confused. Angry at Clara because she'd made him think about *her*, and that'd blurred his focus on Lizzie. Lizzie was the woman he *wanted* to think about, and who was all give, give, give, and not take, as Clara had always been.

And yet Clara was part of what made him what he was. He'd given up long, hard years of his life for her sake. He'd adored her once. Hell, he'd adored her twice . . .

He could still remember his irrational elation when she'd sought him out after he and Caroline had parted. Forgiveness had been easy. He'd been full of hope . . . *This time*, he'd thought. *This time, we'll get it right. She was scared before, thrown into turmoil by what had happened.*

So, he'd given her a second chance, and for time a she'd moved in. He'd thought about marriage. And so had she . . . but not to him. Staying with him had been her bolt-hole while she'd formulated bigger plans. She'd targeted another prize, even greater than the vast wealth he'd amassed by then.

And when she'd snagged what she wanted, she'd been away, and laughing. 'Surely you knew it was just fun, darling. It could never really be serious again between us.'

Now she was poison to him. She'd made him hate himself and feel like a lovesick fool. And she'd soured the whole experience that he'd called 'love'.

Meeting at Caroline's, he'd all but cringed when Clara had touched him, almost wanted to physically shove her away, brush off the taint. He could almost feel that soft hand on his arm now, so insidious. He could still sense the iron will beneath her understated flirtatiousness. Clara had a habit of fighting dirty for what she wanted, and getting it. And he'd had an almost sickening feeling that it might be *him* she wanted again, despite their chequered history.

Oh Lizzie, if only you were here. You're my Amazon princess, and one touch from you could wipe away the memories, and make me feel whole again. With you I'm a man, not a dupe. A strong, unsullied man who dares to feel...*something.*

But Lizzie wasn't here. She was back home, thousands of miles away, and the elegantly smiling spectre of Clara was squeezing her out of his mind. He eyed his laptop, tempted to fire up Skype again, and pour his heart out to his beautiful accidental lover, even though it was only a few minutes since they'd broken the connection.

Don't be a selfish git. She needs her rest.

Instead, he pulled up a screen-grab he'd taken. Her lovely smiling face. Not the clearest shot, but enough.

He set the laptop on the broad bed at his side, the image of Lizzie as his guardian angel, fending off memories and regrets, battling all unknowingly against a rival she didn't know existed.

Perhaps he'd try to sleep in her presence after all? Either that or lie awake, gazing at her face, so he could blank out that other one.

7

Are You Free, Miss Aitchison?

'So, no more naughty Skyping to tell me about, then?'

Lizzie looked up sharply at Shelley as they ate cereal in the kitchen. It was nearly time for both of them to go out. Shelley to her temp job; Lizzie to a full day at New Again, helping Marie to redo the window and freshen up the stock. Sometimes changing the displays, and bringing some different items out of the backroom, really perked things up. The premises were quite small, and it just wasn't practical to have everything out at once.

'I never said it was *naughty* Skyping, and no, I haven't spoken to him in two days. He's a very busy man and he's there to do some high-powered business stuff. Making deals that'll create jobs for people, not just another ton of money for himself. So I don't expect him to spend all his time over there thinking about *me*.'

Part of her wanted him to, though, selfishly. Mainly because she'd been sure that the other night there'd been something else on his mind, something unpleasant. Something Lizzie sensed was nothing to do with purpose of his trip.

Something personal?

'Your ears were bright pink when you told me he'd called.' Shelley was the queen of knowing grins. 'And that's your "tell" for when nookie or something similar has occurred.'

'Ah, well, they're not pink now, are they?' Actually Lizzie *could* feel them heating up a bit, thinking back to the nicer bits of that Skype exchange. But then again, if he'd been sitting here eating cereal with them now, he'd be a turn-on too. You could put John Smith in Shelley's old dressing gown and bunny slippers and he'd still be a sex god.

He hadn't been completely out of touch, though. There had been texts, and emails. Little thumbnail sketches of his day, and even some rather good photos, sent from his phone. As someone whose own camera-pics often amounted to a loose assembly of out-of-focus blobs, Lizzie was impressed. There was artistry in John's simple shots of New York tourist attractions. Yellow cabs. Skyscrapers. Central Park, from a distance. Even a dazzling nightscape of the skyline.

But his timetable had remained vague. Chafing for more, Lizzie had reminded herself that at least he'd kept in touch, as he'd said he'd do. Boyfriends were always like that, and she supposed that was what he was.

'So, when's he coming back, this billionaire of yours? I still can't get over the fact it could have been me who pulled him in the Lawns…Talk about dumb bad luck.' Shelley's grin belied her words, and swigging down her tea, she came over and gave Lizzie a hug. 'I know you're missing him.'

Yes, missing him now more than she'd even done during their month apart. John was addictive. The more you got of him, the more you wanted.

'I don't know…soon, I think…and I don't think he's actually a billionaire, you know. There are only actually a very, very few of them in the world. Magazines and books always exaggerate.' Somehow, she wanted to defend him. Rebut even the vaguest accusation that he might be a soulless plutocrat. 'I think he's got quite a lot of millions, but, well, he's got responsibilities.'

Shelley looked curious, but Lizzie decided that was enough. The chance of anything she said to her friend getting back to the parties in question was remote in the extreme, but it *was* still supposed to be a secret that John was the person mainly supporting his high-maintenance ancestral home. Without the knowledge of the people actually living in it.

'Look, shouldn't we be getting a shift on here? I need to be in the shop for nine, and don't most offices open around that time too?'

'Oh hell! I'm going to be late!' As was her wont, Shelley raced from the room, ready to get dressed in double-quick time.

But as she made her way to her own bedroom, Lizzie pondered her friend's question.

When indeed was John coming back to England…and to her?

In the office-come-workroom at New Again, Lizzie slid the dress back on to the tailor's form and surveyed it carefully, checking the way it hung now she'd completed the taking in. It would have been so much better if the customer had stayed, so they could double-check the fitting, but she'd dashed off in a hurry, a young woman with haunted eyes.

'There's still so much shopping and cooking to do. I don't know how I'll get it all finished for tonight. You're an angel to help me choose a dress and to alter it at such short notice.'

A cocktail party, thrown to make nice with her husband's

demanding boss; what a nightmare. The poor lass had looked terrified, and been almost in tears in the shop. Marie had been on the phone, delicately negotiating with someone who had a lot of choice items to sell, leaving Lizzie to keep an eye on things. She'd spotted the young wife sniffing into a hankie, eyes a bit red, and an expression of despair on her pale face.

'He said I need to smarten myself up…get something new. He's not usually like this. He's a kind man…it's just he's under incredible pressure at work…there's so much competition for promotion. It's a nightmare.'

Lizzie had sympathised and, sizing the girl up, she'd pulled a few frocks from the rack that she thought would suit her. One was a real winner, and even the woebegone wife's eyes lit up at the sight of it. But it was a bit loose – she said she'd lost weight lately, and no wonder – and when she'd wilted again, seeing it was too big for her, Lizzie had offered to alter it as a priority. Basically it was an act of sympathy, but who knew, if her husband got promoted, Mrs Cox might be back to New Again, for more occasion wear . . .

Still, though, Lizzie couldn't bear to see the young woman's unhappiness, and if the right dress could perk her up tonight, it was worth going the extra mile. Marie had agreed to let her get a taxi, when she'd finished, and take the dress round to the customer's home in Kissley Magna.

Now for the hem. At least that was the simplest task. Lizzie decided to tack first; it wouldn't take that much longer, and tacking always gave a better result.

You poor woman, is this what happens when you're a corporate wife? I don't think I could stick it.

Suddenly, as she sewed, a vision came into her mind. Herself, hostessing for John. Weighed down with the same sort of responsibility as the woman who'd wear this dress, only times a hundred, because John *was* the boss, and his parties would be a hundred times more prestigious.

Don't be daft. You don't have that kind of relationship. How would he introduce you to exalted foreign business associates, and to high society? 'Oh, this is Lizzie. She used to be my temporary sex friend, and now she's accidentally become my mistress.'

Just about to slip the dress into the machine, and start hemming, she shuddered. The shop's outside door had opened. Was it a cold draught? Probably not, it was a gorgeous sunny day. Someone had come in, but from her place at the worktable in the back room, she couldn't see them. She could only hear a very firm and determined tread, approaching the counter, where a glass case held the most high-end accessories.

'Hi! I'm looking for some clothes for my gorgeous girlfriend. I'm thinking of whisking her away to somewhere warm and luxurious sometime soon, so she'll need beachwear, and evening wear…and lots of it.'

Thanking her lucky stars that she hadn't already begun sewing, because she would've zigged-zagged the hem all over the place, Lizzie silently fought for control. The familiar voice, so deep and playful, had her shaking like a sapling in the wind. Draping the dress across the worktable, she drew in a long, deep breath, pausing for a few calming seconds instead of flying out into the shop like a maniac. Taking another breath, she stood up, smoothed down her skirt, and then patted ineffectually at her hair in the mirror, tweaking her fringe into place. She actually did look like a bit of a maniac, her eyes wild and brilliant, and her pale cheeks stained with a blush.

'Ah…um…yes,' she heard Marie say in a slightly breathy

voice. 'I think Miss Aitchison might be the best person to help you.'

The next second, Lizzie's employer shot into the workroom.

'Lizzie, there's this absolutely freaking amazing-looking man in the shop! I think it's your bloke…your John. You'd better get out there.'

'Right ho.' It was all she could manage. Her heart was hammering. She felt faint, and it was ridiculous. He'd only been away a few days.

Drawing together her poise, Lizzie walked out.

It was *her* John, standing in New Again, beaming at the sight of her, dressed in one of his wonderful three-piece suits, and…and just *dazzling* her. He wore mid-grey today, with a snowy white business shirt, and no tie. His hair had that look as if he'd been running his fingers through it again. Was he feeling just as maniacal as she was?

All she knew was that he was heaven to her eyes; the warmth of his beautiful grin seemed to light the entire room, and besides Lizzie, it wasn't only Marie who was gaping at him like an adoring worshipper. Two typical Kissley Magna matrons, who'd previously been proving picky customers, to say the least, now gazed at the newly arrived god like a pair of love-sick puppies.

'Lizzie . . . you look wonderful.' Ignoring the 'customer/staff' divide, John strode around behind the counter and reached for her hand, gripping it tightly as if he was afraid she might bolt. Before she could stop him, he leaned in and kissed her. Hard. On the lips.

Lizzie swayed. How could he affect her like this? Every time anew. Unable to help herself, she leaned in and slid her hand up on to his shoulder, holding him as tightly as he held her. Parting her lips, she welcomed the touch of his tongue seeking hers.

'Oh Lizzie,' he gasped, breaking for a moment, then plunging into the kiss again, arms snaking around her and pulling her close.

She was back in paradise, back in the arms of her angel. A wicked, horny angel, who might well ravish her right here on the counter if she didn't stop him, her boss and customers notwithstanding. In their zone of just the two of them, it didn't seem to matter who was watching.

'So, are you free, Miss Aitchison?' He grinned at her as they broke apart, and drew the backs of his fingertips down the side of her face, the touch feather-light.

Free? In what sense? She was no longer masquerading as a call girl but he was still lavishing his wealth on her, and some might call that 'buying' . . .

'Well . . . as a matter of fact, I've got some urgent work to do. I didn't realise you were even on your way home, never mind back here already.'

'You're a very industrious and responsible young woman, Lizzie, and I admire that. Even if I do just want to throw you over my shoulder, and carry you away so I can ravish you.' He spoke very softly, for her ears only, but somehow New Again seemed to have acquired an entirely new acoustic profile. His protestation seemed to bounce off all the four walls of the little shop and reverberate as if he'd roared it like a lion.

Her glance skittered to their companions. Marie was grinning like an idiot, still clearly sideswiped by the John Smith tsunami of masculine glamour, and even the two customers were smiling. Maybe they'd both had a 'John' in their younger days, and could still remember being swept away as well.

'Take the afternoon off, Lizzie. I can easily manage . . . You go and . . . um . . . be with your friend.'

John blinked, as if he'd suddenly noticed other people around them. Giving Lizzie's shoulder a quick squeeze, he stepped forward and offered his hand to Marie. 'Pardon my atrocious manners, but I've missed Lizzie terribly while I've been away. I'm John Smith. How do you do?'

'Marie Lanscombe . . .' Marie looked as if she was about to expire when John shook her hand. 'And don't worry. I really can spare Lizzie for the afternoon.'

The temptation to just let herself be swept away was almost irresistible, but Lizzie stood firm. 'I have to finish Mrs Cox's dress first. She needs it tonight. It's important. We said we'd deliver it, and I've still to finish the hem.'

The look in John's eyes was amazing. Sexy, but with a different glow. She'd impressed him. The look she saw was pride. Pride in her . . .

'How about you finish the sewing, then you and I deliver the dress together? There's something I want to show you this afternoon, but we can easily make a detour first.'

Show me what?

John's tricky, gleaming smile hinted at something unexpected . . . but for all she knew he might simply mean the ceiling of his room at the Waverley.

'Cool . . . Is that OK?' She turned to Marie, who was already nodding. 'Er…it won't take too long. Do you want to wait here, or is your car outside?' she asked John.

'I'll wait here. After the time I had in New York, I don't want to let you out of my sight more than I have to. And I'd like to watch you sew. I'd like to see you work…that is, see your *real* work.' His voice dropped again and he winked outrageously, reminding her of Bettie, the accidental call girl.

Pink in the face again, Lizzie grabbed his hand and hauled him towards the workroom. 'Come into the back. But you've got to promise to behave yourself, and not distract me. This is important stuff. Probably not by your standards, but it matters to me, and to other people too.'

'I'll be as quiet as a mouse,' he said softly.

Lizzie could almost feel the weight of speculation wash over her as they disappeared into the back together. Marie, the ladies, they must be imagining all sorts. She was imagining it herself, hungry for another of those devastating kisses, even if there wasn't the time or opportunity for anything more elaborate.

The workroom wasn't big, but with John in it, it seemed tiny, like being in a pressure cooker. His presence filled the space, and his golden, knowing smile lit it up. Before she could sit down, he had her in his arms.

'One more kiss before you sew. Just one . . . I'll die without it.'

'What are you like!'

He laughed, but very quietly, barely a breath against her lips. 'Sometimes I'm not so sure...Around you I seem to have more randy uncontrollable hormones than I've ever had in my life.' His lips brushed hers, almost floating. 'God, I've missed you so much.'

And I you, she wanted to say, but he was already kissing her. Harder than when they'd been out in the shop, voracious this time, his tongue darting into her mouth, exploring and owning her.

With him here again, all was right in the world. All her doubts, all the niggles about who he might have met in New York, they were the anxieties of an imaginary person. Her only reality was John, his mouth, his hands roving over her back and buttocks, his hands pressing her close to him; and, of course, his cock, solidly erect against her belly. Her hips rocked, massaging his hardness; she couldn't help herself.

'Yes . . . Yes . . .' he gasped, then peppered her face with gentler kisses, greeting her jawline, her cheekbone, the corner of her eye, then travelling down to explore the uniquely tender spot beneath her ear, before drifting to the line of her throat.

For a few moments, time ticked by in slo-mo, as they kissed on. Lizzie explored too, sliding her open hands over his strong back through the cloth of his jacket, then gripping his fabulous arse to press their loins close together. In a dream world detached from reality, they'd hurry pell-mell to the nearest bed, rug, or even just an available flat surface, and fuck like wildcats. But eventually, a tiny voice at the back of her brain reminded her that they were in the real world, not a dream, and she had work to do.

'Sorry,' said John as they broke apart, catching their breath. 'Fell on you like a slavering dog again, didn't I?' His face was aglow, and his beautiful eyes were merry. There were dashes of pink on his cheekbones.

Lizzie grinned back at him. 'Don't worry. I like it. And when I've got this little job out of the way, I'm looking forward to a whole lot more of it.'

'Attagirl,' he replied, then pulled out a chair from against the wall and subsided gracefully into it. 'Do your thing . . . Then later we'll do *our* thing, eh?'

Shaking, Lizzie gave him a nod, and then returned her attention to the dress, slipping it into the machine and taking up where she'd left off. The act of sewing calmed her, even under John's scrutiny, and soon she was slipping the garment back on to the tailor's dummy. Drawing in a deep breath to centre herself, she sank to a crouch, scrutinising the hem one last time, and checking it was level all the way round. Luckily, it was spot-on, so she whipped the frock off the form for the final touches.

John had remained silent while she worked, but his presence still filled the room. She could feel his sharp eyes observing every action, and surveillance like that should have rattled her, but somehow it didn't. She was totally excited by him being there, yet at the same time, inexplicably, she could still function and wield her craft. It was almost as if her fingers had moved even more confidently than usual as she'd handled the luxury fabric, double-checking that the stitching was even and perfect.

'There,' she said, to herself as much as to him, donning her thimble and taking up a needle to fine-finish the hem.

'That's a pretty dress,' said John at last, as if he'd been waiting for the task to be near complete before disturbing her. 'It reminds me a little of your golden dress, the one you wore at the Eyes Wide Shut party. I bet you look just as sensational in blue, though.' His smile widened. 'But then, you look sensational in everything...and also out of it.'

'Mr Smith! I'm trying to work here.' She smiled, though, because she'd thought the same thing about Mrs Cox's blue dress. It'd reminded her of that night, and the party. An event she could look back on and relish now that Brent was doing well again.

John was lounging in the chair, one long leg crossed over the other, but she could still somehow see him kneeling before her, his face pressed to her crotch. Then a little later, bent over that fine old desk, his fabulous rear presented for her somewhat inept but surprisingly effective attempts at discipline.

She knew that wouldn't happen all that often – John's nature was too powerfully dominant – but she hoped that some day not too far away, she'd get another chance to play the dominatrix. To rule him with the strength that he inspired in her.

'What are you thinking about? It's not the dress, is it?' His blue eyes had sharpened. He could see right through her. He knew, he knew . . .

'If you must know, I was thinking about how it felt to wear that dress. And the state of mind I experienced that night. I just hope that Mrs Cox can feel something like that wearing this one.' She touched the blue fabric. 'Not the spanking and demanding to be called "mistress" part, of course . . . although you never know. Just a bit of that confidence. She seems to need it.'

'Really? What's her situation?' He leaned forward a little.

'Poor woman. She's got this mega cocktail party thing for her husband's boss, landed on her at the last minute. Reading between the lines, I'd say it's causing awful friction, the whole situation. Her hubby's desperately worried about losing his job, and she's worried too, and because things are so fraught, they're falling out.' Lizzie frowned. 'I wish I could do more to help, but at least I can make sure she has the right dress for the night, and it fits properly.'

'Business is tough, Lizzie. But I understand the pressures,' said John thoughtfully. 'You're a sweet girl to care so much about some woman you barely know. Are you like this with everyone you sew for?'

'No, not really. It's just the occasional nice person, like Mrs Cox. I could tell she was upset.'

'You have a kind heart, love. Now, shall we deliver Cinderella's frock and hope that the mean boss turns into a frog? I've heard that these business martinets can be total bastards.' He quirked his blond brows at her. Was he just as tough and mean to his many subordinates? She didn't think so. But you never knew . . .

'I have to press it first. You know, use an iron? You probably don't even know what an iron is, with hundreds of drones to do everything for you.'

'I've ironed,' protested John with a smile, 'although admittedly not for a long time. I'll iron that for you, if you like? Just to prove I can.'

'I'll believe you, I'll believe you. But it's better I do it. I'll be quicker!'

A short while later, they were all set to go, with Mrs Cox's blue dress in a box, and Lizzie all spruced up after a swift few minutes in Marie's tiny cloakroom while John summoned Jeffrey and the car. The chauffeur couldn't have been all that far away, because the long dark limousine drew up to the kerb as they exited the shop.

'Where are we going to?' John asked from just behind her, as Jeffrey held open the back passenger door.

'Number Two, The Limes, in Kissley Magna.'

'Kissley Magna?'

Lizzie slid into the passenger seat and looked up at John, alerted by the note in his voice. 'Yes, what about it?'

'That's interesting. The thing I have to show you is in Kissley Magna. A happy coincidence.'

'What is it?' she asked, curiosity rampant as he slid into the seat beside her. 'What's this mysterious thing you want to show me?'

'Tsk tsk . . . patience . . . Wait until we get there.'

'Can't you even give me a smidgen of a hint?'

'It'll spoil the surprise.'

'Oh, go on . . .'

John's blue eyes shone with a slow glitter that was oh, so familiar, and as the smooth car accelerated away, he pressed the switch to raise the privacy screen between them and Jeffrey. Encircled in tinted glass and fine coachwork, they were alone, undisturbed.

'A hint will cost you, Lizzie.' His voice was low, and suggestive. Lizzie's heart leapt, and low in her belly, lust that had been only sleeping, sprang awake.

She weighed the odds. They were barely ten minutes away from Kissley Magna. What could he do in that time?

Just about anything he wants, you dolt. And anything you want too.

'OK, then . . . I'll take my chances. Give me a hint?'

With that familiar teasing glitter in his eyes, he studied her a moment, playing his tongue over his lower lip. The devil, he *knew* how much that little tongue quirk turned her on. And he seemed to love watching her watching him as he did it.

'Well, it's a place, as much as a thing. That's all I'm saying. Now . . . show me those delicious thighs of yours. I've been obsessing about them since I first walked into your shop.'

'It's not my shop.' Her heart was thudding, and it was the first thing that rose to her lips.

John narrowed his eyes, and there was something else in there, mixed with the glow of desire, something calculating. 'Ah, but it *could* be.'

'What do you mean?' She knew, of course, but it seemed important to challenge him.

'I could make your boss an offer she couldn't refuse. If you wanted it, the business could be yours.'

'But I don't want it! I love working with Marie, and she loves the shop and the business. Don't you go making things complicated by throwing money at her. You can't just buy everything, John, even if you *can* afford it.'

Everything was quiet for a few heartbeats. Lizzie could almost hear the cogs of John's brain turning over. She felt guilty, ungrateful, but she knew she was right.

Good God, are we arguing? Well, that didn't take long . . .

But then he smiled. And it was bright, decisive, as if he'd weighed everything up, and already come to a satisfactory conclusion. 'You're right, of course.' He laid his hand lightly on her thigh, just above her knee, where her slim skirt had ridden up. 'Money isn't everything . . . although "buying" you in the first place did bring us together.' His fingers flexed, not quite caressing, but creating pressure.

'I know that. But it wasn't really buying. I was only playing. I always intended to give the money back . . . well, as much of it as I could.'

'And I never wanted it. I only want you.'

He still spoke quietly, but there was ferocity there too. It was as if he'd compartmentalised their little debate over the shop, and whether he might buy it for her, and had now returned to the realm of the senses.

Lizzie opened her mouth to speak, but he silenced her, running a slow, caressing fingertip up and down the inner slope of her thigh, pushing up her hem and rucking up the fabric of her skirt. Each stroke went higher, until he was almost touching her panties.

'No stockings today?' he enquired, his thumb barely a millimetre from her crotch.

It was hard to breathe, hard to speak. She fought not to bear down. 'No, it's too warm. Sometimes I just put on fake tan instead.'

'It looks exquisite, like honey over cream. I've thought

about touching you all the time I was in New York. And now, here I am, and you're all mine to enjoy.'

So possessive, perhaps a bit obsessive, but she wasn't in a fit state to argue. *She'd* thought about being touched all the time he was in New York, and no amount of powerful orgasms with high-end sex toys could outdo the simple caress of his fingers.

'Surely not *all* the time? Surely not in meetings?' They'd covered this ground before, with John claiming he could still think about her and be sharp as a business rapier.

'A lot of the time.' He leaned close, his breath against her throat as he pressed lightly, with the side of his hand, against her pussy. 'Do you want me to make you come? I'll have to be swift . . .' She saw him glance beyond her, out of the tinted window. 'Because I've a feeling we've almost reached our destination.'

Lizzie swivelled, and God, yes, there it was. Even as he slid his fingers to and fro against the gusset of her knickers, outside, the sign for 'The Limes' passed by the window. They were almost at the Cox residence, in a short cul de sac.

'We haven't time,' she protested, even though her body screamed for it. If he played with her and made her climax, she'd be crimson in the face and all of a flurry when they delivered the dress.

'Do you deny me?' His voice was arch. He was playing the dominant, but more in fun than earnest.

'You know I don't easily come on demand.'

'Wilful . . . that's what you are.'

'Then punish me,' she shot back at him, driven crazy.

'I will!' Pushing up her skirt right up to her crotch, he laid his hand flat on her thigh again, as if measuring . . . then landed a hard slap on the land of cream and honey.

'Ouch!' she yelped, less at the shock and the pain than at the electric jolt of desire at the same time. Her pussy fluttered, surging with lust, and she was on the point of changing her mind and begging…yes, begging…that he get her off, when he gripped the hem of her skirt, and smoothly and efficiently slid it down over her thighs, one pale, one fiery pink.

'I'll inspect that later,' he said, Mr Brisk and Efficient as the car slid to a halt, 'after we've delivered the dress to your Mrs Cox.' Almost before the engine was off, John was out and darting around to the kerb-side. As Jeffrey opened the door, it was John himself who helped Lizzie out, handing her from the car, a courtier to his queen. And when Jeffrey retrieved the dress box from the boot, it was John who carried it, following two steps behind her, as if pretending to be subservient.

Lizzie still felt shock from the stinging slap to her thigh, but when Angela Cox opened the door, the young wife was so frazzled and flurried that Lizzie felt like an iceberg of composure. Angela was red in the face and had flour on her cheeks and even in her hair. She looked on the point of tears, almost, and fell upon Lizzie as if they were best friends.

'Oh God, I'm so glad you're here . . . At least one thing will be right. You did manage to alter the dress, didn't you? I was so worried . . . with my weight loss and all.'

'Yes, all done. And very beautifully, I assure you,' announced John, from the rear, tapping the box, then reaching over, offering his hand to Angela. 'I'm John Smith, by the way. I'm Lizzie's boyfriend.' The way he winked told the woman on the doorstep he considered the term 'boy' a slight misnomer.

Angela's worried face lit up, unsurprisingly. John's dazzling smile could do that, lift the spirits, even when they were sinking to the pit. She ran her hand through her floury hair. 'Please…please come in. And pleased to meet you, Mr Smith.'

The kitchen was a scene of disorder, but there was a nice smell of cooking, something very savoury, cheesy nibbles of some kind. 'It's all a frightful mess, but I think I've got things more or less under control, though, just about . . .' She shrugged her shoulders.

'Shall we nip upstairs and try the dress on? Just in case there's a last tweak that needs doing. I've brought my needle.' Lizzie tapped her capacious tote bag, in which she'd stowed a basic sewing kit.

Angela glanced dubiously at the oven.

'Don't worry, I'll watch your baking,' said John, then his eyes narrowed. 'Have you had lunch yet?'

'Er…no. I haven't had time.'

'Shall I make some while you're having your fitting? A sandwich, at least?'

Angela looked a bit befuddled, but then succumbed to the smile again. 'Um, yes . . . There's some ham in the fridge . . . a pack of honey roast, not the whole one for the party . . . Er, would you like some too? I could make . . .'

'Oh no, I'll make the lunch. You girls nip off upstairs.' Before either of them could protest, he had his jacket over the back of one of the kitchen chairs, his sleeves rolled up, and he was at the sink, pumping the liquid soap dispenser, ready to wash his hands.

'What a lovely, lovely man!' exclaimed Angela once they were installed in her pistachio-decorated bedroom, and she was pulling her top off over her head. 'You're very lucky, Lizzie . . . He's so gorgeous he could be a film star. What a smile.'

'I know. He is rather lush, isn't he?' As she drew the dress out from amongst its tissue paper, Lizzie was acutely aware of the hot glow in her thigh. What would Angela think if she knew the 'gorgeous man' was into BDSM? She might be horrified . . . or she might think him even more gorgeous.

'How did you two meet?' asked Angela as her head popped out when the dress slid down over her.

Something in her tone seemed to be asking more than that. How did Lizzie come to be involved with a man so much older, clearly more sophisticated, and loaded with money? There was no way she could tell this good customer of New Again that she'd been pretending to be a whore when she'd met him.

'Purely by chance, actually. A case of mistaken identity, in the Lawns bar at the Waverley Grange Hotel. We just struck up a conversation, and sort of . . . clicked.'

'Lucky you. He's a bit of a dish.'

'I know he's a bit older than me, but I like that. He's a grown-up. He knows what he's doing. I feel safe with him.'

Yes, safe. Despite everything. Despite his sexual proclivities and his many secrets. In a short space of time, John had become her rock.

The dress fitted perfectly, and despite Lizzie's offer to give it another pressing, they decided that hanging it up would deal with any creases. The two women descended the stairs again, and Lizzie was relieved that Angela seemed calmer now, and not so fearful.

The kitchen smelt fabulous. The savoury smell was ten times as strong now, and emanating from a tray of cheesy, pastry-looking things cooling on a tray.

'Your first batch of nibbles is done,' announced John, looking pleased with himself, 'and I've put in the next lot. They shouldn't take long.' Turning to the kitchen table, he made a flourishing gesture. 'Lunch is served.'

He'd made a plateful of sandwiches, set out plates, cups and made tea, which was keeping warm under a cosy. Lizzie felt like laughing with delight, to see him so domesticated, but instead she just smiled her thanks at him. Angela looked almost tearful again, but still she smiled as she sank down on to a kitchen chair.

'Have you had lunch? Please stay and have a bite...Unless you're dashing off somewhere?' There was a pleading look in her eyes. She was feeling better, but Lizzie sensed a bit more moral support was needed to shore her up.

'A bite would be great,' said John, flashing Lizzie a quick look. He understood.

'Absolutely,' she concurred, taking the seat that John drew out for her.

Over their meal, Angela opened up, telling them a bit more of her and her husband's situation. The backstabbing, the office politics; the precarious financial situation with a standard of living to maintain.

'I've told him he should resign, and try to find something ... well, a bit less crappy. I'm happy to go out to work myself. I've got secretarial skills ... we could manage.'

Lizzie nodded and did her best to look sympathetic, but as they were on their way out, it was John who took Angela's hand and squeezed it, looking into her eyes.

'Now, about tonight. I recommend a little nip of gin before they all arrive. Just a drop, to take the edge off. Don't get legless.' He grinned, so beautiful and dazzling that Angela's stress seemed to fade without benefit of alcohol. 'And all the time, tell yourself, "I am amazing. I look fabulous. I'm wearing a really great dress".' Releasing her hand, he fished in his inner jacket pocket and brought out a business card. 'And if everything does go pear shaped, get your man to ring this number.' He jotted a number on the back of the card. 'It's my P.A., and he'll know anyone contacting him on this line is bona fide. I'm about to set up a northern centre of operations in this area, and there might be something for your husband. He'll have to apply on his merits, of course, but at least this way, he'll have an inside track.' He pressed the card into Angela's hand.

Another woman hopelessly smitten with you, John Smith. Is there anyone you can't charm and bewitch?

As they left Angela Cox behind, Lizzie thought that unlikely. It would be a steep learning curve, not to be jealous of the ever growing horde of John's admirers...

Fat chance really, though, when she loved him to distraction!

8

To the Manor Born

Once they were on the move again, Lizzie said, 'That was a kind thing to do . . . about the job for her husband . . . and the other stuff.' She moved close, and gave him a quick kiss on the cheek. Any moment now they'd be playing games again, but she wanted to thank him first, while things were still 'normal'.

John shrugged. 'Well, he won't get a job if he's not up to scratch. But if he is, then he'll get a shot. I'll bring in some of my existing people, but I'd like to make work for people in the area too.'

'So . . . this "northern outpost" . . . what's brought that on?'

A slow smile played around John's mouth, and his eyes searched hers. 'Don't be naïve, Lizzie. You *know* the answer, well, some of it at least.'

No! Not really? Surely not . . .

'Why not?' he answered her silent question. 'You're here, and I want to be where you are, at least some of the time. I'll still be travelling, so there'll be some to and fro, but I'd like to have a base in this area.' His look was steady, challenging.

'And it's practical too. I've made a lot of acquisitions here in the north, and up in Scotland too. It makes sense . . .' A little shadow crossed his face . . . 'And this way I'm close to Montcalm too, in case I want to build a few more of those bridges.'

'Oh, I see.'

But where would he live? Not at the Waverley, surely? And not at Montcalm either. The rapprochement with his aristocratic family was probably still far too fragile, and liable to crumble again, for him to be able to live at their famous stately home.

And then, the light-bulb moment. The thing he was going to show her that was also a place. It must have been clear on her face, because John laughed.

'Quite right, sharp girl. I'm looking at property. In fact, this afternoon, *we're* looking at property.' He did his eyebrow quirk thing, teasing and provocative. 'In fact, if I'm not mistaken, we're almost there.'

Lizzie frowned. They were still in Kissley Magna, on the outskirts, at least. What sort of house was there in Kissley Magna for a man like John Smith, billionaire entrepreneur? There were a lot of rich people living here, in the ultra-posh area of the Borough, but there was a big difference between a few local toffs and bigwigs and someone on John's rarefied level of wealth. He was a bona fide aristocrat too, when all was said and done.

Unless . . .

Perusing the property websites was one of the fun pastimes she shared with Brent and Shelley when they were bored and there was nothing on the telly. They'd trawl RightMove and Zoopla, doing searches for the most expensive houses in the area, then weave silly fantasies about living in them.

Sometimes they'd even see who could design the most bizarre alterations and extensions.

'Not Dalethwaite Manor?' It was one of their recent favourites, and Lizzie's dream house, because she'd once actually been there. 'They don't seem to be able to sell it because they're asking ridiculous money.'

'I've *got* ridiculous money, sweetheart.' John grinned, pleased with himself again. 'And I was hoping you'd look it over with me this afternoon, and give me your considered opinion.'

'What's to consider? It's the most gorgeous house in the area!'

'There, you've helped already. "Gorgeous" sounds like an endorsement to me.'

'But it's a honking great manor house, John. It's like a mini Montcalm, really.' Once, a couple of years ago, she'd helped out as a temporary waitress at a big garden party, falling half in love with the place, even though she'd never expected to see it again. Fond of all vintage and historical styles, she had a soft spot for Victoriana, and Dalethwaite Manor was a gem of a house from that era. Not exactly 'honking great' really, by the standards of John's ancestral home, but still palatial to a girl who currently shared a modest-sized semi.

But there was no more time to protest. They were pulling up to imposing wrought iron gates set back from the road. It was a bit like the set-up at the Eyes Wide Shut mansion, but not so forbidding. The car slowed to a halt, but a second later, the gates swung open.

'Before you ask…preferred prospective buyers are sent a remote for the gates, which Jeffrey just activated.' John smiled, and Lizzie wondered what other privileges 'preferred' prospective buyers might be granted.

The limo glided along a long, immaculately manicured drive, flanked by tall, mature trees that must have been planted when the house was first built.

'"Last night I dreamed I went to Manderley again",' Lizzie intoned, and peering out, she saw rhododendrons and azaleas, just like at Du Maurier's fictional house.

'Not nearly so grim,' countered John, 'and no Mrs Danvers either. If I decide to buy, I'll bring in my own staff, and there'll be no gorgons with weird obsessions and long black dresses.'

'You've got it all sussed out, then?'

Had he actually already bought the place? And, if so, why did she feel so unsettled over such a fait accompli?

Don't be idiotic, Lizzie. He doesn't have to check anything with you first, before he does stuff. It's not that kind of relationship!

But whether he'd bought it or not, or asked her opinion or not, getting a chance to explore her dream house was still a thrill. There'd been barely any time to look around during that waitressing gig, and the hired help hadn't been encouraged to go wandering.

'Pretty much. Come on, let's explore.'

When they stepped out of the car, John instructed Jeffrey to return in a couple of hours.

'It's all ours for the time being,' he said to Lizzie as they ascended the front steps. 'I told the agents that I didn't want anyone hovering over me when I viewed the house. I just want *your* impressions, Lizzie, and I don't want you to have to be polite because someone is shadowing us while we look around.' He let them in, stepping back with a grand flourish to allow her to enter, and then quickly deactivated the alarm.

How come you know the key-code off by heart, Mr Smith?

More fishiness . . .

Dalethwaite was just as magical as it had been at the time of the garden party. It might be Victorian, but there was nothing dark or oppressively cluttered about it. She remembered it as being surprisingly light and airy, and redecoration in the interim had only increased that effect. The décor was contemporary, but it didn't argue with the nineteenth-century structure; the two had had a harmonious conversation across the years, and the estate agent's online brochure hadn't done the renovations justice, by a long shot. Sunshine poured in through windows wherever she turned, and the ambience had a soft quality too; a liveable, easy warmth, despite the luxurious elegance of many of the rooms.

'I've been here before,' Lizzie finally told John as they entered the gorgeous orangery, a giant conservatory space that was at least as big as the entire ground floor of the house at St Patrick's Road. 'There was a big garden party, and I was doing a bit of on and off waitressing for a catering company at the time. It was like being in fairyland, and the guests were so glam in full evening wear and everything.'

'Now you're the one who's glamorous,' said John, flinging himself down on one of two low, cream-coloured settees that were set facing each other. 'You look amazingly at home in this room. Like a film star. To the manor born.'

'Not really . . .'

'Yes, really. Don't be stubborn. False modesty doesn't become you, Lizzie.' The words were stern, but his expression was sultry and indulgent. 'Now come over here and stop drifting around like a supermodel. I had a hellish time in New York, and all I really want to do is touch you.' He paused, his brilliant blue eyes taking her in from top to toe, making her feel as if she'd been swept by a ray of heat. 'And to fuck you in every goddamn room in this place. And believe me, there are a *lot* of rooms.' He held out his hand, palm up, but it was more a gesture of command than supplication.

Her feet frozen to the spot, Lizzie said, 'But we're only viewing the house, John. Someone could come at any minute.' Her heart raced.

'I certainly hope so,' he replied, with a soft, fruity laugh, 'that's my intention at the very least. And as I'm feeling generous, I don't mind if it's you. Despite the fact I've got the most savage hard-on.'

Oh, he certainly had!

Even though she probably looked at John's groin far more often than was decent, Lizzie hadn't ogled his crotch for at least several minutes. Surely he hadn't had that enormous erection a few minutes ago? Although maybe he had, and his jacket had hidden it?

Either way, he was sporting the most sumptuous bulge now.

'Lizzie.' Her name was softly spoken; a tantalising warning.

She walked towards him, helpless to resist. He really was the most crazy man. They were only viewing the house, and anyone really could arrive at any moment. Yet still she knew she'd let him do anything to her, anything at all.

She was like heaven walking towards him. Beautiful, bright, a dream of sensuality to rouse the cock of any man with breath in his body. Her clothing was modest – a slim skirt, a neat vintage blouse and a soft, light cardigan, unbuttoned – but her shoes had a kinky look that stirred his blood. They weren't high, but they were shapely, making her slender feet an object of fetish sex.

Oh, Lizzie . . .

Paused in front of him, she struck an elegant pose, but he still detected a faint touch of anxiousness. She was worried about being discovered, even though he had a feeling that she suspected that he'd already as good as bought this place.

But Lizzie was ever the diplomat. She wouldn't get into it now, because she didn't want to spoil things. And she wanted him as much as he wanted her.

Her tongue ran along the seam of her rose-tinted lips, and he almost cried out, racked with the desire to slip his aching cock into her sweet mouth.

'Do you know what I want, Lizzie?' To his own ears, his voice sounded odd. Ragged. The wait had been agonising. He'd been happy to help her with the stressed-out Mrs Cox and her dress, but all the time he'd been battling down his gouging urges. Bio-feedback was useless. He was a rampant dog, barely keeping himself in check. But he didn't have to fight it any more. He could have what he wanted now. What she wanted too. He could see it in her eyes, dark and hungry.

'I think so.' She glanced around. The room was all glass, but even nervy as she was, she was prepared to serve him. 'But are you sure there's no one about? What if there's some handyman lurking around the garden, waiting for a free show?'

'Ah, but wouldn't you enjoy that? The randy gardener watching while the Lord and Lady of the Manor cavort?'

'I . . . I'm no lady, I'm just Ms Average. And even if you *are* a lord, it's not your manor.'

'Average?' he cried, 'Don't you ever describe yourself as fucking average, Lizzie Aitchison! You're the least average woman I've ever met!' He calmed his anger. He hated it when she undervalued herself. But he supposed it came from family background, and he of all people knew how that could screw a person up. There'd been hints of a rigorous father, with rigid standards. And female siblings too, over-achievers in purely conventional terms.

'All right, then, I'm a lady. I'll not argue with you. Now, what precisely is it that you want, Your Lordship?' She glanced down at his crotch, clearly knowing *exactly* what he wanted.

'Your mouth, beautiful Lizzie. Your mouth on my cock. Your lips and your tongue, taking me to paradise.'

She gave him a long look, her eyes roving over him in an assessing glide. It felt astonishingly masculine somehow. She was cataloguing his charms, as a man would check out a woman. Even as she sank to her knees, he felt as if he were the one who should be kneeling.

Offering no words, she continued to hold his gaze, even while she reached out and laid a hand over his crotch. His cock leapt wildly, pushing hard against his clothing, and her fingers flexed around him. Her steady expression commanded him. He couldn't move, only wait. To enjoy.

With swift efficiency, she unbuttoned his waistcoat and parted the panels. Then she tackled his shirt, pulling out the tails from his waistband and baring his chest. Leaning forward, she kissed his nipples, then lightly nibbled them. He wanted to dig his hands into her hair, but just as he was about to do it, she looked up at him, her eyes warning. His hands loosened at his sides, inert.

Next, she dealt with his belt, flicking it open, making the buckle jingle. His trousers she unzipped roughly, not seeming quite so poised now, and then she tugged furiously at his underwear, getting impatient with it until he shook off his inertia and helped her, dragging down his jersey trunks and freeing his stiff, reddened cock.

If the mythical gardener looked in now, it was he, John, who was vulnerable. Lizzie was still primly clothed, not a hair of her exquisite, accurate fringe out of place, and her divine body unrevealed, except to his ravenous mind's eye.

He imagined her naked before him as she laid her slender seamstress's fingertips against the hot aching length of his erection. Bare, she would still have the power and the dignity. There was no way to diminish her. Even when she allowed him to punish her, and to prance around like a dominant dickhead, she was still subtly and completely in charge.

He was in her thrall. He was in . . .

Really? Am I? I don't know . . . but I do care, Lizzie, I do care.

'Suck me, love,' he said softly, aching for the solace of that perfect mouth.

God, he was so tempting!

Lizzie enjoyed giving head, but she'd never relished a man's cock the way she yearned for John's. Leaning forward, she extended her tongue, furled it to a point and started out with an experimental lick, scooping up the clear beads of pre-come gathered at his tip, welling from the love-eye. She curled her fist around his shaft, and lapped at him like a lollipop, loving the clean yet salty flavour of him. Against the skin of her palm she could feel the blood pulsing, pulsing, pulsing in the veins of his cock, the beautiful beat of life, and of man.

Opening her mouth wider, she engulfed his glans, cradling it, just holding it and cherishing it. Looking up for a moment, she saw his eyes rapt, watching her. But when she sucked fast and hard, he slumped back against the settee, his head falling back, his golden curls gleaming against the pale upholstery.

'Oh my dear, dear girl,' he gasped, his hips bucking, his hands curling into tight fists against the seat cushions, 'your mouth is perfect. There's nobody like you.'

Holding him, she kept on sucking, and sometimes licking, sometimes teasing. Sometimes even grazing him slightly with the edges of her teeth, in a light but playful threat.

Was he holding out on her? The cords of his neck were taut with stress, and he swallowed hard.

Devil!

She jabbed hard with her tongue at a tender spot, the little notch beneath the head of his cock. She'd tipped him over before, working there, but this time he resisted her, stirred from his passivity to grasp her head. Holding her, he asserted his control and took back his power.

'Oh no you don't, Miss Aitchison. I'm in charge here...I think...'

John laughed, hissing through his teeth as she tried to goad him again, darting her tongue to that sweet spot she always found so accurately. 'Stay still, beautiful girl. Just let me rest on your tongue.'

Her mouth relaxed, and she obeyed him. He drew in a few deep breaths, steadying himself as he gazed down at her lovely face, and her lovely mouth around him. A sudden urge ripped through him, prompted by the neat perfection of her clothing; the innocent almost prissy little collar, the unbreached buttons of her pale-blue blouse.

What did she have on beneath? Lace and underwires? Satin, low cut, deep, deep cleavage. Or was it something more austere? She hadn't been expecting him . . . Dressing this morning, she'd had no reason to don her seductive call girl's lingerie.

Suddenly he had to see. To enjoy. To wickedly ravish her and make his mark on her sweet, saintly underthings.

'Back off now, Lizzie. I want to see you.' Leaning forward and cradling her face, he edged her back. She seemed reluctant to relinquish him, but she obeyed, licking her lips as he slid out, the little action automatic, yet electric. His cock gleamed where she'd lavished it with attention and, if anything, he felt himself stiffen more, get even harder, loving that shine she'd created.

Her eyes were huge and dark, and her gaze darted from his face to his erection and back again, to and fro. He almost laughed; it was as if she were hypnotised by the sight of him, his serpent flesh.

'Unfasten your blouse. Show me your gorgeous breasts.'

Still staring at his cock, she started to slip the buttons through the buttonholes purely by touch. They were small and pearly, very delicate and pretty. Her fingertips were neat and deft, as they always were, whether on him, or otherwise. He sighed at the sight of her divine cleavage revealed to him. Her bra was simple and white, cotton, very pure. His cock swayed as he leaned forward and pushed her blouse and cardigan down off her shoulders, exposing them. Then he plucked at the straps of her bra, sliding them down over her shoulders too. Greedily, he cupped her breasts in his hands, baring them.

'Exquisite,' he whispered, meaning it from the bottom of his soul. Everything about her was adorable. 'Now, suck me again. But don't use your hands.' Giving her nipples a playful tweak, he released her and lounged back again.

Her lashes fluttered, and she looked down, perfectly demure. Well, almost…For a moment he saw the greedy salacious glitter in her eyes, the bright boldness that aroused him so. She gave herself away with a slow, wet swipe of her tongue over her lower lip.

'You teasing trollop, come on…get on with it.'

'Of course, master.' Her poise was indomitable and her face was a picture, a beautiful canvas of elegant submission, and devilment. She'd never be a thoroughgoing sub, her will was too strong, but to please him she could wear obedience like a glamour, a magic spell that made him believe, for the moment, that he had the upper hand. 'May I rest my hands upon your thighs, to brace myself? I'll be able to pleasure you all the better.'

'What's good for you is better for me, gorgeous.' He nodded assent, adjusting his position, letting her get in close and rest her hands on him. 'Ah! Oh yes,' he gasped, breathtaken as she quickly and deeply engulfed him, instantly rubbing the underside of his glans with her tongue in a fast flicking action, amazingly flexible. His hips bucked of their own accord, propelling him deeper. He placed his hands over hers on his thighs, squeezing and holding, loving the more tender contact almost, but not quite, as much as having his dick in the embrace of her mouth.

Slowly, meticulously, she worked him, leaning in, letting him in, relaxing her entire throat, not panicking. Her control of her gag reflex was awe inspiring, making him toss his head as she accepted more of him into the wet heat. Instinctively, he laced his fingers with hers, bonding with her.

'Oh baby…baby,' he crooned, all stress falling away, all memory of the angst and anger of New York. Lizzie's beautiful mouth erased Clara from existence for the moment, rubbing her out as if as if she were an ugly drawing sketched in pencil. The aggravating memory stab of her would return…but not while he was here, like this, with his lovely young Lizzie.

*

I love you.

The words popped lightly into her mind as she worshipped his flesh. There was no touch and caress for her in this act, but somehow, it still excited her. Her pussy was latent yet energised, waiting and ready, graced by need.

He let her control this act, though. He couldn't stop his hips moving; the reaction was ancient, autonomous. But she was calling the shots. She was letting him in deep one minute, and then backing off again, to lavish him with tongue work. It wasn't a thing she'd ever consciously practised, but with John, she discovered an almost inexhaustible wealth of tricks and techniques. Even the muscles of her jaw seemed to have new, enduring powers.

Would he come in her mouth? Give her that gift? Suddenly she sensed not. She could almost read him as he so often read her, and looking up at him from beneath her lashes, she slowly and daringly let him slip from between her lips.

'Oh, you wicked girl…you know, don't you? You know what I want?'

Their eyes met, sparking, clashing.

'I…I'm sure I don't know, master.' She tried not to grin, but couldn't help herself. Sliding her fingers out from under his, she caught the edge of her clothing – bra, blouse, cardigan – and drew them back a bit further, offering her breasts to him. They were aching, and she could swear her nipples were harder than they'd ever been, dark with blood. She wanted them to tempt him into wickedness, to make him mark her and anoint her with his seed.

'Oh yes, you do, Miss Aitchison. You *know* what I want.' His blue eyes were like sapphires illuminated with starlight.

She could see his chest heaving. Good God, he was panting with lust, or with the effort of control.

'I do . . .'

'Do you permit it?'

'Of course, master . . . how could I not?'

Triumph soared as he grasped his cock in his fist and began to pump. She came up a bit more on her knees, making a better target. Sliding her palms beneath her breasts, she offered them up.

'Oh God…Oh yes…Oh yes . . .' Smart, articulate John devolved into just a man holding his cock, working himself. His hand moving in a blur almost, he snarled an oath, then another, the crude words a canticle of male exultation as his semen spurted forth and landed in droplets on the upper curves of Lizzie's breasts.

It was wickedly dirty, and like something out of a porn movie, but she couldn't help but grin. There was nothing demeaning about it. It was fun, erotic fun, and John was the one who'd made himself vulnerable, revealing the way he handled himself in privacy. Afterwards, he fell back against the upholstery, his chest heaving and his penis still in his fist, but losing its hardness.

'Oh . . . my . . . God . . .' His eyes were closed, but they flipped open, and his mouth curved provocatively as he zeroed in on the white pearls and trails of his spunk on her skin. 'Oh hell, that looks so horny. If I hadn't only just come I'd start all over again.'

It seemed a bit insulting to him to wipe it away with her hankie, so Lizzie scooped a little of the white fluid with her finger and tasted it, making John moan like a happy man in torment.

His semen didn't taste of much. A bit salty, a bit ammoniac, but only faintly. It wasn't horrid, just bland, so mild for something born in wild, thrashing tumult. She swept up some more, and did a little pantomime of smacking her lips and savouring it as if it were Crème Chantilly or a whisky cream liqueur.

'Dirty girl . . . so dirty . . .' He grinned at her, his eyes dancing as he tucked his cock away in his clothing and zipped up. She wondered if, had he been a younger man, he might already have been hard again, but she wasn't worried. She'd get hers. That was one of the most beautiful things about John. He was generous, and he'd give her pleasure, and get her off, by other means.

Slowly, she massaged the remains of his emission into her skin, watching his eyes every second as she did it.

'Here.' Whipping a snow-white handkerchief from his pocket, he leaned forward and dabbed her chest with it. Then he wiped her lips. 'There, that's better.'

She didn't mind. But he was right, it would make her clothes stick to her. When she'd handed back the hankie, she started to set her bra to rights, but he caught her by the hand.

'No, leave it. I like you as you are.'

Desire thrummed deep in her vitals. She loved being displayed to him, and loved it even more for the little frisson of danger, the slim threat of discovery. He'd probably given the strictest of instructions, but still…someone might not have got the message about the preferred client and his foibles; someone might blunder in on them any minute and discover her with her tits out. The room was warm, but her nipples tightened, stirred by the possibility.

'We should inspect the upstairs now,' announced John, rising to his feet and pocketing his handkerchief. With Lizzie still on her knees, her eyes almost at the level of his groin. He *was* already getting hard again. So much for his protestations that he didn't have the recuperative powers of a younger man.

You're a horndog, Mr Smith, and I suspect you'll still be one for decades yet.

And especially so with that glint in his eyes. He had plans for the upstairs that went far beyond just inspecting the amenities.

'John!' she protested, for form's sake.

'Don't fret, love. Estate agents can be pretty accommodating when their client doesn't balk at the asking price.'

With a wink, he handed her to her feet, his hold light, but masterful. As she followed him from the orangery, her blouse still open and her breasts still revealed, she allowed herself a little smirk at the thought of what he clearly intended.

9

Upstairs, Upstairs

Once on the first floor, John ignored most of the open, inviting doors, and the hints of equally beautiful redecorations beyond, and made a beeline for one room in particular.

The master suite – decorated in soft, country meadow colours and with elegant ceiling mouldings. It was on a corner of the house, with stunning garden views in two directions.

'And this will be your room.' He presented it all to her with an elegant, courtly gesture – the vast bed with its mahogany head and footboards and wild flower-print duvet. Although his glance did flick momentarily upwards.

'Now, wait a minute... It's a bit soon to talk *my* room, isn't it? Moving in and all that... If you count up all the time we've spent together, it can't be more than a week or two.' It was difficult to argue cogently with John at the best of times, but it was doubly hard now, like this. 'I can't just up sticks and leave my friends, just like that.'

For a fraction of a second, as he followed her into the quiet, harmonious room, and she turned to him, a stubborn, steely expression flashed across his face. The look of a super-rich man and a ruthless negotiator who could buy a hotel chain or beautiful mansion house without a second thought. Then he pursed his lips, and made the slightest of huffing sounds.

'You're right, of course. I'm making assumptions when I shouldn't. Let me rephrase that. When you stay for a sleep-over, which I hope you often will, this will be your room.'

His eyes were persuasive now, but she'd seen that other side of him. When John wanted something, he usually got it, by fair means or foul. It was thrilling in a way, but also troubling. Being ordered about in the bedroom was the deepest of delights for her, but outside of it, not so much. She didn't respond well; she never had. Just look what had happened when her father had tried to steer her life, and how disastrous the rigours of university life had been – predicated by rules and teachers, authority figures.

And she'd always been the worst of office temps too. Rebellious against bosses, even if they only held sway over her for a day or two; which was why she was a full-time seamstress now, and working with Marie, who treated her as equal.

'But you're the master of the house, John. You should have the master bedroom.'

'Ah, but while you're sleeping over, Lizzie, you're the mistress,' he countered, pacing to the nearest window and pulling aside the filmy, cream-white voile inner curtains, to glance quickly across the park. 'And therefore the principal bedroom is yours.' He spun back to her, his eyes still a boss's eyes.

Yes, a mistress, that was what she was now, and the word was dual. It did mean a dominant, powerful woman, but it could also describe the companion of a multi-millionaire who was subtly trying to assert control over her life with his wealth. Calling herself his 'girlfriend' seemed suddenly too freewheeling.

'I don't know...'

'What's not to know? I know that actually sleeping together is still...well, it's still a way off. But how are we supposed to work on that if we don't sleep in the same house occasionally, Lizzie? You're a very stubborn woman sometimes.'

'I'm not. It's you...you always get your way, John.'

'Ah, but don't you like it that way?'

'Yes...to a certain extent.'

She pursed her lips, knowing she was being just as stubborn as he claimed, yet inside still melting with desire.

Desire. Lust. Passion. All so much easier than grappling with 'real' life.

For an instant, her fingers itched to fly to her clothing, to cover herself. She did want to have it out with him, and exposed like this, she couldn't negotiate. But . . . They were in a beautiful bedroom, a quietly seductive space, and John was John. And he too was still exposed, his strong chest a panel of golden temptation, framed by the white of his shirt.

They would return to this issue between them, probably go there quite soon. But not now. He'd only been home from travelling a few hours, and her priorities were elsewhere.

She gave him a firm look, and sashayed across to where he was, still by the window. 'We're not going to argue about this, are we?' She laid her hand on his bare chest, where the skin was hot and silky. Energy shot through her from the contact. 'Let's put a pin in it. I can see you're determined to ravish me in this bedroom whether it belongs to you or not, so shall we get on with that instead, and have a row or discussion or whatever at some later date?'

'Consider it pinned.' He placed his hand over hers, fingers curving. 'No row.'

His blue eyes were lambent, all sex again. Maybe the source of their first conflict was simmering somewhere in the back of his sharp brain, but most of that organ, and other organs, had returned their attention to the matter in hand.

Reaching up, she drew him down to her, making him kiss her. It was barely moments since their last kiss, but it all seemed new, sweet and hot. His tongue pressed, then plunged in, and he whipped his arms around her, pressing their bodies together, her breasts to his naked chest, skin to skin. Against her belly, his cock had risen again, ready and potent beneath the fine cloth of his trousers.

'What if the gardener is watching again?' Lizzie was breathless when he freed her mouth, and her glance darted to the garden, beyond the window, and further, the parkland, rolling and serene. And all fortunately deserted given that she was still exposed. She imagined the view of that imaginary worker, maybe out there pruning one of the formal flower beds, when he looked up at the window. He'd see two figures together, breaking from a tight embrace: a golden god of a man, and a brazen brunette, bare breasted, clinging to him.

John kissed her brow, then the side of her face, nuzzling her hair. 'Oh, let him watch. In fact, let's really give him something to watch!' Grabbing her by the shoulders, he turned her, face towards the glass, and set her hands, one by one on the window sill.

'What are you doing?'

But she knew what he was doing, and she was right with him, excited. Standing behind her, his hands roved her body, roughly caressing her bare breasts, squeezing her and rubbing her nipples with his thumbs. When she moaned, he slid one hand down to her crotch, cupping her there and working her through her skirt and her panties. What he was doing down there was probably out of the view of the mythical randy, voyeuristic gardener, but the way she rocked, and tossed her head would reveal all.

'That's it, baby, work it,' hissed John in her ear, squeezing her harder, massaging her sex in a fierce rhythm and pinching her nipple. 'That randy beast of a gardener wants you ... he wants to touch you the way I'm touching you. But he can't have you ... you're my lady of the manor, not his.'

Again with the possessiveness, but she didn't care. It just made her hotter. Her pussy ached, crying silently for more of the same treatment, more pressure. For real contact. She surged against his hand, inciting him to go further, faster, rougher. Wanting more.

'He's out there ... he can see your writhing body...he wants to fuck you.' John's finger pressed hard through her skirt, dividing her sex lips and settling on her clit, making her jerk, and gasp. Then moan as he jammed the cloth of her knickers and skirt against her, rocking. 'He's a big dirty bastard with a big hot cock...all ready and primed for Your Ladyship.' Behind her, the only cock she was interested in jabbed against her buttocks, also ready and primed.

John leaned his weight against her; she had to hold on to the sill. Her arms were taut with the effort, but her fingers clenched, longing to cover John's and to encourage him to work her even harder.

'Do you want him? Do you want his cock inside you? He's a very nasty man and he'll be rough with you, and use you...Do you want that?' Oh, he was enjoying this. She could hear the glee in his voice.

'Yes! Yes, I fucking well do! I don't care how nasty he is . . . the nastier the better. Bring it on.'

Her own voice sounded harsh to her ears, cracking with lust. It was either that, or scream at him, demanding he fill her.

'Very well, Your Ladyship. I'm going to take your knickers off now, and I'm going to play with your pussy before I fuck your brains out. You posh birds are all the same. You like a bit of finger first.'

Lizzie laughed, despite the raving tension, the aching need. John *was* the gardener now, the rough man with the big hot dick and the crude vocabulary.

'Oh, you think it's funny, do you, milady?' John was laughing too, his words full of unsupressed mirth. 'You think you're too good for the likes of me? Well, I'll show you.'

His hands left her body, and started wrenching at her clothes. She'd thought he was going to pull her skirt up, but suddenly he was fishing around for the zip, and in a flash, he'd got it undone and was pulling the garment down, around her ankles.

'Step out of it,' he commanded, a gardener prince. When she did so, he kicked it away across the carpet.

'Now…let's get these knickers down, shall we?' His hand slid into the back of her panties, teasing her bottom, squeezing the firm rounds as crudely as he'd manipulated her breasts. Crooking his wrist, he slid one long, flexible finger into her sex from behind, brushing her entrance, then plunging in, just a little way. 'You like that, don't you? Something in you…finger, cock…a bit of dildo now and again. Dirty slut.' He flexed his finger, pressing, hooking, almost controlling her completely with the digit.

Lizzie let out a sob, her mind and body confused, loving what he did, but not knowing if she was Lizzie, begging for more of it, or the fantasy noblewoman, awash with shame and degradation, being pawed by the crude man from her own garden who was bent on humbling her.

'I bet you want me to finger your clit now, don't you, ma'am? To give you a bit of something before I get mine?' John's face was in her hair, his voice in her brain. 'Tell me, Your Ladyship! Tell me, you mucky trollop. Do you want your bit of rough to diddle your clit?'

'Yes! Oh God, yes! Do me! Do me now, you obnoxious clod!' Lizzie laughed again, loving the shadow-play as much as John clearly was.

'Obnoxious clod? I'll give you "obnoxious clod", you stuck up mare!' Jubilation in his voice, he shoved his other hand down the front of her knickers, diving in and going straight for her clit. 'Is this obnoxious?' he growled, rubbing furiously at her, pressing and knocking and kneading, and at the same time, flexing his other wrist more to get his finger further into her. With it deeply lodged, he lifted her, making her rise on her toes while he mercilessly drove her towards higher pleasure.

'Do you like that?' His mouth was against her ear, and a beat later, she felt the long, lascivious lap of his tongue as he licked her neck. His thumb and fingertip closed on her clitoris and he squeezed it.

From her mouth came a noise that might have been 'yes' but which sounded more like the uncouth, gulping cry of a woman enduring an intense, wrenching orgasm.

Somehow, Lizzie clung on to the sill, her pelvis jerking crazily as she came. Her hair flew everywhere as she tossed her head, lashing against John's face in floating black clouds. His fingers were merciless, maintaining station, tasking her harder, sending her higher.

'That's it…come, baby, come…you can do it. You can come again, you sweet, sweet girl.' She was his lover now; he was hers. The *dramatis personae* were gone.

Staggering, she slumped back against him, no longer able to brace herself. He was rock behind her, supporting her with his body even as he still played with her flesh. Tears were in her eyes, but they were tears of intense, sweet pleasure . . . and joy.

'You're amazing, Lizzie. You're so gorgeous when you come . . . so raw . . . unbelievable . . . please . . . please . . . again . . .'

His fingers flickered and feathered her, gentler now, but still potent. Somehow, he wrung another from her and she shouted, cursing the air.

'Fuck you, John! I want you in me…I fucking well want you in me. Now.' She pitched forward again, filled with new strength, finding power from somewhere. Dragging in a deep breath, she looked over her shoulder, commanding him with her eyes.

'Hell, yes!' he cried, his blue eyes wild. His hands slid from her sex, but hooked at her knickers, dragging them down off her, baring her from the waist down, except for her shoes. Her underwear floated away across the thick, rosy-beige carpet to join her skirt. She watched him as he unbuckled and unzipped again, dragging his underwear down out of the way, then taking his cock in his hand, pointing rudely, and rigid again.

'I hope you've got a condom for that.'

'Always, love, always. Whenever I'm around you, I have to be ready to be in you.' He rummaged in his pocket, bringing one out, the familiar packet. Within seconds the wrapping was on the floor and the contents wrapped around him.

Feeling shameless and lewd, Lizzie widened her stance, inviting him to mount her. She didn't need mad thoughts about randy gardeners now, just John, behind her, fitting the hot, latex-clad head of his cock against her entrance.

'You know...I might take up gardening when I move in here,' he said as he pushed on into her, coasting the well of silk that was overflowing her and oozing down her inner thighs. 'Imagining me as some horny-thumbed son of the soil has got you incredibly wet, baby...You're gorgeously slippery. Tight, but slippery...just how I like you.'

Lizzie's head pitched forward. She was overcome. He was so huge, he filled the whole world, not just her. 'Imagining you as *you* gets me incredibly wet, genius. I thought you might have worked that out by now...ooh! Agh!' The breath left her body as he shoved in hard, right to the hilt.

'I'm glad,' he said. She could tell his teeth were gritted in concentration. 'I like to know I make you wet. I like to think about it. Imagine it...all the time. You, wet for me.' He rubbed his face against her hair again, nuzzling her, and all the time, working his hips, pushing. Thrusting. 'When I'm away from you, I think about touching your pussy and finding it all slippery and warm, primed and ready. Sometimes it's the only thing that gets me through the day.'

He had to be exaggerating, but it was still a thrill to hear. And a thrill to have him huge and hard inside her, thundering away. Every thrust knocked and stretched her, driving her up again, up, up to orgasm. When he reached around, to touch her clit, she hit the summit. Her cries echoed around the room, bouncing off the glass just in front of her.

It was hard to stay upright, but John supported her, his hand cupping her crotch while he braced them both against the wall, by the window. Lizzie's arms had no strength left, as if her whole body had been wrung out, and she swayed, almost falling.

'Lean against the wall, love,' gasped John, still hammering into her, still holding her pussy, cradling it.

His voice gave her strength and she shuffled a little, widening her legs, tilting her hips to let him in deeper. Her eyelids fluttered and she started to see things, the real world again. 'Oh fuck!' she cried, when a dark shape beyond the glass caught her eye.

There was a car tootling up the long drive towards the front of the house.

'What? What's . . .?'

'There's a car coming . . . someone coming to the house!'

'What the blessed fuck? I said no one should interrupt us while we were viewing. They must have had a trip sensor on the gate,' John growled, still pounding her. But as the car approached closer, he grabbed her and whipped her away from window, holding her against the wall.

Feeling him tense to withdraw, Lizzie growled back at him, 'No! Finish, you bastard, finish! There's time.'

John laughed, his voice cracking as he grabbed her hips hard, and thrust in three or four short, fierce strokes, obeying her. 'Lizzie, Lizzie, Lizzie!' he cried.

There was no time for afterglow and tenderness, only frantic rearrangement of clothing, punctuated by a bit of cursing, and Lizzie's helpless giggles.

'If I didn't like this place so much, I'd tell them to stuff it,' John muttered, zipping up, then negotiating his belt and his waistcoat buttons.

'Yep, it's definitely an estate agent,' said Lizzie, peeking from behind the edge of the window as she fastened her blouse. 'He's got a portfolio, and he's got that look, smooth and predatory, a bit like you.'

'Cheeky madam,' said John, straightening up from swooping down to retrieve her knickers and her skirt. 'Look, I'll go down and see him. You take your time, love.' He paused to kiss her cheek, a quick chaste peck, so at odds with what had gone before, and the fact that she was still pretty much naked from the waist down. 'Do I smell of sex?' He wrinkled his nose, sniffing the air.

Lizzie sniffed too. She was pretty sure she smelled a bit raunchy, but John seemed OK. Nevertheless, she scooted across the room and picked up her bag, rummaging inside. 'Try a bit of this. It's just a very light body spray. It's not too sweet or girly. It should mask anything more dubious, if you're worried.' She held out a small atomiser.

John pulled a doubtful face, but all the same, he puffed a couple of squirts of the spray beneath his jacket.

'Smells much better on you, sweetheart,' he said with a shrug, flapping his lapels. 'I hope he doesn't fall madly in love with me.' Flashing her a swift wink, he sped away, heading for the door. 'Don't worry, I'll engage him in conversation, and I'll give him a piece of my mind too. Just come down when you're ready.' And with that, he disappeared, out into the small vestibule, closing the door carefully behind him.

Hysteria surged up, but Lizzie fought to control it. What would the estate agent guy think if he heard someone guffawing like a loony upstairs while he was talking to John? Wriggling into her knickers and then her skirt, she cast around for a door to the bathroom. Ah, there it was. Back the way they'd come.

In the vestibule she tried two doors. The first was obviously a huge dressing room, but the second led into a lovely, light airy bathroom, all cream and mellow gold, and with a vast sunken tub, his and hers sinks, and even his and hers lavatories in inset cubicles. When she tried the taps, she found the water was turned on, and even whatever heated the hot water was working too. She managed a swift wash, punctuated by suppressed fits of the giggles as she smirked at her pink, flustered face in the gilt-surrounded mirror.

What a scrape. What a near thing. Memories of herself and John cavorting in the ladies' room at The Bluebell Café, not all that long ago, returned to her. She could still hear the high, squeaky, dowager's voice he'd assumed to inform the unwary soul outside that their cubicle was occupied. And now he was likely to be behaving all righteous with the hapless estate agent, knowing that he'd just fucked his girlfriend in the bedroom of the house he was viewing, and was now liberally perfumed with her body spray.

And you can't stay up here all day either, Lizzie Aitchison! Get a move on!

Swiftly, she gave her hair a last once over, tweaking stray strands of her black fringe into place. She gave herself a good dowsing with body spray too. If the estate agent twigged that both she and John were wearing the same fragrance, well, that was tough. Realistically, she didn't think they were the first couple ever to have sex in a house they were viewing; far from it, if stories in magazines were to be believed.

Making her way down the stairs, she listened to the voices drifting up. John, as ever, sounded completely poised and in charge, not making a fuss about the disobeyed stipulation, but managing to assert his displeasure subtly, all the same. The estate agent sounded petrified, and probably was, fearful that he'd lost a considerable commission. When Lizzie reached a bend in the staircase, she could see him. He was smooth and over-groomed, but quite a young man. The anxiety in his eyes, in the presence of a high-rolling and possibly temperamental buyer, was plain to see.

'So, what do you think of the upstairs, darling?' John beamed at her as she reached the ground floor, and strode towards her, touching her arm possessively and steering her towards the young estate agent. 'This is Jason, from Blackthornes, and I think he's a bit nervous that you won't like this prime piece of real estate of his.' He winked at nervous Jason, then dusted a kiss on Lizzie's cheek. 'This is my friend, Miss Aitchison, on whose opinion the sale or no sale hinges.'

Oh really? I'm sure you've already made your decision, you tricky devil!

'It's a gorgeous house! I love everything I've seen so far.' She smiled and held out her hand and, apparently as spooked by her as he was by John, Jason did a juggling act with files and a briefcase in order to shake it.

'So?' John gave her a long, provocative look.

Oh fuck, it did all hinge on her.

Lizzie glanced around. The lobby was a perfect snapshot of the rest of the house, light and warm and welcoming, a sort of sunshine Victoriana. She couldn't imagine ever getting tired of walking into this space, or of the memories they'd already forged here.

In the orangery. In the meadow sweetness of the master bedroom.

'You should buy it,' she said firmly. 'I haven't seen all of it, but if the rooms I have seen are anything to go by, it's far too lovely to pass up.'

John's eyes flared, and Lizzie glowed inside. She'd impressed him, and she'd impressed herself. For someone who'd always had a lack of confidence about choices, especially the big ones, she gained a new decisiveness around him.

'Right. I will.' He beamed at her, and then turned to Jason. 'Do you have paper?'

'Er…yes…yes, of course.' The young man fumbled with the catch on his briefcase. 'I have the documents all here…er…do you want to sign them now?'

'I don't sign anything without reading it first, but if you let me have them, I think I'll slip into the orangery to read things over. Then I'll make the call to my P.A. to have the asking price wired over by bank transfer.'

I'm not half so decisive as you, lover. Awe, and a new surge of lust, rampaged through her. This was what John did: make the big decisions, without hesitation, unshakably sure of his own judgement. Regardless of what she might have said, she knew he'd already settled on this house, and if there'd been any remote chance that *she* didn't like it, somehow he'd have won her round, and made her love it.

'The asking price?' Jason seemed gobsmacked.

'Indeed. Admittedly, it's a tad steep, but I think it's well worth it.' John was enjoying the young man's shock. The fact that Jason had expected a struggle, especially after turning up when he shouldn't have, and wasn't getting one. 'Why don't you take Lizzie and show her round a few more of the house's features while I'll get all this sorted?' He gestured expansively with the sales portfolio as if he was just about to buy a second-hand garden shed for fifty quid.

'Yes, of course. Do please come this way, Miss Aitchison,' said Jason, visibly relaxing, as if relieved to get away from the intimidating presence of a man like John, who could probably compel anybody to anything, even without the benefit of his millions.

'Enjoy!' called out John as they walked away.

Jason launched into his spiel, but really, he didn't need to. Dalethwaite Manor was exquisite. Lizzie had loved it on sight, back when she'd waitressed for the garden party, and the additions and renovations since had only enhanced its intrinsic charm and made it yet more desirable.

They toured the cosy kitchen, with all mod cons; the conservatory, a small gymnasium, and a new addition, a pool with an all-weather canopy roof that could retract on sunny days. A huge home office for John, with every amenity for high-speed business communications; and a lovely, well lit workroom-come-studio, which Jason said had been used by a previous owner for his painting hobby, but which Lizzie could see set up for sewing, with a full-size cutting table for laying out patterns and pieces.

After struggling in her room at home, this would be all-out luxury. She could really get ambitious here; perhaps even design from scratch after all. Closing her eyes, she imagined racks to hang the finished garments on, a little cadre of tailor's dummies, and space, space, space in which to work and dream.

'Do you paint, Miss Aitchison?' asked Jason politely.

'No, I'm a dressmaker actually, but this room would be ideal for my work.'

She didn't say 'will' . . . somehow that was a step too far.

After a brief foray around the gardens, the ancillary buildings, the hangar-sized garage and the hard-standing tennis court, Lizzie sensed Jason getting edgy.

He wants to know if John's done the deal.

As she thought that, the young man's mobile phone rang, and when he excused himself to answer it, she saw his eyebrows shoot up. 'Crikey, just like that?'

When he ended the call, he looked around, first towards the heart of the house, then back in the direction of the grounds. Then he whistled. 'Well, Mr Smith is now the proud owner of Dalethwaite Manor. That was a call to say the money's already been transferred. In full. I believe there's always a bottle or two of Champagne kept in the refrigerator for occasions like this. Do you think he'd like to toast the purchase?'

Butterflies battered about in Lizzie's chest and she felt as if she'd already downed a bottle of Champagne. Just like that indeed. She knew, empirically, that John was rich, but to have it demonstrated to her so graphically was a bit scary.

And she had to know . . .

'Um . . . he hasn't said, and it's probably terribly nosy of me to ask . . . but what is . . . was . . . the asking price for this place?'

Jason smiled, looking as if he was slightly scared too.

'Five point three million.'

'Jesus Christ!'

10

Anything for You

'So, five point three million? That's quite a commitment.'

They were drinking Champagne, sitting on the front step, waiting for Jeffrey to arrive with the car. Jason had drunk half a glass and gone, the smile on his face so wide he clearly didn't need booze to feel happy. No doubt his commission on five point three mill was sufficiently intoxicating.

John looked at her thoughtfully over the rim of his glass. 'Yes. Yes, it is. But I'd just as soon buy a shack on a council estate if it'd make you happy and convince you to move in with me.'

So determined. He wasn't going to give up. Lizzie wondered why she just couldn't say 'yes' and be done with it. But it was such a giant step, even to be with him.

'I'm sorry . . . I know you think I'm being a dithering idiot, and you're wondering why I won't do what any woman in her right mind would do without a second thought. But, I need a bit of time to make big decisions. I've made some stupid ones at speed in my time, and I'm trying to be a bit older and wiser and all that.'

'It didn't take you long to make up your mind that night at the Waverley.'

Touché.

'No...that decision was pretty easy to make.'

John smiled, and lifted his glass towards hers, clinking them together. 'For me too. And I'm sorry...I know I'm trying to pressure you. I can't help myself. But I will endeavour to let you make your own decision in your own time.' He gave her a seductive smile, something he excelled at. Lizzie's heart fluttered, and despite everything they'd done that afternoon, she hungered for him again. 'But you will come and stay with me sometimes, eh? Just throw me a few crumbs. After all, we're barely any further from the centre of town here than you are at St Patrick's Road.'

'Of course I will . . . Sometimes . . . Believe me.'

'Good! Thank God for that! I've managed to wring something out of you.' His eyes went dark. He was thinking of other things he'd wrung out of her, up in the master bedroom. 'So, what do you think of the rest of the house? How was Jason's pitch? I'm sure he knew that if you had misgivings, I'd give back word in a heartbeat.'

'He was very competent. Very good at his job. He does sell a good pitch, but he's not pushy.' She took a sip of the Champagne. 'And I do love the house . . . and the swimming pool . . . and the tennis court . . . Do you play, by the way?'

'I have in my time, but I must be very rusty by now. We'll have to give it a bash when we're not exercising in other ways.' He flashed her a wink, and reached for the Champagne bottle. There was just a drop left, but he shared it scrupulously between them.

'I was always rubbish on grass, but I'm not too bad on a

hard court. I'm looking forward to giving you a damn good thrashing.'

John let out a bark of laughter. 'And playing a few sets of tennis too, I hope.'

Oh yes, that too. It had been a strange night, at that party held in the unknown mansion, the one she called the Eyes Wide Shut party. Being John's dominatrix for an hour or so had been so new to her, but she could still remember the delicious dark thrill of it. Maybe if he kept badgering her about moving in, and spending ridiculous amounts of money on her, she might have to have another go at that too, sooner or later.

'So, what else did you discover on your tour?'

'Well, there's a rather spooky wine cellar . . . Not much in it. In fact, just a couple more of these and some dusty-looking reds.'

'That's soon rectified,' remarked John roundly. 'What else?'

Ooh, yes, something! Something that made her smile.

'When we were passing through the utility room, guess what I saw? There's a cat flap in the outer door, and there was a water dish and a mat...for a little someone called "Alice" . . .' Without even stopping to think, she'd called out, hoping the owner of the dish and mat was around. 'Jason said there *is* a cat that lives here. She was bought for the children of the former owners, but she took more to the house than the kids, and when they went, she managed to find her way back. The old housekeeper had been feeding her . . . but she's in a cattery at the moment.' She glanced at John sideways. 'Jason said they'd find another home for her, of course. Unless we wanted to keep her?'

'I guess we're keeping her, then?' John grinned at her.

'Well…yes…I said she could stay.' She gave him a steady look. He wanted her to move in. He wanted her to be happy. Well, he could indulge her in this, if he wanted to entertain hopes. 'I'll miss Mulder when I'm not at St Patrick's Road, so it'll be nice to have a moggie here too. Make it more like a proper home…if you can call a five point three million pound mansion house a home.'

'I intend to. It's my plan to spend most of my time here, when I'm not travelling. I'll keep my London flat on, but this will be my base.'

Crikey …

She opened her mouth to speak, but John beat her to it. He was staring down the drive. 'Here's Jeffrey. We'd better swig this lot down, then close up and set the alarm.'

Five minutes later they were speeding away from Dalethwaite Manor. Lizzie turned around and looked out of the rear window, fixing it in her mind just as it disappeared out of view behind the stands of trees that lined the drive.

John's home now. And hers, if she wanted it.

'Where shall we eat dinner?' John's voice, and the touch of his hand on her shoulder, forestalled her inner debate. 'Do you want to go back to the Waverley, or perhaps try somewhere else? I know of one or two decent restaurants near here.'

Much as she loved walking into a crowded room with John, and feeling that electric thrill, knowing everybody was looking at them, Lizzie suddenly felt tired. It had been a long, strange day, and it was barely more than early evening yet. When she'd woken up and set off for New Again this morning, she hadn't even anticipated seeing him – and now they'd helped Mrs Cox, he'd bought himself a blooming great mansion, and they'd even christened two of the rooms there, by making love in them after a fashion.

I want something normal now. Something I'd do if everything in my life hadn't changed. Something from before John…but something I can share with him.

'I don't really fancy eating out.' She bit her lip, watching his face. 'What do you say we call for some fish and chips and eat them back at St Patrick's Road, watching the telly? You know…live life how the other half live, Mr Gazillionaire?'

John beamed at her. 'Sounds great to me! I love fish and chips.'

'Yeah, right.'

'I do! It's a while since I had decent ones too. They don't know how to make them in these awful Michelin star gaffs I have to eat in all the time, and they get really narked if you ask the chef to serve them in newspaper.'

'Stop taking the piss!' She punched him on the shoulder, but didn't seem to make much impact on the hard muscle beneath his beautiful suit.

'No, I'm serious. I would love to have fish and chips. In fact, I can't think of anything better. Where's the nearest good chippy?'

When Jeffrey had been directed to the Barracuda Fisheries, Lizzie said, 'Crikey . . . I forgot . . . You don't mind eating with Shelley, do you? I'd forgotten all about her. Isn't that *awful*? I'd better ring and see if she wants chips too. She was supposed to be dieting but I'm not sure how that's going now.'

Before she could reach for her phone, John took her hand. 'Of course I don't mind eating with Shelley. She's your friend and she's in your life. So she's in my life too.' He kissed her fingers. 'Anything for you, love. You know that, don't you?'

Lizzie started to shake. She couldn't stop herself. John frowned, then swept her into his arms. 'Hey . . . hey . . . it's all right. I know this is all new . . . but we'll muddle through. Don't worry.'

Lizzie leaned against him. He was so strong. Like a rock. And he smelt of her own body spray. Which made her smile.

'Oops, sorry, I'm not usually a fainting miss, you know. It's just that it's been a really sort of weird day. So much has happened.'

His arms tightened around her. 'Yes, it has…but good stuff, isn't it?' She felt his lips move against her hair, and his breath wafting her fringe.

'Yes…yes, it is.' She slid her arms around him, savouring the beautiful feel of his body. 'But I think I need a quiet night in now. How about you?'

'Absolutely.' Gently easing her away from him, John gave her a quick kiss on the cheek. 'Now ring Shelley and we'll call in for our supper, and I'll check the listings and see what's on the box tonight. Does that sound like a plan?'

She nodded. He seemed to understand that she needed some things in their relationship to be 'normal' and not a fairy-tale sex adventure all the time.

Shelley answered after a few rings, sounding breathless.

'Nice thought, but I'm going out tonight. I'll probably have left by the time you get home.'

A date? Lizzie felt a rush of guilt. She'd not really been taking as much notice of her friend's life as she should have been lately. John had commandeered her time, eating it up even when he wasn't around. Lizzie had been vaguely aware that Shelley had been preoccupied, certainly, but she hadn't probed. Maybe she should have? Shelley was normally a person who liked to share, rather than keep things close to her chest.

'Oh, that's super! Anyone I know? How did you meet?'

'No . . . you won't know him. I don't really . . . it's sort of a blind date thing.'

Something was up. The girl who liked to share sounded distinctly cagey. There was a definite 'don't ask' subtext going on that troubled Lizzie, compounding her guilt. She'd just have to make time for a girly night in, or out, with Shelley soon, regardless of John, and Shelley's mystery man.

'Ah well…Hope you have a fabulous time. Don't do anything I wouldn't do…which gives you a pretty wide latitude, I'd say.' She was pleased to hear her friend giggle in response.

'Yep, I'll need a wide latitude. In fact I'm counting on it!' Shelley paused. 'Look, I'm running late, but we need to catch up. I'll tell you all about my…um…date, when I get in. Will you be home tonight? Or will you be with John?'

'I'm not sure. I don't know yet.'

Would he stay over? Did she even want him to? He'd shared her bed briefly at St Patrick's Road before; but it hadn't really been for much sleep, and certainly not sex. It didn't seem right, somehow, to fuck him in the house she shared with the others, weird as that seemed.

'Don't worry, we'll catch up,' said Shelley cheerfully, 'Somehow. I've got quite a lot to tell you, and I hope to have more after tonight. Look, gotta hustle . . . talk to you later!'

Lizzie stared at the suddenly silent phone, intrigued. She thought about quickly calling Brent, to see if he knew anything about this mysterious date of Shelley's. Perhaps the other girl was confiding in their male house-mate more now? Lizzie knew she'd been preoccupied with John Smith, almost to the exclusion of the whole world, and she'd barely exchanged more than a few brief texts with Brent since he'd left to stay with his parents. He was probably due to come home any day now…but Lizzie didn't have a clue about his intentions, so wound up in herself and her lover had she been.

'She's got a date. So it'll be just us. Some new bloke that she's being very close-mouthed about. I hope he's all right . . . Shelley's had some bad luck on the romance front, and she's ended up with some very dubious characters sometimes.'

'Bit like you, then,' said John teasingly, reaching out to squeeze her arm. 'Don't worry. I'm sure she'll be fine. She knows to call you, if there's a problem, presumably?'

'Er, yes, I think so.'

Within moments, the car was drawing up in the small layby, where the fish and chip shop and a cluster of other small outlets was situated.

'Do you have wine in the house?' John nodded towards the off licence two doors down from the Barracuda. 'Something white, to go with fish?'

'I don't think so. Brent's usually the one who buys wine. He knows more about it than Shelley and I. We just drink any old rubbish. And we usually drink beer or pop with fish and chips…or the traditional cup of tea.'

'I'll get us a bottle,' said John, reaching for the door handle, just as the ever efficient Jeffrey opened the door for them. 'What do you usually get at the chippy? Fish and chips apiece? And mushy peas?' he added gleefully.

'Don't mock! They're delicious!' Lizzie scurried out of the car after him. 'And the fish and chips are my treat, if you're buying the wine.'

John's eyes widened. When was the last time a woman had paid the tab? Might it be as long ago as his marriage? Whatever, he looked bemused for a moment, then grinned. 'OK, it's a deal. I'll see you back here in a few minutes, then?'

Luckily, the Barracuda was quiet, and Lizzie didn't have to wait. Within a couple of minutes she was heading back to the car, with her warm bundle. Would this be a first? She'd lay good money on the fact that there'd never been fish and chips wrapped in paper in the back of John's limousine before.

'I think these will do.' She nearly jumped out of her skin. He'd come up behind her so quietly she hadn't heard him.

'Um…yes. I guess they will. They're white at least.'

John was carrying a transparent plastic carrier bag, with what looked like two tissue-wrapped bottles of Champagne inside it.

'I couldn't resist,' he said, as he settled into the back seat beside her. 'I rather got a taste for it this afternoon, and it's not every day one buys a house, is it? Five point three million is a significant purchase, even for me.'

'It's a lot of money.'

It terrified her. Perhaps he would have bought Dalethwaite anyway, wanting to gradually creep closer to a rapprochement with his family, and needing a base from which to do it?

But she had the feeling it had been more about her. And the weight of five point three million pounds was a heavy responsibility.

A giant commitment, for her, as well as him.

'Don't worry, sweetheart,' he said, in that sudden way of his, that spooky way that suggested her thoughts were an open book to him. 'It'll be all right. We'll work things out. We'll do it together.'

Lizzie smiled back at him. She was being silly again. Just getting the collywobbles, overwhelmed by changes in her life.

Perhaps it would all be all right? After all, change was good…and they had fish and chips, and Champagne, and they were together.

11

Shelley Steps Out

'Thanks, I need this,' murmured Shelley, grateful as the barman set her glass of wine in front of her, a large one. It was a bit drier than she normally drank, but it seemed quite strong and she needed the sudden heat, glowing in her belly.

'Enjoy!' replied the handsome young man, giving her a nod and a wink before moving away down the long bar to serve another punter.

I wish it was you. You're really cute, she thought, following his progress but trying not to be too obvious. He had lovely firm, boyish buttocks in his tight uniform trousers, but she'd have to lean right over the counter if she wanted to see them for much longer, and tipsy letch would not be a good look on her.

Opening her bag on the bar counter, she slipped out her phone, checking the details.

Seven-thirty, Room 217, the Sorrel Hotel.

She'd half hoped he'd suggest the Waverley Grange. Then lightning might strike twice, and she'd pull someone as fabulous as Lizzie had. Hardly likely, though, given that the guy she was meeting was an escort.

I still can't believe you did it, Shell.

But here she was, fifteen minutes away from meeting a man she was going to pay to have sex with her. OK, on the website, she'd actually selected 'sensual massage' from a menu of so-called 'fantasies', but she supposed they *had* to say that, for legal reasons.

Brent would go nuts. It was his old agency, Indulgence. But it was the only one Shelley had ever actually heard of, and if Brent had been on their books, they must be OK.

And certainly better than the last man she'd been out with, Julian. What a git.

Automatically, Shelley's lips thinned, something else she knew didn't look good on her. Slipping out her mirror, she checked her minimal make-up, trying to relax her face. She fluffed her hair a bit, poked her tongue out at herself, and breathed deeply as she straightened her spine.

Tonight is fun. Tonight is all about me. Tonight is ... hell, tonight is sex, sex, sex, unless I've got it all wrong and sensual massage is just sensual massage!

Taking another long swallow of wine, she breathed deeply while a ribbon of fire curled down into her belly, and beyond. Actually, the dry wine wasn't at all bad. Perhaps it had aphrodisiac qualities? She was beginning to feel more and more in the mood with every sip.

Oh yeah ... So, where's Mr Sensual Massage, then?

Sholto Kraft. What the hell kind of name was that? It must be made up.

The meeting wasn't exactly supposed to take place here, but she glanced around the busy, softly lit bar anyway. She'd kind of, sort of hoped she might find him in here first to break the ice. Or that he might find her and introduce himself. A chat would be nice. A chat might make things easier, especially over a drink or two. They could get to know each other in a safe setting where it'd be easier to do a runner if she needed to.

Scanning the room, she didn't recognise anyone who looked like his picture on the website, but then, it'd been an arty, shadowy shot, more about showing his rather fab body than his face. If that was even his body at all. Brent said some of the guys cheated, even though he'd always used his own picture.

No, not everybody you picked up in bars or in hotel rooms was going to be a looker like darkly handsome Brent, or have the sheer drop-dead movie star glamour that Lizzie's John did. Not that he was an escort, and anyway, Shelley wasn't quite sure she fancied the idea of getting involved with a chap twenty years her senior, even if he did look like a worldly-wise angel.

But Lizzie seemed to adore him, and you couldn't fault the guy for generosity. Not everybody would lavish you with high-speed broadband, a deluxe digital telly package, and a huge great television to watch it on, just because you were the *friend* of their girlfriend!

But, back to her own prospective, if temporary, man. And so far, nothing. No click of unspoken recognition. No suave sexy approach by 'Sholto'. No broken ice, or first hurdle hopped over. Surely an experienced escort could spot his client easily in a place like this? Her sense of anticipation – and nerves – must be screaming out.

There were plenty of men drinking alone at this early evening cocktail hour. Muted conversation hummed, but it seemed to be business mostly. Attaché cases abounded. Sharp, corporate ties were already loosened.

Shelley shifted on her seat, heating up from the wine, and

excitement. She still couldn't tell whether it was an alarming sensation, or a thrilling one, but she was prepared to stick with it for a little while yet.

Before the night's out, I'll probably be in bed with a man, doing the wild thing, his cock inside me.

Vibrators were fun, but they didn't come with a man attached to them, and in a shared house, you had to wait until the others had gone out. A man could kiss you afterwards as if he cared, even if he didn't, and had a warm, willing body to give you a hug, even if it was just paid for.

Cautiously rubber-necking around, she still couldn't see anyone who looked like the website picture. None of them looked at her with that promising smile she was hoping for.

But then, a man *did* glance her way, just for a second. A hard-faced, craggy man with brutally short, dark blond hair and startling eyes, light coloured but piercing. He looked away before she could 'click' with him, and continued his perusal of a newspaper. He had a closed attaché case set in front of him on a low table, but he was no groomed cosmopolitan male. He was wearing a rough-looking leather jacket, black t-shirt and black jeans tucked into low, soft leather boots.

No, definitely not Mr Sholto 'Sensual Massage' Kraft. Too threatening. Too aloof. He looked far more like one of those guys who was into kink, a bit like Lizzie's John, and his icy gaze had accidentally traversed the space she occupied and then dismissed her.

Irrationally angry, Shelley drank the rest of her wine and slid off the stool. She didn't like the bar any more, and she wanted to get out of it, even though she'd found the ambience exciting when she'd first entered. She flung down a note to pay for her drink and walked out into the foyer, head held high. A lift was opening up and she darted forward to take it.

I could still just go home.

'How cosy is this, eh?' said John

Lizzie grinned at him, her eyes teasing as they clinked their Champagne glasses. The fish and chips were long gone, and had been so good he'd almost sighed, and now they were watching the television, he with his legs stretched out like the man of the house, and Lizzie tucked up next to him, snuggled against his shoulder.

It was so normal. Like nothing he'd experienced since university days, when he'd shared a scruffy house with other students. He'd had no idea until now how much he'd missed it.

'It's great,' he said, imagining how they might share the same togetherness at Dalethwaite too. It was a big house, and beautiful, but also homely. Nothing to say they couldn't have fish and chips in front of the telly there too, sometimes.

'We don't normally have Champers with our chips, though, but I must admit, they do go together. You won't mind if I share the second bottle with the others one night, would you?'

No. He didn't mind. No, he didn't…did he?

'Go ahead, love. They might get a taste for it.' He paused, half watching the screen, a Victorian police drama, and pretty good. Why didn't he watch more television? 'Fish and chips and Champagne is a perfect combo, don't you think? It's sort of like how life should be, don't you think? A bit of luxury, and a bit of keeping it real too.'

Lizzie remained silent for a few moments, her eyes on the screen. In the low light of just the television and a table lamp, her profile looked perfect and pure, like a Renaissance masterpiece. His cock stirred lazily, but not insistently. It was OK to get aroused, but be quiescent too, keeping it real but enjoying the thing of beauty.

'Yes...I think you're right,' she said at length, 'that makes sense.' Her lips curved in a wise little smile.

The Victorian programme came to an end and they discussed it. He loved the way Lizzie was excited by the well-researched nature of the plot, and raised a few points he'd not been aware of. Smart as a whip, she constantly surprised him. He imagined her at a dinner party, holding her own in the toughest of rooms, charming everybody with her dazzling natural beauty and her sense of fun. She could exist in his world, probably far better than he'd manage in hers, and he wanted to show her off.

But did she *want* to be shown off?

'You're into all sorts of things, aren't you?' he said as she flicked through channels with the remote, rejecting trash with a discerning ruthlessness.

'Yes, I suppose I am.' She turned to him, her eyes narrowing a little. 'I'm not just some kind of dropout bimbo, you know. Just because I look like Bettie Page, it doesn't mean I don't have a mind. And Bettie wasn't dim, either. She was an intelligent woman who knew how to use her natural gifts.'

'I never said you were dim, did I?' he protested, instantly feeling guilty, in case, by some fault of his own he'd inadvertently made her feel that way.

Lizzie laughed. 'No, don't worry! You haven't.' She squeezed his thigh in a way that he knew was just supposed to be reassuring, but which made his cock lurch alarmingly. Thank God she wasn't looking south. 'It's just me...I do have a bit of a chip on my shoulder sometimes, because I left university, and most of my contemporaries stayed on, and got degrees and good jobs. Some of them *do* look down on me. But I just couldn't stay there. I couldn't hack it.'

Curiosity overcame the beast in him. He ignored his erection, burning to know what had happened. Why someone so bright, and who seemed so well adjusted, had chosen such a course.

'Why was that? I mean ... only if you want to talk about it, Lizzie. But clearly you're a smart, intelligent woman. I would have thought you'd have breezed through.'

Muting the television, she turned in his arms, and looked straight at him. In doing so, she pulled away a little, and something in him cried out, at the closeness lost.

'I don't do well in groups. I hate "structures". Regimes . . . you know? I could have done the work but I didn't like *having* to do it.' She frowned, and he wanted to reach out and gently caress her forehead, beneath her sleek black fringe, and smooth away what had caused the hurt and the unhappiness. 'It's all pressure, expectation. Either from academia itself or just from my father. He wanted me to be like my sisters. Even though they're younger than me, they were both enthusiasts at school, and he could see something in them that was lacking in me. They've both ended up doing fabulously at uni . . .' She shrugged, and leaned down to put aside her glass. He did the same, and reached for her hand. 'Me being a bit of a drifter by his standards, doing a bit of sewing and temping and even waitressing in my time . . . well, he considers that I've wasted the education he lavished on me.'

John wanted to shake this as yet un-met father of hers. Give him a stern talking to. 'That's unfortunate. Surely he must see that you have other gifts. That you excel in many areas. The academic world isn't for everybody. I learnt far more when I'd left uni than while I was there.'

'He's resigned to it now. In fact, he's accepted it quite well, and we get on much better. I know it's a battle for him, but he always makes a point of asking me about sewing when I visit now.' She laughed softly, and his heart turned over. Always she impressed him. For all she'd said about chips on shoulders, he sensed no real bitterness or resentment in her.

But at the same time, he thought again about that dinner party. That world was structured in its way. She *could* fit in. She had the charm and grace. But would she want to? Should he even think about imposing it on her? Ever . . .

As he leaned forward, and kissed her lightly, he was befuddled. Why did he keep on thinking 'for ever'? He wanted it, in some way, shape or form, but was it fair on her? Especially given the difference in their ages. When she responded to his kiss he was momentarily frozen.

She'd spoken of her father, and being the eldest.

Good God, what if he's younger than I am?

12

The Man from the Bar

Dressed or undressed?

Answer the door or 'Enter!'?

Drink or no drink?

Decisions, decisions, decisions, decisions!

Shelley stared out across the rooftops of the city centre. The hotel was high rise, so from here she could see quite a lot of it. The shopping centre. The Piazza, down by the canal. Borough Hall and the library nearby. The familiar yet unfamiliar sights calmed her. She'd never seen it all from this angle before.

This was her treat. There was no need to stress. She was in charge here; it was her entertainment, her pleasure, all paid for. This was no accidentally blundering into a relationship, like Lizzie; this was under control. And if she ended up just wanting a massage, that was all she had to have. In fact, a massage sounded good! Her shoulders were rigid and her stomach was in knots, but Sholto the Sensual Massage Guy would soon set that to rights.

She took off her dress and slipped into the big fluffy robe she'd found in the bathroom. Then immediately flung that off and wriggled back into her frock.

For pity's sake! What did I just say about not stressing?

She eyed the mini bar. No, not yet, why spoil the night by getting wasted?

'Fuck!' She laughed, remembering that was exactly what she'd *planned*, despite her qualms.

The man in the bar had got under her skin, she realised. Arrogant pig, dismissing her like that. Well, his loss. At least her massage man would be attentive and flattering, even if all the niceness was bought and paid for.

For the duration of the date, she'd imagine it was real. No harm in that.

Settling down on the side of the bed, she swung her legs up on to the duvet and settled back against the mass of white pillows, savouring their depth and fluffiness. She closed her eyes and let her head fall back, sinking, sinking, sinking.

A cool, craggy, dismissive face appeared in her mind, and as she shot up straight again, there was a soft knock at the door.

Answer, call out, answer, call out?

Springing to her feet she bounded for the door barefoot, her heart giddy in her chest. She flung back the door far more energetically than she meant to, and as it bounced on its hinges, she met a pair of green eyes staring back at her. The green eyes that'd dismissed her, belonging to the man from the bar, who was all attention now.

'Oh, it's you!'

Oh great, Shelley, really convince him you're a dummy.

'Yes, indeed, it's me.'

The ice melted with his smile and his eyes were warm, a clear golden green. Though the rest of him was pretty stunning too, close up. Not much like his online photos, but even more to Shelley's taste, brawny and muscular. Just the way she liked them!

'May I come in, then?'

What am I just standing here staring for?

'Yes, please do.' She skittered back, aware how big he was, big and lithe and vaguely menacing in his dark clothing as he strode past her. His presence dwarfed both her and everything else in room around her. When he'd been sitting down in the bar it had been impossible to gauge his height, but he was tall, very tall.

Already he was in control of the situation, and he'd barely spoken yet.

'I'm Shelley Moore. How do you do?' She stepped cautiously forward as he spun towards her and looked down at her. His eyes were sharp, darting to every part of her in the space of a few instants, sizing her up like the expert in the female form he probably was. She felt like a piece of meat, and even though she couldn't work out why, that excited her even more.

The way he looked at her seemed to vaporise her clothes and leave her naked and vulnerable before him. She held out her hand and his smile shifted, quirked.

'Pleased to meet you, Shelley,' he said in his pleasant low voice that was already doing strange things to her innards. 'I'm Sholto. Sholto Kraft.' He laughed softly. 'At your service, you might say. Shall we have a drink and get the formalities out of the way?'

Shelley let out a nervous laugh of her own, but her new friend just looked at her, his expression friendly enough but unrevealing. She handed him the envelope of money from her bag, and he slipped it into the pocket of his leather jacket.

Sholto Kraft? Surely it wasn't a real name. Dare she ask him?

They stood looking at each other for several long moments until it suddenly dawned on her that he was waiting for her to get him a drink. That was a bit odd. Wasn't he supposed to be the one doing the serving and pleasing?

'I'll have a whisky.' Turning away from her, he set his attaché case down on the bed, and flicked open the latches, but didn't open it. Looking over his shoulder, he added, 'Nothing with it, just ice, if you please.'

Suddenly something dawned on her, in a plume of anger.

'So you *did* see me in the bar. I looked at you, but it was as if you looked straight through me. Even though you must have known who I was.'

'Of course I saw you. But some women prefer not to be approached in public, and it's better to err on the side of discretion.'

What a cool customer. Her first impressions had been spot on. He was detached and arrogant, a clinician rather than a lover. Unease stirred in her gut, along with more wayward feelings. A strange, whirling, out-of-control sensation, dizziness of the head, but also a wild apprehension, a physical tightening. Of everything.

Jesus, here I was thinking I was in control, and I'm just as much in over my head as Lizzie was. And *I'm paying for it!*

Without knowing when she'd done it, she realised she'd clenched her fists, and as she loosened them, Sholto's eyes flicked, registering the small movement. His rather hard mouth quirked, skirting around the edges of amusement.

'We're here now, anyway. Let's have that drink?' he suggested. He spoke mildly, but Shelley instinctively shuddered, sensing steel beneath the bland words.

She stomped to the mini bar, wishing she'd kept her shoes on for a more effective stomping technique. This was ridiculous. He was supposed to be her treat and he was making her feel weird, and slightly cross and unsettled. It wasn't what she'd expected, but her blood was racing around her body, disturbing areas that shouldn't be disturbed by anger. Heating her up.

The drinks she made were approximate, stupidly strong. She coughed when she sipped hers and poured in more ginger ale. Still too potent, but she made a point of lingering over it before bringing Sholto his.

But he was smiling properly now, his eyes alight. He knew her tactics. He thought them hilarious.

'What kind of a name is "Sholto", then? Surely not your real one?'

He took a sip of whisky and pursed his lips as if he wasn't immune to its peaty bite.

'Actually, yes, it's my real name,' he said, taking another sip and then putting the glass aside. In a swift economical gesture, he shed his leather jacket and tossed it across the chair. 'My parents were a little fanciful. I took hell in school because of it…until I learnt to give hell back again.'

Shelley couldn't bring a schoolboy with a strange name to mind. She was too busy staring, open-mouthed, at a man. At muscles. At power. At elegant flexion in upper arms and shoulders beneath smooth black cotton. And a belt, a heavy leather belt, circling his narrow waist.

He threw her scrutiny back at her, his green eyes coasting over her breasts, her thighs, the area of her crotch beneath her dress. Lifting his glass again to his lips, he drank more whisky. He was a gentleman at a sporting club appraising an example of fine horseflesh.

Shelley was that example, a trembling filly, her nostrils flaring as she scented danger in his faint spicy fragrance.

Right! I've had enough of this. I'm not supposed to feel this way!

'I'm going to get changed. Won't be a minute.' Why was she making excuses, apologising. He was the one who should be seeking her approval, not the other way around.

'Good idea.'

With her heart fluttering and her face scarlet, Shelley turned and strode into the bathroom, only just managing to keep from slamming the door behind her.

How dare he be so casual? He was supposed to make her feel relaxed and mellow, and at every turn he seemed to be deliberately unsettling her. And worse, the more he unsettled her, the more it made her belly crawl with desire and her sex moisten. It was hard to understand. It made her head feel strange, filled with a sort of anti-euphoria. She felt guilty and angry with herself.

And it was like he was watching her too, even though there was a wall between them.

Bloody hell, this isn't what I wanted at all. This isn't relaxing and all about me.

Still, though, she stripped off her clothes and slid into the soft fluffy robe again. Developing her prevarications skills, she cleaned off some of her make-up, justifying the time spent by telling herself she didn't want to get foundation on the hotel bedding when she lay down for her massage. The mini containers of beauty products supplied were luxurious, and she made a note to slip them into her bag before she left. Might as well get as much as she could out of this experience, seeing as how her Sensual Massage Guy hadn't turned out quite as she'd expected...and wanted.

Well, I'm not having sex with you, mister! Massage only. If I feel horny, I'll deal with myself, thank you very much.

But in her mind, those green eyes flashed, as if daring her to take on Sholto Kraft and make the most of what he had to offer. Which she suspected was quite a lot. She'd set out with the plan to enjoy lots of foreplay and, especially, oral...but what would it be like to just have hard sex with a hard man like the one who was out there waiting for her?

His body was superb. All muscle, but not in a gross way. And down below, a sizeable package, which she realised now she'd automatically checked out, even though she'd instantly *not* liked him.

Stop faffing about, Shelley, get the hell out there! You've paid good money for this. More than you can afford. Don't let it go to waste.

Head up, she turned the handle, almost flung open the door and marched out of the bathroom. All business.

Only to stop, her jaw dropping, when she saw what her new nemesis had laid out on the bed.

A blindfold. Buckled restraints. A nasty-looking ball and strap device that could only be a gag of some kind. Various implements that were obviously for inflicting corporal punishment.

'What the hell is all this?'

'Just a small selection of the tools of my trade. I have more in my case, if you want to see them.'

The voice from the shadows was richly amused, like double cream poured over gravel. Shelley spun on the ball of her foot, and found Sholto sitting in an armchair by the big window that looked out across the city. He'd removed his black t-shirt, and the tanned skin of his arms, his shoulders and his deep chest gleamed, catching errant light from the small lamps that were dotted around the room. Shelley had never seen menace look so delectable.

'No! I don't want to see any more. I don't even want to see those.' Her heart bashed in her chest as her imagination threw scenarios at her...images of herself, bound, gagged. She almost squirmed where she stood as a jolt of arousal speared her belly and, to her astonishment, her pussy quickened. 'I don't know what's going on here, but this isn't what I requested. Not at all.'

Ah, but you want it. You've been desperate to try this, ever since Lizzie told you what she gets up to with John!

The news came on the television, and Lizzie smiled. Like all men, John leaned forward, avidly attentive. He muttered during the financial reports, tutting and shaking his head.

'Oh dear, does that mean you'll have lost a few million? Will you have to give Dalethwaite Manor back?' she teased.

He shrugged. 'No, don't worry. I'm always careful. I cover all my positions. Eggs in baskets and all that. But I think everyone wishes the recovery was going a helluva lot better.'

'You can say that again. Mrs Briggs had to put the rent up again last month.' It was true. They were managing all right, but she'd thought twice about her gamble to give up temping and throw herself into sewing full time. She'd grabbed at the opportunity when Marie had offered her part-time work in New Again to top up her income.

John gave her a sharp look. 'I can help you with that. There's no need for you to struggle in any way. You have me to take care of your needs now.' He waggled his blond eyebrows at her. 'And that means *all* your needs.'

She grinned back at him, but beneath it, her unease stirred. He only wanted to help, so why did she always feel so uncomfortable about taking things from him? It was stupid really. He gave generously, and without thought of return, and it made him *happy* to give.

'Don't worry, you'll be the first to know if I can't pay my rent.'

The weather came on next – mostly fine, a bit of rain tomorrow evening – then local news. It was almost always lightweight stuff, and far too many novelty stories for her liking, but tonight, the presenter assumed a grim face, announcing a serious car accident on a local bypass, with two fatalities at the hands of a drunken driver.

Regrettable as it seemed, Lizzie sometimes let stories like that flow over her. There was nothing she could do to help the victims, so faux woe on their behalves seemed hypocritical. But suddenly, tonight, the account tolled like a dark bell through the shadowed room, almost dampening the flickers of light from the screen.

A fatal car accident. Dangerous, drunken driving. It was almost as if the victims and grieving families were in the room with them, heavy with sorrow, like Marley's ghost…and all pointing the finger of guilt at John.

He didn't move, not a muscle, but even in the dark, Lizzie could see his whole demeanour had changed.

Another news item came on – local pigeon fanciers – but still he stared at the screen, as if turned to stone, the beautiful line of his jaw so taut she was sure it must actually hurt.

This wasn't something they could brush off, or get around. She reached out and laid her hand on his shoulder, aching when he flinched, his whole body tense.

'You paid for what you did, love,' she said softly. It was almost as if he were a wild horse and if she spoke too sharply, he might spook. 'You can't change it now, especially after all these years. Please don't beat yourself up any more. You are a good man…you just made a mistake. Everybody does.'

'But not everybody's mistake leads to someone's death, Lizzie.' His body trembled beneath her touch. Trembled hard. 'I'm a killer…that's what it boils down to.' He turned to her and she saw a sheen in his eyes, a polish on the clear sky blue. 'Can you really care for a killer and bear to have him touch you?'

After all these years, his remorse was so keen. A lesser man might have brushed it off by now, but not John. Not her John. She slid her arms around him, and drew his head down on her shoulder, holding him tight. Was he weeping? She didn't know…If he wasn't, he was still bottling it up, even now. There was nothing she could do but keep on holding him. That and press a kiss to his golden curls, as if that might somehow heal him and allow him to heal himself.

But it could never be that easy. Twenty plus years was a long time to carry such guilt and pain. It might never fade or get better if it was still so strong after all this time.

'If you'd committed a deliberately evil act, it might bother me. But even then if you felt remorse for it, I could give you the benefit of the doubt. None of us are perfect, but I know in my heart you're not a bad man . . .' She hugged him tighter…'And I'm never happier than when you're touching me, or I'm touching you. Here's another thing I'm going to put out there…with a pin in it…I love you, John, whether you killed somebody or not.'

Turning to her, his eyes were wide, full of emotion, jumbled emotion. Had she made a huge mistake? It was hard to tell. He opened his mouth to speak but she pressed a finger against his lips, against their plush yet resilient surface that she loved to kiss.

'Say nothing,' she whispered. 'Pinned, remember? No need for a response. I know you care about me. You show it in a million ways. That's enough...'

He kissed the tip of her finger. 'You're a wise woman, Lizzie. Perhaps the wisest I've ever met.' Twisting around in her hold, he slid his arms around her, and she in turn offered her mouth to him.

He sighed as he kissed her, as if her lips were a precious gift, beyond all price.

13

Oops!

'Ah . . . role play . . . Excellent. Always a better experience.'

What the hell was he talking about? Shelley's heart thudded hard, as, suddenly, she remembered something. Oh God . . .

She remembered checkboxes, and dithering, then bottling out and thinking, 'Nah . . . not really.'

But I did click it, didn't I? I clicked it . . . and I didn't unclick it. What an idiot!

And now here she was in Lizzie's accidental territory, but not sure she really wanted to be there.

Sholto's mouth curved into a hard smile, then suddenly and shockingly, he sprang to his feet, lithe and powerful, approaching her. In a heartbeat, he was towering over her, looking down, his icy eyes glittering, hard and bright. Heat seemed to pour out of him, like waves from the smooth, shiny skin of his chest.

As he reached for her, Shelley darted away from him, so panicked that she stumbled. In a move of scary speed, Sholto had her by the arm, holding her up.

'Hush! Be careful . . . you need to relax, behave yourself. Be a good girl.'

Shelley's pulse hammered, and even though she tried to shake free of him, he held her, his grip on her strangely gentle, but also unyielding.

'Look, I don't know what your game is, but this isn't what I requested.' Green eyes narrowed. 'I mean it! It isn't!'

The grip on her arm relaxed.

'Do you know, I think you really mean it.' There was no remorse or apology in his voice.

'Do you have any sort of record of my booking? Check it, you'll see.' He set her free, dropped his hands, then raised one again, tapping his chin contemplatively.

'I think I'd better, don't you?' Still amused, he strode to his attaché case on top of one of the vanity units, and fished out his phone. After a few moments' scrolling, he said, 'Dear me, I think there has been a mistake, hasn't there?'

Still no apology. He seemed to be having fun.

'What do you mean? What did you think we were supposed to do?'

Still smiling, Sholto nodded at the fearsome toys laid out on the bed. 'Well, as far as I can tell, you accidentally selected "BDSM Fantasy", and I came prepared accordingly.'

Oh hell . . . just what she'd feared.

'I saw it on the list, but it's not my thing. No way.' Liar, liar, liar; she'd thought about little else since Lizzie had come home from her first adventure with John.

'Are you sure you're not curious?'

The way Sholto's mouth quirked seemed to suggest he'd read her mind, not to mention the dark gleam in his eyes.

'Not in the slightest,' she lied. 'I'm sorry you've been brought here on false pretences. Maybe you'd better leave. I'll just stay and enjoy some room service . . . watch the cable. It's all right.'

What am I babbling about? He's laughing at me. I must shut up!

But Sholto wasn't laughing. Smiling, yes, but not laughing at her. In fact, he seemed strangely sympathetic. Almost as if he was sorry for her, and she didn't like that.

Opening her mouth to speak, she shut it again. Sholto was already gathering up his things, and returning them to the case.

'Do you want another drink before you go?'

The words were out of her mouth before she could stop them.

Sholto spun around.

'No thank you, I'm all right for the moment.' In his hand was a small bottle, full of golden fluid. 'But I'll stay a while . . .' He held up the bottle. 'I can give you that massage, if you still want it? I'm a man of many talents. I don't *only* do BDSM scenes.'

Caught by surprise, Shelley dithered. She'd wanted massage, and a bit of sex, naturally. Why else would she have blown money she couldn't really afford? When she'd visited Auntie Mae last, she wasn't sure her aunt had pressed a bunch of notes into her hand to pay for a male escort! But why did the vanilla stuff seem like second best now? She didn't really want a spanking, did she? Or any of the weird stuff she imagined Lizzie and John doing?

Sholto was watching her steadily. 'Go on. Try it. If you think I'm a terrible masseur, you can always ask me to stop.' His green eyes were serious. 'And whatever you choose, I'll give you a full refund anyway, and then you can book a new appointment for something you really want. You'll probably feel better with another guy after this, eh?'

'No! I'll stick with you . . . if you don't mind? A massage sounds great.'

What had she to lose? She looked at his hands. They were large and strong, but looked capable. She'd no doubt he was a fantastic masseur, as well as being good at all the other things. She flashed him a nervous smile.

'Good girl.' Brisk now, he strode to the bathroom door. 'We'll need towels. I'll take that drink after all. Just a small one. Will you fix it for me?'

Still bossing me around, even though I'm supposed to be the one getting a treat!

But her heart was pounding. She felt ridiculously thrilled and excited. Those hands were going to touch her, massage her. The idea of them made it difficult to breathe or concentrate. Her thoughts skittered about and she slopped whisky on to the surface of the tray. *Calm down*, she told herself, mopping up the mess.

But she was still jittering about when Sholto reappeared, bearing an armful of the hotel's thick, luxurious towels. Quickly, he spread out the largest on the bed.

'Well?' He nodded to it. The look in his eyes said he wasn't sure if she dare even have a massage.

Shelley wasn't sure either. He was so male, so muscle packed. Bigger than himself, somehow, like a god of dangerous sexuality. His beautiful but intimidating body threatened her.

'Come on, I won't bite.' He wasn't laughing, at least not out loud, but she could sense his amusement. And why wouldn't he be amused? She was being a fool. So much for the enlightened woman who could buy a man. Lizzie wouldn't still be faffing about now. She'd have gone for it, big style. *She* had the guts to reach for the big prize...and it'd paid off!

And I'm still hiding in my robe like a dried-up spinster, hiding every square inch of flesh ... Well, fuck this!

Wrenching open the sash, she dropped her robe on the

floor and walked as smoothly as she could to the bed, every step an act to hide her trembling and quivering.

Sholto's green eyes took in her bra and pants. She felt like a fool for keeping them on, but it'd seemed like a bridge too far to take them off.

What were you imagining, Shelley, you twit? That they'd magically dissolve when he started to make love to you?

Make love? Who was she kidding? She imagined both Brent and Lizzie laughing at her. Brent especially, kindly warning her not to get delusions that she was anything more than a client, no matter how attentive the escort might seem.

Pulling herself together, she slithered on to the broad, soft bed, trying to look graceful, and was pretty sure she wasn't achieving it.

Put a pin in it, she'd said.

John tried to, as he tasted Lizzie's luscious lips, and the sweetness of her flowed from them, through his body. His cock stirred, rising to full hardness with shocking rapidity, even though his mind still whirled with the simple words she'd said.

I love you.

He'd heard her say it before, of course, but only in those moments when most people said crazy things they didn't mean at other times: when they were coming, or pretty soon afterwards. This time, though, he knew it was a statement of honest truth, and it was how she'd been feeling for a while. Despite her innate sophistication, and her natural zest for erotic games, when it came to playing games with the finer emotions, she was an innocent, and unsullied. She was guileless. Completely unlike the other significant women in his life before her.

He squeezed his eyes tight, not wanting to think of those women right now, not wanting to insult Lizzie with their phantom presence. Even his ex-wife, Caroline, for whom he only had benign feelings of fondness and gratitude.

'What is it? Have I mucked things up, saying what I said? Don't think about it. Forget it.' Lizzie eased away from him, peering into his face. She looked worried, and he wanted to kick himself for being an insensitive fool. He desperately wanted to be able to say the words himself, but somehow he couldn't. When he'd said them before, they'd been thrown back in his face . . . not just once, but twice, the beauty of them sullied, perhaps for ever.

'No, no, you haven't. Not at all. You're a beautiful, honest girl, Lizzie, and you know that I adore you. But . . .' He paused, sighing. 'I want to say what you said, but I don't think I'm able to. It probably sounds stupid, but I don't think those words have enough meaning for me any more. They've been spoilt.' He took her face between his two hands, marvelling again at the purity of her features, the innocence despite her magnificently carnal nature. 'But they haven't for you, so don't feel bad. And . . . I'm honoured and touched.'

God, it sounded so stilted. So tight-arsed. Like the very worst of the repressed background he'd tried so hard to ignore all these years. And fuck it; he knew it must hurt her.

Unable to bear seeing that pain in her eyes, he almost threw himself at her, kissing her with all the energy he had in him, but cursing himself for a lousy coward at the same time. For a moment, she seemed to hesitate, holding a back a little, but then, in a heartbeat, she was there with him, kissing him back with all the generosity in her soul. Accepting and affirming with the sweet way her lips yielded to him, and the bolder way that her tongue fought back against his.

Something was on the television, some meaningless words and flickering pictures, but it was like a silent movie from another age, incomprehensible. Barely breaking the kiss apart, they rearranged themselves on the settee, kicking off shoes and half lying alongside each other, bodies pressed together. He growled in his throat when Lizzie rocked her hips invitingly against him, caressing his erection with her belly. Her arms were around him, travelling over his back and arse, exploring and encouraging him. All qualms about making out in the house where she lived were forgotten, by both of them.

John couldn't stop now. He didn't want to. And he could feel Lizzie with him, her bold, daring spirit rising to him, laughing at inhibitions. That was the great wonder of her, always seeking the best and happiest and most vivid parts of life, not dwelling on disappointments.

Maybe I do love you, my darling? Even if I can't say it . . .

He slid a hand up her blouse, loving the feel of her hot skin against his searching fingers. Simply exploring her ribcage excited him. His cock surged. He kissed and kissed her, stroking her back, then, when he could hold out no more, he slid his hand around and pushed up her bra so he could cup her breast, just as hot, just as perfect. She made a thrilling, female sound, a tiny roar of encouragement as his fingertips settled on her hard little nipple. Beneath him, her thighs moved restlessly, parting and creating a cradle for his sex. Gladly, he shifted position, moving into that gracious space, pressing the very essence of his libido against the essence of hers.

'Yes,' he muttered against her mouth, using the arm of the settee to brace himself, so he could push, push against her, massaging her. The friction was heavenly, yet he wished that their clothing would spontaneously disappear so they were naked and he could work himself into the cleft of her sex, unhindered. When he squeezed her breast and rubbed himself against her, she moaned, almost as if the clothes *were* gone and he was stimulating her directly. Her hands closed tight against his buttocks, squeezing and massaging him in return, her deft seamstress's fingertips pressing into the groove of his bottom and tantalising his anus.

'Jesus, Lizzie, yes ... Oh, that's nice.' Her fingers dipped and teased as he dry humped her. He could feel himself rising up, the excitement climbing through his entire body, encompassing more than just his groin, even while his genitals grew more and more ready, closer and closer to crisis. Sensing he might hit critical long before he wanted to, he tugged at her skirt. 'Take your knickers off, baby...I need to touch you. I need to be in you before I explode.'

Still kissing him, she began to scrabble, dashing away his hands from her skirt, so she could get to it better. As she did so, he worked at her upper clothing – her blouse, her bra – so he could get to her beautiful breasts.

Switching his hands to himself, he was just unbuckling his belt when a series of small sounds filtered through to him, penetrating a hot haze of lust that was both tactile and auditory.

It was a key turning in the old Yale lock of the front door, barely yards away from them, then the creak of hinges. Then a voice cried out, masculine, and known to him, but in a put-on, sing-song tone:

'Honey, I'm home!'

Brent Westhead, home from his travels, and heading for the room where they were.

'Shit!'

'Shit!'

Lizzie's hiss of shock was accompanied by her jerking, jack-knifing upright with all the sudden force of panic. A force that sent both of them sliding off the sofa.

With a double thump, they landed on the rug, tangled together, already fumbling to put Lizzie's clothes to rights.

Keys jangled, and there was a thump out in the passage too, a heavy bag being dropped. As Brent's footsteps sounded, Lizzie shoved John's hands away and fastened the buttons of her blouse at lightning speed.

As a rectangle of light appeared in the corner of the room, she was just about decent. If somewhat dishevelled . . .

Silhouetted in the illumination from the hall, John saw Brent Westhead's hand reaching for the light switch, but before he could speak, Lizzie cried out, 'Don't put the light on, B, you'll dazzle us . . . wait a minute.'

'Us? Oh . . . oh my God, I'm so sorry! Beg your pardon . . .' John could hear amusement as well as surprise in the other man's voice. 'Don't mind me. I'll be in the kitchen, putting the kettle on, for when you're decent.' With that he disappeared, and they heard him laugh as he went, heading down the passage.

'Oops,' whispered Lizzie, her eyes merry in the lamplight, and her face rosy.

'Oops, indeed,' echoed John . . . then he laughed too.

Caught making out on the settee, like a teenager. Whatever next?

But as they stood up, and shook out the creases, he felt strangely light and young, renewed by Lizzie.

He smiled at her, trying to communicate that in silence, and through the flicker of light and shade from the television . . . and thank God, she smiled right back, as if she knew.

14

Hands On

Shuffling about, Shelley felt like a body on a slab, waiting for a bunch of medical students to scrutinise her. It wasn't sexy at all, and she had no idea how she should lie. If only she could relax and enjoy what she was paying for! Compelling herself to stop squirming, she lay with her face to one side, every muscle in her body as hard as a board. Sholto was going to have his work cut out with her, that was for sure.

'Don't worry, Shelley . . . just relax.' His voice was softer now, low and almost hypnotic. One or two muscles loosened just a smidge. 'It's only a massage. Nothing more unless you want it.'

With that, his hands settled lightly on her shoulders. They were warm, unoiled as yet, pleasantly dry and smooth.

I want more already, a traitorous voice muttered inside her. *A lot more.*

Still barely floating across her skin, he smoothed his fingertips over her shoulders, her upper arms, her upper back. He was introducing her to his touch, letting her flesh simply make friends with his. It should have been innocent and impersonal, yet it was the most erotic experience of her life, more exciting than the wildest, sweatiest fuck she'd ever had. As he leaned over her, she caught a whiff of some faint but delicious cologne he was wearing, very fresh and green. It went straight to her head like a drug, and to her pussy like a triple-X aphrodisiac.

She drew a sharp breath as he unfastened her bra and eased the straps off her shoulders.

'Easier to work on your upper back with straps out of the way,' he observed, adjusting the scraps of lace again, fingertips brushing her bare back in the process, like points of flame drawn across her skin. Unable to control herself, she shuddered.

Sholto let out a small sigh, as if exasperated, and even though she had her eyes firmly shut, Shelley could sense him shake his head.

Screw you. You make me nervous. What do you expect?

His hands withdrew, and she heard the small sounds of him uncapping the oil bottle, then the slippery-slap noise of him coating his hands with it. She drew in a breath, braced herself, then had to let the air out again when she realised she'd have to breathe at least once during the process ahead.

And then, almost before she realised, he was working on her, moving his strong fingers in circles, quite gentle at first, hardly noticeable, just pushing lightly on her super-tense muscles.

'Hey, come on…you're still not very relaxed, are you?' He pressed a little harder, digging into the knots in her shoulders, but not unkindly. 'Just let yourself go loose or you won't get the benefit of this.' Circling, circling, he worked his thumbs more vigorously, but still far from hurting or going in tough. 'Why so wound up, Shelley? You're like a board . . . Chill out. Breathe . . . enjoy . . .'

She tried to breathe steadily and evenly, to let herself go loose.

'I keep thinking of what you might do to me.'

There, it was out. She'd paid for him; she didn't really trust him. If it'd been Brent, she'd have trusted him, but even thinking about that was weird. She loved Brent as a friend, but she'd never fancied him, even though Lizzie and he had been an item once.

But Sholto was from the same agency as Brent had worked for, so they, and he, must be bona fide.

His hands stilled on her back, spread and resting softly. 'Look, I told you I won't do anything you don't want.' He paused, and his fingers flexed ever so slightly.

'All I want is a massage,' she muttered, knowing that her mulish stubbornness was denying her what she *did* want. Which was more. Everything. All he had to offer.

Totally beyond her control, her body shook again.

'Are you OK? Are you cold?' Lifting his hands from her shoulders, he reached down towards the bottom of the bed and grabbed a soft fleece comforter. Then, as if she were some kind of invalid, he spread it over her bottom and her legs. 'Better?'

She felt like a complete fool, but she sort of liked his solicitousness. In the past, she'd been unlucky and not really scored with the type of man who was like that. Hence this escort experience...But what would it be like to have a proper date with him? Not straight to massage...or sex...or even spanking or whatever. Just a meal out somewhere, maybe, or a few drinks, or a summer's evening walk. A few kisses, maybe. Normal, delicious sex.

I bet even straight missionary is sensational with you.

'Yes...thanks.'

His hands alit on her shoulders again, and he resumed the massage.

'There, that *is* better, isn't it?' He sounded pleased with her, and it dawned on Shelley that sometime during the little exchange for the blanket, she *had* actually started to relax at last.

And the massage had started to be heavenly. Sholto was a genius, a gifted masseur, and even if he did do 'BDSM Fantasy', 'Sensual Massage' was obviously one of his special talents too. His strong, dextrous fingers found all the right spots as if by magic; all the knots and nadges that stressing about the awful offices she sometimes ended up in created. All the tension of wanting to be pleased and happy for her friend, who had this glorious new boyfriend…and at the same time being jealous. Sholto dug into these tough spots with authority, and yet still with gentleness, and unwound the entanglements and apprehension in a way that made her loose and calm and sensualised.

She sighed out loud, and then laughed, astonished.

'You should specialise in massage. You're bloody good at it.' She shimmied her shoulders beneath his touch, and then wriggled her whole body, biting her lips when she realised she was incredibly wet, and even though she was relaxed, her pussy was almost humming with need and hunger. He'd turned her on, without even trying. Or maybe he *was* trying? But had a brilliant and sly way of going about it?

'I try to be all things to all women, Shelley, but I do rather enjoy the other thing.' She sensed him shrugging towards the case where his 'toys' were stowed away again.

Not pausing, his hands slid down her back until they reached her waist and the comforter. He eased it down a little way and began working deftly on the areas of muscle over her hips and the upper edges of her buttocks. Acutely aware of where he was heading, Shelley tensed again.

'Uh oh, naughty, naughty,' Sholto chided. His voice was friendly, but there was a hint, just a breath of something more there too. Perhaps the authority, the discipline he often wielded? It was barely detectable, but it made Shelley's heart beat fast.

That, and her wayward pussy clench in yearning.

What the hell is the matter with me? Do I want the BDSM thing or not? I hate pain…but how will I know if I can like it too, if I don't try?

Damn Lizzie for having sown those seeds, with her thrilling talk about John.

Shelley imagined Sholto looming over her, large and commanding as she knelt at his feet. She imagined him putting her across his knees and then spanking her bottom. She couldn't imagine the actual pain, but the idea of lying there, exposed and trembling, made heat bubble through her and wild energy build up in her body. Her pussy seemed to scream for attention, and unable to stop herself, she pressed her pelvis against the mattress, seeking some ease for it even though Sholto was still actively massaging her.

Then his hands stilled. And not only his hands. It was as if every molecule of air in the room fell still too. As if it and she were waiting for something. Some change. Some sign.

After what seemed an eternity, Sholto moved on to the bed beside her, and she felt his warm breath, which smelt faintly of aromatic whisky, waft against the side of her face.

'Relax,' he said again, but it was as if he were speaking a foreign language, or the single word was a code or cipher, meaning something else entirely.

Involuntarily, Shelley shuddered deeply, the ripple flowing

through her. She felt a sensation of opening and shifting, as if everything had indeed changed, quite radically.

There were new rules between them now, new boundaries, new expectations.

Sholto began to massage again, but it was no longer just massage. He was touching now, exploring, caressing. Searching and owning. His hands slid up her back again, and then slyly around the side of her ribcage and beyond. She moaned as he reached beneath her and cupped her breasts.

As he thumbed her nipples, his lips settled on the soft crook of her neck and shoulder, kissing and nibbling.

Was it these kisses, or the way he was handling her breasts that affected her most? She couldn't tell. She was suffused with a kind of blossoming pleasure and energy that was impossible to contain in a still, pliant body. She had to move. She had to writhe. Her hips rocked and circled against the towel beneath her, and she parted her thighs, trying to press her pussy hard against the mattress to bump and grind.

'Good?' enquired Sholto, pausing to lick sudden salty sweat off the side of her neck. His breath was like a tropical breeze against her skin.

She couldn't speak, but her approximation of a nod made his lips curve. She could feel his smile pressed against the nape of her neck.

We've moved out of Sensual Massage territory now, haven't we? she wanted to ask him, but she couldn't. There was no need to ask anyway. He knew. He knew all. He was deciphering her needs with the touch of his hands and his lips. Experienced in the ways of stirring women, he was feeding her desire as he rolled and fondled her nipples.

His smooth chest was hot against her back as he inclined over her. His skin felt moist and seemed to bloom against her, like a blanket both protecting and arousing. She longed to feel the press of his crotch against her bottom, and the rough denim of his jeans on her bare skin.

She wanted more than that, much more, but her dreaming, floating mind could only negotiate one step at a time.

As his lips tracked down the vertebrae of her spine, his hands moved too, first flipping away the comforter completely, then slipping beneath the elastic of her briefs, both at once, to cup her buttocks. The way he squeezed the rounds of flesh was both rude...and delicious.

Somehow she knew that he would never spank her without some clear signal that she wanted to go that way, and she wasn't even sure she wanted to give such a signal yet. The touching and caressing was so gorgeous that she wanted more of that first...more, more, more.

She parted her thighs again, churning her hips, encouraging him to touch her where it mattered.

Sholto's fingertips strayed into the groove of her bottom, patting and stroking and teasing and making Shelley almost choke with excitement. There was something dark and forbidden about being touched there, and her clit tingled hotter and hotter the more he fondled her.

'You like that, don't you?' he whispered, bending low again, his voice unexpectedly tender. His teeth closed on her earlobe and he nipped lightly as he flicked at her perineum.

Shelley groaned, making a sound she didn't think she'd ever heard come out of her mouth before. It was raw, almost feral, an expression of pure desire without any kind of prevarication.

'Tell me you like it,' he persisted, nipping again, then gentling the tiny hurt with a kiss as his fingertip went forward and paddled delicately around the entrance to her sex.

'Yes . . . yes, I like it,' she sobbed, her hips jerking, her body seeking his touch. 'Please . . . Please . . .' Her words petered away as he pressed his middle finger right inside her. It was such a slight penetration, but still it felt huge, the impact monumental.

They were in uncharted territory now, off the map. He was serving her needs, but expanding them too. She gasped as he wiggled his finger.

Of course these things happened. They probably happened with every single goddamned client of his.

'Relax,' he purred again, his mantra.

Her sticky body softened around his digit and he pushed it in further, right up to the knuckle.

Shelley let out a sob, her inner walls rippling around him.

Please touch my clit.

She knew she hadn't said it aloud. Her brain didn't seem to be working sufficiently well to frame actual words.

But still he knew what to do.

Sholto's other hand slid beneath her, sliding under her belly, inveigling its way into her panties. His middle finger dove in amongst the soft curls of her bush and settled unerringly on her clitoris.

'Oh! Oh God!'

She didn't come. It was just the shock of the touch, even though she'd been expecting it. Her hands clutched at the duvet beneath her, grabbing bunches of the cloth as she writhed, pressing against the tiny, firm pressure of Sholto's fingertip against her clit. Despite her wriggling and jerking, he stayed with her, spearing her body between two delicious nodes of contact.

'And you like that too, don't you?'

His voice was so male, so possessive. So . . . so dominant.

A sweet sense of weakening flooded through her, unlike anything she'd experienced before. It was so sumptuous, so wanton just to be a toy, a reacting bundle of nerves and pleasure. It was like fainting, but still being wide awake.

'Shelley?' he prompted, moving the finger inside her for emphasis.

'Yes! Oh yes!'

His answer to her was infernal, exquisite, precise. A delicate circling of his finger against her clitoris. How could he be so accurate when she was flailing about so much?

The question dissolved. Her ability to think went with it. All lost in the sweet golden glow of orgasm, made all the sweeter and more dazzling for a soft kiss on her neck, beneath her ear, as the waves and waves of pleasure surged through her.

Afterwards she lay gasping, dimly aware that Sholto was no longer touching her, but not too worried about it. The way she'd come had left her tingling in every nerve and cell and she wasn't sure she could even tolerate anything more, for the moment. She buried her face in the duvet, wondering if she should feel guilty or cheap or just massively pleased with herself because she'd *chosen* this treat. She'd made the right decision for once.

Yikes, I paid for sex. How cool is that?

Well-being washed away all qualms, and she smiled against the duvet, suddenly wanting to laugh. Slowly, she rolled over and on to her side, wanting to see Sholto's face. He was sitting on the bed at her side, cross-legged, watching her, with a cryptic little smile on his face.

Immediately, Shelley felt embarrassed. Her bra was twisted and not covering her in any significant way, and hot blood rushed to her face when his cool green gaze flicked to her nipples. She grappled with the bra, but it was too tangled and, before she could stop him, Sholto reached over, eased narrow straps out of her fingers and drew it away from her body entirely. He tossed it away, and instead, retrieved the comforter and wrapped it around her shoulders.

'OK now?' His voice was soft, and Shelley bridled inside, sensing he was laughing at her. How easy it must be for a man with looks like his, and hands like his, to turn clients into pliant, whimpering little puddles.

It was all just a job to him. Business as usual. He probably wasn't even aroused himself.

But when she glanced at his crotch, she got a surprise.

There was a hard-looking bulge beneath the black denim. A big and hard-looking bulge.

'Well, that was nice,' she said, slipping off the bed and heading for the sideboard. On the point of getting more whisky, she chose mineral water instead. She was befuddled enough; she didn't want her faculties dulled. She wanted it all, and she wanted to get the best from it.

Sipping the cold fluid, she realised how parched her throat was, and almost sighed at a different kind of pleasure.

'What else is on the menu?' she asked. Sholto was exactly where she'd left him, with that understated, unreadable smile on his face. And the huge erection still there in his jeans.

'That depends.' He stared her squarely in the eye, unmoving.

'Well, isn't sex usually included in these deals?'

'Not officially, but usually, yes,' he drawled as he swung his legs off the bed, dropped lightly on to his feet and strolled across to where she stood. Not taking his eyes off her, he poured water for himself and took a sip, studying her over the rim of the glass. 'We can't technically advertise or offer sex, but everybody knows the score.' After another swallow of water, he set the glass down again.

Something in his slow arrogance made her fume. 'Right. OK. So I have to pay *extra* for that, then?' she demanded, stomping to where her bag lay on a chair. She was conscious that she was wearing just knickers and a blanket, and she felt incredibly foolish, especially in light of what she'd just let this infuriating man do to her. But if she wanted a proper seeing to, there was an additional fee, apparently.

'Don't be ridiculous,' said Sholto, beside her in a couple of strides. Gently but firmly he took the bag from her, dropped it on to the chair, then gripped her shoulders, making her face him. 'We've only just started. It isn't a one orgasm and run deal, Shelley. I'm a full service guy . . . we're just taking time out.'

'Well you might have said so.'

She knew she sounded petulant and childish, but the way he'd touched her had been so exquisite, so perfect and intense, she'd almost believed it was *real*. That somehow, even though it was a job to him, he'd *wanted* to do it, stupid as that seemed.

His fingers tightened around her upper arms, unremitting through the blanket. His face looked dark, intense, angry. Why the hell was she goading him? This was all supposed to be light, and fun, but he just seemed to bring out a combative spirit in her that no man ever had done before.

'I'm saying so now, Shelley.' His words were low and gritty, a world away from the flattering soft soap one might have expected from an escort.

A feeling like warm honey being stirred inside her made Shelley swallow, and her knees feel as if they were going to buckle. She wasn't sure she'd ever even wanted that soft soap.

This harder, provocative man was infinitely more exciting. A million words and questions buzzed inside her, but before she could capture and use any of them, Sholto leaned forward and began to kiss her.

His mouth was fierce, almost cruel, deliciously dominating.

This is what you do, isn't it? You just take a woman over, swamp every part of her with yourself, drench her in your power, make her hunger for what you can give, whether it be pleasure ... or pain.

She let herself drift, sink into the kiss, her tongue soft and languorous beneath the onslaught of his hard, muscular one. His mouth tasted fresh and hot, still faintly of whisky, but the intoxication came from the man himself. Her breasts tingled as he still held on to her, and her pussy fluttered, running anew, wanting and wanting him.

She moaned, the sound muffled by the kiss.

'What do you want, Shelley?' he whispered as he broke away from her, his mouth still roving across her face, dusting kisses on her cheek, her jaw, her neck, nipping and nibbling.

'I ... I want ... I want to go to bed.' It was the only way she could describe it. Her brain wasn't working properly. She wanted far more than bed, a simple tumble, but with him kissing her throat, and her pulse point, and pouring some sort of arcane power into her from his gripping fingers, she couldn't quite express it.

'Good. So do I,' he said crisply, drawing back, and looking into her eyes, 'for starters.'

15

House Meeting

'This is a really stupid time to have a house meeting. I'm exhausted. Can't we do it tomorrow?'

Lizzie was inclined to agree with Shelley. It wasn't an ideal time for a sit-down, even though midnight meetings were sort of a tradition at St Patrick's Road, with Brent often calling them late at night, on the spur of the moment.

'We're all up now,' he pointed out, 'and we're all in. Tomorrow we might all be busy all day. I'll certainly be out. I need to get back to the centre as soon as poss, or I'll be out of a job. They've been very patient with me through my…um…little difficulty. But they're not a charity and they won't hold my job for me for ever.'

'It was a bit more than a "little difficulty", B,' Lizzie pointed out, remembering the terror she'd felt; the shock that John had helped her through, in his competent, compassionate way. It was a joy, though, now, that Brent looked so much better after his brief visit to his parents. His black curls were as untidy as ever, but his colour was better, and he was just lean now, not unsettlingly thin. His suicide attempt had shaken him up, and turned him around, but in the wake of it, and a course of counselling, he seemed grounded, and ready to heal. If not fully yet, well certainly in time.

She could smile now. It was wonderful to have him back, although she'd been less than delighted by the suddenness of his reappearance.

Oh, that had been a nightmare. Like a farce or an old *Carry On* film. Almost caught in the act, she still felt like an idiot, even though John's perfect sangfroid had kicked in straight away. And he'd seen the funny side more easily than she had at the time . . . Perfectly composed, he'd chatted with Brent afterwards as if they were the oldest of friends, while all the time she'd been puce in the face, and convinced that her house-mate was scrutinising her for incriminating signs of what had oh so nearly happened on the sofa.

John had left soon after. Apparently unruffled until they were outside on the step, he'd caught hold of her once they were out of Brent's earshot, and embraced her almost as if they might never see each other again. Setting inner alarms ringing . . .

'I'm sorry,' she'd whispered, breathless from his kiss, 'I had no idea he was coming home.'

'Don't worry, sweetheart.' His fingers had flickered down her face, as if imprinting the feel of her skin. 'It could have been worse. We might have been fucking. At least we got away with our dignity intact.' He kissed her lips again. 'Just about . . .' He snatched another kiss, this time more hungry, more desperate, as if revisiting the broken moment just before they'd tumbled off the sofa together.

'I'm back to London tomorrow. I should have been there today, but I couldn't bear not to see you.' He kissed her again, as if he couldn't stop, but gentler this time. 'I'll call and see you before I set off, though . . . either here, or at the shop . . . is that all right?'

'Of course it's all right!' She hated the dark and troubled look in his eyes. A look she'd probably put there with her sudden protestations of love and her incessant misgivings over important things like moving in with him. She wanted to beg him not to take her sudden avowal seriously, but at the same time she wanted to quiz him for specifics about when he'd be back.

Too needy, too pathetic!

John had a busy life, with many demands; she couldn't ask him to disrupt it for her, especially when she'd made such a ridiculous big deal over him *not* taking over her life whenever it suited him.

Jesus, relationships were amazing, but they could be hard, bloody hard. She tried to focus on the memory of his kisses, and the pleasure of his company . . . not all the prickliness of partings and arrangements, and the wrenching feeling in her heart when, having summoned the ever efficient Jeffrey, John had climbed into the limousine and let it spirit him away.

'Yes, I know,' said Brent, his gentle tone snapping Lizzie back into the room. There'd be time to brood about John later, and miss him, even though it was barely an hour since she'd seen him. She focused on her friend, glad he looked so calm and normal. 'I was in trouble . . . but I'm feeling so much better now, believe me. Even managed not to argue with my folks.' He paused and grinned. 'Although it was probably best I left when I did, or we might have started scrapping again. Now, shall we get back to the matter in hand?'

'Yes, please, let's . . . and then some of us can get some sleep!' Shelley sounded tired and there was a wild, bleary look in her eyes too, that Lizzie recognised. She'd seen it in her own face, in the mirror, after being with John.

What's happening, love? What's going on?

However Shelley's date had gone, it hadn't been . . . normal. Her instinct tuned by her own 'not normal', Lizzie longed to ask, but this wasn't the moment. They'd have to snatch some girl talk when Brent was out at work.

'This house he's bought . . . are you moving in?'

Jesus, right to the crux of the matter!

'I . . . I don't know . . .' Two pairs of eyes seemed to drill into her. Well, three actually . . . Mulder had wandered in, and jumped up on to Shelley's lap, and even the cat seemed to be hanging on her words. 'Not yet, at least. I mean . . . It's really early days between him and me, and moving in is a huge step.' She shrugged, glancing around at the small, familiar kitchen with all their mugs and their pictures on the fridge. Familiarity. Safety. The world she knew, and in which she knew her place. 'And I like it here, with you guys.'

'I'd miss you big time if you went,' said Shelley, fondling the cat on her lap, looking more and more preoccupied. 'Not to mention the fact that Mrs B's just put the rent up, and it's a struggle as it is.'

'I'd never leave you in the lurch.'

John would pay it. The sum they had to find to enjoy the comforts of such a nice, big house was nothing to him. A pin-prick. She could ask him and he'd arrange a standing order, and then move on without any further mention, barely noting that he'd done it.

'Couldn't *he* pay the rent for you?' Shelley voiced Lizzie's own thought.

'He could, and he would. But I don't want to put him in a position where he feels obliged to . . . There's no easy answer, and he's already paid for the telly and the broadband. I don't like taking advantage.'

'I doubt he looks at it that way,' said Brent. 'From what I can see, he just likes to make life easier and more pleasant for someone he cares about . . . and her lucky friends.' He grinned. 'Jesus, Lizzie, the broadband is blazing now . . . Please don't go all moral high ground on us and insist on going back to our old package.'

'No! Please don't! I love all the new channels,' chimed in Shelley.

'Panic not! I won't! But seriously, you guys…What if I split up with him, what happens then?' Lizzie reached for her tea, and gulped some down. It wasn't very warm, but the sudden horrid thought had made her feel ill, physically ill. 'I don't want that to happen, far from it, but you know what life's like. You can't bank on anything or anybody for ever…I mean, I love him and all that, but there might come a time…I don't know . . .'

'Are you all right, love? You've gone all white.' Brent rose and leaned across the table, to top up her mug from the teapot.

'I'm fine. Don't fuss.'

'You're not pregnant, are you?' Shelley's eyes were wide.

'No! Of course not!'

'Seriously, though,' said Brent, 'he does really care for you. He cares for you a lot. He pretty much told me that, when we were in contact.'

Lizzie swung towards him. 'And yes, I have a fair old bag of bones to pick with you over that. Going behind my back, you sneak!'

'It worked out OK, though, didn't it?'

It was impossible not to smile at him, and be grateful. He was the *other* man in her life, and he'd conspired with the love of her life…to bring that man right back to her.

'Yes, but still…' She shrugged. Bracing up. No use worrying about stuff that hadn't happened yet. 'Anyway, back to the main point of order. I'll be staying here a while yet, at least. I think he's OK with that. I might not be here some nights, and maybe some weekends, but technically I'll still be on the rent book and paying my whack. After all, I won't be paying any rent for staying at Dalethwaite, so it doesn't make any difference to us, does it? Not on that score.'

'OK, then. That's one thing sorted,' said Brent crisply, as if he was marking agenda items off a mental checklist. 'Next order of business…What about you, Mizz Moore?' He turned to Shelley. 'What have you been up to this evening? You've got a decidedly furtive look about you.'

Shelley shifted the cat on her knee like a feline shield, stroking in a swift, repetitive action. 'I haven't been up to anything.'

'She's got a new boyfriend too,' Lizzie pointed out, glad to have the spotlight off her and John at last.

'He's not a boyfriend, as such. It's early days…and not serious.'

'Pull the other one,' said Brent. Even though, not all that long ago, he'd blinkered himself in respect of his own problems, Brent had always been sharp, and able to spot anxiety and prevarication in Shelley and Lizzie. 'Who is this guy? Do we know him?'

Shelley gave Mulder a kiss on top of the head, and let the cat down. The little feline had been struggling, as if she too detected her favourite human's stress.

'No…Yes…You might, but don't go all Papa Brent on me! I'm a grown-up and I can run my own life perfectly well.' Shelley's eyes were bright, and defensive. Her chin came up, and Lizzie had a sinking feeling. Oh Shelley . . . 'And even if I do get into a scrape, I won't be the first one. Look at Lizzie, she got into the biggest scrape you could imagine, and she's ended up pulling a billionaire!'

'Is this guy of yours a billionaire too?' Brent gave her a long look.

'No.'

'How did you meet him, Shell?' Lizzie said, wanting to know, but knowing how she herself hated cross-questioning. 'You never said.'

Shelley looked away, her face tense, as she pushed a hand through her short, blonde hair. Still silence.

'Shelley, what is it? What are you hiding? What is it you don't want us to know about this new chap of yours?' Brent looked worried now too.

Shelley got up and walked to the sink, and braced her hands on its edge, her back to them. 'He's not my boyfriend. Or my chap. He's a male escort, if you must know. I bought him because I'm fed up of not meeting any decent men . . . and I'm fed up of not getting any decent sex.'

'Shelley! What the hell?' cried Brent. He started to rise, but Lizzie grabbed him by the arm and made him sit again, pulling a face at him, urging him to calm down.

Shelley spun round, her face fiery. 'I really don't see what the big deal is. I had some money from Auntie Mae, and she said to buy myself something nice . . . a treat . . . so I did. I wanted a good time, and some sex with a guy who'd put me first, and an escort seemed like the only way to be sure of that.' She looked from Brent, to Lizzie, and back again. 'And neither of you are in a position to say anything bad about escorts, seeing as you've both *been* escorts yourselves, after a fashion.'

Brent huffed. Lizzie smiled. Shelley was right on that score, certainly.

'You should be very, very careful, Shell,' said Brent, quietening.

'Why? You were an escort, Brent. And you're a good person…Why shouldn't Sholto be a good person too?'

'Sholto Kraft? Oh, please don't tell me you went to my old agency.'

'Yes, I did,' said Shelley defiantly.

Lizzie sighed. This was all going to get combative again if they weren't careful. 'Perhaps Shell chose your agency, B, because she thought the guys were all likely to be nice, like you. Better the devils you know, sort of…eh?'

Shelley returned to the table and sat down again. 'Do you know Sholto?' she asked Brent.

'Slightly.'

'Well, then…There's nothing wrong with him, is there?'

Brent drummed his fingers on the table. 'No … not that I know of. As far as I know, he's a straight-up guy. Tends to do the kinky gigs…but who hasn't done that?' He broke into a grin, winking at Lizzie. 'I do know he's had some shitty luck in his life, which is why he's on the game, probably, but yes, he seems OK as a person.'

'Good! Because I like him, and I think I might see him again.'

'All right, then. As long as you don't spend your rent money on buying his body, and as long as you don't start entertaining ideas of morphing him into a proper boyfriend.' He cast a sideways glance at Lizzie. 'We all know it doesn't work that way, except in *Pretty Woman* and in certain very special, specific cases where the escort isn't really an escort at all…and when the fairy tale *can* occur.'

'All right, all right . . .' Lizzie flipped the V sign at him.

'I'm not entertaining those ideas,' Shelley said firmly, 'but I am going to see him again. At the risk of revealing too much information, his services are *worth* paying for, and he's showing me things I might never have experienced otherwise...like Lizzie with her kinky billionaire.'

'Look, can we leave the subject of John's sexual quirks alone for the time being,' Lizzie said equally firmly. 'We're all grown-ups here, and we can manage our own relationships.'

'Chance would be a fine thing,' remarked Brent, with a rueful shrug.

Lizzie and Shelley exchanged looks, but Brent grinned back at them.

'Don't worry, bitches, I'm OK. Really, I am...I'm happier than I've been in a long, long time, and do you know? I just might be ready to get out there again.'

'Well, good for you, man-bitch!' Shelley came around and gave him a hug, and Lizzie reached out to squeeze his hand.

'That's brilliant, B. Mr Right will come along, just you see.'

'Well, I'll settle for a bit of fun with Mr OK For Now, to be honest.'

'I'm sure he'll come along too.' Lizzie rose. 'Now, if these proceedings are concluded, shall we all get to bed at last? I need some sleep!'

I thought you wanted sleep, Lizzie?

Brent stared down into the road, from behind his bedroom curtain, and watched Lizzie climb into a taxi. It was six-thirty in the morning, and she was smartly dressed – as if already on her way to work at that dress agency of hers – but he'd no doubt whatsoever where she was really going.

To the Waverley Grange Hotel, and the bedroom of her man.

Brent hugged his blanket around him. He shivered, even though it wasn't particularly cold. Had he done the right thing, helping to bring John Smith back into Lizzie's life? Nothing could be totally straightforward and plain sailing for two people of such different ages, and from such different backgrounds...but since when had Lizzie ever been one to settle for plain sailing? If she had, she'd have followed her father's plan for her, and finished her university education. She certainly had the brains for it, and she could buckle down and work like the very devil if she had to. But instead she'd chosen the rocky path of defying parental expectations.

And now she was on another rocky path, albeit one that offered brilliant happiness too.

Don't over-think things, man. She's a grown-up, and she knows what she wants. And Smith isn't an ogre or an exploiter. Just a pretty decent man with a bit of a chequered past...and which of us doesn't have one of those?

As the taxi sped away, he wished his dear friend God speed, and a happy time of it, and as the black cab disappeared around the corner, in the distance, he turned his attention to other chequered pasts, and his other friend and house-mate.

Shelley...and Sholto Kraft. Now there was a turn-up.

Savouring the absurdity of his own instinctive objections, he reviewed what he knew of the man, which was fairly minimal. They'd met once or twice, during gigs where a client had booked two men. Always female clients, and he was fairly certain, pretty much one hundred per cent really, that Kraft was wholly heterosexual. Gaydar, or whatever it was, had not pinged once.

Another older man, but this time only slightly. Sholto Kraft was in his thirties: a widower and a man who'd suffered some bloody cruel knocks, with which Brent could sympathise. Kraft had lost his wife, his business, his home; he'd lost his love to cancer, and the rest to the damned recession. He was another man who'd been driven to extreme measures by hard times. Did he even enjoy servicing the women who paid for him? Who knew . . .?

Brent had no reason to think that Sholto Kraft was anything other than a decent man who'd sought to pay his way in life by an unorthodox career change...but still, he was troubled.

Shelley was sweet and smart, but like Lizzie, she could be impetuous, perhaps even more so. And she was looking for love. Brent only hoped that Kraft could see this, and treat her accordingly. With compassion, but also professional detachment.

I'll have a word . . .

Sholto Kraft also worked part time at the Waverley Grange, filling in with a second, perhaps more morally palatable, job to cover his debts. Bar work, Brent thought, or possibly a bit of management cover? He wasn't sure. Either way, there might be a chance to catch him there for a man-to-man chat.

It seemed strange, both his house-mates involved with men who were connected in some way to that crazy hotel.

Brent smiled, thinking about what he'd said earlier. It had been a long, tough road, since Steven's death, and there'd been times when he'd thought it would never end. But astonishingly, he did feel that, now, he wanted to...to start looking again. Even if just for some fun, a friendship, something casual...maybe a bit of sex.

Maybe I'll find someone at the Waverley too?

16

Morning Glory

Just swan in. Don't think about it. They know you're John Smith's girlfriend. Just ask for his room number. It isn't a big deal.

Before seven o'clock, the foyer at the Waverley Grange Country House Hotel was understandably quiet. The manager, handsome Signor Guidetti, was already behind the desk, frowning at his computer monitor over something; and a cleaner was polishing the woodwork diligently, sending a cloud of Pledge aroma out to join the fresh smells of cut flowers in a scattering of large vases. But they were the only ones around. All the guests were still abed, or maybe taking an early breakfast in the restaurant.

'Could you tell me which room my friend, Mr Smith, is staying in, please?' The confidence in her own voice shocked her, this early in the morning, but the admiring smile from the Italian manager told her the confidence ploy had worked. Or perhaps it was because any friend of their beneficent investor was a best friend of the Waverley too?

'Of course, Miss Aitchison. He's in Nineteen, and I believe he's not yet gone out if you want to go up. I'd be happy to escort you.' Signor Guidetti's smile was ineffably courteous, but also twinkling with masculine admiration.

Lizzie flashed him her best 'Bettie Page' smile in return, knowing full well he recognised her 'look'. It was obvious the man was a thoroughgoing sensualist, a person well acquainted with the notorious pin-up goddess, and he appreciated Lizzie's slim skirt, chunky high heels and her pretty blouse tucked into a wide belt. 'That's so nice of you, but I can find my own way, thank you. Good morning!'

During the short lift ride, Lizzie drew in deep breaths. She might look the part, but underneath, she was fluttering. Sleep had eluded her, evaporating every time she'd thought she was drifting off. By the time she'd seen shreds of dawn through the gap in the curtains, it had been impossible to just lie around, turning things over in her head, and missing John. She still wondered if telling him outright that she loved him had been a horrible mistake. Would it have been better to try and keep things light, hide her feelings?

Hurrying along the corridor reminded her of the first time they'd been together here, her original call girl adventure. Her foolhardy agenda that night had been so simple. No expectations or hopes of anything more than a hot one-nighter, or maybe a couple of delicious dates with an attractive businessman who'd be gone again before she even got to know him.

It'd been silly, but uncomplicated.

Maybe I'll take it back to that . . . at least as a game.

Reaching the door marked 'Nineteen', Lizzie found she wasn't the first person there. A handsome young waiter in his smart uniform had his hand raised to knock. His trolley was loaded with morning tea trays.

'I'll take Mr Smith's tray in, if you like. If you'll knock and announce it?'

The young man grinned. He knew the score. At the Waverley, it was probably nothing out of the ordinary for people to be sneaking into their lovers' rooms for a spot of Morning Glory. He rapped sharply, called out 'Your tea, Mr Smith', and then tried the door.

'Come!' was John's answer, the sound of his voice like a pure thrill through Lizzie's body.

She reached quickly into her bag, looking for her purse, not wanting to deny the young waiter his tip, but he shook his head and winked, then handled the door for her as she slid in with the tray.

'Here's your tea, Mr Smith,' she said, trying to keep a straight face and a straight voice, and failing miserably, 'and the…um…other thing you ordered.'

John spun around from the desk where he was seated, already working on his laptop, all business, business, business. But he was still in his bathrobe, he didn't look as if he'd shaved yet, and his blond curls were shaggy and awry, as yet uncombed.

Good. Man in the raw. Just how she liked him.

His smile was immediate, and like the sun that had barely yet risen outside. All anew, it bowled her over, and only a supreme effort at presence of mind prevented her from making the crockery clatter and the tea slop. Controlling herself, she placed the tray carefully on the sideboard.

'Ah yes,' he said softly, rising from his seat, 'I remember now . . . I *did* tick the box for "breathtaking sex goddess" when I filled in my order for this morning. How could I have forgotten?'

'I don't know about that . . . I'm just an escort, sir.'

His blue eyes sparkled, full of fun, right on the same page without prompting. There was nobody like John for being quick on the uptake, especially where sex was involved.

'There's no "just" about it, young woman,' he said, striding towards her. 'How do you feel about scruffy, half-asleep middle-aged businessmen who haven't even had their first shower of the day? Can you handle that?'

'I love handling sexy, handsome businessmen in their dressing gowns. It's what I live for.'

'Good,' he said, putting his hands on her shoulders, and staring into her eyes. His were already darkening, brilliant cerulean turning from morning to midnight as she watched. 'And think yourself lucky that I've at least cleaned my teeth, even if I haven't had a shave.'

He gave her no time to respond. Instead he proved the veracity of his toothpaste claim by taking her mouth in a hard and deliciously minty kiss. Lizzie gave her all in return, dropping her bag on to the floor so she could wind her arms tightly around him, pressing her body to his.

His body was already on the same page too, his cock pressing hard against her belly. Moving fast, she slid her hand down, gripping the firm muscular round of his buttock, then working the towelling robe up and out of the way, so she could caress his bare arse.

'Mmm...bold,' he whispered against her lips. 'So what now?'

'We finish what we were up to when we were so rudely interrupted.' She squeezed him, letting her fingers float and explore.

'I like a woman who knows what she wants.' He rocked his hips, pushing himself at her.

'And I like a man who does what he's told...sometimes.'

Now where had that come from? She hadn't come here intending to take the upper hand, but touching him, and feeling his erection kick, filled her with power. And with the lust that had been thwarted last night. He was a beautiful man of power himself, but she could command him when she chose to, and she chose now.

'Really?' There was challenge in his voice, as his mouth roved over the side of her face. Last chance to change her mind and slip into their delicious, familiar roles.

'Really,' she affirmed, her own voice bordering on sharp. Letting her fingertips settle against his testicles, she twisted her face, then took the lobe of his ear between her teeth, capturing him in a dual threat.

He fell perfectly still, but it was a wild, energised stillness as he fought his urges. He'd told her he'd only occasionally subbed in his life, and she wasn't sure it came particularly easily to him. It might even be a stressor.

But John was a controlling man, and if she wasn't careful, he'd overwhelm her: with houses, presents, simply with his breathtaking charisma. He wouldn't do it in a bad way... But he'd still do it, and even though she revelled in his dominance, it wouldn't hurt to redress the balance now and again.

'Of course,' he said in a quiet, vague voice, as if he'd fallen into a fugue of some kind, compelled there by her touch. Lightly, oh so lightly, she closed her teeth a little more, just nipping, and then, crooking her wrist, she cupped his balls and held them.

A divine shiver went through him. Power all contained. His breathing skittered, and got ragged. She still wondered if he was smiling, though, out of her sight.

She released his ear, but not his testicles. They were hot and firm to her hand. She didn't squeeze them. That was a pain too far. She was only a playful mistress, not a cruel one.

But she could be the kind who'd make him serve her.

'I'm horny, John. I've barely slept a wink. I've lain awake, frustrated. Wanting what I didn't get from you last night.'

He opened his mouth against the side of her face, but she said, 'No, don't speak. No words.'

Instead of words, he stole a kiss, his lips like velvet against her cheek, his tongue flickering against her skin.

'Uh oh, watch the make-up,' she warned, even though she wore neither foundation nor powder, and her lips were defined by her usual long-lasting lip pen.

He kissed again, defiant.

'Wicked man. Wicked, wilful man. I ought to punish you for that, but I don't want to get all hot and bothered and sweaty when I have to go to work.' She imposed her hold on him, infinitesimally, and his mouth stilled against her face.

It was a fine balance of power. But not active enough for her somehow. She released him, and then pushed him away a little, looking him up and down. Somewhere in their clinch, his robe had come unfastened and his cock poked out rudely, fully erect.

'Did I say you could point that thing at me?'

He shook his head, his uncombed hair ruffling. His face was composed, but his eyes were full of merriment. He was just as terrible a sub as she was herself.

'Wipe that smirk off your face and take your robe off. Let me see all the goods.'

All grace, he shrugged off the bathrobe and tossed it in the general direction of a chair, where, amazingly, it landed and stayed even though he'd not looked. Show off!

Lizzie kept her own expression cool and appraising, even though everything in her was silently wolf-whistling.

She would never tire of looking at John, naked. His lean, beautifully proportioned body was a joy. Regardless of his world-weary remarks about his years, he was in far better condition than most men half his age.

He was clearly expecting her to give an order, so instead she asked a question.

'So...apart from the obvious . . .' – she nodded at his quivering cock – 'what do you want?'

Still smiling with his eyes, despite what she'd said, he answered, 'Thank you for your kindness, mistress. I think I should like to service you. If you wish it.'

If I wish it? You wave a gorgeous dick like that at me and ask me if I wish it?

'Yes, perhaps that would be amenable. But nothing rough, nothing untidy. You can kiss me...down there...if you like, but don't make a mess of my clothes. No mauling and grabbing in the process.'

Struggling to keep her face straight, she remembered how he'd given her head on command, at the Eyes Wide Shut party. He'd been so obedient, and so diligent, what a trip!

Without allowing him much time to absorb her words, she turned and sashayed over to the bed, and sat right on its edge. Keeping her gaze locked on his, she smoothed up her slim skirt, slowly revealing her thighs, the tops of her stockings and her suspenders...and finally her naked crotch and her dark bush.

Ta da!

John's eyes widened and his tongue darted out, stroking over his plush lower lip. He probably didn't realise he'd done that...but then again, maybe he did?

'Thank you, mistress.' She'd given him no permission to speak, but still, he thanked her for his gift.

A reprimand would be too obvious, so she narrowed her eyes at him. Bingo! He dropped his own gaze immediately, and a touch of colour gathered on his cheekbones. Whether this was a genuine response, or simply a combination of his phenomenal dramatic skills and his mastery of bio-feedback, she couldn't tell. But the way his cock looked stiffer than ever was certainly real.

'Well, then? What are you waiting for?' She paused a beat. 'And no, you needn't crawl . . . you've got fabulous knees and I don't fancy spoiling them with carpet burns. Now come on.'

He walked the few steps towards her, eyes still downcast, his erection bouncing meatily. When he reached her, he sank gracefully to his knees, like some kinky naked choirboy before an altar. He did look up then, and she could tell he wanted to lick his lips again; she could see fine tension in his mouth and jawline as if he was actively controlling the response. The sight was so stirring that she could only nod for him to proceed, rather than form the words. Leaning back on her elbows, she parted her thighs further.

John dipped lower, swooping in. She expected him to go right for her pussy, attacking with his heavenly skills, and swinging the balance of power back to himself when the sensations overwhelmed her.

But he resisted, pressing his lips very delicately to the pit of her belly, just above her pubic hair. The kiss was light, and reverent, not even a flick of tongue, and he followed it with more of the same, visiting and worshipping every inch of the slight curve there, and the grooves of her groin, before circling back and laying a closed-mouth kiss against the dink of her navel.

Lizzie gasped. How could that be so bloody; arousing? He wasn't even exploring her belly button; he was barely touching it, and yet she squirmed uneasily, feeling the see-saw start to tip towards John. He was hardly doing anything, yet he was getting the better of her.

'More action,' she commanded, her voice roughened by a sudden dry throat.

He gave the faintest of nods, then laid his hands on her, combing apart her pubic hair with his thumbs, parting her labia, and exposing her clit. But, again, instead of storming in to lick and suck her, he kissed her there with the same dry, slight kiss, lips still together. He was almost nuzzling her in a way, gently saying hello, letting his mouth travel respectfully over the geography of her sex. It was about as far from the expression 'eating out' as she could have imagined.

When he'd travelled the entire area, he looked up at her, nothing submissive in his gaze, just questioning. She nodded again.

Then he returned, lips parted, tongue working.

It was still slow, still full of reverence, but thorough, so thorough. He licked at her neatly, painstakingly, coating a zone that was already swimming with additional moisture from his tongue. She was burning hot, burning up, but somehow his lips and tongue were cool, like balm, both infinitely provocative but also soothing. Subsiding fully on to her back, she reached down and buried her fingers in his untidy blond curls.

'Mmm . . .' She could no longer keep quiet, even though she knew she was in danger of undermining her dominance through her uncontrolled response to his majestic skills.

From beneath heavy eyelids, she looked down at him, both venerating and tormenting her. Sex wasn't the answer to all life's questions and complications, far from it, but like this, it was a bloody good place to start.

'More,' she urged again, falling back against the mattress.

He went to work with a fury now, tongue lashing and flickering, diving around, but again and again, jabbing and jostling her clit. Pleasure gathered in great surges, racking up and up and up, while her body, with a mind of its own, surged as well. She jerked against him, goading and commanding, more and more. Digging her fingers into his scalp, she twined and twisted at the silky strands of hair.

'You bastard!' she shouted, over-tipping into climax as he redoubled his devilish efforts. Mashing herself against his face, she squirmed and squirrelled about, riding the delicious cascade, gasping and yipping the cliché, 'Yes, yes, yes.'

With the fine arts of his tongue, he coaxed her through another climax, and then another, until a pale shadow of her domina act whispered, *Enough, he's ruling you with it!*

Hitching herself half-upright, and grabbing him by his hair and ears, she hauled his greedy face from out between her legs.

'You really are a devil, you know,' she gasped, trying to glare, but ending up grinning at him.

'I'm sorry, mistress,' he said, his smile and his half-laughing voice telling her he was having at least as much trouble with his role as she was having with hers.

'You're insolent, and you get above yourself all the time. Don't think I don't know what your tricks are? Trying to get control over me with your infernal tongue skills? There's a difference between giving someone pleasure, you know, and driving them completely off their heads with it!'

'Forgive me. I'll try not to do it again.'

'My arse . . .' she jeered, loving the play-acting.

'If you wish it, madam.'

Lizzie had to bite her lips, fighting the laughter. How

could a sophisticated man of forty-six look like a wicked imp of a randy teenaged boy? Kneeling there, smirking at her, with his shiny-wet lips and the gleam of her even on his chin?

'Wicked, wicked man,' she growled, feeling desire start roiling again, building in the still warm embers of orgasm. God, she wanted him in her now. In deep, probably too deep to maintain any kind of decorum or uncrumpled condition in her skirt. 'You don't deserve any kind of relief for that monster . . .' She nodded down at his rearing, reaching cock, so thick and ruddy. 'But because I'm a fair mistress and a nice person, I think I'm going to have to let you have me.'

'That would be wonderful, mistress.' His beautiful, beaming smile was like gold, dazzling her and turning her head.

'Yes, and to be even more wonderful, you can have me in your choice of position, you rogue. Just as long as you behave yourself and don't rip my skirt or anything with your antics.'

'I'll try to contain myself.'

She noted the lack of 'mistress' now. The sense of tilt made her giddy, like sipping Champagne before breakfast. John, on an empty stomach, was intoxicating.

'So, what's it to be? How do you propose to service me?' She chose the word carefully, to redress the teetering balance.

'Doggie style would be nice.'

More than nice. Her entire body rippled, as if every cell had just gone, 'Ooh yes . . .'

'Ah, that takes me back to our first time,' she said, reaching out to touch his face, where her silk still shone on his lips and his stubble-clad chin. She'd barely noticed the morning whiskers when he'd been pleasuring her, but she wondered now if she might have a bit of beard-burn on the insides of her thighs.

'Happy days,' he replied, cupping her hand, then drawing her fingertips to his lips and kissing them.

'Indeed, but don't you want to see my face?' she challenged. 'You always claim that you love to see my face as I come...or you come...or we both come.'

'You have the most beautiful face in the world, mistress.' He pressed a kiss against her palm, stroking it with his tongue and creating infernal echoes of what he'd just done below the border. 'But when I'm fucking you, I also love to lean over your back and bury my face in your gorgeous hair while I'm deep inside you.' He gave her a saturnine look. 'And you also have an arse that would launch a thousand...no, a million ships!'

'Cheeky!'

'Precisely.'

'Oh, get on with it, then.' She snatched away her hand, and cuffed him lightly on the chin.

'Perhaps you could take your skirt off? So it won't get mangled if I lose my head?'

Lizzie grabbed him by the back of the neck, and kissed him hard, then stared into his dazzling blue eyes, holding her nerve by just a thread. 'You're just trying to get me to pander to your filthy kinks again, aren't you, Mr Smith? To exhibit myself to you, naked from the waist down, just in my stockings?'

His eyes were like fire, a fierce flame, a torch. 'And your heels,' he added, slyly.

'You're incorrigible.'

'I know. But you like it.'

'Fuck you...yes I do!'

Without replying in words, he rose to his feet and drew her up too. Pausing now and then to kiss her lips or her hair, he unbuckled her belt, and then laid it over a chair. Then he tackled her slim skirt, which had slid down to cover her modesty, undoing the button and the zip, then sliding it over her hips. He offered his shoulder for her to lean against as she stepped out of it.

Then he waited, and Lizzie smiled at him, sensing the baton of proactivity passed to her. She could have stripped completely, but instead, she unbuttoned her blouse and let it hang open. From amongst the wealth of pretty lingerie he'd bought her, she'd chosen a front-fastening white lace bra this morning, just for a moment exactly like this. Popping the clip, she drew apart the cups, another gift to him.

Exposed and presented, she still felt strong, in control. She was Mistress. Goddess. Queen. His blazing eyes told her he thought that too. He was happy with his gifts, smiling and her equal now yet still mindful of her status.

'Lizzie,' he whispered, stepping forward to kiss her again, his naked loins pressed to hers, as he caressed her thighs and buttocks. Her trim little blouse was short, and his hands roamed unhindered over her curves, exploring and honouring.

'Shall we?' she suggested, her voice trembling a little as he broke the luscious, deep kiss just as she was on the point of swooning.

'Oh yes . . .' Taking her by the hand, he helped her on to the bed. Guided by him, she took her position, head resting on the arm supporting her weight, bottom up, thighs parted. Offered, yet not shamed. Another bountiful gift to him, of her own choosing.

'Lizzie . . . Lizzie . . .' His voice sounded as awed as hers as he got behind her, and laid his hands on her bottom, stroking and savouring the touch of her skin. He could have spanked her so easily like that, but they weren't playing that particular game today. His fingers were as gentle as they could be ferocious, when she wished them to be. 'Touch yourself, love,' he said, leaning over her back, his cock against her thigh as he drew the edge of his thumb along the inner slope of her bottom cheek, making her sway and work her hips a bit.

Gladly . . . oh gladly.

Her pussy was slick again, ready for him, her clitoris swollen and edgy. She rolled it slowly, gasping, almost ready to come again.

'I hope you've got a condom handy.' It was a nonsense statement. He always had them because he always wanted her.

'Don't worry, even if I didn't, the Waverley always provisions their bedside drawers with a more than adequate supply. Thoughtful of them, eh?'

'It's a very naughty hotel,' she said, almost ready to assume her mistress role again and order him to fuck her, and be quick about it.

Ever attuned to her, he said nothing, but quickly clad himself, his small movements efficient and purposeful.

'Baby,' he murmured vaguely, his voice spaced as he presented his cock to her, nestling the warm, latex-clad head right where she wanted it to nestle...and more.

He stayed poised for a moment, as if teasing her, then pushed in, long and deep. Lizzie gasped at the solid feel of him, the sure, imposing size. He always felt new to her, always a wonder.

'Yes . . .'

'Yes!'

They both laughed, even though the shaking of John's body did extraordinary things to Lizzie. With his cock inside her, she was so much in sync with him that he barely had to breathe and she could feel it as a caress. She could swear that his heartbeat and the very pulse of his blood around his body was a tattoo that passed from his flesh into hers.

'Stroke yourself, sweetheart,' he said, voice low and thrilling. He was in charge again, and she didn't mind a bit. 'Make yourself come while I fuck you. Go on, Lizzie, do it.'

Holding her by the hip, he swung his body, pumping and thrusting in a sweet, hard rhythm, knocking at nerve-endings and zones of sensitivity with each stroke. She barely had to touch her own flesh; friction, possession and push-pull, push-pull were driving her and lifting her to her goal.

But because he'd bade her touch her clit, she did so, slicking and circling, matching his beat. It took barely a moment, and she was shouting. Crying out his name, the pit of her belly and her sex awash with bliss.

'Yes, oh god, John…you bastard! Yes!'

The flexing muscles of her pussy gripped him, rippling and clenching again and again. Her hand dropped away from her flesh…not necessary now…but his hand replaced it, slipping around, yet also accurate, relentless.

Lights went off in her head, and she thrashed about, squirming, half collapsing, engulfed by John as he surged into her, climbing over her back, his hips hammering and hammering, his own vocabulary, as he ploughed her, more salty by a thousand-fold than hers.

Moaning, she came again, and again, feeling the pulse of his climax inside her as he pinned her to the mattress, still fondling her clit. The wild waves crested, tossing her high and dizzying her, but eventually, like any storm, they ebbed and calmed.

The crisp chintz cotton of the duvet cover was deliciously

cool against her cheek as she lay there, beneath him. The source of their never used 'safe word', it smelt clean and freshly laundered. Immaculate. Just as pristine as it'd been on their first night, when the patterned duvet had caught her eye, right at the moment John had instructed her to choose a word.

Yes, pristine . . . Not like me, though. Despite my orders and instructions.

She grinned against the cloth, laughing inside at her own intentions to stay in control with him and not to let him take her over.

But at least it had all been light and fun and crazy and not in the least muddled by issues of 'relationships' and her impetuous announcement that she loved him.

'Well, I'm glad I took my skirt off,' she said, stirring and wriggling beneath him, 'because my blouse probably looks as if it's fit to mop the floor with now.'

John snaked his arms around her and, holding her tight, rolled on to his back. His softened cock slid out of her as they settled against each other again, but she could still feel him against the back of her thigh, intimate and companionable. With a happy sigh, she relaxed against him. They'd both have to go soon, no doubt, but not just yet. There was time just to chill and lie together.

'You always look gorgeous,' he murmured, his breath making strands of her hair flutter, 'whether you're done up like a supermodel, or naked with your hair all over the place, or any state in between. It's impossible for you to look anything less than both elegant and fuckable.'

'You're such a shameless flatterer…but I like it. Don't stop.'

He shifted against her, his hand still cupping her sex while he tweaked at her crumpled blouse. 'We can get housekeeping to run a quick iron over this for you, if you like? They're very good, and it's still early. We could have breakfast together. I'll bet you've come out without your cornflakes, haven't you?'

She had come out without breakfast. Without coffee or tea, even. And now she was starving.

'Mm...breakfast. Yes! Something's made me very, very hungry!'

'Me too.'

Was his cock stiffening again? Well, maybe there was just a hint of it.

'I know . . . I'm a pig. But I'm satisfied, really.' He kissed the side of her cheek. 'Thank you for coming to me, Lizzie. It was beautiful. I don't deserve you, really I don't.'

But you do. You're everything wonderful to me, and I love you.

But she didn't say that. It was too much. 'I'm glad I came too. We missed out last night. We needed it.'

John gave her a hug, then sat up, pushing her up with him. 'We certainly did. And now we need breakfast! And lots of it! I usually eat fruit and yogurt, and high fibre cereal, trying to preserve the ageing constitution and all that, but this morning, I want eggs! And possibly bacon! To hell with it!'

'Yum!' She could almost smell the bacon already, and coffee too.

'And lots of wicked strong coffee too,' he said, as if he'd read her mind, 'with toast and marmalade.' He slid his hands on to her shoulders, and gave her a squeeze, almost a mini massage. 'Now, wiggle into your clothes again, and I'll hit the bathroom, then we can pig out on calories and cholesterol to our heart's content. Or ruin . . .'

'Can I take a turn in the bathroom first? A girl likes to be dainty, you know. Especially at breakfast.' She slithered from the bed, conscious of her naked belly, and her crotch, on show.

'Of course, sweetheart. Do you want to get your blouse ironed? I'll ask for housekeeping as well as breakfast.' With easy grace, he slid to his feet beside her, and retrieved his robe, holding it open, offering it to her.

'Oh, I think it'll be fine. It doesn't look in the least bit mop-like, surprisingly enough.' Suddenly, unaccountably shy, she darted for the bathroom door. 'Back in a trice…Order *lots* of breakfast!'

Oh, she was glorious!

John hugged his robe around him. He wanted to whirl about, like Maria on the hillside, like a callow youth infatuated by his first sweetheart.

A woman could not be more perfect than Lizzie. She was a supreme bed-mate and the most sophisticated empathic companion too. She did not probe. She did not wheedle. She simply gave her heart and her body, unstintingly and with generosity.

Do I love her? Do I know what love is…after Clara?

Whatever love was, what he had with Lizzie was the closest he'd come to it since. Maybe the closest ever. Who knew? His concept of love, the way to *be* with a woman, had become so distorted by what he'd felt for Clara, and then by his marriage to her mother. He hardly knew what the normal way to have a relationship was.

But Lizzie cut through all that. She *was* sophisticated, but she was also unsophisticated. It was easy to be with her, and he knew that was what he wanted. He mustn't rush her, but within those parameters, he'd do everything he could to have her with him. And everything he could to make her happy, and fulfilled, and yes *free*, while she was there.

Reaching for the house phone, he thought of the delicious breakfast they'd share. God, it'd been the truth when he'd said he was hungry. Suddenly, the prospect of eggs, bacon, and all the trimmings seemed all the more delectable and enticing for having his bright, beautiful angel there to share them with him.

He ordered everything, his stomach rumbling in anticipation.

17

Breakfast of Champions

The smell of coffee that hit Lizzie when she stepped out of the bathroom was so aromatic it was almost like downing an espresso without even having to taste it.

'Oh my God, that smells divine!'

'Doesn't it just,' said John, smiling across at her. Decent in his bathrobe now, he was sitting on the bed, working on his laptop, with a cup beside him. 'The breakfast won't be long, but I asked them to send up coffee straight away. They do a very nice Blue Mountain roast here, and it's really hitting the spot.'

Setting his computer aside, he hopped off the bed, and came to her, cradling her face in his hands when they stood eye to eye.

'You look exquisite. Very dainty indeed. Nobody would know you'd been mauled by a randy old goat-man this morning. You look like an unsullied virgin.'

Lizzie laughed, and gave him a quick kiss on the lips. 'What the hell else do they put in that coffee, Mr Smith, besides Blue Mountain? The nonsense you talk, anybody would think you were tripping.'

'You're my trip, Lizzie,' he said. His smile was as dazzling as ever, but there was seriousness in his eyes, something a little dark and strangely moving. 'My escape…my solace.' His fingers drifted over her face, as though he were seeing her, but not seeing her, and the touch was telling him just as much as the sight. 'I've had a good life, with many advantages…but there's been some bad stuff, too, and you erase all that.'

Lizzie shivered. She frowned. The sense of something deeper going on intensified. It touched her, but scared her too. She wanted to know what it was about; she wanted to know everything about this beautiful man she adored…but at the same time, perhaps, she didn't.

'Hey, don't worry,' he whispered, giving her a short, sweet kiss. 'We're keeping it light. Don't let me bring you down with my doomy old man's talk.'

'If you don't stop calling yourself an old man, I'll be the one bringing you down. With a clip round the ear, you blinking idiot!'

'All right! I won't do it again!' He laughed, and he *did* sound young, like a happy boy, rejuvenated in the blink of an eye. 'Now come on, enjoy some of this gorgeous coffee while I have my shower. And if the breakfast arrives, don't wait for me, just dig in.'

Taking her by the hand, he drew her to the large, comfortable chintz-upholstered chair, and pushed her down into it. When she was settled, he poured a big breakfast mug of coffee from the pot, and added milk to it, just how she liked. 'Enjoy! I'll be back in a little while.' Setting it beside her, he shot forward, gave her a kiss on the forehead, and then strode to the bathroom, closing the door behind him.

Ah, the bliss of caffeine! She couldn't argue in respect of the coffee; it was some of the best she'd ever tasted. A pure pleasure, just like John himself. There was no need to worry about being a 'trip', or a 'solace', or even a rich man's fancy mistress, at moments like this. Sinking back into the armchair, she sipped slowly, savouring each mouthful and clearing her mind of as much else as she could while she listened to the running of the shower behind the bathroom door.

For a few minutes, that was enough. The drumming of the shower was soporific, and she'd had very little sleep. How easy would it be just to nod off, waiting for him? She almost did . . .

But after a moment or two, her eyes snapped open again, and her attention was drawn to the laptop John had left open on the bed.

She'd been in this position before. Alone with his laptop, and his secrets. Last time he'd actively encouraged her to Google him. This time, he hadn't mentioned the machine. But might the fact that he'd left it there, live, be a tacit invitation?

She sidled over, sipping her coffee. Look? Not look?

Not your business, Lizzie. He cares for you, but that doesn't give you an access all areas pass. Get real...And anyway, compulsively checking up on people is weasly.

Yet still, she set aside the cup and hunkered down on the bed beside the laptop. Her heart thudded when she realised a program was open, a personal organiser of some kind, week to a view. There were a number of entries in blue, clearly business orientated, and one in red.

Sotheby's – Twentieth Century English Watercolourists – gift for Rose? Willis re. bid. Also tea at Claridges?

Rose. Who was Rose? Clearly somebody important to him, if he, or his P.A., was bidding on a gift for her and taking her to Claridges.

Lizzie scrolled through a mental address book of people he'd mentioned. Women he'd mentioned. There weren't many. It wasn't his ex-wife, because she was called Caroline. Maybe his sister-in-law? Or his niece? Were they close enough for him to expend so much thought on a gift? And take them to Claridges for tea? John was generous to a fault, but Lizzie's unease still roiled. Something she could only describe as a gut feeling told her this 'Rose' was incredibly important to him, more even than family.

And more important than me?

'Shut up, you silly moo,' she muttered, barely audibly, 'don't go there.'

Of course there would be women from his past, lovers he still cared about. He'd already said he was still on good terms with Caroline. He might still harbour genuine affection for women he hadn't married as well as the one he had.

Walk away from the laptop. Do it now.

But, of course, she didn't. She reached out to the touchpad, scrolled a page or two ahead, and a couple more.

Visit Rose.

Damnit. Now she'd seen it, she couldn't unsee it. She flicked forward still further, and found another entry, and another. The visits seemed to be planned, and more or less monthly. Scrolling back revealed more of them, on the same schedule.

He saw this woman every month, without fail. Was she someone he simply couldn't ever fully break from? Someone who'd wormed her way into his heart and soul, despite his claims that he wasn't into hearts and flowers and all that stuff?

Someone you'll still see, even if you and I are living together, John?

Swigging down some of the gorgeous coffee, but not

tasting it at all, she marched away from the laptop. Then raced back to it, and returned the organiser to the page she'd first discovered open. The urge to barge into the bathroom and cross-question him was ridiculously powerful. But it was a stupid thing to do. She wasn't even supposed to have seen the organiser...or was she? Maybe it was his subtle way of telling her to back off, after that foolishly blurted out *I love you*?

Buggeration, if only she'd just chilled out in the big chintz armchair, enjoying her coffee and thinking back to the delicious fuck they'd just shared. She'd be feeling fine and mellow now, happy with her decision to keep things light and comfortable with the idea that in a while . . . sooner or later...it might be more.

Now there was a 'Rose' festering around in the back of her brain, and no amount of being sensible, and just ignoring the fact she'd ever seen the name, would work.

The brisk rap at the door could not have been more welcome. Thank God for something to break her out of her deranged spiral of speculation, or at least slow it down. When she opened the door, the smiling waiter who'd let her take the tea tray earlier now stood in the corridor with a trolley, one from which heavenly smells of bacon and toast were emanating. Despite her Rose-thoughts, Lizzie's stomach suddenly growled, indicating that her appetite at least hadn't been affected.

'Ooh, that smells lovely. I'm starving!' she exclaimed as her waiter friend pushed in his glorious chariot of fried food, baked goods, fruit juice and what looked like yet more magnificent coffee.

'I think you'll enjoy this, ma'am...We do a great breakfast here, though I say it myself.'

After he'd deployed the trolley into a mini-breakfast table, they did the dance of the tips again. Lizzie tried to give him a gratuity, but the friendly waiter shook his head. She fished in her bag for her purse, not sure what the going rate was, but he beat a retreat and was out of the door with a cheerful, 'Enjoy your breakfast!' before she could find the blessed thing or extract any cash from it.

Pushing 'Rose' to the back of her mind with only moderate success, Lizzie investigated the covered dishes, and discovered, as she'd suspected, a mountain of divinely crispy bacon and a bumpy yellow lake of creamy scrambled eggs. There was toast and croissants too, various jams, and two kinds of juice, plus fresh fruit and mini cartons of cereal, yeah right.

If I was a proper lady, and emotionally refined, I'd pick at a handful of grapes and sip weak tea, and brood about John and his fucking ex-girlfriend, for whom he buys pictures at Sotheby's...But instead I'm just me, Ms Lizzie Average, and I'm so sodding hungry that I'm going to eat the breakfast of champions!

She wasn't sure scrambled eggs and bacon would help her forget her suspicions and insecurities, but she was damned well going to give them a shot at it.

When the bathroom door swung open and John appeared, robe-clad and rubbing his hair with a towel, she was halfway through her plate of eggs and bacon, and convinced they were definitely working.

'Mm, that smells good . . .' Beaming, he tossed his towel over the back of the chair and surveyed the trolley. 'How is it?' He glanced at her plate.

'Fabulous!' She surveyed the damage herself. She'd eaten quite a bit. 'I'll have to hope the others go out tonight, so I can do some Zumba or something, in front of the telly.'

John winked. 'I'd pay good money to see that. Wonder if I could rearrange my schedule?' She watched him fill his plate, ruefully noting he didn't take as much food as she had.

'I'd rather you didn't. I look like a hippo when I'm exercising.' She picked up a crispy strip of bacon and nibbled it, Zumba be damned.

'Not during any of the kinds of exercise I've shared with you,' John said, giving her an arch look. 'You always look like a goddess of grace and beauty when you're with me. Especially when you're in the throes of ecstasy.'

'Please...I'm eating!'

Chuckling, he pulled up a chair to the trolley, and began his breakfast. They ate in silence for a few moments, but it was a companionable one. John topped up her coffee cup; she handed him the marmalade, then realised he hadn't asked for it, but clearly wanted it.

It could be like this, every day. Breakfast together. All the other stuff, as well as sex. It was so tempting. So wonderful, yet scary too.

Pushing her plate aside, she swirled her teaspoon in her cup, even though she didn't take sugar. When she looked up, John was watching her, his own plate abandoned.

'You're amazing, you know that, don't you?'

Lizzie blinked. What had brought that on? The expression on his face was admiring. She saw affection there, desire quiet for the moment.

'Er...not really. I'm just me.'

'That's what's amazing. I love the way you are. I can see you're making a conscious effort not to ask me about something.' His eyes were very clear, very blue. He could see everything. For a moment, panic swirled. Was he going to ask her if she'd read his appointments? He hadn't once looked at the laptop himself since he'd returned from the bathroom, though.

'You can ask, you know,' he went on, a little smile playing around his lips. 'You're important in my life, Lizzie . . . entitled to know things . . . yet you still don't push.'

Yes, why didn't she push? Good God, she wanted to know who this Rose was. 'It's just not my way, I suppose. I prefer to let things come to me. People only get cranky when you pester them. Especially men . . . And who needs a cranky man?'

He leaned forward a little, and she caught a whiff of lovely cologne. 'You're as wise as you are gorgeous, sweetheart, and I'm very lucky. But I don't mind a few questions, you know. I might not give you the answers, but still, you should ask. Really.'

Lizzie took a deep breath. What simple question could she ask? The words 'Who's Rose?' drummed in her brain but she pushed them aside. In their place, she recalled a conversation. Their Skype chat. Hadn't he told her then that he'd tell her what had been troubling him?

And if it was Rose-related, well . . .

'You said you'd tell me about stuff from New York. You were tired, and you seemed out of sorts, and you said you'd tell me about it when you got back.'

'So I did.' He cocked his head on one side. His blond hair was drying from his shower and looked very soft, very youthful.

'It's OK if you don't want to,' said Lizzie quickly, her nerves thrumming. 'It's not only women who're entitled to change their minds.'

'No, it's all right.' He paused a moment, and took a sip of coffee. 'I saw my ex-wife while I was in New York. She and her husband have a rather nice place on the Upper East Side, and I called in for drinks.'

Caroline? Was that it?

'But I thought you and she were still good friends? Still fond of each other.'

'We are, and it was cool. I was glad to see her, and she's very well.' He smiled, and Lizzie could see the affection in his eyes. She tried not to feel a pang. Jealousy was stupid, and for the immature. And it didn't do to be immature with a man who was…mature.

'I was glad to see that, because she had a little bit of a heart scare last year. But she's fine now. Fitter than ever.'

One question *had* to be asked. 'How old is she?'

'She was seventy last month,' he said with a quirk of his blond brows, challenging her reaction.

'Ohmigod!'

An ex-wife of seventy and a mistress of twenty-four. What about the women in between, how old were they? How old was Rose?

'I guess you can say I've always thrived on age gaps,' he said softly.

'So it was her health that had you worried?'

Suddenly, his beautiful mouth thinned, and a plume of anger filled his eyes. Hypnotised to stillness by him, Lizzie inwardly reeled back. But then he smiled again, and reached out to place his hand over hers, sweet reassurance.

'No, I wasn't out of sorts about Caroline, and I don't mind you asking about her. It was something else that had put me in a shitty mood. Someone else . . .'

Who? Rose? Shut up, Lizzie!

'Another ex, alas.'

'Oh dear.'

John's hand tightened over hers. 'It wasn't so great to see her. Too much history between us. I'm afraid I got angry inside. I tried not to show it, but underneath, I really let her get to me.'

Despite her intention to play it cool, Lizzie frowned. Who the hell was this one? Could it be this mysterious Rose, or was it some other woman? The entries in his organiser suggested he saw Rose on a regular basis, and the gifts, at least, suggested fondness, not antagonism.

Good grief, the man's forty-six. He's bound to have had dozens of women in his time. Get real, Lizzie. It's no big deal.

But it was a big deal. Well, biggish . . .

She opened her mouth, to ask she knew not what, but before she could get a word out, the sound of her mobile ringing cut off her train of thought. Who the hell was ringing at this time? Astonishingly, it wasn't even eight o'clock yet!

Mum, said the caller ID.

'Oh bollocks, it's my mother. I'll have to answer.'

'Do you want me to leave?' said John quickly. 'I can throw on some clothes and slip downstairs. I need to see Signor Guidetti about a few things anyway.'

'No, it's OK. I won't be long.' At least she hoped not. She loved her mother dearly, but she knew her parent constantly worried about her.

John nodded, and Lizzie answered the call.

'Hello, Mum, how are you?'

'I'm perfectly fine, Elizabeth, but as I haven't heard from you in a week or so, I just wanted to check that nothing was wrong . . . I thought I'd ring early, just in case you had a busy day ahead. I'm not even sure what you're doing these days . . . now that you're not temping any more.'

Lizzie suppressed a sigh. That was the constant bone of contention with her parents. Her lack of some clearly definable career. The 'future' that they believed would have been assured by her getting a good degree, even despite the fact that graduate unemployment was at an all-time high.

'I'm fine, Mum. I'm doing a lot of sewing, remember? And I'm working in New Again with Marie, which I also told you about. It's regular work now . . . you mustn't worry. I won't starve.'

She glanced across at John, and her heart revved. She wasn't sure whether he was being deliberately provocative or not, but he'd slipped off his robe and was reaching for his clothes. When he reached for his boxer briefs, stepped into them, then adjusted the disposition of his cock inside them, Lizzie zoned out of her mother's conversation completely for a second, and didn't snap back into it until she registered a concerned demand from the phone's speaker.

'Elizabeth, are you there?'

'Yes . . . just got distracted a minute. Sorry, what were you saying?'

Across the airwaves, Lizzie sensed maternal antennae pinging. 'Are you alone, Lizzie? Is there someone there? You're not with a man, are you?' Her mother huffed out a breath. 'Is it your friends, or is it . . . someone else?'

Another bone of contention. Her parents weren't old fossils, far from it. But they were a touch old-fashioned on some issues, and neither of them seemed to be quite able to get their heads round her continuing relationship with Brent. Both conveniently forgot their own apparently fairly wild student days, and expressed mild disapproval of her living with a man she'd once had a romantic relationship with.

Lizzie wanted to tell her mother to leave it, but she knew that was pointless.

'I'm with a friend, Mum. It's…um…somebody I've been seeing a while. His name's John and don't worry, he's very steady and he's got a proper job and everything.'

The man with the proper job grinned at her from across the room, pausing in the action of slipping in his white gold cufflinks. He was decent now, wearing the trousers of one of his breathtaking suits and a powder-blue shirt.

A machine-gun volley of questions issued from her phone, and Lizzie wished she'd told a fib. She'd been settled comfortably in the armchair, but now she perched on the edge, grinding her teeth as she listened.

'He's a businessman, Mum, and yes, he's quite well off . . . Yes, of course he's single! Oh, I don't know . . . stuff . . . he has a lot of different business interests . . . Shouldn't you just be asking if he's nice, rather than cross-questioning me about his bank balance?'

John moved closer, his inquisitive expression morphing into a slight frown.

'It's only because I worry about you, Elizabeth,' said her mother. 'I don't mean to pry, really, but I just want you to be happy.'

'I am happy, Mum. And I'm happy with John.'

Her mother said nothing, but Lizzie could feel the doubt. She looked up to find that John, moving like lightning, was standing right over her. Miming, 'Let me . . .' he put out his hand for her phone.

Lizzie shook her head, but he waggled his fingers. 'It'll be OK,' he whispered, and suddenly she was handing the mobile over.

'Hello, Mrs Aitchison, my name is John Smith, and I'm Elizabeth's friend. Nice to speak to you.'

How the hell did he know that her parents always called her 'Elizabeth'? Surely he didn't have super hearing, and had heard her mother's voice? Cringing inside, but also intensely curious to see how John would handle this, she strained her own hearing to try and catch both sides of the conversation.

'Yes, Elizabeth and I have been seeing each other for a while now. I think she's an amazing woman, and I'm very fond of her. You should be very proud of your daughter. She's very bright and talented.'

In spite of the hideously awkward situation, Lizzie giggled, stifling it with her hand. John winked at her as he listened to her mother. Lizzie couldn't bear to contemplate what he was being asked. Whatever it was, it sounded as if it could well be a form of the third degree.

'Yes, indeed, Mrs Aitchison. I have quite a number of holdings. Property, some light industry, hotels, communications, leisure facilities, shopping centres . . .' There was a pause, more interrogation. 'Oh no . . . they're my own holdings. Yes, I own them . . . Yes, all of them . . . Yes, several times over . . .' His brow crumpled, and he snagged his lower lip. Damn her mother, what was she quizzing him about now?

'I'm forty-six . . . Yes, it is quite a bit older than Elizabeth, but she's very mature for her age. She's one of the most grounded and sensible women I've ever met.'

Lizzie spluttered, profoundly grateful that she'd not chosen that moment to be drinking coffee. 'Oh, for heaven's sake!' She reached out for the phone, getting a slight purchase on it, only for John to whisk it out of her reach again. Leaping to her feet, she almost danced with frustration, desperate to stop her mother bombarding John with even more personal questions, and getting more and more alarmed by his answers.

'That would be wonderful . . . I'd love to . . . I look forward to meeting you and your husband. I'll see you then. Here's Elizabeth again . . . It's been lovely to speak to you.'

Glaring at him ferociously, Lizzie grabbed the phone back.

'What on earth do you think you're doing, Mother, cross-questioning John like that? What he earns and how old he is are none of your business! And what the hell does that mean, "Look forward to meeting you"?'

Still scowling, she watched John calmly buttoning his shirt, a serene expression on his face, as if nothing untoward had occurred.

'I just wanted to be sure he was suitable for you, Elizabeth, that's all. And he sounds very nice, very urbane . . .' There was a pause, and Lizzie braced herself for what was coming next. 'But isn't he a bit old for you? I mean . . . you're only twenty-four. And he's . . . he's . . .'

'Nearly twice my age? Yes, he is, Mum, but it doesn't make any difference. I don't even notice. He's like a young man to me. He's . . . um . . . very fit and all that.'

Now it was John's turn to supress laughter. She could see him biting his lip again as he knotted his navy blue tie, and then slipped into his waistcoat.

'I'm sure he is,' replied her mother primly, 'but I'm a bit uneasy, you know . . . I . . . Are you sleeping with him, Elizabeth? A man so much older than yourself?'

'Of course I'm fucking well sleeping with him, Mother!' Across the room, John burst out laughing, then clapped his hand across his mouth in an elaborate pantomime. 'And don't be so shocked and uptight . . . after all, when you were my age, you'd given birth to *me*, so you must have had sex with Dad before you were twenty-four. Give me strength!'

'Don't be coarse, Elizabeth. It's just that I worry about you. You know it's only because I love you, sweetheart, and want the best for you.'

Lizzie sighed, cross with herself for getting cross. She imagined if the positions were reversed, she'd be just the same. 'I know, Mum, but don't worry. I'm well, and I'm happy in the work I'm doing, and I'm very happy with my rich, handsome, mature boyfriend. Life couldn't be better!'

'Is he very handsome, then?' Mum was lightening up. Lizzie relaxed a bit.

'He's drop-dead gorgeous, Mum. Believe me…he's like a film star.'

Across the room, the movie star grin twinkled as John combed his hair.

'Ooh, I'll look forward to meeting him, then.'

'Ah, yes, I gather you've invited him to visit…Dad's birthday, I guess?'

Her father's birthday was coming up, and her mother liked to plan ahead, and ensure that the family always gathered if they could.

'Yes, nothing fancy, but I just thought it would be nice if Mr Smith could come along with you.'

'His name's John, Mum.'

They chatted for a few minutes more, about her father, and her sisters, and about Brent and Shelley, but eventually, Lizzie sensed her mother was ready to ring off, her mission accomplished.

'Right ho, Mum, I'll see you soon . . . but I'll be in touch beforehand about the arrangements. And in the meantime, you can tell everybody you know that your Elizabeth's pulled a real-life multi-millionaire and she's bringing him home with her so you can show him off to everybody!'

'You're a very wicked girl, Elizabeth Aitchison,' said John, coming to her as she stuffed her phone into her bag after her mother had rung off. 'Using such disgusting language to your mother. I ought to smack your bottom for that.'

Filled with stress adrenaline from the last ten minutes of mother/daughter shadow-boxing, Lizzie bristled. Her chin came up, and she held his gaze, unflinching. 'Why don't you then, Mr "I own half the county" Businessman? Show *your* real side, and not the sleek, smooth-talking, mother-pleasing performance you just put on. Mum would've had a fit if I'd told her what a raving pervert you are.'

'Ah, but you like it,' he said, his voice as silky as when he'd been speaking to her mother, 'and you're just as much a pervert as I am, Miss Elizabeth, aren't you?' His eyes flashed like a hot summer sky, and between one breath and the next, all the desire she'd felt earlier, all the lust she'd believed assuaged, was back and rampaging through her body.

'Yes, I am . . . so sue me.'

'I'd rather spank you.'

'Do that, then.'

He took her by the upper arms, fingers fierce against her flesh, holding her tight. His blue gaze bored into her, mastering her with its brilliance, dominating her without need for words or rituals. Her fighting spirit melted and mutated; she was still strong, but she channelled it within her, creating endurance.

Slowly, slowly, she lowered her gaze, giving her true assent. His lips settled on her brow, nuzzling her thick dark fringe. She felt the shape of his smile.

'Kneel in the armchair, smart-mouthed girl,' he whispered, making the hair flutter. 'Show me that beautiful arse of yours again...you know I can't resist it.'

She nodded, and he released her. Shaking, she moved to the big chintz-upholstered armchair, reconnoitring it. It was firm and well-padded beneath her knees as she assumed her position, putting her arms forward to support herself, and heeling off her shoes.

How do I get myself into this every time? Why do I love it so?

Submissive, yet not cowed in the slightest, she relaxed, waiting for him. Moments ticked by, and she imagined him surveying her like a god, unhurried.

'Raise your skirt, Elizabeth. Show yourself to me.'

Reaching back, she shuffled up her skirt. She had her knickers on now, prim, white, sensible knickers, which she'd been planning to wear all day. After this, she might have to treat herself to a pair of Sloggis or something from the hotel's little boutique. It stocked a variety of personal items that guests might have forgotten to pack, and it was a good job it did, because John was getting her all hot and bothered again, teasing her with his scrutiny and the leisurely way he studied her. Surely time was flying by now, and soon he'd have to leave, but he was behaving as if they both had all the day to themselves.

When he touched her, she jerked in the chair. Not from shock, but from the weight of yearning.

'Easy . . . easy . . .' His fingertips travelled slowly over the cotton of her knickers, and strangely the contact was more intimate than if she'd been bare. 'Just a couple of slaps, my sweet darling. A glow to take with you so you'll think of me today.'

Lizzie almost laughed. As if there was any chance she *wouldn't* think of him! He was the centre of her thoughts at all times, no matter how much she might assert her independence and convince herself she was still her own woman and not ruled or controlled by him.

'And every time I touch something today, I'll remember the touch of you,' he went on, his fingertips spreading until his palm pressed against her bottom cheeks, 'firm . . . resilient

. . . and yet sometimes yielding. Like you, Elizabeth . . . my beautiful Lizzie.'

Her skin trembled finely beneath his examination. She wanted to move and wriggle, but she tried to keep still. It was so hard and even more so when he hooked the waistband of her knickers and eased it down to the top of her thighs, exposing the rounds of her bottom.

'I wish we had more time.' He squeezed her flesh, testing it. 'But people will be waiting for me. In fact, they probably already *are* waiting.' Leaning close, he whispered in her ear, 'I'll cancel it all if you want me to.'

Did she? Could she make him do that, in a show of *her* power? It would prove her importance to him, that *she* was the 'first lady' in his life now, not these others from his past; his wife, the mysterious Rose.

She gasped, as he stroked her cleft, and the words rose almost to her lips, *Yes, cancel it all, do it for me!*

And yet she couldn't. She couldn't be that petulant, demanding mistress, playing havoc with her lover's business and schedules. She wasn't fickle and she wasn't difficult. She was Lizzie, who'd once been Bettie, but who lived in the real world, where it was a crappy thing to mess up dozens of people's days, just to have some fun and make a point.

'No, don't do that,' she said quietly, trying to stop her voice from quavering because he was almost touching her sex. 'We'll have plenty of time when you get back. No need to bollocks up everybody's day just for me.' She squirmed as the tip of his finger slid between her labia. 'Not that I don't appreciate the thought.'

'I adore you,' said John, fire in his voice. He meant it, she could tell, and he was awed by her choice. 'I adore you...and I'm going to spank you . . . *because* I adore you.'

Before she could react, before she could catch another breath, he landed a crisp, open-handed slap across the cheek he'd so recently fondled. And before she could react to that, he landed another, square on the other cheek.

White fire flamed, in her flesh and in her mind. She rocked her hips, emitting a yelp as the first shock dissipated and the spanks came to life.

'Yes!' He gave her two more, and two more, his hand, that could be so gentle and so meticulous, impacting like a length of tropical hardwood against her arse.

Heat surged through her, filling her body, settling in the pit of her belly but also travelling, spreading out. It was in the tips of her toes, her earlobes, every strand of her hair. And where it burned, she felt pure need, desire reborn.

'Oh please...please touch me,' she cried, shaking her hips, stirring up the pain to make alchemical pleasure.

In an instant, he caught her to him, hauling her up. She still knelt in the chair, but he was right behind her, cradling her body against his, pressing the sore lobes of her bottom against his strong thighs and the hardness of his loins.

But he didn't seem interested in his own body. As if unaware of his own condition, he slid his hand between her thighs, fingertips going straight for her clitoris, as he hugged her tight with his other arm, drawing her closer.

'Lizzie . . . oh, my Lizzie,' he purred into her hair, his lips seeking the side of her neck, and finding it in a fierce, desperate pressure.

As he kissed her, and praised her name, he made her come.

18

To and Fro

John's fingertip shook against the surface of the tablet, making the figures he was studying fly and skip about. When he'd told Lizzie that whenever he touched something today, he'd think of touching her, it had been a figure of speech, lovers' mad talk, and they'd both known it was delicious nonsense of the moment.

But now, he feared it was true. He *was* thinking about touching her all the time.

As the motorway heading south slid grimly along beyond the tinted windows of the limousine, John stared at his fingers. He'd probably washed his hands any number of times since he'd caressed her, but he still imagined her intimate fragrance there. It was a rare gift, vouchsafed only to him. And he could still feel her, as if the echo of her firm, beautiful bottom and her delicate, silky sex were forever imprinted in the surface of his skin.

Oh, for God's sake, man, you're losing it! Your head's full of the most bizarre ideas these days.

It was true, though. Notions kept popping into his mind, and he kept entertaining ideas that he'd long ago locked away. The fact that he couldn't keep them in line now was disturbing. His ability to compartmentalise was eroding.

He had to talk to someone. To bounce ideas. And yet the only person who sprang to mind was Lizzie herself. She was the one he wanted as the mirror for his life, just as he wanted to be the mirror for hers.

It was hopeless. Fucking hopeless. He was happier than he'd ever been in his life, but equally, more confused than he'd ever been. Accustomed to total confidence, not being sure of himself, one hundred per cent, shook him hard.

He closed the cover on the tablet, and reached into his pocket for his phone. There was one person whose judgement he trusted. Someone wise, and sorted, who'd come through tough choices and watersheds of his own, and arrived at the other end of an emotional journey intact and comfortable. Despite a good deal of opposition.

The number rang twice, and then was answered by a familiar well-loved voice.

'Hello, Jonny, you old git, how the devil are you?'

'Very well thanks, brother. And yourself?'

'Not too bad … not too bad … same old shit from the usual quarters, but all's pretty cordial, and I think I'm wearing them down gradually.' John could hear the wry humour in his brother's voice. They were both family black sheep in their separate ways, but Tom was perhaps the braver sheep, still living at Montcalm as he did.

'I should bloody well think so! Montcalm and the estate would be chaos without you. They should be grateful, especially the Old Man.'

'Well, it'd all probably have crumbled into dust long ago without you, Jonny,' said Tom Wyngarde Smith, 'if only they knew it. I think it's about time Father knew who's really funding the place. It's getting increasingly hard to sustain the fantasy that opening the house a few days a week, and the income from the rare breed sheep, the organic wheat, and the odd bit of Montcalm honey is paying for the annual maintenance and restoration bill.'

'In time…in time.' John had a shrewd idea that his father was already fully aware of the situation, yet was choosing to blank it out, the same way he did with the fact that Tom, his youngest son, was gay. 'Look, can you and I meet for a drink? Neutral territory somewhere? I'm in London for a few days, but there's something I'd really like to talk over with you when I come back north again. Something that I need to discuss face to face. I'm not quite sure of my movements, but I'll text you…that OK?'

'Of course. I'm intrigued now. Just let me know when you're back.'

He'd have to make his own choices, and those that were best for Lizzie in both the short and the longer run, but Tom was smart, sensible and humane, the perfect sounding board where matters of the heart were concerned.

As he rang off, John smiled. Happily as he would race back north again to be with Lizzie, he couldn't help but look forward to seeing his brother again too.

And perhaps, afterwards, introducing them to each other? He had a feeling they'd get on famously.

Good grief, man, you've really got it bad!

The last time he'd introduced a woman friend to a member of his family, it'd been Caroline…and his father had threatened him with a shotgun and told him to fuck off and never come back again!

*

He'd sent her roses! Roses of all things. A huge great posy of white roses, that looked almost like a wedding bouquet. Everybody in New Again had been enormously impressed by the delivery. The shop had been quite full with ladies browsing, and murmurs of 'How romantic . . .' and 'Ooh, *Jardiniere* . . . they must have been pricey' had hummed amongst the gently worn finery.

Roses ,though, the flower name of her mysterious 'rival', from his organiser.

Don't be idiotic, Lizzie. If this Rose was some kind of long-time secret love of his that he doesn't want you to know about, firstly, he wouldn't have left his organiser open when you were around on your own like that; and secondly, he wouldn't send you roses. Do try to think like a rational grown-up, and not a neurotic teenage emo...and please, please, please don't start Googling!

But no amount of rationalisation could still the niggling inner voice, the soft, feminine whisper that plagued her when she woke up in the dead of night. Half asleep, she was helpless when the spectre of the unknown Rose plagued her, and there was nothing to do but get up, get a cup of tea, and sip it until common sense returned. The grown-up thing to do would be to ask him outright who the woman was. It wasn't as if he hadn't told her to ask him things...But every time they chatted on the phone, even if the question was on the tip of her tongue, she was just too happy to be talking to John, and laughing with John, and sharing fun little incidents from their days. Only an idiot would spoil that, especially when she wasn't even supposed to have been nosing about in his organiser in the first place.

They discussed Dalethwaite Manor quite a bit too, although Lizzie suspected that John had ulterior motives on that score. He was making it sound far too tempting, with his plans and enthusiasm, luring her with more talk of that light airy studio room where she could spread out and work on her dressmaking projects. Space to lay things out at St Patrick's Road was always at a premium, and with thin walls the hum of the sewing machine could be irritating when the others were watching the television. They never complained, but she knew it was a bother.

If she lived at Dalethwaite, it would be easy to work. She'd be mistress of her own space, able to tackle more ambitious projects. She could dream. She could even design. Marie had begun to encourage her; another person tempting her with shining, challenging dreams.

But even if she didn't technically move in to Dalethwaite for a while yet, perhaps she could still use the space? John would at least feel he'd partially won the skirmish.

I'll sound him out, see how he feels.

He'd be back tomorrow. She could tackle him in person . . . In between kissing him and climbing all over his body!

'Mrs B called this lunchtime, just before I was heading out,' said Brent as the three house-mates gathered at teatime. 'She was very excited . . . but it's a bit of a bombshell, really.'

Lizzie swung around, alarmed. Their landlady wasn't a young woman, and for a while now, she'd been hinting that she might sell up in the not-too-distant future, and move down to Devon to live near her sister.

'What kind of a bombshell?' demanded Shelley, scratching the head of Mulder, who'd jumped on the table. 'Not another rent increase? She only put it up last month!'

'That wasn't her fault, though . . . everything's going up at the moment . . . electricity, water, council tax . . . you name it,' said Lizzie, hoping the others wouldn't point out – again – that she no longer had to worry about things like that, having a boyfriend who was loaded. 'I'm amazed she didn't put it up sooner.'

'No, not that,' said Brent, fiddling with his teaspoon. 'She's sold the house.'

'What?'

'What the fuck?' Mulder leapt away at Shelley's exclamation, then snuck back again.

'Yes, just like that. To a property company, an outfit called Oldacre Holdings, she said. I'm not surprised; she's been dropping all sorts of hints about her sister in Devon for ages. I suppose it was only a matter of waiting until she could get a decent price.'

'But it's all rather sudden.' Unease coiled in Lizzie's mind. Unease and suspicion.

'Sudden indeed,' said Brent slowly. 'Apparently she got an offer yesterday morning, right out of the blue…and it was five times the price she'd been thinking of asking!' Brent turned towards Lizzie and narrowed his eyes. 'You wouldn't happen to know anything about this, would you? It seems this Oldacre lot are taking the house on as is, services and taxes included, and say that they're quite happy to let the existing tenants stay put.'

Lizzie scowled. She took a sip of tea, barely tasting it.

All the existing tenants, but one . . . Damn you, John Smith, I know what you're up to! Oldacre Holdings, my arse!

'No, I don't know anything about it.'

'Are you sure? Are you absolutely sure?' Brent persisted, a wry look on his face.

'It's him, isn't it? Your billionaire? He's a property guy…I hope *he* doesn't put the rent up. I just can't afford any more at the moment.' Shelley frowned.

Brent swung round to her. 'No, you wouldn't be able to.

Not with your expensive new tastes on only a temp's money. Us male escorts don't run cheap, do we?'

'Oh, shut up! It's none of your business.'

'Oh, but it is…I care about you, and I know him. I'm worried about you.'

'I can take care of myself . . . and Sholto is . . . well, in his own way, he's very nice. And he's just as pukka as *you* ever were.'

'Oh, please stop squabbling!' cried Lizzie, wincing at the shrill sound of her own voice. 'Shelley, you need to be careful . . . and Brent, you need to let her run her own life. And as for fucking Oldacre Holdings, yes, it probably is John, and I suspect he's just doing it to make sure you two aren't left in the financial shit if I move in with him…which is what he wants.' Her whole body felt tight, wound up like a spring. But she couldn't let fly at her friends. It wasn't their fault. 'We'll probably get a letter to say that the rent's been reduced to about five quid a month, or something ludicrous like that.'

'Well, since you mention it . . .' Brent pursed his lips, and Lizzie knew she was right, or thereabouts. 'There was a phone call just before you got home, some geezer…the lettings manager from Oldacre. Our new rent is apparently twenty pounds a month, inclusive of utilities and council tax.'

'John, you bastard! You fucking, manipulating bastard,' she hissed, but even cursing and swearing didn't help. It was as if he'd suddenly invented an innovative form of torture, a way of tearing her two ways at once.

'What on earth are you complaining about? This is fabulous,' cried Shelley. 'We . . . we'll all be rolling in it, with no rent to speak of. Please, for God's sake, don't tell him he can't do it, Lizzie! Please don't cut off your nose to spite *our* faces!'

She couldn't do anything. It was a fait accompli. John knew Lizzie couldn't deny her friends. She had to go along with it for Brent and Shelley. To coin a Mafia cliché, the all-powerful master negotiator who always got all his own way had made them an offer that *she* couldn't refuse.

She sighed. 'No, I won't ask him to change things…but I will give him a piece of my mind. He can be a controlling git sometimes.' It was meant kindly, she knew, if pragmatically. A generous act towards her friends *and* Mrs B, as well as a means to getting what *he* wanted. 'I've a good mind to say, yes, thanks, that's very kind of you, John. I'm going to enjoy living *here* virtually rent free for the foreseeable future…just to teach him a lesson.'

'Are you insane? Don't you want to move in with him?' said Shelley gently, reaching across the table to pat her hand. 'It's obvious that he's bonkers about you and wants to be with you. What on earth's the matter with that? He's gorgeous and he's got tons of money, I don't see what the problem is. And, I mean, it's for *you* he's made all these changes you've told us about. You should be flattered that someone like him would turn his life upside down for you.'

Lizzie's eyes watered. She was being an idiot, and ungrateful. Any other woman would be over the moon . . . But the idea of being manoeuvred and controlled, even by the man she adored, filled her with panic – and an irrational, primitive defiance. John cared about her. He *had* turned his life upside down for her. And yet the way he operated sometimes had sneaky echoes of previous efforts to control her life. The way her father had tried to propel her along the path he'd had mapped out for her.

I'm going to have to grow up and face this. This . . . and the other stuff. Age, background, bloody Rose, whoever she is . . .

She knew, deep down, that in his own way John probably loved her, even if he couldn't come out and say it. But even if he was her dream man, this was real life, with bumps and awkward stuff, and loving someone one minute and wanting to throttle them the next.

Bugger, relationships were hard.

'What's wrong?'

'What do you mean, what's wrong?'

'I can tell by the tone of your voice something's bothering you.' The tone of John's voice, over the phone, was frustratingly measured and reasonable, even though it was what she'd been longing to hear all night.

It wasn't long after her conversation with Brent and Shelley, but they'd both already gone out, destinations suspiciously vague. Lizzie had a feeling that Brent might be on a mission, to 'have a word' with the mysterious Sholto Kraft, and she just hoped and prayed that it wouldn't develop into a three-way slanging match if Shelley was there too.

God, everyone's in a muddle at the moment!

'Well, I do have some stuff on my mind, but it's probably better not to get into it on the phone. Better face to face.'

John made a soft 'huff' of almost-laughter. He knew . . . yes, he knew she knew what he'd done, the bugger! His crafty little stunt with 'Oldacre Holdings' . . .

'That sounds ominous.'

'Don't give me that . . . *You* know!'

Then he did laugh, and the pendulum swung towards throttling rather than wanting to jump his bones.

'Oh dear, I take it you're not pleased.'

Agh, he was the most beautiful man in the world, and he

could be the kindest, too. But he was so confident he sailed dangerously near to smugness sometimes.

'It's not that I'm not pleased.' She drew in a sharp breath, feeling her hackles rise. 'No . . . I told you I won't get into it on the phone, and I won't. When will you be back?'

She could almost feel him regrouping, setting aside the potential conflict, preparing to prevail at a later time. He'd probably win the argument, but she wasn't going to let him get away without at least hearing her objections.

'I'm not sure, love. I intended to be back at Dalethwaite early evening. The plan was to call for a swift drink with my brother on the way, then straight back to you. But there's been a chemical tanker overturned on the motorway, so I've a feeling I won't be back until very late. I'm sorry, Lizzie . . . I was so looking forward to us having dinner together . . . and afters.' He laughed wryly. 'It's at times like these that I really could do with that helicopter.'

'Don't be silly. All that fuel, just for an hour or two extra with me. That's not very green, is it?' She knew she was being perverse, but it was just another example of him throwing about vast amounts of money in pursuit of getting what he wanted. But then, why wouldn't he? He had millions and millions . . .

'I suppose not, but still.' He paused and she sensed a hint of a less secure John. 'I know you've got some issues with me . . . but we can see each other when I get back, eh? Maybe you could nip over to Dalethwaite? We could eat together if I'm not too late. Thrash out a few things.' She imagined him grinning now. Her mind had gone *that* way too. 'And maybe you could stay over? As an experiment . . . Just to see how you like it?'

'You're trying to get round me, aren't you?'

He was doing a good job of it too. In spite of all her objections and misgivings, the idea of trying a night at Dalethwaite Manor *was* enticing.

'OK, but it's just the one night, you hear me? We still have to deal with stuff . . . I'll get a cab and I'll see you whenever. Are you still meeting your brother first?'

'No, we've agreed to take a rain check. Had a bit of a pow-wow on the phone instead.' His voice went quiet, almost solemn. 'But you and I will have our discussion. It's important to me that you're happy. You know that, don't you?'

'Yes . . . I do.' Suddenly she felt tired. Did she really want to get into a taxi tonight?

Yes, she did.

'OK, then, sweetheart, I'll see you as soon as I can. Get your gorgeous arse into gear and pack an overnight bag. I'll let Thursgood know, and he'll be over to collect you, in . . . say . . . about half an hour. Have you eaten? Mrs Thursgood's a wonderful cook – she can rustle up just about anything you fancy if you're too hungry to wait for me.'

'*Thursgoods*? Who are these Thursgoods?'

'My butler and my housekeeper, a man and wife team of irreplaceable treasures. You didn't think I was going to mop the floors and leave notes out for the milkman myself, did you? It's a big house. It needs staff.' He did laugh now. Oh, he could be bloody insufferable!

There was a silence, a heavy one. Across the airwaves, she could feel him shifting gears, moving from teasing and arch, to serious. Honest.

'Lizzie, don't worry. I know there's a lot to think about . . . but you and me, it's not all about sex. You know that, don't you? Not all about control.' His voice was so quiet, so intense. 'I love fucking you and I love the games we play . . .

But it's *being* with you that matters most of all, just believe that.'

She *did* believe it. She *wanted* to believe it. But could he change the habits of a lifetime? Really? Even if he tried . . .

And as they said their goodbyes, and she rang off, she *made* herself set her qualms aside for the moment. Brooding over them would get her nowhere. Better to wait and discuss things rationally with John, work them out.

But still the worms of disquiet wiggled and gnawed at her.

When it had just been fun, just 'temporary sex friends' as she'd described them, this stuff hadn't mattered, not his controlling nature, not the women of his past, none of it. But now they were serious, it was a whole new ball game, and a future coloured by the past. John's past . . .

Hurry home, my love. When you're close, it'll be so much easier to deal with. You make me strong.

19

Lightning Can Strike Twice

Although the conversation with Sholto Kraft hadn't been entirely pleasant, Brent was satisfied that he'd got his point across. The man was prickly, but basically honest and straightforward, and if Shelley was going to go with an escort, Brent would rather it was someone like Kraft than some sketchy independent or a chancer from some dubious agency he had no knowledge of.

So, on the face of it, Shelley was safe with the guy. That should have been it, but still Brent's instincts had sounded an alarm. Sholto Kraft did seem genuinely to like Shelley, and that could lead to a whole new can of complications down the line. Business sex and affection sex just shouldn't mix, which was why he'd been so worried about Lizzie and her adventures. Although that seemed to be working out well enough, as far as he could see.

I'd better still keep an eye on both of them.

Having done the best he could tonight, Brent decided he deserved a real drink now, even if the prices here at the Waverley were a bit steep, compared to their local, around the corner from St Patrick's Road.

Over whisky and soda, he scanned the Lawns Bar. He
hadn't really taken any notice of his fellow patrons earlier,
with his focus on getting some answers from Sholto Kraft,
but now, his thought from a few days ago resurfaced. Lizzie
wasn't the only one who could have an adventure, here at
the notorious Waverley Grange. Pity the odds were so long
that he might find a handsome, *gay* billionaire in the hotel
tonight, but you never knew. Just a fairly fit guy, who could
also hold a decent conversation, would be nice. It had been
so long since Brent had been out there – for himself rather
than on an appointment – that a frisson of nerves prickled
the back of his neck, like the ice from his whisky melting
down his spine.

Would he still know *how* to play the game, to do the
dance? And even if he could score, did he even *want* it to go
any further than just a simple chat-up in a bar?

But he wouldn't know if he didn't try. And he couldn't try
if he didn't scope out the potential!

There were plenty of nice-looking men in the Lawns.
Even the barman who'd now replaced Sholto Kraft was
pretty tasty. But Brent couldn't see any men who he thought
would fancy *him*. Most of the guys were with women, or
clearly waiting for women, or waiting for the opportunity to
meet a woman.

Strike out. Zilch. But . . . Good God! Wait a minute . . .

A few stools down at the bar sat a man Brent recognised.
More than recognised. It was a man he'd met in a club several
years ago. A man he'd had a night with, in a hotel . . . and
who'd most definitely fancied him back then.

Don't stare, idiot. He might not remember you, or he might not
want to remember an insignificant one-night stand.

Shame, though, because the man at the bar was gorgeous.

Just Brent's type, both then and tonight. Older than himself, mid-thirties now, probably. He'd been friendly yet refined that night, but clearly out for some fun, and comfortable with a slightly younger man. Brent had sensed that the man at the bar didn't do one-nighters all that often, but still found him irresistibly confident and sexy . . . with a great body and a fantastic, good-sized cock.

What the hell was his name? They'd never even exchanged surnames . . . but what was his first name? Something short, no nonsense.

Tom! Your name's Tom.

As if he'd heard his own name, the man turned and their eyes met. Adrenaline surged, fired by the sight of a smile that Brent realised he'd never forgotten. It was open, a bit playful, but intelligent. The man, Tom, cocked his head on one side, and Brent's excitement flared. God, he was glad the guy hadn't changed his look in the interim. Still the same great hair, wildish brown curls, a little on the long side, deliciously Bohemian.

Psyching himself up, he slid off his stool, and some god or goddess must have smiled on him, because the stool next to Tom was suddenly vacated when the man who'd been sitting there strode off across the room.

'Tom, isn't it?' Brent said as he slid on to the empty seat. 'I don't suppose you remember me, but we met at Sylvestros . . . must be three, four years ago.'

The smile that had turned him to jelly back then widened, and he discovered that it still had that star quality, making him feel ridiculous and fluttery.

'Brent. Yes, of course I remember you. What's a nice boy like you doing in a rum old place like this?' He looked around, his blue eyes gleaming. 'It's a tad recherché, but I rather like it, don't you?' He nodded to Brent's glass, and the bare mouthful of whisky and soda that remained in it. 'Another of those?'

'Yes, thanks. That'd be great.' He'd had a few drinks when they'd met last time, a bit more than his usual limit, but he hadn't been wasted. Just sufficiently cheerful to be up for an adventure…and here was that very same adventure, newly returned to him.

As Tom ordered more drinks, Brent scrutinised him. The passage of years had seasoned the man, and made him more desirable than ever, if anything. He had a lean and whippy look about him, and an air of athletic strength. His face was more tanned, as if he'd been spending time outdoors. And there was something else. Something Brent couldn't quantify; a kind of familiarity that went beyond his own memories of that one-night stand, an overlay that seemed to refer to a different kind of recognition completely.

'Do you live round here?' asked Tom when their whiskies were settled before them. 'This isn't your local, is it?'

'Not really, although I don't live all that far away.' Shit, did that sound as if he was already propositioning? 'I was here to meet someone, a guy I know slightly.'

Was that disappointment he saw in Tom's face? Oh God, quick…he had to put that right.

'Not a date or anything,' he went on swiftly, 'just a guy who's seeing a friend of mine. I'm a bit worried about her, and I wanted to sound him out and make sure he was on the level. Sort of a concerned brother/uncle type thing, although she's not a relation, just a house-mate.'

God, he must think I'm a complete twerp.

'And is the guy on the level?' Tom sounded interested, almost intrigued.

'Well, yes, I think so, but it's all a bit torrid and complicated. He's an escort, and she's paying him for sex, but I think they actually really like each other too, and I know how bloody difficult that can get.'

Tom's brows shot up.

'Well, yeah, I've done some escorting myself, so I'd know.' There, he'd put that out…he wasn't sure why. It was risky. Especially when he knew, deep in his gut, that he really, really wanted to go to bed with Tom again, even after all this time, and after only a moment or two's conversation.

'Really? Hmm…that's interesting. Do you go with women or with men? I'd imagine you're much in demand with either sex.'

'I'm not escorting now . . . but yes, both. Although . . . um . . . when it's for me, I . . .'

'Ah, that's cool,' said Tom, his eyes glittering. He took a sip of his drink, and Brent felt as if he was going to faint, watching the undulation of the other man's throat and imagining him sucking, swallowing…something else. 'I'm glad,' he added. 'Really, really glad.'

Oh hell! Oh shit!

Brent took a swallow of his whisky, grateful for the powerful peaty belt of the spirit. How could this be going so well? After all this time, the man was *still* interested.

But into the excitement, a suddenly cold shard sliced across Brent's mind. What…what would have happened if that night hadn't just been one night? He'd fucked Tom before Steve came on the horizon. What if they'd got to know each other? Could they still have been together? Happy?

'Are you OK, you look a bit dazed, man,' said Tom with a kind smile, 'as if you've seen a ghost. Would you like another drink?'

'No, I'm fine...thanks. I just, well, haven't been out much lately, and it's all a bit strange to me. I mean, out for *me*...you know? Not on an appointment.'

Tom clinked his glass to Brent's. 'Well, here's to being out and about again. Good thing you met me, then, isn't it? Someone you already know...That might make things a bit easier, eh?'

The urge to punch the air and shout 'Yes!' was insane. This was pure, dumb luck, meeting this decent, good-humoured and downright-drop-dead hot man again out of the blue, just when he needed him. Brent tried to calm down, but it was like being a giddy young stud out on the pull again ... a young stud meeting the man of his dreams, even if for just one night.

'So, what brings you here tonight?' It was a sensible, non-crazy question. With luck, Tom wouldn't think he was a loony.

'I was supposed to be meeting my brother for a drink. And to be a fraternal sounding board, I suspect. He's met someone, and he's crazy about her by the sound of it . . . but he's not had the best history with relationships, so he's after the advice of little bro . . . Who probably knows even *less* about them than he does.' Tom laughed softly. He didn't sound bitter, or unhappy; more philosophical than anything.

But Brent's heart sank. The brother would arrive any minute. Tom would smile, and say cheerio, enjoyed the drink and all that . . . and then be gone again.

'Look, I guess your brother will be here soon . . . but, do you think we could exchange numbers or something? I wish we had done that last time.'

Tom did smile then, a big happy grin. And he reached out, and placed his hand over Brent's, almost but not quite lacing their fingers. 'We *can* do that. But actually, my brother just phoned to say he's going to be very late, and he's decided to go straight to see his girlfriend. So . . .' His fingers tightened. 'It's rain-check time, and I'm all alone in a strange bar…a *very* strange bar if the stuff I've heard about this hotel is to be believed…and I'd be very glad of some company.'

Tom had the most beautiful blue eyes. So intensely blue they dazzled Brent, so brilliant that they seemed to make the whole bar glow and turn into the happiest place in the world, strange or not. He glanced quickly around, seeing other couples, smiling at each other, with *that* look in their eyes, the look of the game, the dance, anticipation of pleasure to come.

'Cool,' was all he could say, and he laughed, wondering what some of his clients would think of the smooth, confident Brent Westhead now, usually so unflappable and, yes, really quite suave. Even after all the appointments he'd done, and after the relationships he'd had, both the fleeting ones, and those of more moment, like Steve…he'd never been as excited and full of hope in his life.

'Cool,' concurred Tom, mirrored excitement in those blue eyes, and a promise on his sculpted, shapely lips.

Brent wondered what it would be like to kiss that mouth right now, and why, again, he felt that strange sense of double familiarity.

Hopefully soon he'd get answers to both those questions.

'Have you worked for Mr Smith long?'

Lizzie stole a sideways glance at the stocky, slightly greying man sitting beside her. She wasn't quite sure how to address him. Thursgood? Mr Thursgood? Whatever his first name was? Who knew what the protocol for addressing your boyfriend's butler was? Presumably it must be somewhere in a Debrett or something, and probably on the internet, but while she was frantically shoving clothes and bits and pieces in a holdall, she hadn't had the time to look up obscure stuff like that. She'd have to wing it, and hope she didn't insult anybody. If only she'd paid more attention to *Downton Abbey*!

'Why yes indeed, miss. My wife and I have been lucky enough to work for Mr Smith several times, on and off, over the years. Although not recently.'

So, if not with John, where had they been? And how did they come to be with him now? She knew so little of his life beyond his visits to the Waverley Grange. She knew he had a flat in London and that he didn't ever visit Montcalm. Presumably he lived in hotels a lot of the time, maybe the ones he owned.

Thursgood kept his eyes on the road, focused on his driving. He seemed completely unperturbed by her silence, and she supposed that good staff didn't expect the people who they were looking after to chat to them. She thought she'd noticed a slightly raised eyebrow when she'd climbed into the passenger seat beside him, but his demeanour was pleasant and good-humoured.

If only she dared ask exactly when and how the Thursgoods had been engaged for Dalethwaite. John had barely owned the place more than a week or two.

'Um…where have you been working most recently?'

'Mrs Thursgood and I were employed by a Russian gentleman, running his London residence, but he decided to close the house so our services were no longer required. Fortunately, our severance payment was generous, so we were in the process of taking what you might call a little holiday when Mr Smith offered us a position at Dalethwaite, and we were able to move in more or less straight away.'

'That's lucky.' Lizzie frowned. The couple must have just dropped everything, upped sticks and moved halfway across the country, just to work for John. He must be a good employer, then! 'But didn't you mind moving all the way up here?'

Thursgood gave her a quick, sideways smile. 'Not at all, miss. My wife and I are both originally from this part of the country, so we have family and friends close by. We were already considering looking for a position in this area when Mr Smith contacted us.' As the car slowed, Lizzie realised they'd reached their destination, and Thursgood took a small remote from his pocket to open Dalethwaite's imposing wrought iron gates.

'We both know Mr Smith from our early days in service at Montcalm,' continued Thursgood, as the Range Rover sped up the long drive, carving between the avenues of mature trees. 'Of course we knew him as Lord Jonathan back in those days.'

Yikes, they'd known John in the time before he'd shaken off his aristo heritage.

'Oh, wow, you worked at Montcalm?'

'Indeed, miss. Although we were both in fairly lowly capacities on the domestic team then.' A broad smile creased the man's amiable face. 'That's how I met Mrs Thursgood. We've been married twenty-three years and we've been lucky enough to work together ever since.'

'That's wonderful!'

'We think so, miss.'

When they reached the house, the lucky Mrs Thursgood was on the doorstep to meet her, a thin, dark woman with a wide, merry smile and friendly eyes.

They were both nice, in fact she had a feeling they were probably completely lovely, but it was weird, so weird, being waited on. She had to stop herself trotting around to the back of the Range Rover to grab her own bag.

Mrs Thursgood escorted her upstairs, to the bedroom where she and John had made love, not that long ago, the beautiful master suite.

'Shall I unpack for you, miss?'

'Er…no, it's fine, really. I think I'm probably only staying the one night…for now.'

The older woman's pleasant face remained impassive. 'Very well, miss. Will you be requiring supper? There's a fully stocked pantry . . . It won't take me but a moment to prepare a cooked dish, or you could have something cold, if you prefer?'

Lizzie blinked. At a loss. She'd eaten, but it seemed rude not to accept something.

'Or perhaps just tea, or coffee? I made a lemon cake this afternoon that I think you might enjoy, if you'd prefer just a snack? It's very good, though I say it myself.' Mrs Thursgood beamed. 'It's one of Mr Smith's particular favourites.'

Relief washed through Lizzie. Yes, that was easier. Cake always made things better.

'Shall I serve it in the sitting room, miss? It's rather cool for the time of year, and there's a fire laid in there. It's a lovely cosy room and you can read or watch the television while you wait for Mr Smith to get home. I'm sure he won't be very long now.'

'That all sounds brilliant! Thank you very much . . . I . . . er . . . all this is a bit strange to me. Thank you . . .'

'Don't you worry, miss. This is a lovely house. I'm sure you'll soon feel completely at home. And if there's anything you need, anything at all, just dial "0" on the house phone, to let us know. We'll be in our flat, but it's just a step away across the back courtyard, and it won't be any trouble.'

A little while later, in front of the comforting fire, and with two slices of the most awesome lemon cake she'd ever tasted in her belly, Lizzie tried to relax and watch one of her late evening junk viewing favourites on the television. The sitting room was lovely, and under any other circumstances, she would have been thoroughly content there, especially as the cat – whose dish she'd seen on her previous visit to Dalethwaite – had crept in to see her.

'Alice', an incredibly pretty-looking tortoiseshell, had sniffed her, sounded her out and pronounced her acceptable. She'd stayed for a little while, then gone off about her inscrutable feline way. Lizzie was fond of Mulder, the house cat at St Patrick's Road – whom she'd fed before she'd set out, just to be on the safe side – and she was glad there was a feline presence at Dalethwaite too.

Staring at the screen, though, she still saw nothing. Nothing but John, with a knowing, confident look in his eyes.

You're doing your utmost, aren't you? Doing everything to tempt me. The most beautiful house I've ever seen, the one that I've always wanted to live in. Lovely, friendly staff to pick up after me and make my life easy, and cater to my every whim. Even a cat, you crafty devil!

Like the iron hand in the velvet glove, he was making it ever less and less rational to resist moving in. And she sensed he was increasingly sure she'd succumb. The bathroom in the master suite was filled with all her favourite bath and beauty products. He must have taken note of everything during their visit to that grand hotel at the seaside, when he'd taken her with him on that business trip, not long after they'd met. Or perhaps he'd made a mental list when he'd stayed over at St Patrick's Road on their return, after they'd visited Brent at the hospital.

The drawers in the dressing room were filled with lingerie in her size too, and nightclothes. A gorgeous, thick velour robe hung on the back of the door, and there were slippers to match. And even though he'd not gone so far as to furnish her with an entire alternative wardrobe here, there was a lavish selection of comfy, lounging type clothes in the drawers and cupboards. He'd captured her taste, with simple t-shirts and also the sort of 1950s casual tops that Bettie or Bardot might have worn; a couple of pairs of jeans and some jersey dance pants; soft ballet flats for mooching about the place in and a pair of adorably silly bunny slippers. Not to mention trainers, workout gear and also several bathing suits, so she could take a dip in their gorgeous swimming pool.

Everything was in colours she liked, or neutrals she'd probably also choose.

These were all an example of his kindness, she knew that, and his thoughtfulness. But it still felt as if he believed her moving in with him was virtually a done deal.

But why not? Why do I resist? I love him.

Yet still, it was a huge step. The hugest of her life. Even more radical than abandoning university or any other decision she'd made.

And all the time, she felt the gentle but determined hand of John at her back, pushing her, pushing her into making it, into making that final step.

20

A Rubicon of Sorts

After another whisky, Brent was gently buzzed, but his senses were pin sharp. The perfect state in which to enjoy a man like Tom.

They'd spent a little time in the bar, slipping into easy chat, a bit of fun; people-watching. The Waverley was the perfect venue for that sort of thing, with its sexy ambience and its reputation for naughty goings-on, discreetly handled. Their game had been 'Guess what position the observed couple would end up in', and it had been the simplest thing in the world to laugh with Tom.

Their meeting in Silvestros had been frantic, wild, all about the body, but now, even though he was almost certain they'd get together before the night was out, Brent felt no hurry. It was good just to hang out . . . like friends.

Until, in a sudden, sharp moment, their eyes met in the mirror behind the bar. Tom's lips curved in a mysterious little smile, that hinted, suggested . . . enticed. And Brent couldn't do anything else but answer, with his own grin.

'Shall we stop dancing around this?' suggested Tom, reaching out and running a finger over the back of Brent's hand. The thing is . . . I know I want to revisit what we had, that night, but I don't want to pressure you. I've a feeling you might have been to hell and back since we last met, and . . . well . . . you might not be quite ready.'

How did he know? Well, not exactly know, but somehow, Tom had sensed something.

'I won't know until I try, though, will I?' said Brent quietly. 'I mean . . . if you're prepared for me bottling out at a critical moment, I'd like to . . . I'd like to try.'

Tom's face lit up; a glow of triumph, anticipation, maybe a bit of apprehension of his own? His fingers spread, and he covered Brent's hand, then squeezed. 'Good man...you won't regret it. Even just trying can be fun, eh?'

His heart thudding, and his cock on sudden red alert, Brent grinned. There was something vaguely old-fashioned about that 'Good man . . .' – sort of county and aristocratic. He wondered for a moment about Tom's background, then dismissed the curiosity. At least for now. There'd be time for finding out who they each really were later...he hoped.

'I don't live all that far away. We could get a taxi. I think both my house-mates are out this evening.' At least he hoped so. He knew Shelley and Sholto were meeting, at their own neutral ground, a hotel in the city centre, but he wasn't sure about Lizzie. If things had gone to plan, she'd be out somewhere with John Smith now. Maybe dinner and then back to Dalethwaite Manor. It was still hard to believe that Lizzie was likely to be living there before long. That her sudden, wonderful boyfriend had literally bought the finest house in the whole Borough area, just for her.

'There's no need. I've got a room here. When my brother suggested we meet at the Waverley Grange, it was too good a chance to miss.' Tom looked around the bar, taking in the soft lighting, and the general ambience of something simmering beneath the outwardly respectable surface. 'This place has quite a reputation and I've never stayed here before.'

'That's great,' said Brent, his nervousness ramping up. No taxi ride, then, no time to acclimatise himself to the idea of going to bed with this stranger who wasn't a stranger.

'Don't worry. We'll take it slow.' Tom slid from his stool and tossed a couple of notes from his wallet on to the bar, nodding to the barman. 'Come on...I won't bite. Unless you want me to.'

Brent fell into step, just behind, as Tom wove through the tables towards the door to the lobby. God, the man had a great body. How could he have forgotten that? Long lean legs, and a gorgeous arse. It was like scoring a prince or something. Even Tom's bearing and the way he walked had a regal quality to it, the grace of a warrior angel or a knight.

I can't believe my luck. What are the odds of meeting him again? This is just the best coincidence ever.

They strolled through the lobby, and took the stairs to the first floor. Brent had done this any number of times, in any number of hotels, even in this one, when he'd been escorting, but this was so, so different. This time it was like he was the punter, and Tom the deluxe, high-class treat he'd bought for himself. Only he hadn't had to buy him. The goodies were being given to him willingly.

For a fleeting second, he wished Shelley and Sholto *could* be a real relationship. She deserved that, and Kraft had endured enough bad luck in his life to deserve something good for a change.

Maybe it would happen? Who knew . . .?

'You look thoughtful,' said Tom as they reached his room, Number Eight. 'Don't have second thoughts. If things don't work out, we can watch the television in the room, and maybe have some room service. I've been told the food here is great.'

Brent's heart swelled with gratitude. The other man was doing everything he could to make things no pressure. 'No, it was something else I was thinking about. I was hoping for good things for my house-mates, seeing as my own evening is working out so great. They've both got newish men in their lives and I was hoping...well...that all would go smoothly for them.'

Tom pushed open the door, and laid a hand on Brent's shoulder. 'Well, I don't know these friends of yours, but I hope life is good to them too.' The pressure of his hand increased, urging Brent to cross the threshold...and a Rubicon of sorts.

Ah, the familiar Waverley chintz. He'd been here before, although not this particular room, and experienced the hotel's distinctive kitsch décor. It was a combination of mildly luxurious, laughably twee...and yet, like the bar, there was the undercurrent of naughtiness, and a hint of kink. It reminded him of a room he'd read about, described in an erotic novel once, but for the life of him, he couldn't remember its name.

The door snicked shut behind him, and Tom's presence reached out to him like a warm aura, embracing him without even touching him. There was furniture aplenty in the room – a couple of chairs, chests of drawers, a sort of sideboard with the usual hotel bits, coffee, tea, kettle – but it was the wide bed with its thick downy duvet that owned the space. It seemed impossible to look anywhere but there, and he wandered into the centre of the room, just staring at it.

A warm hand took his, and gently spun him round. Tom's eyes were brilliantly blue in the low light, and his smile slight, but tempting.

'What now?' said Brent, unable to believe how absurdly naïve and unschooled he felt, even with his history as an escort. His first time ever, years ago, hadn't seemed half the step that this was…or anywhere near as magical.

'Let's try kissing, shall we?' Tom ran his tongue over his lower lip, preparing the way. 'Nothing too scary in that, is there?'

Brent laughed, and inclined forward, confidence growing.

Tom's lips were warm, their surface soft, but with a strong hint of muscularity beneath. This man could kiss hard, and be voracious, Brent remembered, but for the moment, the touch was measured, delicate…and utterly delicious. He slid his arms around Tom, pulling him close, and the feel of his lean strength and the hard knot at his groin was familiar, much, much more so than he could ever have thought possible.

How can this be? How can a one-night stand, several years ago, have had an impact on me like this? How can it seem so memorable now, when in the interim I swear I'd completely forgotten it?

But enough with the questions. Tom's tongue was questing for entrance, and he was eager to let it in, to taste and duel with it. Like his body, it was lean and muscular, a poem in understated power. Brent relaxed, allowing the dominance, thrilling to it, and to the way Tom's hands slid down his back and gripped his buttocks, holding their bodies together. Rocking against each other, they fell into a natural rhythm, working their cocks in a hungry dance, through their clothes.

'See . . . nothing scary,' said Tom playfully as they broke apart, gasping.

'Not scary at all,' announced Brent, his heart soaring as he cradled the other man's head and brought his lips back, to another kiss. This time Brent probed, loving the moist heat and the play of Tom's tongue, not quite fighting back, but not entirely yielding either. It didn't seem to matter which of them was dominant. Maybe they both were, and it was a kind of seesaw, this way and that.

'Shall we lie on the bed,' he asked, his lips moving against Tom's.

'You bet,' said the other man, already pulling him towards the generous expanse of crisp chintz. Kicking off their shoes, they fell on to the duvet, almost as one.

From a dream where she was some kind of sacrifice, spread on a slab before an all-powerful god-man, Lizzie snapped awake with a gasp. She'd fallen asleep on the thick, fluffy hearth rug before the fire, in the sitting room, half-draped across the low, thickly upholstered ottoman that was heaped with magazines and newspapers. Her knees were warm from the fire, and around her shoulders someone had draped a thick, woven throw.

An all-powerful god-man was observing her from his seat in one of the deeply upholstered chairs by the side of the fire.

'John! When did you get home? What time is it?' She rubbed her eyes furiously, blinking around. There were just a couple of small lamps lit in the corner of the room, and the main light came from the slow burning fire.

'It's about twelve-thirty,' said John, after a quick glance at the clock on the mantelpiece. He sat forward, his blue eyes scanning her. 'I was just wondering if I should wake you, or let you sleep on. Are you all right?'

He'd changed, presumably, since his arrival home. A soft, blue cotton long-sleeved top clung to the shape of his chest, arms and shoulders, and he wore old, well-worn jeans. His narrow elegant feet were bare.

'Yes...I'm fine. I was watching the telly and I must have

nodded off. This is a lovely room…but then, they all are here.'

In the low light, John's expression was inscrutable, but somehow she got the sense of him saying, *Yes, they are.* And suggesting, without saying so, that there was no good reason on earth for her not to live in this house, and share all these lovely rooms with him on a regular basis.

'Any more where that came from?' She nodded to a cut-crystal glass set on the little carved table set beside him. It had about a quarter of an inch of clear fluid in it: gin.

'Yes,' he replied, rising to his feet, all smooth elegance, perfectly at home in this romantic yet luxurious space. This was how he was used to living. As he strode across to the sideboard, she saw the gin bottle on a silver tray, along with ice in a clear bucket, slices of lime on a saucer, and several little bottles of tonic. It barely took him a moment to return to her with a lavish G&T.

'Thanks.' She took a sip immediately, sensing confrontation ahead. It was super strong, but delicious all the same. 'Lovely!'

It would have been so easy if he'd just kissed her . . . and then ravished her. Bypassing everything else, to get to the simple, straightforward, wonderful place. But that would have been the craven route, and that wasn't John. Or her either. Better to get issues out in the open…then fuck.

'So, you're my landlord now. That's convenient.'

John tapped his finger against his glass. 'Ah, so that's it . . . the thing that's bothering you.'

Lizzie contained herself. And the urge to toss back her entire and very strong gin and tonic. Did he think it wasn't a problem, taking over all aspects of her life and controlling them with his money? Her head seemed to whirl, even though she'd barely sipped her drink, conflicting thoughts and urges bashing around in her mind, cannoning off each other. She'd never really thought about the expression 'in two minds' much before . . . but now she knew it intimately. Love and gratitude, for John's boundless generosity and desire to further her welfare, were completely at war with her frustration at being manoeuvred and steamrollered into things.

'You mean you didn't know? You didn't expect me to be at least concerned?' She did sip then, taking a big mouthful, only just avoiding coughing at the jolt of silvery spirit. 'I mean, I know you mean well. And you're the kindest, most generous man I've ever met . . . but don't deny that some of the motivation behind it is to get what *you* want!'

'Why would I deny that? I'd be a liar if I did.' He was very still in his chair, utterly relaxed, and yet that finger still slid over the cut design of his glass, again and again. 'I want you, Lizzie. I need you. I desire you. I admire you. I want you to be with me . . . the maximum amount of time.' For a moment he gnawed his lower lip, and despite the conflict simmering between them, Lizzie nearly melted with desire, just from that tiny little thing. 'For the good sex . . . and for the games . . . but also for everything. I've effectively been alone for a long time, and that's been my choice. Because I couldn't find anyone I wanted to spend time with. But now I have found someone. And I'll do anything I can to get what I want.'

A little silver thrill ran through her. Like the gin, but not the gin. His determination was intoxicating, despite her qualms. It would be so easy just to give in, go with his flow . . . but that wasn't her way. She'd been swept along before, doing what other people wanted when she had reservations herself, and that had nearly taken her along a life path that would've made her miserable.

Worse still, that path would almost certainly never have crossed John's!

'You can't just manipulate people and buy everything.'

'Why not? It usually works.' That tricky little smile of his appeared. So confident. The man who never lost when he gambled. The man not used to losing. And yet…sometimes there were deep shadows. Had he lost, once? More than once? Something to do with 'Rose', who may or may not be the woman who'd made him angry in New York?

He'd certainly made a bad choice, the worst possible choice, that time he'd got behind the wheel, over twenty years ago…and driven like a fool. With alcohol in his blood.

Was that it? Why he didn't like to gamble and lose now? Why his choices were so calculated?

She took another sip of gin, knowing she was making her own stupid decision where alcohol was concerned, but hating the edge between them, and wanting to take it off.

Her head swum a bit and she said, 'But don't you think you're behaving like a big kid, trying to fix everything with money? I . . . I'm not sure yet. I do care for you, but you're forcing big changes on me.'

'A big kid?' He gave a small, bitter laugh, and set his glass aside. 'I wish . . .'

'What do you mean?' She knew, though. That again.

'Don't forget I'm nearly twice your age, love. Would that I were a young man again. A kid. A young stud. Someone who hadn't, well, done some of the things I've done. If I were a young man, maybe I wouldn't push myself so hard, or push you.' Without warning, he slipped on to his knees, and shuffled along the rug, to sit facing her. Somehow he did it so elegantly, though, and Lizzie almost laughed thinking how she'd have looked like a wombat or some other pudgy animal, slithering along on her haunches.

His blue eyes like flames, he stared at her intently. 'You're so young and beautiful. So bright . . . so glowing. I always feel that some younger man might come along and steal you away.' His jaw tightened, a warrior look passing over his beautiful face. 'So I have to use the weapons in my arsenal that a younger man, a man in his twenties, a man *your* age, probably wouldn't have at his disposal. My money and the resources that come with it.'

Putting aside the last of her gin, because she didn't need it or want it, Lizzie returned his fierce look with one of her own. 'Don't be stupid, John. I never even stop to think about the age gap between us.' It was true; she only remembered it when he brought it up. 'I think of you as someone my own age . . . well, maybe a smidge older, thirties perhaps, with slightly better sense than me.' She narrowed her eyes. 'Well, more sense, most of the time. And as for the money, I've told you before . . . this lot . . .' She waved her hand, hoping to encompass Dalethwaite, his fortune . . . the whole shebang. 'It isn't what I love. It's you, you fucking idiot. You!'

John's lips twitched, as if he wanted to laugh at her outburst, but to his credit, he remained straight-faced.

'You don't need money to make me care for you. You have *this*!' She reached out and touched his temple, the seat of his mind. 'And *this*!' She curved her fingers down the side of his face and jaw, so handsome. 'And *this*!' She pressed her hand over his heart, his great, kind heart. 'And *this*!' Letting herself grin, she slid her hand down his body and cupped his groin.

For an instant John blinked. It could have been emotion, or perhaps just surprise at her pre-emptive cock strike.

Then the little smile escaped his control; as did his erection, instantly hardening. She watched him fighting to stay serious, and on top of his words. It was like a poem across his face.

'I appreciate that, love . . . I do . . . but if you care for me, you care for me as the man who's been shaped by his circumstances.' He lifted her hand from his groin, then kissed her palm, before sliding his fingers around hers. 'I'm what my past has made me. And what my money has made me too. I'm as used to my life as you are to yours. I can't just give it all away and live what you'd call a normal life. It's only in romantic melodrama that people do that. In real life, everybody makes accommodations, no matter how much they care for someone, and no matter how "good" a person they are.' He squeezed her hand, then let it loose. 'I do care for you, more than I ever imagined I could…but, I must admit, I'm not that admirable a person really. And I like the good life. I like fine things and comfort.'

'I do too…but it's all new.'

He winked at her. 'And let's face it, can you see me living with you at St Patrick's Road, wading through all the clothes and coffee cups and magazines in your bedroom to get to you?' His grin widened again. 'You're the most wonderful woman in the world, Lizzie, but you must admit, in housework terms, you're a bit of a slob.'

'You cheeky sod!' She was laughing, though. It was true. Her room at St Patrick's Road was mostly a terrible mess, and she'd been just as much a slattern when she'd lived at home, to the despair of her mother. So, that was one huge tick in the box of moving in with John. He had first-rate staff to keep on top of her untidiness.

'I bet you'd be just as untidy if you'd never had people to pick up after you!' she went on. 'Who knows what sort of a scruffbag you'd be if you lived down amongst the lower orders like the rest of us.'

'Now who's a cheeky sod?'

Without warning, he lunged at her, grabbed her in his arms and ravished her with a fierce, hard kiss. Holding her tight, he laid her back on to the hearthrug, looming over her, smoothing back her hair, then launched into kisses again.

I know what you're doing. You're trying to distract me with sex, and your sheer, bloody gorgeousness. You're doing it because you know you can . . . because it's easier than debating the 'issues'.

She didn't mind, though. Not for the moment. Enjoying him *was* easier. And wonderful. Her body came alive, every cell tingling. How many days had it been since they'd been together? It seemed like a lifetime.

But some time, tomorrow or the next day or the next…things would have to be faced up to. By both of them.

21

Sex Matters

Brent fell back against the pillows, gently urged by Tom. As he closed his eyes, he felt the other man working on the buttons of his shirt, drawing it open and allowing the soft air of the room to caress his chest.

The bedroom smelt divinely old-fashioned, with pot-pourri and furniture polish, but neither of those scents hid the lusciously crisp aroma of Tom's fresh aftershave. It was green, yet rich, with a hint of spice. Brent drew in a deep breath, then gasped again as Tom's warm lips settled against his nipple. The contact was light, yet tantalising, and when Tom began to lick and nibble, Brent couldn't prevent himself squirming in simple pleasure.

He grinned as he gave himself up to the sensations, thinking of the times he'd done this sort of thing himself, lavishing kisses on an exposed nipple as part of a total pleasure package to arouse a punter.

He'd mostly done women here at the Waverley, though, and he'd never dreamed in all that time that the tables might be turned, and he'd be the one ravished and overwhelmed by a generous lover.

'Good?' enquired Tom, looking up at him, then extending his tongue to wickedly flick and tease, swirling it around the erect little nub.

'Yes! Hell, yes!' Brent growled, digging his hands into Tom's thick curly hair, forbidding him from interrupting his task. It was such a simple thing, but so exciting it made him pant for air, lifting his hips and pushing himself against his lover's body. He nearly howled when Tom began to stroke and tweak the other nipple as he sucked.

The man was divine. He knew just what to do, and older now, he was far slower and more subtle than on their first encounter. And Brent, older now, could appreciate him so much better.

After kissing and teasing Brent's nipples until he was half out of his head, Tom shimmied back up to kiss him again. Fired up, Brent attacked eagerly with his tongue, gripping hold of the other man, and rolling both their bodies over the bed, until he was on top. It wasn't an act of dominance . . . he wasn't sure what it was . . . but he wanted to give now, to pay back for the delights he'd received.

He kissed Tom hard, rocking against him, working their groins together, loving the pressure of an equally hard cock against his. Slithering a hand beneath his partner, he gripped and squeezed the firm musculature of Tom's glorious arse.

'Jesus, man . . . yes,' gasped Tom. He was the man straining and arching now, pressing back against Brent. 'Yes!'

For several minutes, they worked themselves against each other, rocking on the bed, muttering, laughing, touching, smiling.

'Shall we strip off?' said Tom eventually, the slight shyness in his eyes, despite everything, completely adorable. Brent longed for him to strip, so he could kiss this new angel in his life all over, every inch.

'Hell, yes,' he said, then kissed Tom again. 'But let me undress you. I'd really like to do that. Unwrap my gift . . .' He grabbed another kiss, like another delicious treat.

'OK.' Tom sat up, his eyes on Brent's, his demeanour softening, becoming passive. A great, atavistic surge of possessiveness rose through Brent like a wave, and he reached for the buttons on Tom's shirt, working them open quickly and parting the garment.

Ooh, nice, just as tempting as he remembered. The lean physique, latent with whippy strength. A little dark body hair, but not too much, just the right amount that Brent admired . . . especially the provocative arrowing that pointed south, beneath Tom's waistband.

Unfastening his lover's cuffs first, Brent eased the shirt off Tom's shoulders, first one, then the other, letting the fabric rest at his wrists in a slight, yet meaningful containment. Leaving it thus, he kissed Tom again, his mouth plundering, then moving on, kissing the other man's jawline, and his throat and the sensitive spot beneath his ear. As he kissed and nipped he could sense Tom wanting to shake off his shirt, but not doing so, respecting the way it bound him. Brent's mouth moved onwards, and just as Tom had done to him before, he bent down and sucked the older man's nipples, first one, then the other, delicately biting.

Tom shuddered wildly beneath his mouth, inciting him. Brent nibbled, teasing with little nips, and tugs, savouring his lover's grunts and exclamations of pleasure.

'God, strip me off, man. I need to be naked,' Tom cried at last, shaking at the sleeves of his shirt. Brent sprang to comply, tugging at the garment, then going for Tom's fly, manipulating the button and zip in double-quick time.

Tom's underwear was dark grey, and his erection huge beneath it, pushing at the cloth. Brent scooted down the bed, and peeled off the other man's socks, then pulled down his jeans, as Tom came up on his elbows, lifting his bottom.

The denims went flying across the room, and Brent doubled right down to kiss the mighty bulge beneath the soft dark jersey. Tom's cock stirred from the contact, lively, eager. Even as he rubbed his face against the hidden cock he yearned to see again, he could feel Tom himself plucking at his waistband to rid himself of his underwear.

As Brent sat up again, clutching his own groin, the yearning was so great, Tom stripped off the last barrier, and the briefs went the way of all the other clothing, to the floor.

Oh, what a gorgeous cock . . . Thick and sturdy, well-shaped, pointing high and ready. Brent bent forward again and kissed it, loving the heat and the velvety texture of Tom's shaft. He let it slip and slide against his cheek, bussing it with his closed lips, then opening his lips and kissing, but not taking it in. Tom gasped, 'Oh man . . .' when Brent lingeringly licked him.

The taste was foxy, but celestial. Brent used his tongue boldly, but after a moment, Tom caught him lightly by a lock of his hair and made him look up.

'Oh Brent . . . Brent . . . let me see you too. I want your skin against mine. All of it.'

Brent struggled to comply without shaking. His fingers wouldn't work properly as he tried to unbutton his cuffs, but Tom helped him. They worked as a team, divesting Brent of shirt, socks, jeans, shorts . . .

'Oh baby, yes,' whispered Tom, and a great wave of yearning crested inside Brent's heart as the other man pulled their bodies together. It had been so long since they'd touched each other, so long since Brent had wanted to be touched, so long since he'd done anything sexual that mattered. Mattered for *him*.

But Tom and his body and his . . . his magic, did matter. Brent's eyes misted as they lay along each other, chest to chest, belly to belly, cock to cock. He dug his hands into Tom's thick nut-brown curls and manoeuvred their mouths into perfect alignment for another perfect kiss. A full body kiss as well as a meeting of lips.

They kissed and licked and tasted each other for minutes on end, swirling their tongues, as they swirled their hips, pelvises against each other. Their hands travelled, meeting again the zones they'd met those years ago, but more leisurely now, touching with maturity and with a greater wealth of experience and emotion. Brent shivered finely, again and again, almost overcome. Not with lust, well, not with lust alone, but more, so much more.

'We don't have to do the Full Monty, you know,' said the older man, nipping at Brent's ear. 'We don't have to rush anything. I . . . I think I want this to be the start of a thing, not a thing in itself.' He kissed where he'd nipped, gentle and soothing. 'Maybe I *am* rushing . . . in a way . . . but hell, I do want to know you better. In other ways, not just cock stuff, you know?'

Brent almost sobbed, astonished by the intimacy. By the offer of what he'd been wondering whether he might ask for himself, at the right moment. Hearing Tom's words was like liquid happiness being poured over them, as they lay there, body to body. It ripped away the fatalistic ennui that always hovered over encounters like these, the emptiness that came from the knowledge that this was all it would be.

This wasn't all it would be. There could be more. More than he dare contemplate right now.

'Thanks…yes…I don't know . . .' He laughed, and felt Tom's body shake lightly as he shared the laughter. 'Hell, just listen to me…like a virgin on his first date. Barely believable, isn't it? I don't know quite what I want, but I know I want something.'

'Me too…Me too…All I know is that I want to come, with you, and that I want you to come.' Tom's hand moved over Brent's arse as he spoke, caressing, a slow gentle stroke. 'I'm not sure I want to fuck yet…or to be fucked…but I *will*…soon. When the time's right.'

Sex, for himself, with men, had always been frantic, Brent realised, rocking in time to Tom's stroking hand. Even with Steve, it'd often been kind of desperate.

But this wasn't desperate. It was easy. There was no need to strive, to fret. All good things would come, in time.

'Well, if you don't want to fuck,' he said, feeling a rush of mischief now, of power born of a lack of pressure and expectation, 'how about this?' Slithering his hand between their bodies, he took a measured but decisive hold on Tom's cock. 'And this?' Slowly he began to pump, letting his cradling fingers glide over the hot skin, the vibrant, pronounced veins.

Tom pressed his face against the side of Brent's neck, and Brent could feel the smile, and then, the beginnings of heavy, panting breaths.

'Mmm . . . yes,' the older man said, working his hips, riding the strokes, 'that will do nicely…oh yes, very, very nicely . . .' He kissed Brent's throat, his tongue matching the motion of his hips, and Brent's fingers. 'And afterwards . . . something nice . . .' His breath caught as the flesh Brent was cradling jerked and leapt . . . 'something just as nice for you.'

And it would be nice. Very nice. Unbelievably nice.

As nice as the warm, silky semen pulsing and spurting over Brent's fingers and on to his thigh.

'You're trying to distract me,' accused Lizzie, panting. John's kisses were voracious, but was there a bit of calculation about them? Was he trying to dazzle her with lips and tongue, with his hands and the weight of his body?

Trying to make her breathless so she simply couldn't task him and quiz him about anything but matters of sex?

'Yes, I am,' he answered, lifting his face from hers just an inch, bewitching her with his eyes, this time, from the closest of close quarters. His pupils were black, like dark stars, glinting in the firelight. 'I've been away from you for days, and I haven't fucked you. What do you expect me to do? I'm just an idiot man with a raging hard-on.' He gave her a hard kiss, and rocked his pelvis against her. 'And I had it all the time you were taking me to task about being too controlling. I can't help myself.'

'And now you're still trying to control me...with this.' She wiggled her hand between their bodies and cupped him. With a flex of her fingers, she exerted her own kind of control. Her blond devil-angel was not going to have it all his own way.

John fell still. She had him now. He could shake her hand off him if he wanted. Dominate her with his body and his strength, and the force of his personality, but she could almost taste his effort of will, as he fought *not* to do that. He knew his own nature, but for the moment, it seemed, he was choosing to subsume it. To hers.

'Guilty as charged!' he gasped when she ever-so-slightly tightened her grip on him.

Still holding him, Lizzie sat up, compelling him to move, her hand still curved around his crotch. He rocked back, settling on his knees beside her. His golden hair glinted in the radiance cast by the low fire, and with her free hand, she reached out and dug her fingers in it, bringing his face back to hers, for another kiss, one of her choosing. She dove in with her tongue, teasing and flicking at his, feeling his cock kick against her palm as she challenged and chivvied him.

'Mm . . .' he purred as she freed his mouth, but not his erection. He dove back at her, seeking another kiss, but she denied him.

'Don't you get carried away, just because I've decided to grope you. We still have to deal with our issues, you know.'

'I do know.' His expression was serious, intense. Somehow both provocative yet humane. 'It's just that it's been a long time since I couldn't get what I wanted using money, and I don't like the sensation.' He bobbed forward, stealing a tiny kiss. The solemnity in his eyes intensified. 'Last time it happened, it was like being gutted, Lizzie. It made me swore never to let myself be bested again. Never to be weak and give in to my heart. Can you blame me for fighting dirty?'

Lizzie withdrew her hand, looking into his eyes, trying to divine what he was talking about; what that gutting experience could have been. Would he ever tell her those secrets? Was it Rose? She dove both hands into his hair now, making him face her.

'I don't want to make you weak or get the better of you. I just don't want to be manipulated. I . . . oh, this is so complicated.' She sensed they were both seeking the same thing, or seeking to avoid it.

'Yes, it bloody well is,' he cried, and she felt his energy gathering, ready to surge. 'But *this* isn't!' He lunged forward

again, kissing with power. Thrilling to him, Lizzie met his
advance.

They were combatants again, but in the joust of passion.
Each of them strong; each of them fighting vulnerabilities.
Who was going to yield? With a great gathering of her will,
she pushed at him, making him subside this time, forcing
him on to his back on the rug.

But even though he was supine, he was still a force of
nature.

'So, little girl, are you going to fuck me? To ride me? Do
you think you can stay on top?' He flirted his pelvis upwards,
challenging her with the mighty bulge there.

'I'm sure I fucking well can!' she cried, attacking the
button of his jeans before he could react. 'I hope to God
you've got a condom tucked somewhere about your person.'
Dragging down his zip, she rummaged at his boxer briefs and
flicked his erect cock out into the open. It looked like a pagan
fertility totem, harsh and gleaming in the firelight.

'Hell, yes!' Lifting his hips again, making his erection
sway, he reached into his back pocket and brought out a
condom packet. With a flick of his wrist, he tossed it to her
and she caught it.

'You randy beast . . . I might have known. Always at the
ready.' Lightly, she batted at his cock with the backs of her
fingers, making it dance again.

'You know me so well,' he replied, but she could see him
tensing, as if genuinely apprehensive about her handling of
his tackle.

Lizzie narrowed her eyes, in mock threat.

*But I don't know you well . . . In some ways I barely know you
at all. And that's the problem.*

Squaring her shoulders, she dismissed the shadows for

the moment. Why spoil the delicious prospect that lay before her? A girl should never pass up the chance of mounting such a magnificent erection.

Her mind might be uneasy, but her body was ready for him. Desire surged in her belly; silk pooled in the vale of her sex. She unwrapped the condom as fast as was careful, and rolled it down over him with no further ado. Even clothed in latex, his cock was an object of primal beauty, and her pussy ached for it.

She wanted him in her, now; no preliminaries. The quickest way was the best, avoiding complications, avoiding talk. Before she could change her mind or even think, she was wriggling out of her yoga pants, and kicking them away.

Then, pulling the crotch of her knickers to one side, she crouched over him, positioning herself right over his glans.

'What, no foreplay?'

'I don't need it.' Wriggling, she settled on him, then let herself descend, quite fast, panting as his length filled her up.

'What about me?' His grin was wicked. He didn't need it either. He was ready now as he was always ready, although he gasped out loud when she rocked, and swivelled a little, striving for the maximum, for all of him.

'You'll manage,' she replied through gritted teeth, engulfed in sensation. Every time he was in her, it was as if she'd forgotten how big he was, or simply how big he *felt*, and the sensation surprised her, filling her heart with wonder as he filled her with himself.

'I feel like your sex toy.' He moved uneasily beneath her, then cursed a blue streak when she gripped him fiercely, flexing her inner muscles.

'Women feel like that a lot of the time. Get used to it.' She was talking nonsense, but the way he was bucking up against her played havoc with rational thought. Rising up, she slammed down hard again, forcing another oath from his lips. His fingers dug into her hips, through her knickers, as he gripped her tightly, reciprocating her action with an upward thrust of his own.

'But I don't treat you like a sex toy, Lizzie,' he hissed, 'I never have . . . even at first, when I still thought you were "working". I've always tried to respect women, and you most of all!'

Her eyes snapped open, and she stared down at him. Something in his voice, some shadow in his eyes, drew her out of her sex fugue for a moment. What other women had he respected? His wife, of course . . . But what about Rose? Had he respected her? Had he gone out of his way to coax her to live with him? What if he'd wanted *her* to marry him, whereas now he'd given up on matrimony?

'What is it, Lizzie?' His voice was softer, concerned all of a sudden. Even in the midst of a wild ride he was acute, reading her every nuance. 'You went away for a moment there. What's wrong?'

'Nothing,' she growled, rocking again, shaking her head, making her hair fly as if to eject all stupid, possessive thoughts from her mind. Fuck Rose! She wasn't here. She, Lizzie, was the one sitting on John's beautiful cock, with her eyes nearly starting from her head because he was in so deep.

Inclining forward a little, she slid her hands beneath his cotton top, palms flat, coasting over the smooth hot skin, savouring the friction of the light, crisp body hair. Making pincers of her fingers and thumbs, she trapped his nipples, squeezing him and making him squirm anew beneath her.

'Oh yes, oh God,' he burbled, tensing, his heels dragging on the rug. 'You're a demoness, sometimes . . . you know that, don't you?' She pinched him again and once more the air was blue. His fingers tightened, digging cruelly into her hips, but she didn't care. God, she wanted more of it. Twisting his nipples, she clamped hard on him, with her sex.

John rolled his head from side to side on the rug, his flaxen curls tossing. His face was like a tortured saint's, in extremis, yet strong. Always strong.

'You get the better of me, Lizzie…I…I should hate that. But it's never seemed so right.' He slid a hand up her body, over her ribs, and then hooking round her shoulder. With a rough tug, he pulled her down, her face to his. 'Hell, this is always right…no matter what…always good.'

There was only one thing to do. Kiss him. Her lips settled on him softly at first, but then, in a swift rearrangement of limbs, he was holding her more tightly, a hand buried in her hair. Gripping her scalp, he took control of the kiss, even though she was in the superior position. He held the back of her head with his powerful spread fingers, and thrust his tongue into her mouth, searching and subduing.

Lying completely still beneath her now, he was dominant again, mastering her with the hot hard flesh inside her and the jab and dart of his tongue. The balance had tipped, but who cared? For the moment it was marvellous, just pure sex, no complications. She moaned into his mouth when he slid a hand to her breast and squeezed it quite hard. She tried to retaliate, punishing his nipples, but he shook her away from them with barely any effort.

Play-acting resistance, she didn't fight at all. Her sex rippled around him, the palpitation involuntary, not her conscious doing this time. She was close, hair-trigger close, to the bliss of orgasm. Gasping, she reached down between their bodies and flicked her swollen clit.

'I'll do that.' John's voice was low, husky and ragged, almost unrecognisable from his usual cultured tones. As she shook and trembled, he grabbed her by the waist and lifted her from him, then guided her on to her back. There wasn't much space between the edge of the fireplace and the ottoman, but somehow, he made some, nimbly moving over her. For a moment he was poised, kneeling between her rudely spread thighs, his cock pointing at her face. Was he going to whip off the condom and come all over her? Mark her with his dominion, like some savage male beast?

An almost primal smile crossed his glorious face, and she could read his thoughts as he considered that very thing. Then he shook his head, and moved into a new configuration, settling between her legs, pushing his cock towards her entrance. Drawing aside her knickers, just as she'd done, he found the sweet spot, then thrust home, his flesh filling her again. As they readjusted their bodies, he reared up on one elbow and his eyes fixed on her face as his fingers found her clitoris.

His expression was pure male confidence and power, but she didn't back down from it. She stared back at him, knowing she was his equal, holding that fiery golden gaze of his, even as he caressed her, teased her, wound her up tighter and tighter and tighter until with a hoarse cry, she climaxed hard. Reaching up, even as her body pulsed with pleasure, she dug her fingers into his curls, compelling him to observe the results of his manipulations in her eyes.

'Lizzie,' he growled, his voice a homage, his blue eyes near black with lust. Half out of her head, she knew that it was the look in her eyes that was exciting him as much as the embrace of her flesh, rippling around him.

And he looked away first, tipping back his head, his eyes

closing as he gripped her harder, now with both hands, and powered into her. She'd come already; he could do his thing now, claim his own prize.

Grabbing at him, she doubled up her knees, her ankles at the small of his back, drawing him in deeper. All the time, still half coming, pulsing, soaring higher, higher. John took her gift, following the siren call of her utter surrender to him, and within moments, he was coming too, shouting her name.

22

Quietly, Afterwards

For two minutes, or perhaps five, they were just a heap on the rug, bodies tangled, chests heaving as if they'd both completed a marathon with a hundred yard dash. John was a lean man, his body lithe, but shattered by pleasure, he felt like a dead weight upon her. Lizzie was dazed, and coming back to her senses, she wondered whether she was suffering from oxygen deprivation. But just as she was about to push at John and nudge him into getting off her, he levered himself away, murmuring, 'Sorry, love, I must be crushing you.'

'Just a bit, but I'll live.' Filling her lungs, she lay where she was, still getting her breath back and watching John right his clothing, and deal with the condom, wrapping it carefully in a thick handful of tissues that he'd pulled from the box encased in a chased silver holder.

'There are some things that even the most broadminded staff shouldn't have to deal with,' he said, grinning, as he tossed the bundle in the fire, and then jabbed it with the poker to ensure incineration.

Lizzie sat up, tweaking her knickers back into place. 'I'm

glad their flat is over in the stable block.' She answered his grin. 'At least that way they won't hear all the racket we make sometimes.'

'Indeed,' answered John, casting around for her yoga pants, finding them, and passing them to her so she could wiggle them on again. As he watched her, he asked, 'More gin?' and gestured to their abandoned glasses.

It was late, and a bit shell-shocked by the sex, Lizzie didn't want alcohol. 'I think I'd rather have some tea.' Pushing off from the ottoman, she stood up, half expecting to sway, but managing to stay upright. 'Shall we go and make some? We are allowed in the kitchen, aren't we?'

John laughed. 'Yes, of course. This isn't *Upstairs Downstairs*, you know. The Thursgoods won't have a fit of the vapours if we do a bit of fending for ourselves sometimes.' He swooped down and collected the glasses. 'Come on. I could just fancy a cup of tea too.'

Lizzie collected her tray, and they made their way to the kitchen together. It was a warm, lovely space, all done out in country greens and browns, full of high-tech cooking equipment, yet not in the least intimidating.

As John ran water into the sink, to wash the glasses, it dawned on Lizzie that she needed the bathroom. 'Is there a downstairs cloakroom?'

'Several, sweetheart, but the nearest is back the way we came, second door on the right.' He winked at her. 'Some people will do anything to avoid washing the pots.'

Lizzie stuck out her tongue and fled the room.

A little while later, she surveyed herself in the mirror, her face still aglow from sex, her hair mussed, not tamed, her fringe floppy. Her clothes were rumpled from rolling about on the rug. But she felt comfortable that way.

Perhaps I could live here. Like this. It's like a palace and there are staff . . . but it isn't really intimidating.

And yet . . . it was so different to all she'd known.

Shaking her head, she abandoned the bathroom and hurried back to the kitchen.

The tea was made. John was sitting at the kitchen table, presiding over the pot and two mugs. No bone china tea service, thank heavens. Just normal black earthenware; she'd seen the same ones in Homebase last time she'd been in buying some new bits and pieces for St Patrick's Road.

'What I said before . . . I'm not ungrateful, John. You do the most wonderful things. You're the kindest man. But you just do them and you don't . . . um . . . keep me in the picture.' She took the tea he pushed towards her, and took a sip. 'It makes me feel out of control, as if I'm being buffeted along, and I don't like that because I've felt it before. It took me such a long time to get control of my life, and it was a big step to make my own choices and abandon uni. I don't want to give up that self-determination.'

'I understand that. Completely,' said John quietly, stirring his tea, although she knew for a fact that he didn't take sugar. 'And the supreme irony is that it's exactly why I do what I do . . . take control, that is. There have been times in my life when I've not been in control myself. In prison. In relationships . . . well, *a* relationship. And I just can't allow it to happen again, so I tend to take these "executive actions" to keep a firm hand on everything.'

Relationship? What relationship? He must mean Rose, who could only be the New York woman. Had he loved this mysterious siren so much that he'd given up his natural urge to be in command of things? Lizzie knew that his marriage had been egalitarian, and a happy balance, even if his wife had initially had the upper hand, moneywise.

'So, we understand each other, really.' She reached out, and took his hand. 'Perhaps we're just rushing along too fast?'

John's smile was gentle, wise, full of admiration.

'You're such a smart girl, Lizzie. Such a realist. I wish I had half the emotional sense that you do.' He twisted his wrist and cradled her hand, holding her as if she *were* porcelain, not like their bargain basement drinking vessels. 'I'll move at your speed from now on, I promise. I won't do anything without consulting you.' He raised her hand quickly to his lips and kissed it passionately. 'At least I'll *try* not to.'

He would try. She knew that. But would he ever tell her about Rose?

'What's bothering you, Lizzie? Something is. And something more than this business of moving in, I can tell.'

He didn't miss a trick. Those blue eyes were so sharp, like lasers, seeing right through to her soul and its qualms.

'Come on, love, you can ask me anything. I know I've not been too forthcoming about my life, and my past, but that's something else I'll try to change.' The look on his face was almost hypnotic, inviting her to be bold; to ask.

Don't do it, Lizzie. Don't spoil things. He says he wants to tell all, but he's a man. I bet he doesn't really.

And still, she took a deep breath, and asked:

'Who's "Rose"?'

Two days later, she still didn't really know. But she soon would. They were in the Bentley Continental, scudding along the motorway, heading out to meet the woman who Lizzie feared, in her most irrational moments, might be her nemesis.

It had been a busy couple of days. John had spent long hours at the new JS North office complex, in meetings with his new staff: managers and executives, and workers at the sharp edge alike. Lizzie had thrown herself hard into sewing and helping out at New Again. Something interesting had come to them. A bridal commission. A client had been let down by a big wedding gown firm and, furiously upset, had told them, basically, to stuff it. And she'd come to New Again, begging them to help her. Could Lizzie make a dress? Marie had casually raised the issue of creating their own mini 'label' again . . . but then didn't press, as if she'd sensed Lizzie's deep preoccupation.

Two days of poring over patterns, online catalogues of trims and fabrics, and in intense meetings and fittings with Serena, potentially the first ever New Again Bride, had occupied Lizzie's mind usefully, and deflected her from a continuous stream of pointless and irrational brooding about Rose. She hadn't even had a proper chance to touch base with Brent and Shelley; it seemed that when *she* was at St Patrick's Road, neither of them were around, and vice versa. The only occupant who was there consistently was Mulder the cat. Lizzie had a strong suspicion that the two other human occupants were at least as deeply absorbed in their own love lives as she was in hers, although whoever Brent was seeing was someone new and unknown to her. She would have to quiz him a bit when they next found time for a chat. The same with Shelley, about her escort man, Sholto.

Lizzie glanced at John, beside her, still almost as unknown, in many ways, as the new lovers her two friends had found.

Does he really want to do this?

Outwardly he seemed serene. In high good humour, as he tapped his fingers on the steering wheel in time to the 1980s music pouring from the radio. A weird choice, she'd thought, until he pointed out to her that these were the sounds of his impressionable youth and, somehow, he'd never grown out of them.

Yet when she looked closer, she could see tension. A tightness in the immaculately shaven line of his jaw. The occasional hint of frown, which quickly dispersed as if he were exerting a conscious effort to appear untroubled.

He'd certainly responded calmly to her request, back in the kitchen.

'Rose? How did you know about her?' he'd said, and Lizzie had been forced to own up to her snooping.

'I can't blame you. I haven't really told you anything much about my past, have I? I'm amazed you haven't bombarded me with questions before now. Or found out whatever gory details are on Google.'

'I don't like to be nosy,' Lizzie said, staring into her mug. 'People don't like being cross-questioned and checked up on. Especially men . . .' She sipped her tea. Yuck, it was cold already. 'But . . . well . . . I saw that name. And the repetition in your organiser, and I realised it was someone pretty important in your life.'

For a moment, John looked sad, vaguely shattered, his magnificent eyes full of pain. Then he turned to her, with a wry, complex little smile. 'She *is* important in my life. Very much so . . . but not in the way you think, love. Not like that.' There was still sadness in his eyes, but somehow, almost, wonder. 'In an ironic twist of fate, she's become one of my dearest friends, and I don't have many of those.'

But he'd declined to elaborate. It had been late, very late, and despite her desperate curiosity, Lizzie had been exhausted. John had promised to tell her the full story, and to take her to meet Rose in person on Sunday. Then he'd accompanied her to her bedroom door, kissed her very sweetly, but not followed her in.

And now it was Sunday, they were on their way, and they hadn't had sex together since.

I should never have asked.

'So . . . it's about time I told all, isn't it?' said John suddenly, almost as if he'd been following the train of her thoughts. The way he seemed to do that sometimes was scary.

'I suppose so. But I'm beginning to wish I'd never asked. I hate being a nosy parker, and I feel I've forced an issue sooner than I should have done.' She fiddled with her seatbelt. Like everything in the Bentley, it was superbly comfortable, and probably designed by rocket scientists, but still it seemed to oppress her. 'I mean, you never batter me with questions, do you?'

John laughed softly. 'Maybe I will . . . but let's do me first.' He winked at her. 'Well, you know what I mean.'

'OK, then . . . Who *is* Rose, this person who means a lot to you but not like that?'

The car sped on for a few moments, as John steered it assuredly through the Sunday stream of day trippers and others. Lizzie thought for a moment that he'd changed his mind, but then he began to speak.

'Twenty-four years ago, the very year you were born, I was involved in a car crash, as you know. I was driving far too fast and I slammed into a car at a country junction at night, on the way home from a party.' He drew in a deep breath. 'I got away without a scratch, but in the other car, a woman was killed and her ten-year-old daughter was seriously injured. As you'll no doubt have guessed, I'd been drinking.'

'Oh, John . . .'

The words had been so stark, so quiet, that she wondered if she'd almost imagined them. Yet they were out there and her mind was a jumble of reactions. Horror, mostly. Horror for the victims, and horror for John. He wasn't an evil person, she was convinced of that, utterly, but in the year of her birth, he'd done a terrible, horrible, wicked thing.

'Don't say anything. You don't have to. I know what I did. And I was punished, although not enough . . . not nearly enough.' He was talking to her, yet she could tell that at the same time, he was totally focused on the road and the traffic. She felt perfectly safe. He'd learnt a hard lesson, and had it burnt into his psyche. 'But . . . somehow . . . one good thing came out of that. Well, perhaps there are more things, but one major thing. Against all the odds, and after quite a few years, I gained a good friend. A wonderful, inspirational friend.'

Who? And yet strangely, she already knew . . .

'We're going to meet that friend now, love. Her name is Rose, and I killed her mother.'

'Omigod!'

'I know. Not quite what you were expecting, is it?' said John, changing gears smoothly as they climbed the ramp to exit the motorway. 'And for many years, she did hate me, and wanted nothing to do with me. I tried to offer as much financial support as I could, and fortunately her family accepted it because they felt, like me, that it was the least I could do.' For a moment he was silent, as they fed into traffic on a roundabout. 'It was a struggle at first. I was pretty broke. But I managed to persuade an aunt of mine who had a bit of money to let me have her bequest to me early, and then of course when Caroline and I got together, she was more than happy to supply all the funds I needed.'

For a moment, he looked grim again. The tale of this must be difficult for him. But there was something . . . something else. Lizzie couldn't put her finger on it, but she sensed another story, some other angst, that was intertwined with this one, but which he wasn't able – couldn't bring himself – to explore.

'But you did become friends?' she prompted, almost afraid to.

'Yes. I think after she'd had some counselling, with a new therapist, she had some kind of, I don't know, catharsis . . . and she reached out to me.' He heaved a sigh, and she could see him reliving the relief that must have been, despite the difficulties. 'I started going to see her and we talked a lot. It was prickly at first, but eventually, it became something to look forward to . . . for her just as much as me, I realised.'

'That's great!' It was. Miraculous, but great. Lizzie grinned at him, happy to see him quickly return the smile.

'It is. I'm very thankful for it. And, of course, one of the benefits of being a stupidly wealthy man now, I can continue to provide for her financially.' He sighed again, but just a little one this time. 'Would to God I could give her back her mother, and the ability to walk...but not being an angel or having super powers, I just do the best I can.'

Not sure what else to say, Lizzie laid a hand carefully on his arm. He *was* a good man. He'd done something stupid in the past, and hurt people, but his heart was true.

In only a few more minutes, they were gliding down a country lane, flanked by some very nice renovated properties, an area much like the more rural end of Kissley Magna. At the end of the lane, however, there stood a modern bungalow. Clearly a unique design, it still managed to blend in with the surroundings, organic and harmonious. Lizzie could see a long garden spreading out on either side, with lush flower beds set amongst broad paths of hard standing. Beneath a pretty loggia, a swimming pool glittered blue.

Even before the car had pulled fully to a halt, a handsome woman with eye-catchingly red hair propelled her wheelchair down the front door ramp, ready to greet them. Behind her another woman, dark-haired, slender and wiry, and younger by some years, followed in her wake. Both were grinning.

'Eh up, John, you old devil. How are you doing? I hope you're hungry. We've got tons and tons of lunch,' said the redhead, reaching out to embrace John in a bear hug as he leaned down towards her, 'enough to feed an army!'

A bit shy, Lizzie held back as John greeted the pair. The affection between them all was like a warm wave. They were so comfortable together.

'Rose, this is Lizzie, who I've been telling you about.' John drew her forward into the glow, his hand closing around hers, encouraging her. 'Lizzie, this is Rose . . . and Hannah, who keeps her in line.'

'With difficulty,' said Hannah with a soft laugh.

'Hi! Nice to meet you.' Lizzie edged forward, nerves jingling. She wasn't usually uptight about meeting new people, but these women probably knew John far better than she did, and had done for a much longer time. They had a bond with him. She offered her hand to Rose, but found herself pulled down into another of those powerful hugs.

'Wow, you're just as stunning as John said,' Rose announced, looking Lizzie up and down with disturbing frankness, 'and I'm really digging the "Bettie" vibe . . . awesome!'

'Thanks . . . It's just a "thing", you know,' Lizzie stammered. Rose obviously said exactly what she meant, and that was both attractive and a bit unnerving.

'It's fab. Where do you get your Capri pants? I really love them, but mostly all you can get nowadays is horrid shapeless cut-offs. I hate them.'

'I made them. I make a lot of my own clothes…for the look, you know?'

'Fantastic! John said you were a seamstress. You'll have to make some of those for me, if you've time. I'll pay top dollar for something that fits properly.' She turned to Hannah. 'They'd look good on you too, honey. How about it?'

Hannah smiled at Lizzie. 'I bet they wouldn't look nearly as sensational as they do on Lizzie. Why don't we all go in, and eat, eh? I'm starving. Would you like to wash your hands first, Lizzie?'

A few minutes later they all sat down to dine on a lovely patio overlooking the garden and the pool. On pins at first, Lizzie soon found it easy to relax. The two women drew her into their circle as easily as they did John, asking her about her sewing, and New Again, and about Dalethwaite in particular; but the questions weren't too probing, or intrusive. No third degree about the unorthodox way she and John had met, or what their plans might be for the future.

In turn, the conversation drifted on to Rose and Hannah's life. They were both active in the affairs of the nearby village, and Hannah was a part-time journalist on a local newspaper. Rose's passion was art, which stood to reason, given the entry Lizzie had seen in John's organiser. The redhead was both a connoisseur of English watercolours and an exponent of them herself.

'You should exhibit, Rose,' said John, toying with his mineral water glass. The three of them were drinking wine, but Lizzie noted that without anything being said about it, he didn't touch alcohol. A lesson learnt hard, long ago, now always adhered to. 'You know I'd finance a show for you. You just have to say the word.'

'I might . . . I'm thinking about it. But I'm not sure I'm ready yet,' said Rose, her expression firm. She was obviously not the type to be pushed into anything before she was ready. The best way to be, where John was involved.

'Well, if you won't exhibit, will you at least let me buy the canvas I saw last time I was here . . . that clifftop view?'

Rose named a wild price. John called her a robber, but in the end agreed.

'Shall I help you wash up?' he said to Hannah when the pleasant meal was done, and the dark-haired girl began gathering the plates and stacking them on a tray.

'I'll help,' said Lizzie, jumping up.

'No, you stay here and help me finish this bottle,' cut in Rose, splitting the last inch or two of white wine between their glasses. 'Let's go into the shade over there.' She pointed to the loggia beside the pool. 'It's getting a bit hot out in the sun.'

When the others had gone, she manoeuvred her wheel-chair close up against Lizzie's lounger. 'This is when he'll be grilling her about my health, and getting her report. He tries to be subtle about it, bless him, but I know what he's up to.' She took a sip from her glass, and fixed Lizzie with a penetrating stare.

It was good to be out of the sun. A niggle of a headache had been building up behind Lizzie's temple during the meal, despite the fact that she'd quickly been able to relax with Rose and Hannah. She hoped she wasn't coming down with something . . . or maybe it was just an autonomic reaction to the other woman's benign scrutiny?

'You're curious, aren't you?' went on Rose, with a wink.

'Er . . . about what?' Lizzie sipped her wine, wondering if it was a good idea, given her head and the fact it might make her say something daft.

'About Hannah and me. You can't work out whether she's my carer, my friend . . . or something else.'

Crikey, she was sharp. Lizzie *had* been wondering, but had tried not to make any assumptions.

'Well . . . she *was* just my carer at first. Now she's "something else". We're a couple, Lizzie. We have been for a few years now.'

'Oh . . . right. That's fantastic. Hannah is lovely. She's obviously crazy about you.'

Rose beamed. 'And I am about her! We've been toying with the idea of doing the civil partnership thing. But we've decided we'll hang on for the legislation, and get married instead!' She reached out and patted Lizzie's arm. 'You and John will be top of the guest list, natch.'

'Thanks . . . I love weddings.'

Rose gave her a long, impish look. Lizzie wasn't sure what to expect next, a question about her own longer term plans? But instead Rose said:

'And in case you're wondering…yes, we *do* have sex. And yes, it's very, very good!' She winked broadly. 'My legs might be knackered, but certain other, very important bits are still working just fine!'

Lizzie burst out laughing, her headache temporarily forgotten. Rose was a caution. A lovely, good-humoured woman, someone who could grow to be a friend and ally. About as far from the threat, or feared rival for John's affection, as she could possibly be.

'Awesome! That's brilliant!' she said, reaching forward to clink her glass to Rose's. 'I'll drink to that!'

Rose gave her a sly look. 'Don't worry, I'm not going to ask for details of *your* sex life. Although with a gorgeous, charismatic bloke like John, I'd imagine it's a riot. Obviously, I'm into women, basically, but that doesn't stop me admiring beauty in either sex.'

'I...I've never met anyone quite like him,' said Lizzie. It was the truth, but so inadequate. Could she tell this woman she'd known for barely an hour what she really felt? 'I think I love him . . . I think it was pretty much love at first sight, stupid as that sounds.'

There, it was out.

Rose gave her a very level look, acceptance and comprehension in her eyes. 'He's a complicated man, Lizzie, but very worthy of love. I can't imagine he's easy to be with sometimes, but when it comes down to it, he's as beautiful on the inside as he is on the outside. And I can see he's completely dotty about you.'

Lizzie trembled. Perhaps it was Rose's words, perhaps it was the headache, something she was coming down with. She felt rather peculiar.

'I hope so . . .'

Rose put her hand on Lizzie's arm. 'I know so. I've got to know him quite well over the years. Some people can't understand how that could happen, but it has. I hated him at first. I wanted to kill him, really I did . . . but now I know he's a good man. A man of worth. And I want him to be happy.' She squeezed hard. 'And I think his best shot for that might be with you. Do you know, he's never brought a woman here before . . . you're the first. That's got to mean something, eh?'

Perhaps it did? Perhaps it did? Lizzie fought hard to quell her shaking.

'I'm so glad John has a friend like you,' Lizzie said,

feeling it. Ever since she'd first met him, she'd sensed an inner loneliness, an emptiness, but at least he had Rose and Hannah. And that brother she was looking forward to meeting. 'It . . . it must have been quite a journey for you.'

'It has been. I did hate him. With the power of a thousand suns . . . well into my teens. I had a mini breakdown then, but I got some help, very expensive help, funded by John, even though at the time I wanted nothing to do with him personally.' Rose gazed out into the garden for a few moments. 'But the psychologist was brilliant. Really helped me work through issues, and also helped me remember things I'd suppressed. Catharsis and all that, you know?'

'I suppose it does help to face the most horrible things. So you can move on.' Her own traumas in life had been piddling, really, but Lizzie understood the principle.

'Precisely,' said Rose, turning back to face her. 'I remembered almost everything about the night of the crash. I was semi-conscious most of the time, but I'd blocked it. And when I remembered exactly what happened, it put a whole new complexion on things, and completely changed how I felt about John.'

The air suddenly seemed very still. Lizzie could hear a bee buzzing in the pretty climbing plants that covered the loggia.

'I remembered him helping us . . . talking to us . . . trying desperately to help Mum . . . and shouting at that bitch to run to a phone box or whatever, and call an ambulance. But she just sat there like a zombie.'

Lizzie blinked. What 'bitch'?

'Was there someone else in the car with him?'

Rose's eyes flashed. 'Yes, there bloody well was! That bitch . . . she was stoned. She'd told him she hadn't been drinking at the party, but she'd omitted to say she'd crept away amongst all the jollification, and got high. He blamed himself for believing her. He's always blamed himself for believing her, and because he'd had a few to drink himself, he trusted her. He considers the accident totally his fault because of that.'

Something suddenly started to add up. Something weird . . . 'What do you mean, Rose? Who was the woman?'

Rose had released her arm, but now she grabbed it again, nails digging in.

'Clara. The woman John was crazy about at the time. The woman he wanted to marry.' A look of disgust made the redheaded woman's handsome face look ugly for a moment. 'The woman who was *really* driving the car that killed my mother.' Her eyes shone with tears, the tears that would never go away, no matter what. 'The bitch he took the rap for, as they say. The one he spent nearly three years of his life banged up in prison for!'

23

Enter the New Rival

Pain stabbed at Lizzie's head, forcing her to close her eyes.

Damn, damn, damn...just when I finally discover that 'Rose' is an angel, suddenly there's a fucking 'Clara' instead!

Rose's revelation had rocked her, a blow on any number of levels. If a man was going to do what John had done, for a woman he cared about, that degree of entanglement just wasn't going to go away. Even after twenty-four long years.

She couldn't remember much about the rest of the afternoon. Somehow, she'd chatted and even laughed and enjoyed herself...but on a deeper level, she'd brooded and brooded about this 'Clara' that John had loved. Perhaps still loved, even if he wouldn't admit it.

Goddamnit, he'd never even *told* her about the woman.

'Are you all right, sweetheart? You're scowling. What's up?'

John's voice was full of puzzlement. Was he wondering why she'd suddenly gone so quiet on the way home from such a successful afternoon? It must seem weird...and yet her thoughts consumed her mind, gobbling up her ability to make small talk. Even with him.

'It's OK, thanks. I have got a bit of a headache, though. And I'm a bit worried I might have got a little bug or something, and I might have passed it on to Rose and Hannah now.'

'Ah, I thought you looked a little pale. Rose mentioned it to me when you were out of the room.' He paused. 'She asked me if I thought you were pregnant.'

'Ooh, no, it's not that!' Sudden wild thoughts surged, and Lizzie squashed them ruthlessly. No way was she going to let *those* mad sort of fancyings get a hold. 'I think it's just a thing that's going around, or maybe just a migraine or something.'

'Shall we pull in at the next services? You could have a cool drink and we could get some paracetamol. Maybe a spot of fresh air would do you good too?' As he spoke, Lizzie sensed the great car begin to accelerate. She'd noticed he never went over the speed limit, but a quick glance at the speedo said they were hovering right on seventy now. 'Lizzie?'

'No…it's OK, thanks. I've had worse and we'll soon be home. I'm just worried that if it is a bug, Rose might have got it.'

'Don't worry. I'll check in with them when we get home, and mention it. She's actually a very fit person apart from her disability. She and Hannah are very health conscious.' He flashed the quickest of glances her way. 'Are you sure you're all right? I know that this afternoon might have been a bit tense for you…a bit like meeting family for the first time. But Rose and Hannah adored you, and I could see that you've taken to them too.'

'They're lovely, both of them, absolutely lovely. I'm just tired. I think I'll rest my eyes for a bit.'

It was true, what she'd said. Rose *was* wonderful. It was this bloody 'Clara' who was the nemesis now.

*

He ached to ask her what was really troubling her, but he had a suspicion he already knew. What had Rose said to her when they'd been alone?

The accident had been discussed, he was sure of it. Maybe even Clara, damn the bitch! Even now, when she was thousands of miles away, in New York – or maybe back in South America by now – she was still making life difficult for him.

Taking his eyes off the road for just a split second, he stole another glance at Lizzie. In the flashing twilight, she looked ethereal, her creamy skin whiter than usual, and pure drama against her shimmering blue-black hair. Dozing, she looked more like an exquisitely pure Snow White than a provocative Bettie Page, and yet still her magical beauty excited him and made him hard.

Don't be a fucking degenerate, man. She's not well.

Did Lizzie know the truth now? He had a feeling she did, at least some of it. But what difference did it make that he'd not been behind the wheel that fateful night? The responsibility had still been all his, and the punishment he'd taken, all of it, was well deserved. He'd known that Clara was flighty and mercurial, and always did what she wanted. That was – had been – one of her charms, that wild and wayward quality. But he'd trusted her to tell the truth about something as crucial as whether or not she was under the influence, and that trust had been misplaced. With terrible consequences.

He schooled himself to stay calm and drive fast and smoothly. So that he could get Lizzie home, and then she could rest.

Clara, though. Would he ever be free of her? Even after all these years, she had the power to fuck up his life. She'd made an idiot of him, not once but twice, and made him ashamed of his own susceptibility to her. And now she was reaching out to touch the life of his precious Lizzie; troubling her, making her uneasy. Making her ill, goddamnit!

He would have to get at least this one portion of his past life out into the open, for both their sakes. Clean the wound, so it could finally heal and they could both move forward.

But not right now. Not when Lizzie was so fragile, and trying to make light of what looked to him to be something far more serious than the simple headache she claimed.

Lizzie blinked awake from the pain-sodden half-sleep she'd been floating in, haunted by some Medusa-type figure who must be her subconscious mind's representation of the unknown Clara.

'Give me your keys, and I'll collect some things for you. Just let me know what you'll need,' said John, as his hand settled lightly on her arm.

'What do you mean?' She glanced out of the window. It was dark, and they were parked outside the house in St Patrick's Road. There was a lamp lit in the front sitting room, but she recognised it as the one they always left on, just in case, when the house was empty.

'I mean…I'll get a few of your things for you, and then you're coming home to Dalethwaite, where I can take care of you.' John's tone was very crisp, no nonsense. Just the sort of stance she imagined him taking in a meeting when he'd lost patience with the argy-bargy of some dithering negotiator.

'It's only a little headache, John, don't make a big deal of it. All I need is a good night's sleep and I'll be spot on.' She braced up, ignoring a slightly nauseous feeling. 'I think I'll be better off here tonight, in my familiar burrow…Then maybe tomorrow evening, we can have dinner and whatever . . .'

She fabricated a wink and an approximation of a seductress's smile. 'By then I'll be much more fun, just you see.'

'Don't be absurd, Lizzie.' His face was tense. He was clearly trying to control himself, and not get impatient with her. 'You need someone to look after you. And I'll give even money that both your friends are out, and you'd be alone here. That one light in the front room trick doesn't fool anybody.'

'I'm not being absurd. Just sensible. I *will* be fine! And anyway, even if they are out, somebody has to make sure the cat's fed.' It was a straw, and she knew he'd see through her clutching at it.

His mouth thinned to a hard line. She could see him battling with himself, trying not to be all-controlling; trying not to impose his will on her. He was really only thinking of her, but she desperately needed some time to herself to brood, and be a complete idiot over motherfucking Clara!

'OK, then…but at least let me come in for a few minutes to make sure you're all right, and get you settled.'

'Now you're making me feel like an ageing dowager duchess, who needs to be installed in her bath-chair.' At least he seemed to be yielding a bit.

'Believe you me, you're nothing like an ageing dowager duchess, darling. I should know, I've met quite a few in my time.' He gave her a gentler smile, then reached for the door catch.

Of course, he would know duchesses, wouldn't he? She always forgot that he wasn't just plain John Smith, not really. He was an aristo, and the son of a marquess. More complications down the line…if there was a line for them ultimately to go down. Her head throbbed harder at the thought of it.

Walking up the path and letting them into the house felt like a forty-mile yomp over hard country. Sitting down, she'd just about been holding her own, but it was a tough struggle to walk around, pretending to be just a bit headachy, when her knees felt as if they'd disintegrated into blancmange, and everything around her was threatening to whirl. She just hoped that John wouldn't notice her surreptitiously reaching out to hold on to the wall or the bannister for support.

'Back in a trice. Do you think you could feed Mulder for me? The cat food's in the cupboard, next to her dishes.' That should distract him, while she sought sanctuary in the bathroom and put her head between her knees, hoping to settle her vertigo.

But whatever it was that had her in its hold was just getting worse. And five minutes later, she felt dizzier than ever, and her headache was like a war axe straight through the front of her skull, when John's impatient question floated up from the bottom of the stairs.

'Lizzie? Are you all right?'

'Fine,' she answered, appalled at the odd sound of her own voice. She pinched her cheeks furiously, trying to inject a bit of healthy colour. Instead, she just looked like a clown with terminal malaria. 'Won't be a moment.'

Best friends with the bannister again, she proceeded gingerly down the steps, aware of the intense scrutiny of John, who was poised at the foot of the staircase, frowning. When the inevitable happened and she wavered, almost losing her footing, he shot forward, grabbed her in his arms and half carried, half hauled her down to the hall.

'You're coming with me. I won't take no for an answer. There's nobody in the house, and I've left a ton of food for the cat, so she'll manage until either Brent or Shelley get home.' His arm, tight around her middle, was unyielding. He wasn't going to allow her to do anything but go with him, that was obvious.

But still, she tried to assert herself. All his big talk about not taking over was obviously meaningless in this situation. He was acting like a boss – totally – again. She summoned her last wisp of energy.

'I'll be fine. I just need to go to bed and have a sleep. It's nothing.'

'Bullshit. It is something. And you're going to bed and having a sleep at Dalethwaite. It's a bigger, more comfortable bed, for a start.' He started to guide her towards the door, gently, but remorseless. 'Where's your bag? Your keys?'

'Hall table, bully.'

'Whatever,' he said, snatching up both and escorting her, closely, out of the house.

Head like whirling cotton wool, Lizzie found it just too difficult to stage any kind of resistance. It was a monumental struggle putting one foot in front of the other, and if she betrayed even a hint of how hard a task it was, he'd just pick her up and carry her. As it was, she let him settle her in the passenger seat, belt her up, and pop her bag on her knee, before sprinting to the door, and locking up the house.

As he took his seat beside her, he peered at her, his face a hard, white mask. Good God, he was worried. Really worried. If she hadn't felt so vile, Lizzie would almost have been amused. The human male usually ran a mile from illness of any kind, fearing the risk of man flu or whatever, but John was no normal man.

'Just relax, sweetheart. It won't take long to get you home. I'll just make a quick call. You need a doctor.' He reached into his pocket for his phone.

'Oh no, John. They won't come out just for a bit of a bug. They're very strict about out of hours home visits at our surgery!'

'Not your doctor, ninny. A doctor I know . . . the man I'll be seeing when I'm up here.' He paused, reaching out to smooth her hair from her brow, then frowning because it was damp with sweat, even though she was shivering now. 'He's very good. The best general physician in the north. Luckily he lives in the area. Now, just lie back in the seat . . . relax. I'll phone Thursgood too, and tell him to have things ready.'

It was useless to argue and, obeying him, she closed her eyes, listening to the beeps of his mobile phone, as he scrolled through contact lists.

Speaking quickly, John laid out a set of instructions. Prepare extra blankets in the master bedroom, along with hot water bottles, and were there certain basic medicines available? 'Oh, and I'm about to call Sir Richard Spillsey. I doubt he'll get there before us, but it's possible, so expect him.'

When he rang off, he dialled again, and after a moment, said, 'Richard? How are you? I wonder if you could do me a huge favour…I know it's out of hours, but could you come over to Dalethwaite Manor? A friend of mine is ill and I'm taking her there…I'd like you to take a look at her.'

Lizzie tugged at his elbow, and he paused, putting the phone face down beside him. 'What's wrong, sweetheart? We'll be home in a few minutes, and everything will be ready. You'll be fine . . .' His fine eyes gleamed in the low light of the car's interior, and a frown pleated his brow; he was her ministering angel, concerned, but on top of things.

'I don't need Sir Richard Thing, John, really I don't. It's just a bit of a bug . . .'

'Shush . . . He's going to take a look at you whether you like it or not. Just indulge me, love, eh? I'm not prepared to take any chances where your health is concerned, and I won't be happy until I've had a medic's opinion.'

'It's just a bug . . .' The effort of arguing was like a ton of rocks weighing down on her, and even though she opened her mouth, to try and reason with him, the words just seemed too awkward to get out. She subsided back again, grateful for the deep, deep upholstery of the luxury car.

'Sorry about that,' he continued to the eminent man. 'Can you come? Yes…that's wonderful. I'd be so grateful. I don't think it's anything too serious, but I'd feel better if you checked her over. Do you know where Dalethwaite Manor is? Excellent! I'll see you soon. And thank you so much…I'm sorry to trouble you in your free time.'

Agh, doctors. She was sure Sir Richard Wotsit was a lovely man, and at the top of his profession, but to bring in some kind of mega consultant on a Sunday evening was just ridiculous for a little touch of summer flu or whatever it was.

She would have fretted more, but it was too tiring to think now, so she just relaxed as John set the Bentley in motion. The car was such a smooth ride that, with her eyes closed, she was barely aware of their progress along the roads and lanes that led to Dalethwaite. It seemed that hardly had they set off than they were slowing to a stop again.

Squinting out of the window, she saw the lights of the big house burning, and Thursgood hurrying down the steps to greet them. At the door, his wife stood waiting too.

Lizzie almost giggled. It *was* just like *Downton Abbey* or *Upstairs, Downstairs*, and she was the clapped-out dowager duchess, marchioness, or female equivalent of whatever John was...being lifted out of the car, and carried up the steps by him, flanked on either side by his retinue.

But the house lights were bright, and as she buried her face in his shoulder, the pain in her head ramped up ten more notches...and she whimpered.

She felt so wretched that, just for the time being, she didn't even give a shit about bloody Clara!

24

The Best Medicine

As her temperature rose, Lizzie's consciousness wavered. She was in the master bedroom again, *her* bedroom, but barely able to keep her eyes open. She was certainly in no condition to enjoy its luxurious decor. The firm mattress and the crisp bed linen felt heavenly, though, fresh and cool against her overheated body. She lay quite still, not wanting to disturb her pounding head, and just drifted, listening to the sough of the night breeze outside, and the barely audible flutter of the delicate voile inner curtains. Every now and again, there was the sound of a bird or owl in the garden or the park beyond...and the occasional rustle of John's clothing, as he shifted position in the chair at her bedside.

It seemed he was standing – or at least sitting – guard over her. When she essayed a little movement, turning over, he was on his feet, hovering.

'Would you like some iced water, love?'

'Um . . . yes. Yes, please . . .'

As she raised herself up, wincing, he slid one supporting arm around her, and held the glass to her lips, gently helping her to drink the deliciously cool water. When she was done, he settled her down again, tucking the quilt around her, as if he were swathing a priceless crystal figurine in protective cotton wool.

Lizzie wanted to laugh again, but she suspected that even a smirk would kill her head. John made the most adorable nursemaid. And a rampantly sexy one too, if only she'd been in a fit state to appreciate him.

After a period of time that could have been minutes or hours, there was a knock on the door, and Mrs Thursgood quietly announced the doctor and ushered him in.

Helped up again by John, Lizzie allowed herself to be examined: pulse and temperature taken, eyes and throat inspected, glands felt. Sir Richard Spillsey had cool, gentle hands, and an equally gentle and good-humoured bedside manner. He was like a kindly but authoritative uncle, and a world away from her own poor harried GP, who always seemed careworn and bogged down by paperwork.

'I don't think there's too much to worry about. It's just one of those tiresome summer viruses that are going about. Rest, quiet, plenty of fluids and paracetamol for the headache and body pains. In two or three days, I think you'll find yourself feeling much better, Miss Aitchison. Just let John here wait on you hand and foot. That's the best medicine of all.'

'Thank you very much. I'm sure you're right.' Lizzie managed a feathery grin from amongst her bundle of bed-clothes, and John winked at her, before escorting the doctor from the room.

Stupid as it seemed to her, as she burrowed under the quilt, the simple act of being examined had worn her out, and she floated into her netherworld again almost immediately. Soft footsteps returned to her side, and she wanted to emerge, and thank John for just being there, but that too was a huge effort. Summoning all her strength, she pushed a searching hand out from under the bedding, and it was grasped, gently, then kissed.

As she slid into sleep again, she felt John stroking the back of her hand . . . and it soothed her away.

The next time she awoke, he was still there. Well, perhaps not 'still' because when Lizzie cracked open an eye with extreme caution, and then found it safe to open the other, she found John was lying beside her on the bed, on top of the covers, wearing jeans and a t-shirt and with wet hair as if he'd recently showered. He had newspapers, and what looked like work files spread out on his side of the duvet, and he was frowning into the middle distance. Twisting a little, Lizzie discovered he was watching a financial report on the large flat screen television on the far wall. He had the subtitles on and the sound muted. It must be some kind of City morning programme, because judging by the sunlight filtering through the curtains, it was indeed the next day.

Even though she'd barely moved, and not made a sound, he snapped towards her, leaning close.

'How are you feeling, love? You've slept for hours.' He reached out and brushed tangled strands of hair from across her face.

Lizzie breathed deeply, trying to listen to her body and work out how it felt.

Better. Definitely better. A bit weak and washed out, but a vast improvement on last night.

'Better, I think . . . but I'm not sure, because I'm not sure I'm fully awake yet. What time is it?' She wiggled around, carefully, trying to sit up, and all the time bracing herself for jabs of head pain. Mercifully, only faint wisps of discomfort floated around.

John helped her to sit. 'It's ten-thirty. Would you like some tea? Or breakfast?' His blue eyes were intent, full of apprehension, as if monitoring her for the tiniest of signs. Still half holding her upright, he dragged a light fleece throw from further down the bed, and arranged it around her shoulders. Lizzie pulled a face on discovering that she was wearing only her knickers and yesterday's striped t-shirt. There was no sign of her Capri pants, and her bra seemed to have disappeared. John must have helped her out of it at some time during the night but she had absolutely no memory of that.

'Ooh, tea would be good,' she said, wrinkling her nose. She was sweaty and far from fresh, and what her breath was like didn't bear thinking about. 'But don't get too close to me…I smell and I've got disgusting morning breath…and I'm riddled with germs, presumably.'

'Don't fret, woman. You're as adorable as ever.' As if to prove it, he kissed her lightly on the lips, not cringing in the least. 'And I've got the constitution of an ox. I never get ill. So your germs don't stand a chance against me.'

Something in Lizzie seemed to float up, buoyed by him. His beautiful golden smile was like a healing radiance, washing over her. The doctor, last night, had said having John to wait on her was the best medicine, and he'd been right. Or perhaps just the smile alone would do the trick.

'Right, then, how about some toast with that tea?' John stroked her face, relief showing in his. Lizzie realised that bed-hair, gruesome sweaty sleep clothes and morning breath notwithstanding, she must indeed be looking at least a little bit better.

'Er . . . yes . . . maybe . . . please . . .' She frowned. There were other priorities. 'Think I need the bathroom first though, before all that,' she said, starting to wriggle from under the covers.

John sprang up, on to his feet, at the side of the bed. 'I'll take you.'

'No! I can manage. For heaven's sake, John, there are some things a girl has to do alone. I'd have to have Ebola and two broken legs at least before I'd need a loo escort.' She slid her feet over and set them on the floor, praying that when she stood, she wouldn't sway.

Thankfully, she didn't, but she wasn't exactly steady as a rock.

'Very well…but I'll be here if you do need me, and I forbid you to lock the door, just in case.' He gave her a stern, mock-authoritarian look. 'And just the essentials…don't launch into any elaborate beauty routines or bathing. I like you smelly!'

'Yes, but you're a pervert,' she muttered at him as she padded across the carpet.

'Very true…but no dawdling, promise?'

'Promise.'

Ten minutes later, after sneaking a forbidden teeth cleaning, and a smear of moisturiser to soothe skin that felt as if it had turned to parchment, Lizzie crept out again, fleece throw clutched around her shoulders as she tottered through the vestibule and into the bedroom.

The tea and toast had arrived, and John was eating a slice, watching the television again, now with the sound on, down low. He muted it when he saw her, and swung his legs off the bed, as if about to storm over, sweep her up, and carry her back to the bed.

'It's all right. I can manage.' She hurried over and slid into bed beside him.

He gave her an old-fashioned look. Lizzie lifted her chin, defiant.

'So, I cleaned my teeth and put on moisturiser . . . call the cops.'

'Bad girl, I'll spank you when you're better.'

Lizzie grinned, feeling better and better. She grabbed a slice of toast and bit into it. 'I'll look forward to it!' Mm . . . the toast was from a fresh country loaf, and the butter was butter, not 'healthy' spread. Sheer heaven!

'I should ring Brent and Shelley,' she said, still chewing.

Her friends would be wondering where the hell she was, but it was more than that; she needed to know that *they* were OK too. Both of them seemed to be plunging in far too deep with people they barely knew yet . . . although on *that* particular score, she had no right to judge, she acknowledged wryly.

'It's all right. I've put them in the picture,' said John quickly. 'They send their love and their "get well soon" wishes. And I've also contacted Marie and said you won't be in for a few days. She says you've not to worry at all, everything's under control, and you've to concentrate on getting better. Oh, and someone called Serena's decided she doesn't want any more appliqué after all, so the design is good to go and you've "oodles" of time.'

He was taking over again. Running her life for her. Lizzie squashed her feelings of rebellion, though. He did mean well. He always meant well. And having spent most of his adult life controlling things, it was just his standard *modus operandi*. Nobody, least of all her, would ever be able to change that. John was John.

'Thanks…you've saved me a job. I was feeling guilty just disappearing again like that, without telling anybody. Especially with New Again so busy, and the wedding dress and everything.' It was a concession, but the sharp way John looked at her told her he'd sensed her qualms, and his odd little smile, in lieu of a reply, said he didn't particularly want to get into an argument about them.

She smiled back at him. 'Thank you for looking after me, John. You're a very kind man.' In spite of all the revelations of yesterday, he'd made her feel safe. And that touched her. She could cope with a bit of this kind of 'taking over' sometimes.

'A very selfish one, though,' he said. 'You know that it's all part of my strategy to coax you to live here permanently with me, don't you?'

She put her hand on his. 'Yes…I do know that. But it's still kind.'

John laughed softly. 'Am I so transparent?'

'A bit.'

But he wasn't, though, not all the time. As she nibbled a bit more toast, and drank more tea, chatting idly with John, watching the television, Lizzie couldn't help wondering about the layers upon layers of him that were still opaque to her. The details of his past, his relationships, his family; the inside stories that no amount of looking up on the internet would ever reveal. The spectre of Clara rose up, escaping the temporary hiding place afforded it by fever and illness. This . . . this woman was too tangible to be a phantom. And her grip on John reached inexorably across the years, imbued with power by the sacrifice he'd made for her.

She was definitely the woman he rowed with in New York. The one who made him angry.

Which meant he'd seen her recently. She wasn't just a

powerful memory. She was still around…and perhaps she wanted him back?

Don't be stupid, Lizzie, she told herself for the hundredth time. *You're the one he's with. You're the one he's nursing through a summer virus. If he still cared about this Clara the way he used to, he wouldn't even* be *here and he probably wouldn't have ever bought this house. He cares for* you *now, so stop nit-picking about his exes like an idiotic jealous thing.*

But later, as a new wave of exhaustion took her over, and she let John tuck her up again, and mute the television so she could sleep, those nit-picking thoughts still nipped and snapped at her weary consciousness.

John set aside the papers he'd been studying. It was hopeless. He couldn't concentrate. He had to focus on Lizzie, and Lizzie alone.

She seemed feverish again, asleep, yet stirring from time to time, muttering. He ached to be able to hold her, as if the contact could erase what ailed her, yet if she was running a high temperature, he'd most probably make things worse.

Intellectually, he knew it was just a mild summer virus that had afflicted her. It would be over in a day or two, and as a healthy, vital young woman, she'd be quickly back to her magnificent feisty, seductive form, challenging his mind and driving him crazy with lust. But right at this moment, she was ill, and, apart from ensuring her comfort, he couldn't do a damn thing to change that. Even with all his resources, he couldn't just snap his fingers and make her well again.

He smiled wryly, remembering her protestations about looking like death warmed up, and being all sweaty and horrible. Bloody hell, she didn't look horrible to him! She was adorable. All tousled up, delicately pale, yet still his wild, bold Lizzie. The curve of her shoulder was visible above the quilt, and the exquisite, vulnerable patch of skin where her t-shirt had twisted to one side speared him. He wanted to lean over and kiss her there, lick the saltiness of her fevered skin, perhaps nibble a little, while sliding his hands beneath the covers to draw her close to him. The warmth of her body next to him cried out to all his senses; she was all colours, scents and textures that delighted him.

Closing his eyes, he imagined sliding beneath the covers with her, and their clothes magically disappearing so they could be skin to hot skin. The curves of her gorgeous bottom and the sleek lines of her thighs would be heaven, cupped in the palms of his hands. The tender, silky contours of her cunt would weep for him, and when he stroked her clitoris, she'd gasp and moan in pleasure. His heart and his cock ached, wanting her. Wanting her hard.

He grimaced. He was fully erect, ready to fuck.

What kind of a fucking, perverted beast are you, man? You're doing it again . . . She's ill, you pig. She's ill. Give it a rest!

And yet he wanted her fiercely. It was wrong, but it had happened. He should leave her in peace and let her sleep; just check back on her from time to time. He should free her from his presence, which was possibly – in fact, probably – accounting for her unease, and the lack of a true repose. Him…and her speculations about Clara, he suspected, guessing that Rose had been just as forthright as she normally was.

But he couldn't go. He couldn't leave. He had to stay; on guard. Protecting his beloved against things he couldn't change, the past, and things he couldn't alter now, even if he'd give the world to be able to.

And he had to be here, even if his own tumescence was bloody killing him.

Oh Lizzie, please come and live with me. My precious, wonderful, rare and amazing Lizzie. I'll do anything . . .

But as she stirred again, still muttering beneath her breath as she dozed, he wondered if he would or could do anything she wanted. Everything she deserved.

He owed her total honesty. He owed her answers to her questions. After all, he was pretty sure she kept nothing much from him.

And yet, the prospect of bringing Clara . . . and prison . . . out into the open, repelled him just as much as he feared they might repel Lizzie. He could hardly bear the thought of her knowing all, and feeling disappointment in him. Maybe even revulsion. He'd been irredeemably stupid in his life. Just as stupid as he'd been smart and successful. It was long ago now, but still hovering around, still possessing the power to upset this delicate, wondrous thing he had now, with this woman.

As if she'd read his troubled thoughts, she rolled over, her arm flailing out, and falling across him. Her hand rested against his thigh, mercifully not too close to the great, hard knot of his erection, and her slender seamstress's fingers flexed and curved, holding on to him.

With infinite care, he placed his hand over hers, enfolding it.

I think I love you, Lizzie . . . if I really, truly know what that means. And I'd tell you, if I dare, but I don't want to hurt you. It might not be the kind of love you want, and almost certainly not the calibre of love you deserve.

And yet, as he sat there, with the woman he adored restless beside him, he knew he was a coward. A coward for not admitting his love, and a coward for concealing aspects of his life from her.

But I will do better, Lizzie. I will try. Even if I can't give you all

the answers at once, I'll do my best to reveal everything, eventually.
Even if it means I might risk losing you in consequence.

Thinking that, he felt the sudden grip of fatalism, of lightness. The weight of decision was out of his hands now.

The whole fate of his happiness, from this day forward, lay in the smooth and gentle palm that rested against his thigh.

And for a man accustomed to control that was both terrifying . . . and wonderful.

25

Some of the Shadows

Later, when Lizzie woke again, she felt better. Not as hot and light-headed, just low on energy, as if her body was healing but still wasn't quite sure of itself.

Turning to one side, she found John still there, his eyes closed. It was twilight, and the room was not yet lit. He might have managed to nod off…perhaps?

Are you sleeping? With me here?

But his eyes snapped open almost immediately, sharp and completely lucid, with none of the slight blur of someone who'd been dozing.

'How do you feel now?' Straightening up, he laid the back of his hand against her brow. 'Any better? You're not as hot.'

Lizzie shuffled, managed to sit up, and the fact she didn't immediately need to lie down again confirmed her assessment. She *was* better this time.

'I…I think I feel slightly human again.' She grinned at him. 'But I still feel horribly grungy, and in need of a bath.'

He reached out and brushed her tangled hair back from her face, his eyes locked on hers, searching, reading.

'Are you sure? That you feel better? I don't want you

falling and cracking your head in the bathroom.' He cradled her chin, his fingers sure and cool.

'Please…I really, really need a bath. I think I'll feel even more better, if I have one. And clean my teeth again and everything.'

He smiled, and leaned over, kissing her forehead in a chaste gesture.

'OK, then, but leave this door open and the bathroom unlocked again, and when you're ready, give me a shout, and I'll come and wash your back, just to make sure you're not up to anything you shouldn't be.' He winked, then reached for the robe spread over the bottom of the bed. Swirling it around her shoulders, he helped her into it. When she swung her legs to one side and set her feet down, in the slippers thoughtfully set at the side of the bed, he sprang to his feet, and supported her as she rose, a guiding hand beneath her elbow.

'It's OK, I'm not going to keel over, John.' She smiled at him, feeling strong again, buoyed up by the sensation of being looked after so lovingly.

'Shall I get some food organised? More toast?' he enquired, as she stood at the door, looking back at him. She'd never seen a gorgeous, macho stud of a man look so much like a fussing mother hen. It made her want to giggle, but also get better as soon as humanly possible, so she could draw forth again the other side of him, the dominant, exciting lover.

'Bath first…then I'll decide if I'm hungry.' John the mother hen was lovely, but against all the odds, Lizzie suddenly felt vaguely horny.

Must be some wacky 'preserving the species' reaction to feeling better again. How weird.

A little while later, settled in the huge, sunken tub, she

called out to him. The water was heavenly, and even though she'd washed already, the offer of having her back scrubbed by her lover was just too tempting.

'I'm mostly clean,' she told him when he appeared, 'but there're just some bits of my back I can't reach.'

'I thought there might be.' He settled gracefully beside the tub, and she passed him the washcloth. Dipping it into the water, he began to move it in slow circles over her naked back.

The odd little surge of desire had sunk to a low flame now, just a pilot light. The beautiful sense of intimacy between them was too lovely to disrupt with fires of passion, joyous as those were. Companionship, his light touch, and his close presence were just the final dose of sweet medicine that she needed.

And there was always the possibility that any form of crazy, rampant shagging might deplete her hard-won energy levels.

'I bet this wasn't what you had in mind when you decided you wanted to lure me to your lair, was it?' she asked, flexing her back and enjoying the gentle massage. 'You were expecting a kinky sex kitten mistress and you got a fluey, germy, smelly gargoyle who you had to get the doctor for.'

'Maybe I have a thing for gargoyles?' He grinned at her, with that beautiful, playful superstar twinkle of a smile that had hooked her, instantaneously, that first night in the Lawns Bar at the Waverley.

'You're a very peculiar man, Mr Smith.'

His sudden, gusty sigh surprised her. 'Yes, certainly that…but I'm not exactly an easy one either, am I?'

A little chill overcame her, and she shivered. As if he

were monitoring her every breath, her every movement, or symptom, John let the washcloth slide into the bath, and laid his bare hand on to her back.

'Are you cold, sweetheart? Are you OK? Not feeling dizzy again?'

She wasn't. She was convinced she was virtually well now, almost back to herself. But there were shadows from the past that had to be dealt with, and she sensed that was what John felt too. They would have covered that ground by now, and perhaps been in an entirely new place, if she hadn't been taken ill. They'd certainly have brought Clara out of hiding.

'No. I'm good, John. I feel almost back to normal now.' She paused. 'I'm ready to deal with things, and I think we need to discuss some stuff, don't you?'

'Yes,' he said, one word a full answer. He reached for a bath sheet, and as she rose from the water, he swathed it around her.

'Do you think I might have a moment or two to myself again, John?' she said, shimmying against the thick, lush terrycloth. 'Just five minutes or so and then I'll be out again.'

'Of course, love.' His lips settled momentarily on the nape of her neck, then with a squeeze of her shoulders, he strode to the door. Only to pause, turn and give her a look.

'Yes, OK, if I feel weird again, I'll shout for you.'

'Good girl,' he replied, then slid from the room.

When she returned to the bedroom, he was sitting on the padded seat at the further, larger window, looking out over the park. It was dark now, but the moon rode high, and John's face was pure drama where its light shone upon him. Turning to her, he rose, but when she walked forward to join him there, he sat down again.

'Better?' He reached for her hand and held it, rubbing

his other hand up and down the sleeve of her thick velour bathrobe.

'Very much. Barely any gargoyle characteristics left now.'

'You look beautiful. You always look beautiful. When I look at you, I never can quite work out what I've done to deserve you.'

And me, you.

She didn't say it. She just smiled. His sweet compliment didn't seem like an avoiding tactic; it just felt as if he really meant it.

'So . . .' she said.

'Yes...so,' he answered, his hand tightening around hers. 'What did Rose tell you? I suspect she revealed some things I told her she should never ever disclose to anybody.' His expression was rueful, and it made him look so young, a little lost, but ageless.

'She did. But don't be cross with her. She was only trying to help.' She put her own hand around his. He so often embraced her with that double-handed grip, and it felt right to return it to him. 'I know you weren't driving that night, and I know you went to prison for someone called Clara.' He didn't move, but she felt immediate tension in his fingers. 'I guess she was a girlfriend? Someone who meant a lot to you?'

He nodded, his face hardening to a mask. Did he hate Clara now? Or hate himself for still caring for her? It could be either. Determined not to cringe from the worst possibilities, Lizzie pressed on:

'Is she the woman you ran into in New York?'

'Yes.' He seemed to be fighting with himself, wrestling with the old, reticent John who never said anything about the past. Trying to vanquish him, so they could face each other frankly, without secrets.

And yet she could see him in pain. Would it be better to back off?

Suddenly, he turned his hand in hers, and replicated her double-handed grip. 'I loved her once, Lizzie. I was besotted with her…I wanted to marry her, and she led me to believe that she wanted that too, that we were more or less engaged.' With a passion that shocked her, he raised her hand to his lips and covered it with kisses, hungry and desperate. 'It was a good match too. Her … her family knew my family. We were all set.' He kissed the back of her hand again, softer this time. 'And then, when I needed her, when I thought she'd stand by me … she just ran.'

'The fucking ungrateful cow!' It was out before she could stop it, and she was as shocked by her own vehemence as John appeared to be. They sat in stunned silence for a moment, as if set in amber, then suddenly he laughed. And laughed. And Lizzie joined in, overtaken by it, giggling, almost hysterical.

When they settled down again, she said, 'Well, it's true, isn't it? You make an enormous sacrifice for her . . . blacken your good name and all that. And she buggers off. What a bitch!'

He leaned forward and drew her to him, bringing their foreheads together, shaking his against hers.

'You're completely right. She was a bitch. She still is . . . I think. But she has a way of wrapping it all up in a cloak of charm.' He put his fingers beneath her chin, tilted up her face, and kissed her. It was a long, slow, thoughtful kiss, but for all his focus on her, Lizzie sensed a preoccupation…the phantom touch of a devilishly charming woman?

No! He's mine. You can't have him back!

When their lips parted, John gave her a puzzled look, as if he'd heard her silent declaration. Then his expression changed, became almost glowing, as if some other thought, some illumination, had occurred to him.

'I *was* going to say, if only I'd known that at the time...well, perhaps I'd not have succumbed to her. But maybe it's better that things turned out the way they did.' His eyes gleamed in the moonlight. Suspiciously so . . . 'If Clara hadn't right royally fucked me over . . . and then done it all over again . . . I might not have been in the Lawns Bar one night not all that long ago. I might have been leading an entirely different life.' He blinked. 'And then I probably wouldn't have met you, Lizzie.' He grabbed her again, hugging her to him, rocking their bodies. 'Or I might have met you and not been able to do a damn thing about it!'

Lizzie blinked too, horrified by the thought of that near miss, and awed by a more emotional, open John than she'd ever seen. She hugged him back, a sudden, passionate strength banishing the last of her weakness and whatever had ailed her.

But there was more, she knew, much more. Clara had right royally fucked him over *twice*? What was all that about? Lizzie didn't know yet, but it spoke to her of tenacity in this rival she'd never met. A mercurial quality. A woman like that could change her mind. A woman like that really could suddenly decide she wanted John again . . . and reach out to take him.

But for the moment, Lizzie wasn't going to show her own hand, or lose her head. She'd deal with all the twists and layers to John's story all in good time. And knock down the demons – and bloody Clara – as they presented themselves.

Determination surged in her, and she put up her hand, dug her fingers into his golden curls, and drew his mouth down to hers for a kiss. To hell with the germs; he was tough, he'd fight them off.

John was her man, and *she* was going to do some fighting too. She'd fight for him, and fight against all the shadows of his past; the ones he'd revealed to her and the ones as yet still hidden. She had a shrewd idea that they hadn't heard the last of Clara, but this moment was too precious to let thoughts of her spoil it.

Responding to her, John took over the kiss; clearly he wasn't in the slightest bit bothered by germs either. Lizzie had no idea whether he'd 'heard' her inner resolutions, but he drew her to him, kissing hard, his tongue twirling with hers.

'Toothpaste,' he observed, licking his lips as they broke apart.

'Of course…germy gargoyle breath, remember?' She smiled at him, mimicking that swipe of the tongue.

'Oh, hell, love…I forgot. Some bloody nursemaid I am.' He didn't let go of her, though.

'You're not a nursemaid, Mr Smith. You're medicine. And I feel better already.'

He gave her a slow, sweet, tricky, narrow-eyed look. 'No . . . surely not . . .' His hand slid down her body, caressing her through her robe, the quality of his touch suddenly different, exciting. 'What would Sir Richard say? He'd have a fit if he knew what I wanted to do to his patient, so soon.'

'Bollocks to Sir Richard. He's a nice man, but *I* know what's best for me.' Lizzie rose, drawing John with her, and started tugging him towards the bed. 'You can do me nice and gently. I'll survive it…though it's probably best to save the funny stuff until I've got a clean bill of health.'

John stopped her in her tracks, and moved in front of her,

cradling her face between his two hands, looking down at her. His beautiful blue eyes were as brilliant as the moon outside.

'I think I know what it is now, Lizzie,' he said softly.

'What *what* is?'

He kissed her on the forehead, then whispered, 'I love you, Miss Aitchison.'

'And I love you too, Mr Smith.' Her heart hammered, and she hugged him, claiming him as hers and loving that he'd finally spoken the words. Because now, in the shadow of Clara, they *really* mattered.

'Good, that's settled, then!' Voice full of joy, he whisked her up in his arms and carried her to the bed. 'One extremely nice and gentle fuck coming up.'

It's not going to be easy. There's more we have to deal with. Much more…But I love him and he's worth any amount of fighting for.

While John stripped off her robe and then, kneeling over her, started tearing off his own clothes, Lizzie came to a conclusion.

In order to fight effectively for her man, she had to be on the spot, as close as close could be, right by his side.

So, when they'd made love, and when they were sleepy and sated, or maybe energised and hungry again…*that* was when she'd announce that she'd move in with him!

Lizzie and John's story continues in

The Accidental Bride

Coming soon from Black Lace

The Accidental Bride

Marrying a billionaire?

It's every girl's fantasy, but ever since meeting brooding sexy tycoon, John Smith, Lizzie has never been entirely sure of his true feelings for her.

Has he proposed marriage because he truly loves her or just to keep her in his bed?

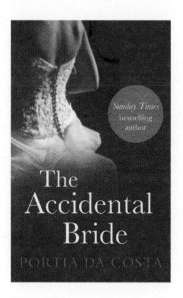